THOSE
WHO CAN

Also by Robin Wilson

To the Sound of Music (with R. W. Shryock)
Death by Degrees

As editor

Clarion
Clarion II
Clarion III
*Paragons: Twelve Science Fiction Writers
Ply Their Craft*

THOSE WHO CAN

A Science Fiction Reader

EDITED BY

Robin Scott Wilson

St. Martin's Griffin ◾ New York

ACKNOWLEDGMENTS

"Jamboree" by Jack Williamson originally appeared in
Galaxy, copyright © 1969 by Universal Publishing and
Distributing Corporation. Reprinted by permission of the
author.
"We, in Some Strange Power's Employ, Move on a Rig-
orous Line" by Samuel R. Delany originally appeared
under the title "Lines of Power" in *The Magazine of
Fantasy and Science Fiction*, copyright © 1968 by
Mercury Press, Inc. Reprinted by permission of the
author.
"Crazy Maro" by Daniel Keyes originally appeared in *The
Magazine of Fantasy and Science Fiction*, copyright ©
1960 by Mercury Press, Inc. Reprinted by permission of
the author.
"Pretty Maggie Moneyeyes" by Harlan Ellison originally
appeared in *Knight Magazine*, copyright © 1967 by
Sirkay Publishing Company. Copyright assigned to
Harlan Ellison, 1967. Reprinted by permission of the
author and the author's agent, Robert P. Mills, Ltd. "The
Whore with a Heart of Iron Pyrites; or, Where Does a
Writer Go to Find a Maggie?" by Harlan Ellison, copyright © 1973.
"The Man Who Could Not See Devils" by Joanna Russ
originally appeared in *Alchemy and Academe*, copyright
© 1970 by Anne McCaffrey. Reprinted by permission of
the author and the author's agent, Virginia Kidd.
"Sundance" by Robert Silverberg originally appeared in
The Magazine of Fantasy and Science Fiction, copyright
© 1969 by Mercury Press, Inc. Reprinted by permission
of the author and the author's agent, Scott Meredith.
"Nine Lives" by Ursula K. Le Guin originally appeared in
Playboy Magazine, copyright © 1969 by Playboy. The
substantially revised version here reprinted first appeared
in *World's Best Science Fiction: 1970*, edited by Donald
A. Wollheim and Terry Carr. Reprinted by permission of

(The following page constitutes an extension of this copyright page.)

Playboy, the author, and the author's agent, Virginia Kidd.

"Masks" by Damon Knight originally appeared in *Playboy Magazine*, copyright © 1968 by HMH Publishing Corp. Reprinted by permission of the author.

"The Planners" by Kate Wilhelm originally appeared in *Orbit 3*, copyright © 1968 by Damon Knight. Reprinted by permission of the author.

"For A While There, Herbert Marcuse, I Thought You Were Maybe Right About Alienation and Eros" by Robin Scott Wilson originally appeared in *The Magazine of Fantasy and Science Fiction*, copyright © 1972 by Mercury Press, Inc. Reprinted by permission of the author.

"The Listeners" by James E. Gunn originally appeared in *Galaxy*, copyright © 1968 by Galaxy Publishing Corporation. Reprinted by permission of the author.

"Grandy Devil" by Frederik Pohl originally appeared in *Galaxy*, copyright © 1955 by Galaxy Publishing Corporation; "Day Million" by Frederik Pohl originally appeared in *Rogue Magazine*, copyright © 1966 by *Rogue Magazine*. Both stories reprinted by permission of the author.

Library of Congress Cataloging-in-Publication Data

Those who can : a science fiction reader / Robin Wilson, editor.
    p. cm.
    ISBN 0-312-14139-4
    1. Science fiction, American.   2. Science fiction—Authorship.   3. Science fiction—History and criticism—Theory, etc.   I. Wilson, Robin Scott.
    PS648.S3T48   1996
    813'.0876208—dc20   95-45205
                                           CIP

First published simultaneously in the United States of America, Canada, and Great Britain by The New American Library Inc., The New American Library of Canada, and the New English Library Limited.

First St. Martin's Griffin Edition: April 1996

10 9 8 7 6 5 4 3 2 1

This one's for
LOUISE and JIM

Contents

INTRODUCTION:
To the Reader

WE INTEND in this volume to bring you—the general reader, the student of science fiction, or the apprentice writer—the work of a dozen highly accomplished craftsmen who have also, not incidentally, distinguished themselves as teachers. Some hold tenured professorships; some have alternated teaching assignments with other work; some have lectured widely at colleges and universities and demonstrated unusual pedagogic ability in the pressure-cooker atmosphere of one or another of the "Clarion" writers' workshops—at Clarion itself, at Tulane University, at the University of Washington, or at the Justin Morrill College of Michigan State University.

I asked each contributor to select one of his stories—one he believed might have certain exemplary qualities—and then comment on its genesis, development, or aims in a brief essay. The essays thus generated are grouped under six topical headings: plot, character, setting, theme, point of view, and style. I make no brief for this rather mechanical method of approaching the complex gestalt that is fiction; it is probably the worst possible way to go about it—except for any other way I can think of. At the very least, however, I believe these terms are consonant with the critical currency of the classroom, and I hope the juxtaposition of pairs of essays on similar subjects will generate a little light.

Why build a collection of fiction written by teachers? I assure you it is not just another attempt to prove the fallacy of Bernard Shaw's "Those who can, do. Those who cannot, teach." Rather, it seems to me that the teacher-writer is likely to be both unusually skilled at analyzing literary accomplishment and deft at communi-

cating his findings to an audience of nonspecialists who
have come to know him through his art.

So the essays in this collection are not to be taken as
exercises in technical criticism. Instead, I think you will
find them mixing prescription with description, find them
free of critical cant and pedagogical rhetoric. They are
above all personal statements—chronicles of an unusual
kind of odyssey, an author's voyage into his own creative
terra incognita. I suspect that some of my colleagues have
found—as I did—that the journey was unusually trying:
what physician enjoys taking his own blood pressure? But
we have all done our best, and I think we may have
learned as much from the effort as we hope you will.

Preceding each grouping of two stories and two essays
is a brief statement about the category at hand for which
I alone am responsible. I do not expect my colleagues in
this volume to agree with my formulations, and—at five
or six hundred words—I do not offer them to the reader
as definitive or comprehensive treatments. I hope that
they will provide some beginning definitions of critical
terms which may be useful to the student, not overly tire-
some to the general reader, and not constrictive to the
teacher, who probably has his own ideas on these matters.

A final note: if there is a critical theme unifying these
essays by twelve very different men and women, it is based
on some version of a definition of the writer's art that runs
like this: "Art is the imposition of form on the materials
of human experience." While I daresay the twelve of us
can find much in the literary vineyard to quarrel about,
we are all—as writers *and* teachers—concerned with the
techniques of imposition, the implications of form, the
nature of our perceptions of the human condition.

Teaching, too, is an art.

THOSE
WHO CAN

PLOT:
The Tangled Web

O what a tangled web we weave,
When first we practice to deceive!

YES INDEED, Sir Walter. And although the writer's business
is truth, his primary tool is a kind of deception achieved
through the (apparently) tangled web of plot.

Some writers plot consciously, building a structure to
which such other elements as character, setting, and style
are tailored. Others plant characters in an opening situation and watch what grows, pruning and shaping the
result until it seems satisfying. Whatever the process, all
plots display certain characteristics: there is a series of
events in time, causally related (although "time" may be
variously interpreted and "cause" may be obscure);
there is conflict (between people, between a person and
nature or society or a machine, or between two aspects of
a single character); and there are some structural elements,
the terms for which have been borrowed from the drama.

Exposition is the explanation of events or circumstances
not given narrative or dramatic treatment in the story.
Sometimes referred to as the "expository lump"—because,
I suppose, it is so hard for the reader to swallow if presented clumsily—exposition is conspicuously thin in much
contemporary fiction, which may work the reader a little
harder, but lets the writer get on with his business without distracting interruptions.

Another structural device is *involution* (or *nouement*
if you prefer the French), the winding together of the
threads of action and motivation which heighten conflict,
add complications, or promise (falsely) an early end to
things.

Climax is the point of maximum conflict, when apparently irreconcilable forces meet, the issue is in maximum
doubt, and some decisive event is demanded.

Last comes the *resolution* (or *denouement*), when the

1

issue is decided, all is clear, a kind of equilibrium has returned to the little world of the story, and wiser or sadder or happier, the reader is released from his contract with the writer.

These structural elements may be combined in a variety of ways and may enjoy greatly varying degrees of emphasis. True climax may not be perceptible to the reader until after the resolution and the new information it conveys; exposition may take place imperceptibly through the implications of events rather than through direct statement; involution may follow or precede climax; the resolution itself may be so equivocal as to leave even the careful reader unsure of the full meaning of what he has read. Writing fiction is not an exact science; there really are no plot formulas for anything worth reading.

Two more words are useful in discussions of plot: an *organic* plot is based upon direct and perceptible relationships between events, each being linked to its predecessor and successor by strong bonds of causality. In an *episodic* plot, events are knit together less by causality than by their common relationship to some central event or character or theme. The plot of Poe's "Cask of Amontillado" is highly organic, a chain of events stretched tightly from opening to resolution; *Tom Jones* is more episodic, a series of events—some causally related, some not—bound together like the spokes of a wheel by their common hub, the theme of Tom's maturation as a good *and* prudent man.

Finally, in plot time is of the essence. Some plots move along a smooth chronological line; others reverse time, or employ it as an element of conflict, or negate it as much as possible to focus the reader's attention on other matters. Then there is *tempo* (the pace of the author's presentation of events in the story, not the ticking of the clocks in the little world that *is* the story). *Normal tempo* is the conventional balance between the realistic slowness of most human happenings and the need to compress these happenings to fit the limitations of the reader's patience. *Retarded tempo* expands time, often to a pace far slower than real time, to allow the writer to examine events in great detail. (*Tristram Shandy* and Henry James's *The American* are examples). *Accelerated tempo* is the pace of the action-adventure tale or the documentary history, the furious rush of events that leaves the hero (and the reader) breathless. Tempo is not necessarily uniform throughout a story; its variation in conformity with the author's intentions is part of his craft, something he achieves as much through stylistic devices as through his selection and arrangements of events in plot.

I will make no apology for the accelerated tempo of this cursory treatment of an enormously complex subject. I will add only that good plotting is the first (if not the most important) skill of the writer, that an understanding of plot is essential to the critical reader, and that—for me—it is the most troublesome aspect of fiction.

JAMBOREE

by Jack Williamson

THE SCOUTMASTER slipped into the camp on black plastic tracks. Its slick yellow hood shone in the cold early light like the shell of a bug. It paused in the door, listening for boys not asleep. Then its glaring eyes began to swivel, darting red beams into every corner, looking for boys out of bed.

"Rise and smile!" Its loud merry voice bounced off the gray iron walls. "Fox Troop rise and smile! Hop for old Pop! Mother says today is Jamboree!"

The Nuke Patrol, next to the door, was mostly tenderfeet, still in their autonomic prams. They all began squalling, because they hadn't learned to love old Pop. The machine's happy voice rose louder than their howling, and it came fast down the narrow aisle to the cubs in the Anthrax Patrol.

"Hop for Pop! Mother says it's Jamboree!"

The cubs jumped up to attention, squealing with delight. Jamboree was bright gold stars to paste on their faces. Jamboree was a whole scoop of pink ice milk and maybe a natural apple. Jamboree was a visit to Mother's.

The older scouts in the Scavanger Patrol and the Skull Patrol were not so noisy, because they knew Mother wouldn't have many more Jamborees for them. Up at the end of the camp, three boys sat up without a sound and looked at Joey's empty pallet.

"Joey's late," Ratbait whispered. He was a pale, scrawny wise-eyed scout who looked too old for twelve. "We oughta save his hide. We oughta fix a dummy and fool old Pop."

"Naw!" muttered Butch. "He'll get us all in bad."

"But we oughta—" Blinkie wheezed. "We oughta help—"

Ratbait began wadding up a pillow to be the dummy's head, but he dropped flat when he saw the scoutmaster rushing down with a noise like wind, red lamps stabbing at the empty bed.

"Now, now, scouts!" Its voice fluttered like a hurt bird. "You can't play pranks on poor old Pop. Not today. You'll make us late for Jamboree."

Ratbait felt a steel whip twitch the blanket from over his head and saw red light burning through his tightshut lids.

"Better wake up, Scout R-8." Its smooth, sad voice dripped over him like warm oil. "Better tell old Pop where J-0 went."

He squirmed under that terrible blaze. He couldn't see and he couldn't breathe and he couldn't think what to say. He gulped at the terror in his throat and tried to shake his head. At last the red glare went on to Blinkie.

"Scout Q-2, you're a twenty-badger." The low, slow voice licked at Blinkie like a friendly pup. "You like to help old Pop keep a tidy camp for Mother. You'll tell us where J-0 went."

Blinkie was a fattish boy. His puffy face was toadstool-pale, and his pallet had a sour smell from being wet. He sat up and ducked back from the steel whip over him.

"Please d-d-d-d-d—" His wheezy stammer stalled his voice, and he couldn't dodge the bright whip that looped around him and dragged him up to the heat and the hum and the hot oil smell of Pop's yellow hood.

"Well, Scout Q-2?"

Blinkie gasped and stuttered and finally sagged against the plastic tracks like gray jelly. The shining coils rippled around him like thin snakes, constricting. His breath wheezed out and his fat arm jerked up, pointing at a black sign on the wall:

DANGER!
Power Access
ROBOTS ONLY!

The whips tossed him back on his sour pallet. He lay there, panting and blinking and dodging, even after the whips were gone. The scoutmaster's eyes flashed to the sign and the square grating under it, and swiveled back to Butch.

Butch was a slow, stocky, bug-eyed boy, young enough to come back from another Jamboree. He had always been afraid of Pop, but he wanted to be the new leader of Skull Patrol in Joey's place, and now he thought he saw his chance.

"Don't hit me, Pop!" His voice squeaked and his face turned red, but he scrambled off his pallet without waiting for the whips. "I'll tell on Joey. I been wantin' all along to tell, but I was afraid they'd beat me."

"Good boy!" the scoutmaster's loud words swelled out like big soap-bubbles bursting in the sun. "Mother wants to know all about Scout J-0."

"He pries that grating—" His voice quavered and caught when he saw the look on Ratbait's face, but when he turned to Pop it came back loud. "Does it every night. Since three Jamborees ago. Sneaks down in the pits where the robots work. I dunno why, except he sees somebody there. An' brings things back. Things he shouldn't have. Things like this!"

He fumbled in his uniform and held up a metal tag.

"This is your good turn today, Scout X-6." The thin tip of a whip took the tag and dangled it close to the hot red lamps. "Whose tag is this?"

"Lookit the number—"

Butch's voice dried up when he saw Ratbait's pale lips making words without a sound. "What's so much about an ID tag?" Ratbait asked. "Anyhow, what were you doing in Joey's bed."

"It's odd!" Butch looked away and squeaked at Pop. "A girl's number!"

The silent shock of that bounced off the iron walls, louder than old Pop's boom. Most of the scouts had never seen a girl. After a long time, the cubs near the door began to whisper and titter.

"Shhhhh!" Pop roared like steam. "Now we can all do a good turn for Mother. And play a little joke on Scout J-0! He didn't know today would be Jamboree, but he'll find out." Pop laughed like a heavy chain clanking. "Back to bed! Quiet as robots!'

Pop rolled close to the wall near the power-pit grating, and the boys lay back on their pallets. Once Ratbait caught his breath to yell, but he saw Butch's bug-eyes watching. Pop's hum sank, and even the tenderfeet in their prams were quiet as robots.

Ratbait heard the grating creak. He saw Joey's head, tangled yellow hair streaked with oil and dust. He frowned and shook his head and saw Joey's sky-blue eyes go wide. Joey tried to duck, but the quick whips caught his neck. They dragged him out of the square black pit and swung him like a puppet toward old Pop's eyes.

"Well, Scout J-0!" Pop laughed like thick oil bubbling. "Mother wants to know where you've been."

Joey fell on his face when the whip uncoiled, but he scrambled to his feet. He gave Ratbait a pale grin before he looked up at Pop, but he didn't say anything.

"Better tell old Pop the truth." The slick whips drew back like lean snakes about to strike. "Or else we'll have to punish you, Scout J-0."

Joey shook his head, and the whips went to work. Still he didn't speak. He didn't even scream. But something fell out of his torn uniform. The whip-tips snatched it off the floor.

"What's this thing, Scout J-0?" The whip-fingers turned it delicately under the furious eyes and nearly dropped it again. "Scout J-0, this is a book!"

Silence echoed in the iron camp.

"Scout J-0, you've stolen a book." Pop's shocked voice changed into a toneless buzz, reading the title. *"Operators' Handbook, Nuclear Reactor, Series 9-Z."*

Quiet sparks of fear crackled through the camp. Two or three tenderfeet began sobbing in their prams. When they were quiet, old Pop made an ominous, throat-clearing sound.

"Scout J-0, what are you doing with a book?"

Joey gulped and bit his under lip till blood seeped down his chin, but he made no sound. Old Pop rolled closer, while the busy whips were stowing the book in a dark compartment under the yellow hood.

"Mother won't like this." Each word clinked hard, like iron on iron. "Books aren't for boys. Books are for robots only. Don't you know that?"

Joey stood still.

"This hurts me, Scout J-0." Pop's voice turned downy soft, the slow words like tears of sadness now. "It hurts your poor Mother. More than anything can ever hurt you."

The whips cracked and cracked and cracked. At last they picked him up and shook him and dropped him like a red-streaked rag on the floor. Old Pop backed away and wheeled around.

"Fox Troop rise and smile!" Its roaring voice turned jolly again, as if it had forgotten Joey. "Hop for Pop. Today is Jamboree, and we're on our way to visit Mother. Fall out in marching order."

The cubs twittered with excitement until their leaders threatened to keep them home from Jamboree, but at last old Pop led the troop out of camp and down the paved trail toward Mother's. Jocy limped from the whips, but he set his teeth and kept his place at the head of his patrol.

Marching through boy territory, they passed the scattered camps of troops whose Jamborees came on other days. A few scouts were out with their masters, but nobody waved or even looked straight at them.

The spring sun was hot and Pop's pace was too fast for the cubs. Some of them began to whimper and fall out of line. Pop rumbled back to warn them that Mother would give no gold stars if they were late for Jamboree. When Pop was gone, Joey glanced at Ratbait and beckoned with his head.

"I gotta get away!" he whispered low and fast. "I gotta get back to the pits—"

Butch ran out of his place, leaning to listen. Ratbait shoved him off the trail.

"You gotta help!" Joey gasped. "There's a thing we gotta do—an' we gotta do it now. 'Cause this will be the last Jamboree for most of us. We'll never get another chance."

Butch came panting along the edge of the trail, trying to hear, but Blinkie got in his way.

"What's all this?" Ratbait breathed. "What you gonna do?"

"It's all in the book," Joey said. "Something called manual over-ride. There's a dusty room, down under Mother's, back of a people-only sign. Two red buttons. Two big levers. With a glass wall between. It takes two people."

"Who? One of us?"

Joey shook his head, waiting for Blinkie to elbow Butch. "I got a friend. We been working together, down in the pits. Watching the robots. Reading the books. Learning what we gotta do—"

He glanced back. Blinkie was scuffling with Butch to keep him busy, but now the scoutmaster came clattering back from the rear, booming merrily, "Hop for Pop! Hop a lot for Pop!"

"How you gonna work it?" Alarm took Ratbait's breath. "Now the robots will be watching—"

"We got a back door," Joey's whisper raced. "A drainage tunnel. Hot water out of the reactor. Comes out under Black Creek bridge. My friend'll be there. If I can dive off this end of the bridge—"

"Hey, Pop!" Butch was screaming. "Ratbait's talking! Blinkie pushed me! Joey's planning something bad!"

"Good boy, Scout X-6!" Pop slowed beside him. "Mother wants to know if they're plotting more mischief."

When Pop rolled on ahead of the troop, Ratbait wanted to ask what would happen when Joey and his friend pushed the two red buttons and pulled the two big levers, but Butch stuck so close they couldn't speak again. He thought it must be something about the reactor. Power was the life of Mother and the robots. If Joey could cut the power off—

Would they die? The idea frightened him. If the prams stopped, who would care for the tenderfeet? Who would make chow? Who would tell anybody what to do? Perhaps the books would help, he thought. Maybe Joey and his friend would know.

With Pop rolling fast in the lead, they climbed a long hill and came in sight of Mother's. Old gray walls that had no windows. Two tall stacks of dun-colored brick. A shimmer of heat in the pale sky.

The trail sloped down. Ratbait saw the crinkled ribbon of green brush along Black Creek, and then the concrete bridge. He watched Butch watching Joey, and listened to Blinkie panting, and tried to think how to help.

The cubs stopped whimpering when they saw Mother's mysterious walls and stacks, and the troop marched fast down the hill. Ratbait slogged along, staring at the yellow sun-dazzle on old Pop's hood. He couldn't think of anything to do.

"I got it!" Blinkie was breathing, close to his ear. "I'll take care of Pop."

"You?" Ratbait scowled. "You were telling on Joey—"

"That's why," Blinkie gasped. "I wanta make it up. I'll handle Pop. You stop Butch—an' give the sign to Joey."

They came to the bridge and Pop started across.

"Wait, Pop!" Blinkie darted out of line, toward the bushy slope above the trail. "I saw a girl! Hiding in the bushes to watch us go by."

Pop roared back off the bridge.

"A girl in boy territory!" Its shocked voice splashed them like cold rain. "What would Mother say?" Black tracks spurting gravel, it lurched past Blinkie and crashed into the brush.

"Listen, Pop!" Butch started after it, waving and squealing. "They ain't no girl—"

Ratbait tripped him and turned to give Joey the sign, but Joey was already gone. Something splashed under the bridge and Ratbait saw a yellow head sliding under the steam that drifted out of a black tunnel-mouth.

"Pop! Pop!" Butch rubbed gravel out of his mouth and danced on the pavement. "Come back, Pop. Joey's in the creek! Ratbait and Blinkie—they helped him get away."

The scoutmaster swung back down the slope, empty whips waving. It skidded across the trail and down the bank to the hot creek. Its yellow hood faded into the stream.

"Tattletale!" Blinkie clenched his fat fists. "You told on Joey."

"An' you'll catch it!" Murky eyes bugging, Butch edged away. "You just wait till Pop gets back."

They waited. The tired cubs sat down to rest and the tenderfeet fretted in their hot prams. Breathing hard, Blinkie kept close to Butch. Ratbait watched till Pop swam back out of the drain.

The whips were wrapped around two small bundles that dripped pink water. Unwinding, the whips dropped Joey and his friend on the trail. They crumpled down like rag dolls, but the whips set them up again.

"How's this, scouts?" Old Pop laughed like steel gears clashing. "We've caught ourselves a real live girl!"

In a bird-quick way, she shook the water out of her sand-colored hair. Standing straight, without the whips to hold her, she faced Pop's glaring lamps. She looked tall for twelve.

Joey was sick when the whips let him go. He leaned off the bridge to heave, and limped back to the girl. She wiped his face with her wet hair. They caught hands and smiled at each other, as if they were all alone.

"They tripped me, Pop." Braver now, Butch thumbed his nose at Blinkie and ran toward the machine. "They tried to stop me telling you—"

"Leave them to Mother," Pop sang happily. "Let them try their silly tricks on her.' It wheeled toward the bridge, and the whips pushed Joey and the girl ahead of the crunching tracks. "Now hop with Pop to Jamboree!"

They climbed that last hill to a tall iron door in Mother's old gray wall. The floors beyond were naked steel, alive with machinery underneath. They filed into a dim round room that echoed to the grating squeal of Pop's hard tracks.

"Fox Troop, here we are for Jamboree!" Pop's jolly voice made a hollow booming on the curved steel wall, and its red lights danced in tall reflections there. "Mother wants you to know why we celebrate this happy time each year."

The machine was rolling to the center of a wide black circle in the middle of the floor. Something drummed far below like a monster heart, and Ratbait saw that the circle was the top of a black steel piston. It slid slowly up, lifting Pop. The drumming died, and Pop's eyes blazed down on the cubs in the Anthrax Patrol, to stop their awed murmuring.

"Once there wasn't any Mother." The shock of that crashed and throbbed and faded. "There wasn't any yearly Jamboree. There wasn't even any Pop, to love and care for little boys."

The cubs were afraid to whisper, but a stir of troubled wonder spread among them.

"You won't believe how tenderfeet were made." There was a breathless hush. "In those bad old days, boys and girls were allowed to change like queer insects. They changed into creatures called adults—"

The whips writhed and the red lamps glared and the black cleats creaked on the steel platform.

"Adults!" Pop spewed the word. "They malfunctioned and wore out and ran down. Their defective logic circuits programmed them to damage one another. In a kind of strange group malfunction called war, they systematically destroyed one another. But their worst malfunction was in making new tenderfeet."

Pop turned slowly on the high platform, sweeping the silent troop with blood-red beams that stopped on Joey and his girl. All the scouts but Ratbait and Blinkie had edged away from them. Her face white and desperate, she was whispering in Joey's ear. Listening with his arm around her, he scowled at Pop.

"Once adults made tenderfeet, strange as that may seem to you. They used a weird natural process we won't go into. It finally broke down, because they had damaged their genes in war. The last adults couldn't make new boys and girls at all."

The red beams darted to freeze a startled cub.

"Fox Troop, that's why we have Mother. Her job is to collect undamaged genes and build them into whole cells with which she can assemble whole boys and girls. She has been doing that a long time now, and she does it better than those adults ever did.

"And that's why we have Jamboree! To fill the world with well-made boys and girls like you, and to keep you happy in the best time of life—even those old adults always said childhood was the happy time. Scouts, clap for Jamboree!"

The cubs clapped, the echo like a spatter of hail on the high iron ceiling.

"Now, Scouts, those bad old days are gone forever," Pop burbled merrily. "Mother has a cozy place for each one of you, and old Pop watches over you, and you'll never be adult—"

"Pop! Pop!" Butch squealed. "Lookit Joey an' his girl!"

Pop spun around on the high platform. It's blinding beams picked up Joey and the girl, sprinting toward a bright sky-slice where the door had opened for the last of the prams.

"Wake up, guys!" Joey's scream shivered against the red steel wall. "That's all wrong. Mother's just a runaway machine. Pop's a crazy robot—"

"Stop for Pop!" The scoutmaster was trapped on top of that huge piston, but its blazing lamps raced after Joey and the girl. "Catch 'em, cubs! Hold 'em tight. Or there'll be no Jamboree!"

"I told you, Pop!" Butch scuttled after them. "Don't forget I'm the one that told—"

Ratbait dived at his heels, and they skidded together on the floor.

"Come on, scouts!" Joey was shouting. "Run away with us. Our own genes are good enough."

The floor shuddered under him and that bright sky-slice grew thinner. Lurching on their little tracks, the prams formed a line to guard it. Joey jumped the shrieking tenderfeet, but the girl stumbled. He stopped to pick her up.

"Help us, scouts!' he gasped. "We gotta get away—"

"Catch 'em for Pop!" that metal bellow belted them. "Or there'll be no gold stars for anybody!"

Screeching cubs swarmed around them. The door clanged shut. Pop plunged off the sinking piston, almost too soon. It crunched down on the yellow hood. Hot oil splashed and smoked, but the whips hauled it upright again.

"Don't mess around with M-M-M-M-Mother!" Its anvil voice came back, with a stuttering croak. "She knows best!"

The quivering whips dragged Joey and the girl away from

the clutching cubs and pushed them into a shallow black pit, where now that great black piston had dropped below the level of the floor.

"Sing for your Mother!" old Pop chortled. "Sing for the Jamborree!"

The cubs howled out their official song, and the Jamboree went on. There were Pop-shaped balloons for the tenderfeet, and double scoops of pink ice milk for the cubs, and gold stars for nearly everybody.

"But Mother wants a few of you." Old Pop was a fat cat purring.

When a pointing whip picked Blinkie out, he jumped into the pit without waiting to be dragged. But Butch turned white and tried to run when it struck at him.

"Pop! Not m-m-m-m-me!" he squeaked. "Don't forget I told on Joey. I'm only going on eleven, and I'm in line for leader, and I'll tell on everybody—"

"That's why Mother wants you." Old Pop laughed like a pneumatic hammer. "You're getting too adult."

The whip snaked Butch into the pit, dull eyes bulging more than ever. He slumped down on the slick black piston and struggled like a squashed bug and then lay moaning in a puddle of terror.

Ratbait stood sweating, as the whip came back to him. His stomach felt cold and strange, and the tall red wall spun like a crazy wheel around him, and he couldn't move till the whip pulled him to the rim of the pit.

But there Blinkie took his hand. He shook the whip off, and stepped down into the pit. Joey nodded, and the girl gave him a white, tiny smile. They all closed around her, arms linked tight, as the piston dropped.

"Now hop along for Pop! You've had your Jamboree—"

That hooting voice died away far above, and the pit's round mouth shrank into a blood-colored moon. The hot dark drummed like thunder all around them, and the slick floor tilted. It spilled them all into Mother's red steel jaws.

PLOTTING "JAMBOREE"
by Jack Williamson

PEOPLE KEEP asking, "Where do you get those crazy—uh —new ideas." It's often hard to say, because story sources are seldom fully conscious. When the writer is lucky, creation can be so subtle and so fast that the finished work appears as a sort of instant mental miracle, complete and begging to be typed. Most fiction, however, is born through care and pain, its origins only half mysterious.

Assisting at the birth, the writer can help in two ways. He can fuse fragments into growing wholes, and he can turn abstract generalities into concrete specifics. The fragments may be bits of character or setting or action; the abstractions may be feelings or patterns or themes.

The initial coming-to-life of a story idea is a little like the fertilization of an egg. Two or more elements—perhaps a glimpse of character, the effect of a place, a spark of emotion—join to form a new unity with life and direction and the power to grow.

The writer can't always control its growth, because the roots extend beneath his full awareness. The story comes out of his whole mental being, not simply from conscious technique. Yet technique is essential to help the growing story find its own best shape, and a good sense of plot is the beginning of technique.

A story speaks through a grammar of its own, a bit more complex than the grammar of the sentence. Its meaning and emotional effect, like the sense of a sentence, depend on unity. Its unity comes from the selection and fusion of many elements—style and point of view, theme and mood, character and setting—all so related that none exists without the rest. The first of them is plot.

Plot is happening—but not all happening is plot. A good plot is a patterned sequence of events, a chain of cause and inevitable effect. Complete with the beginning, middle, and ending first described by Aristotle, it can be defined as the whole response of a set of characters to a situation.

The opening shows us people with problems—a detective with a killer to catch, a wandering Greek longing for his home, a prince with a murdered father to avenge, a spaceman down on an unknown planet. Plot interest depends on how much we like or hate the people, on how new and great their problems are, on how near disaster is.

The body of the story shows us the people in live action, as their responses complicate their problems and reveal their traits of character. The detective displays an uncanny acumen; the Greek demonstrates both cunning and courage; the prince exchanges indecisive innocence for cruel resolution. Plot interest rises as time runs out and problems appear impossible to solve.

Surprise or not, the ending shows the problems solved. The mystery killer is identified. The Greek reclaims his wife and home. The prince carries out his tragic mission. The cycle of response completed, the people are back at rest—usually with a gain or loss of life or fortune, with a lesson learned or not—their real nature now fully manifest.

More simply, perhaps, the plot opening asks a "narrative question." Can X get to Mars? Will Y decide to betray the Terran mission? The body delays the answer. In midflight, X collides with an asteroid. Y falls in love with a loyal Terran girl, whom he can't betray. The ending reveals the answer—using clues and weapons and character traits planted in the beginning.

When plot interest is subordinate to character or atmosphere or theme, the story pattern may shift to "organic form"—from the unity of a single conflict to that of a day or a year or a generation, of a journey or a marriage or an illness. The skillful writer selects a pattern to fit his purpose, but a story without form is seldom readable or saleable.

Since science fiction is about the possible, not the actual, many a story answers a what-if question. Jules Verne asked what if men could fly around the moon or reach the center of the earth. Wells inquired what if Martians invaded England, what if a man could travel in time. Social science questions are more popular now. "Jamboree" came from this one: "What if there were a children's world, with no adults allowed?"

It might have been a delightful Peter Pan sort of place, had I not just attended one of Damon Knight's Milford Conferences. These are nonacademic seminars in science-fiction writing. Each member brings a story to be criticized by the other invited professionals. Damon and his guest are masters of story technique, but they tend to view science and the future through lead-colored glasses. Under their influence, I couldn't help seeing the children's world as a pretty grim one.

Incubating the idea, I looked first for conflict. Conflict is the essence of plot, the two sides drawn up with all their forces in the opening, joining indecisive battle in the body, winning and losing at the end. Here, clearly, the inevitable battleground lay between the children and the machines that ruled their unhappy world. Though the plot of man-against-machine has become badly worn, the war of child-against-machine promised a certain novelty.

The outcome troubled me. Involved with the children, I wanted them to win, yet I soon saw that any sort of victory would dull the point of the story. If the machines can be beaten by children, the implication is that they are weak and vulnerable—which these machines are not.

The plot, in other words, must fit the feeling and the meaning of the story. The beginning sets the children against the insane machines that dominate their lives. The body tests the traits of both, as the forlorn campaign against the machines is interrupted by the jamboree. The ending demonstrates the heartless power of Mother and Old Pop.

I began with plot, though many writers are scornful of it. It's true that the basic plot patterns are few and therefore likely to seem trite. Popular fiction—even science fiction—has often relied on crude plot interest, with little regard for anything else. Yet, for all such misuse, plot remains a powerful tool for commanding interest, for creating character, for vitalizing setting, for demonstrating thematic truth.

The traits of a character shine through his plot action. When the city is in danger, one man joins the defenders on the wall, another hides in his cellar, a third sneaks down to open the gates. An alien setting comes to life in plot conflict with the lost spaceman fighting to survive there. Action has meaning; every plot can be read as support for some general theme, false or true, trivial or profound.

Aware of such uses, some modern writers question plot because of its very power. Plot is order, the patterned flow of effect from cause. In the plotted story, people win or lose their battles and receive their rewards, however ironic. If fiction reflects life, plot implies reason and morality or sometimes malice in the operation of the universe.

Once that was fine, but today we are skeptics. The astronomer and the literary artist and the man in the street all tend to find more chaos than fitness in events. Experimental writers are sometimes tempted to represent the senseless confusion they see in the world with senseless confusion on paper. They find few readers.

James Joyce worked out a better solution to a similar dilemma. He wanted to portray modern life as an unheroic round of random impulse and petty frustration, given meaning neither by conventional rewards for conventional goodness nor by conventional punishments for conventional sins. His brilliant ploy inverts the great plot Homer invented to dramatize the triumphant heroism of Odysseus. Leopold Bloom wanders for less than twenty hours instead of twenty years, all around Dublin instead of beyond the known limits of the world. Home at last, the Greek hero slaughters the suitors to recover his faithful wife. Joyce's Jew merely creeps back to bed—wrong end around—with his unfaithful Molly. So inverted, Homer's old plot states Joyce's new theme.

With a simpler plot for "Jamboree," I began to think of how to tell it. There are many ways to make a story, and whatever works is good. Robert Heinlein often seems to put a strong character into a solidly constructed situation, then let the story grow. Now and then I have killed an idea with too much planning, but I like to know where I'm going.

As far as possible, I wanted to do "Jamboree" in scenes. The theory of the dramatic scene, like the theory of the functional plot, I learned from a one-time teacher of writing named John Gallishaw, whose books I studied faithfully. Some people are cool to his advice, but I have found it useful.

Plot and scene together shape a story, providing a blueprint for the whole structure of language and emotion that is to create the illusion of life. Regulating dramatic tension, they control narrative interest. Though they can be abused to exploit trivial material, the greatest writers have used them to move us most deeply.

A complete dramatic scene has five steps: meeting, purpose, clash, outcome, and result. The meeting brings two people or forces together. One has a purpose, which the other resists. They clash, exchanging words or maybe space torpedoes. The outcome is a win or a loss or a draw. The fifth step, the essential result unit, shows the effect upon the larger action of the whole plot, shows the hero nearer his main goal or in despair of ever reaching it.

Good scenes impinge on all our senses. We see the actors and hear their voices. We know the place and time, sense the social atmosphere—not from abstract statement, but from sensory detail. In "Jamboree," I hope the reader can see Pop's blazing eyes, hear the tenderfeet squalling in their prams, smell the stale piss in Blinkie's blankets.

Gallishaw set the length of the scene at 800 words. A. E. van Vogt used to write his stories in units of that length, forcing the interest by tossing in a new mystery or danger that made each scene almost a tiny story. The trouble came when he sometimes failed to fuse all his frantic scenes into one convincing whole.

Superior scenes were written, I think, by the men Captain Joseph Shaw trained while he edited the old *Black*

Mask magazine. I used to review those in Dashiell Hammett's *Maltese Falcon* every year. They have a thematic implication that I dislike—to get maximum clash into every scene, Hammett has to let every other character attack or betray his lone champion of justice, with the implication that his whole world is totally corrupt. But the scenes always dazzle me.

Being a short story, "Jamboree" has no room for many 800-word blocks. Most of the scenes are telescoped into shorter units, and parts of the story—such as the march from the camp toward Mother's—are told in dramatic narrative. This is summarized action, enriched with sensory detail but still economical of space.

In the opening scene, the meeting is between the scoutmaster and the boys. The clash results when they resist Old Pop's purpose to find the missing scout. Brief as it has to be, we see some of the traits of Ratbait and Blinkie and Butch, as well as Pop's. In the outcome, Joey is caught; the result is exposure of his plan.

Though Joey and the girl have been at work a long time, down in the pits, this scene picks up their plot action near the climax, in the very morning of the jamboree. Since fully developed dramatic scenes take space, they should be reserved for important action, with explanations and transitions kept as smooth and brief as may be.

Thinking out the scenes, I had to reconsider the tone of the story. To be endurable, its darkness needed relief. The simplest sort would have been a brighter ending, but a conquerable grimness isn't really grim. The relief I came to search for, as the story took shape, was that of irony—an indirection of statement that could blacken the blackness, rather than diluting it.

Irony may lie in either language or action. In a great ironic plot, Oedipus discovers that the criminal he has been hunting is himself. The smaller ironies I found for this story are those of character and style—chiefly in the contradiction between Old Pop's speech and its mechanical reality. I hope they support the theme of the story.

On the surface, "Jamboree" is about men—or children—and machines. I first assumed that the theme was going to be some critical comment on technological progress, but I presently found a more universal theme, not planned at all. Discussing themes is always dangerous, because fiction speaks to the emotions, in a different voice to every reader. But now, to me, Mother and Old Pop are only metaphors, their symbolic meaning hinted by their ironic names.

"Jamboree," I now believe, is a satire on society—a bitter outcry of the stricken individual, trapped in the duel with society that none of us escapes. That old revolt of the naked self against the ruling group is the actual human condition, and the mainspring of most fiction. In each of us, a billion years of animal evolution collides with the cruel new claims of social life. Though I sensed it only dimly when I began the story, Mother and Old Pop stand for all the conventions and establishments, all the traditions and the customs and the laws, that maim and kill our natural selves.

The children in the story stand for all children—even the child I was. As happens to us all, they were born into the ambiguous grip of a society that frustrates them lovingly, cripples them kindly, punishes them for their own benefit. Mother and Old Pop are the family, the first and strongest social unit the child ever meets. The half-seen world outside can stand for all the other social machinery that exists to kill the innocent animal in us, for the sake of the social adult.

Thus, I think, "Jamboree" must have grown out of my own largely forgotten pain at finding what happens to a child. Looking back from what I am, a more or less fully conditioned adult, I can see that it has to happen. Social animals, we can't live alone. There's no malice anywhere, nobody at all to blame. I myself have become another cog in the machine. But the story, like a wail in the night, reflects the hopeless terror that one child felt.

WE, IN SOME STRANGE POWER'S EMPLOY, MOVE ON A RIGOROUS LINE

by Samuel R. Delany

—for R. Zelazny

Only the dark and her screaming.

First: sparks glint on her feet, and crack and snap, lighting rocks, dirt. Then no screams. She almost falls, whips erect: silver leggings. Pop-pop-pop. Light laces higher, her arms are waving (trying to tell myself, "But she's dead already—"), and she waves like a woman of white and silver paper, burning on the housing of the great ribbed cable exposed in the gully we'd torn from the earth.

"Thinking about your promotion?"

"Huh?" I looked up on Scott who was poking at me with a freckled finger. Freckles, dime-sized and penny-colored, covered face, lips, arms, shoulders, got lost under the gold hair snarling his chest and belly. "What's it feel like to be a section-devil? I've been opting for it two years now." Freckled fingers snapped. "Pass me up and take you!" He leaned back in his hammock, dug beneath his tool belt to scratch himself.

I shook my head. "No, something else. Something that happened awhile back. Nothing, really."

Night scoured our windows.

The Gila Monster sped.

Light wiped the panes and slipped away.

Scott suddenly sat up, caught his toes, and frowned. "Sometimes I think I'll spend the rest of my working life just a silver-suited line-demon, dancing along them damned strings." He pointed with his chin at the cross-section, sixteen-foot cable chart. "Come thirty-five, when I want to retire—and it's less than ten years off—what'll I be able to say? I did my job well?" He made a fist around the hammock edge. "I didn't do it well enough to make anything out of it." Hand open and up. "Some big black so-and-so like you comes along and three years later—section-devil!"

"You're a better demon than I am Scott."

"Don't think I don't know it, either." Then he laughed. "No, let *me* tell *you*: a good demon doesn't necessarily make a good devil. The skills are different skills. The talents aren't the same. Hell, Blacky, you'd think, as your friend, I'd spare you. Say, when do you check out of this cabin? Gotta get used to somebody else's junk. Will you stay on at the old Monster here?"

"They said something about transferring me to Iguana. What with the red tape, it won't happen for a couple of weeks. I'll probably just give Mabel a hand till then. She gave me a room right over the tread motor. I complained about your snoring, and we agreed it would be an improvement."

That rated a swing; he just nodded.

I thought around for something to say and came up with: "You know I'm due an assistant, and I can choose—"

"Hell!" He flung himself back so I could only see his

feet. (Underneath the hammock: one white woolen sock [gray toe], magazine, three wrenches.) "I'm no clerk. You have me running computers and keeping track of your confusion, filing reclamation plans and trying to hunt them out again—and all that for a drop in salary—"

"I wouldn't drop your salary."

"I'd go up the wall anyway."

"Knew that's what you'd say."

"Knew you'd make me say it."

"Well," I said, "Mabel asked me to come around to her office."

"Yeah. Sure." Release, relief. "Clever devil, Mabel. Hey You'll be screening new applicants for whoever is gonna share my room now you been kicked upstairs. See if you can get a girl in here?"

"If I can." I grinned and stepped outside.

Gila Monster guts?

Three quarters of a mile of corridors (much less than some luxury ocean liners); two engine rooms that power the adjustable treads that carry us over land and sea; a kitchen, cafeteria, electrical room, navigation offices, office offices, tool repair shop, and cetera. With such in its belly, the Gila Monster crawls through the night (at about a hundred and fifty *k*'s cruising speed) sniffing along the great cables (courtesy the Global Power Commission) that net the world, web evening to night, dawn to day, and yesterday to morrow.

"Come in, Blacky," Mabel said at my knock.

She brushed back silver hair from her silver collar (the hair is natural) and closed the folder. "Seems we have a stop coming up just over the Canadian border."

"Pick up Scott's new roommate?"

"Power Cadet Susan Suyaki. Seventeen years old. Graduated third in her class last summer."

"Seventeen? Scott should like that."

"Wish she had some experience. The bright ones come out of school too snooty."

"I didn't."

"You still are."

"Oh, well. Scott prefers them with spirit."

"They're flying her in by helicopter to the site of our next job."

"Which line broke?"

"No break. It's a conversion."

I raised an eyebrow. "A rare experience for Miss Suyaki. I've only been through one, during my first couple of months in Salamander. That was a goodly while ago."

Mabel gave me a super-cynical-over-the-left-cheekbone. "You haven't *been* in the Power Corps a goodly while You're just brilliant, that's all."

"It was a goodly while for *me*. Not all of us have had your thirty years experience, ma'am."

"I've always felt experience was vastly overrated as a teacher." She started to clean her nails with a metal rule. "Otherwise, I would never have recommended you for promotion." Mabel is a fine devil.

"Thankee, thankee," I sat and looked at the ceiling map. "A conversion." Musing. "Salamander covered most of Mongolia. A little village in Tibet had to be connected up to the lines. We put cable through some of the damnedest rock. They were having an epidemic of some fever that gave you oozy blisters, and the medical crew was trying to set itself up at the same time. We worked twenty-four hours a day for three days, running lines, putting in outlets, and hooking up equipment. Three days to pull that primitive enclave of skin huts, caves, and lean-tos into the twenty-first century. Nothing resembling a heater in the whole place and it was snowing when we got there."

Over joined fingertips Mabel bobbed her chin. "And to think, they'd been doddering along like that for the last three thousand years."

"Probably not much more than two hundred. The village had been established by refugees from the Sino-Japanese War. Still, I get your point."

"They were happy when you left?"

"They were happi-*er*," I said. "Still, you look at the maps—you trace cables over the world, and it's pretty hard to think there are still a few places that haven't been converted."

"I'm not as dreamy as you. Every couple of years Gila or Iguana stumbles over a little piece of the planet that's managed to fall through the net. They'll probably be turning them up a hundred years from now. People cling to their backwardness."

"Maybe you're—the border of *Canada!*"

"That is the longest take I've ever seen. Wake up, boy. Here I've been telling everybody how bright you are, recommending you for promotion—"

"Mabel, how can we have a conversion on the border of Canada? You convert villages in upper Anatolia, nameless little islands in the Indian Ocean—Tibet. There's no place you could lay another cable in the Americas. A town converted to Global Power along there?"

Mabel bobbed some more. "I don't like conversions. Always something catastrophic. If everything went by the books, you'd think it would be one of our easiest maneuvers."

"You know me. I never go by the books."

She, musing this time: "True, doll. I still don't like 'em."

"The one I was telling you about in Tibet. We had a bad accident."

Mabel asked what it was with her eyebrows.

"A burning. Middle of the night, when somebody had wandered down into the trough to troubleshoot one of the new connections. She was climbing up on the housing, when the power went on. Some sort of high amperage short. She went up like the proverbial moth."

Mabel stopped bobbing. "Who was she?"

"My wife."

"Oh." After a moment she said. "Burnings are bad. Hell of a waste of power, if nothing else. I wondered why you chose to room with Scott when you first came on the Gila Monster rather than Jane, Judy, or—"

"Julia was the young lady out for my tired, brown body back then."

"You and your wife must have come straight out of the academy together. In your first years? Blacky, that's terrible. . . ."

"We were, it was, and it was."

"I didn't know." Mabel looked adequately sincere.

"Don't tell me you didn't guess?"

"Don't joke . . . well, joke if you want." Mabel is a fine woman. "A conversion just over the Canadian border." She shook her head. "Blacky, we're going to have a problem you and I."

"How so, ma'am?"

"Again: you are going to have a problem with me. I am going to have a problem with you."

"Pray, how, gentle lady?"

"You're a section-devil now. I'm a section-devil. You've been one for just under six hours. I've been one for just over sixteen years. But by the books, we are in equal positions of authority."

"Fair maid," I said, "thou art off thy everloving nut."

"You're the one who doesn't go by the books. I do. Power of authority divided between two people doesn't work."

"If it makes you feel any better, I still consider you boss. You're the best boss I ⸱r had, too. Besides, I like you."

"Blacky," she looked up at the skylight where the moon, outside the frame, still lit the tessellations, "there is something going on out there just across the border that I guess I know more about than you. You only know it's a conversion, and where it is, is odd. Let me warn you: you will want to handle it one way. I will want to handle it another."

"So we do it your way."

"Only I'm not so sure my way is best."

"Mabel—"

"Go, swarthy knight. We meet beyond the Canadian borders to do battle." She stood up looking very serious.

"If you say so."

"See you in the morning, Blacky."

I left the office wondering at knights and days. Oh well, however, anyway: Scott was snoring, so I read until the rush of darkness outside was drifting gray.

II

The dawning sky (working top to bottom):
Sable, azure, gules—
—mountains dexter, sinister a burst of oak, lots of pines, a few maples. The Gila Monster parked itself astride a foamy brook below a waterfall. I went outside on the balcony and got showered as leaves sprinkled the stainless flank of our great striding beast.

"Hello? Hey, hello!"

"Hi." I waved toward where she was climbing down the—whoops! into the water to her knee. She squealed, climbed back up the rock, and looked embarrassed.

"Cadet Suyaki?"

"Eh . . . yes, sir." She tried to rub her leg dry. Canadian streams at dawn are cold.

I took off my shirt, made a ball, and flung it to her. "Section-devil Jones." She caught it. "Blacky'll do. We're pretty informal around here."

"Oh . . . thank you." She lifted her silver legging, removed her boot to dry a very pretty ankle.

I gave the stairway a kick.

Clank-*chchchchc*-thud!

The steps unfolded, and the metal feet stamped into pine needles. I went down to the bank.

"Waiting long?"

She grinned. "Oh, I just got here."

And beyond the rocks there was a corroborative roar and snapping; a helicopter swung up through the trees.

Cadet Suyaki stood quickly and waved.

Somebody in the cockpit waved back till copper glare wiped him out.

"We saw you getting parked—" She looked down the length of Gila Monster.

I have said, or have I?

Cross an armadillo with a football field. Nurse the offspring on a motherly tank. By puberty: one Gila Monster.

"I'll be working under you?"

"Myself and Mabel Whyman."

She looked at me questioningly.

"Section-Devil Whyman—Mabel—is really in charge. I was just promoted from line-demon yesterday."

"Oh. Congratulations!"

"Hey, Blacky! Is that my new roommate?"

"That," I pointed at Scott, all freckled and golden, leaning over the rail, "is your pardner. You'll be rooming together."

Scott came down the steps, barefoot, denims torn off mid-thigh, tool belt full of clippers, meters, and insulation spools.

"Susan Suyaki," I announced, "Scott Mackelway."

She extended her hand. "I'm glad to meet—"

Scott put a big hand on each of little Miss Suyaki's shoulders. "So am I, honey. So am I."

"We'll be working very close together, won't we?" asked Susan brightly. "I like that!" She squeezed one of his forearms. "Oh, I think this'll work out very well."

"Sure it will," Scott said. "I'm . . ." Then I saw an open space on his ear pinken. "I sure hope it does."

"You two demons get over to the chameleon nest!"

Scott, holding Sue's hand, pointed up to the balcony. "That's Mabel. Hey, boss! We going any place I gotta put my shoes on?"

"Just scouting. Get going."

"We keep the chameleon over the port tread." Scott led Sue down the man-high links of the Monster's chain drive.

Thought: some twenty-four hours by, if Mabel yelled, "You two demons . . ." the two demons would have been Scott and me.

She came, all silver, down the steps.

"You smile before the joust, Britomart?"

"Blacky, I'm turning into a dirty old woman." At the

bottom step, she laid her forefinger on my chest, drew it slowly down my stomach and finally hooked my belt. "You're beautiful. And I'm not smiling, I'm leering."

I put my arm around her shoulder, and we walked the pine needles. She put her hands in her silver pockets. Hip on my thigh, shoulder knocking gently on my side, hair over my arm, she pondered the ferns and the oaks, the rocks and the water, the mountain and the flanks of our Gila Monster couchant, the blazes of morning between the branches. "You're a devil. So there are things I can say to you, ostensibly, that would be meaningless to the others." She nodded ahead to where Scott and Sue were just disappearing around the three-meter hub.

"I await thy words most eagerly, Lady."

Mabel gestured at the Monster. "Blacky, do you know what the Monster, and the lines he prowls, really are?"

"I can tell you don't want an answer out of the book from your tone of voice, Miss Rules-and-Regulations."

"They're symbols of a way of life. Global Power Lines keep how many hundreds of thousands of refrigeration units functioning around the equator to facilitate food-storage; they've made the Arctic habitable. Cities like New York and Tokyo have cut population to a third of what they were a century ago. Back then, people used to be afraid they would crowd each other off the planet, would starve from lack of food. Yet the majority of the world was farming less than three percent of the arable land, and living on less than twenty percent of the world's surface. Global Power Lines meant that man could live any place on dry land he wanted, and a good number of places under the sea. National boundaries used to be an excuse for war; now they're only cartographical expedients. Riding in the Monster's belly, it's ironic that we are further from this way of life we're helping to maintain than most. But we still benefit."

"Of course."

"Have you ever asked yourself exactly how?"

"Education, leisure time," I suggested, "early and sliding retirements. . ."

Mabel chuckled. "Oh, much more, Blacky. So much more. Men and women work together; our navigator, Faltaux, is one of the finest poets writing in French today, with an international reputation, and is still the best navigator I've ever had. And Julia, who keeps us so well fed and can pilot us quite as competently as I can, and is such a lousy painter, works with you and me and Faltaux and

Scott on the same Maintenance Station. Or just the fact that you can move out of Scott's room one day and little Miss Suyaki can move in the next with ease that would have amazed your great-great ancestors in Africa as much as mine in Finland. *That's* what this steel egg-crate means."

"Okay," I said. "I'm moved."

We came around the hub. Scott was heaving up the second door of the chameleon's garage and pointing out to Sue where the jack and the graphite can were kept.

"Some people." Mabel went on as I dropped my arm from her shoulder, "don't particularly like this way of life. Which is why we are about to attempt a conversion here on the Canadian border."

"A conversion?" Sue popped up. "Isn't that when you switch an area or a dwelling to Global—"

At which point Scott swung at Mabel. He caught her upside the head. She yelled and went tumbling into the leaves.

I jumped back, and Sue did a thing with her Adam's apple.

Something went *Nnnnnnnnnnn* against the hub, then chattered away through the ferns. Ferns fell.

"Look!" Sue cried.

I was staring at the eight-inch scratch in the Gila Monster's very hard hide, at about the level where Mabel's carotid had been a moment back.

But across the water, scrambling up the rocks, was a yellow-headed kid wearing a little less than Scott.

Sue ran through the weeds and picked up the blade. "Were they trying to *kill* somebody?"

Mabel shrugged. "You're Cadet Suyaki? We're going to explore the conversion site. Dear me, that looks vicious."

"I used to hunt with a bolo," Sue said warily. "At home. But one of these . . . ?" Two blades were bolted in a twisted cross, all four prongs sharpened.

"My first too. Hope it's my last." Mabel looked around the clearing. "Am I ever optimistic. Pleased to meet you, Suyaki. Well, come on. Crank up Nelly. And for Pete's sake, let's get *in*."

The chameleon, ten feet long, is mostly transparent plastic, which means you can see sea, sunset, or forest right through.

Scott drove with Mabel beside him.

Me and Sue sat in back.

We found the chewed-up asphalt of an old road and crawled right along up the mountain.

"Where are . . . we going, exactly?" Sue asked.

"Honey," Mabel said, "I'll let you know when we get there." She put the throwing blade in the glove compartment with a grunt. Which does a lot of good with transparent plastic.

III

Sue leaned against the door. "Oh, look! Look down!"

We'd wound high enough and looped back far enough on the abominable road so that you could gaze down through the breaks; beyond the trees and rocks you could see the Gila Monster. It still looked big.

"Eh . . . look up," suggested Scott and slowed the chameleon. A good-sized tree had come up by the roots and fallen across the road.

The man standing in front of it was very dirty. The kid behind, peering through the Medusa of roots, was the one who had tried to decapitate Mabel.

"What . . . are they?" Sue whispered.

"Scott and Sue, you stay right here and keep the door open so we can get in fast. Blacky, we go on up."

The man's hair, under the grease, was brass-colored. Some time ago his left cheek had been opened up, then sewn so clumsily you could see the cross-stitching. The lobe of his left ear was a rag of flesh. His sleeve-ripped shirt hung buttonless and too short to tuck in, even if he had a mind to. A second welt plowed an inch furrow through chest hair, wrecked his right nipple, and disappeared under his collar.

As we came up, Mabel took the lead; I overtook her, she gave me a faint-subtle-nasty and stepped ahead again.

He was a hard guy, but the beginning of a gut was showing over the double bar and chain contraption he used to fasten his studded belt. At first I thought he was wearing mismatched shoes: one knee-high, scuffed, and crack-soled boot. The other foot was bare, a length of black chain around the ankle, two toes, little and middle, gone.

I looked back at his face to see his eyes come up to mine.

Well, I was still sans shirt; back at the chameleon Sue's pants leg was still rolled up. Mabel was the only one of us proofed neat and proper.

He looked at Mabel. He looked at me. He looked at Mabel. Then he bent his head and said. "Rchht-*ah*-pt, what are you doing up here, huh?" That first word produced a yellow oyster about eight inches north of Mabel's boot toe, six south of his bare one. His head came up, the lower lip glistening and hanging away from long, yellow teeth.

"Good morning." I offered my hand. "We're . . ." He looked at it. ". . . surveying."

He took his thumb from his torn pocket; we shook. A lot of grease, a lot of callus, it was the hand of a very big man who had bitten his nails since he was a very small boy.

"Yeah? What are you surveying?"

He wore a marvelous ring.

"We're from Global Power Commission."

Take a raw, irregular nugget of gold—

"Figured. I saw your machine down the road."

—a nugget three times the size either taste or expediency might allow a ring—

"We've had reports that the area is underpowered for the number of people living here."

—punch a finger-sized hole, so that most of the irregularities are on one side—

"Them bastards down in Hainesville probably registered a complaint. Well, we don't live in Hainesville. Don't see why it should bother them."

—off center in the golden crater place an opal, big as his—*my* thumbnail—

"We have to check it out. Inadequate power doesn't do anybody any good."

—put small diamonds in the tips of the three prongs that curved to cage the opal—

"You think so?"

—and in the ledges and folds of bright metal capping his enlarged knuckle, bits of spodumene, pyrope, and spinel, all abstract, all magnificent.

"Look, mister," I said, "the Hainesville report says there are over two dozen people living on this mountain. The power commission doesn't register a *single* outlet."

He slipped his hands into his back pockets. "Don't believe I have seen any, now you mention it."

Mabel said, "The law governs how much power and how many outlets must be available and accessible to each person. We'll be laying lines up here this afternoon and tomorrow morning. We're not here to make trouble. We don't want to find any."

"What makes you think you might?"

"Well, your friend over there already tried to cut my head off."

He frowned, glanced back through the roots. Suddenly he leaned back over the trunk and took a huge swipe. "Get out of here, Pitt!"

The kid squeaked. The face flashed in the roots (lank hair, a spray of acne across flat cheek and sharp chin), and jangling at her hip was a hank of throwing blades. She disappeared into the woods.

As the man turned, I saw, tattooed on the bowl of his shoulder, a winged dragon, coiled about and gnawing at a swastika.

Mabel ignored the whole thing:

"We'll be finished down the mountain this morning and will start bringing the lines up here this afternoon."

He gave half a nod—lowered his head and didn't bring it up—and that was when it dawned on me we were doing this thing wrong.

"We do want to do this easily," I said. "We're not here to make problems for you."

His hands crawled from his knees back to his waist.

"You can help us by letting people know that. If anyone has any questions about what we're doing, or doesn't understand something they can come and ask for me. I'm Section-Devil Jones. Just ask for Blacky down at the Gila Monster."

"My name's Roger . . ." followed by something Polish and unpronounceable that began with Z and ended in Y. "If you have problems, you can come to me. Only I ain't saying I can do anything."

Good exit line. But Roger stayed where he was. And Mabel beside me was projecting stark disapproval.

"Where do most of the folks around here live?" I asked, to break the silence.

He nodded up. "On High Haven."

"Is there somebody in charge, a mayor or something like that I could talk to?"

Roger looked at me like he was deciding where I'd break easiest if he hit. "That's why I'm down here talking to you.'"

"You?" I didn't ask. What I did say was: "Then perhaps we could go up and see the community. I'd like to see how many people are up there, perhaps suggest some equipment, determine where things have to be done."

"You want to visit on High?"

"'If we might."

He made a fist, and scratched his neck with the prongs of his ring. "All right." He gestured back toward the chameleon. "You can't get that any further up the road."

"Will you take us, then?"

He thought awhile. "Sure." He let a grin open over the yellow cage of teeth. "Get you back down, too." Small victory.

"Just a moment," Mabel said, "while we go back and tell the driver."

We strolled to the chameleon.

"You don't sound very happy with my attempt to make peace."

"Have I said a word?"

"*Just* what I mean. Can you imagine how these people live, Mabel, if Roger there is the head of the Chamber of Commerce?"

"I can imagine."

"He looks as bad as any of those villagers in Tibet. Did you *see* the little girl? This, in the middle of the twenty-first century!"

". . . just over the Canadian border. Scott," Mabel said, "take me and Sue back down to the Monster. If you are not back by noon, Blacky, we will come looking for you."

"Huh? You mean you're not going with me? Look," I told Scott's puzzled frown, "don't worry, I'll be back. Sue, can I have my shirt?"

"Oh, I'm terribly sorry! Here you are. It may be damp—"

"Mabel, if we did go up there together—"

"Blacky, running this operation with two devils admittedly presents problems. Running it with none at all is something else entirely. You're a big devil now. You know what you're doing. I even know. I just think you're crazy."

"*Ma*-bel—"

"On up there with you! And sow as much goodwill as you can. If it avoids one tenth the problems I know we're going to have in the next twelve hours, I will be eternally grateful."

Then Mabel, looking determined, and Sue and Scott, looking bewildered, climbed into the chameleon.

"Oh." She leaned out the door. "Give this back to them." She handed me the throwing blade. "See you by noon." The chameleon swayed off down the road. I put my shirt on, stuck the blade in my belt and walked back to Roger.

He glanced at it, and we both thought nasty-nasty-evilness at one another. "Come on." He climbed over the tree. I climbed over after.

Parked behind the trunk was an old twin-turbo pteracycle. Roger lifted it by one black and chrome, bat-form wing. The chrome was slightly flaked. With one hand he grasped the steering shaft and twisted the choke ring gently. The other hand passed down the wing with the indifference we use to mask the grosser passions. "Hop on my broomstick and I'll take you up to where the angels make their Haven." He grinned.

And I understood many things.

So:

Small Essay

on a phenomenon current some fifty years back when the date had three zeroes. (Same time as the first cables were being laid and demons were beginning to sniff about the world in silver armor, doctoring breaks, repairing relays, replacing worn housings. Make the fancy sociological connections, please.) That's when peteracycles first became popular as a means of short-(and sometimes not so short-) range transportation. Then they were suddenly taken up by a particularly odd set of asocials. Calling themselves individualists, they moved in veritable flocks; dissatisfied with society, they wracked the ages for symbols from the most destructive epochs: skull and bones, fasces, swastika, and guillotine. They were accused of the most malicious and depraved acts, sometimes with cause, sometimes without. They took the generic name of angels (Night's Angels, Red Angels, Hell's Angels, Bloody Angels, one of these lifted from a similar cult popular another half century before. But then most of their mythic accouterments were borrowed). The common sociological explanation: they were a reaction to population decentralization, the last elements of violence in a neutral world. Psychological: well, after all, what does a pteracycle look like?—two round cam-turbines on which you sit between the wings, then this six-foot metal shaft sprouting up between your legs that you steer with (hence the sobriquet "broomstick") and nothing else but goggles between you and the sky. You figure it. Concluding remarks: angels were a product of the turn of the century. But nobody's heard anything serious about them for thirty years. They went out with neon buttons, the common cold, and transparent vinyl jockey shorts. Oh, the teens of *siècle* twenty-one saw some goodies! The End.

I climbed on the back seat. Roger got on the front, toed one of the buttons on the stirrup (to do any fancy flying you have to do some pretty fast button-pushing; ergo, the bare foot), twisted the throttle ring, and lots of leaves shot up around my legs. The cycle skidded up the road, bounced twice on cracks, then swerved over the edge. We dropped ten feet before we caught the draft and began the long arc out and up. Roger flew without goggles.

The wind over his shoulder carried a smell I first thought was the machine. Imagine a still that hasn't bathed for three months. He flew *very* well.

"How many people are there in High Haven?" I called.

"What?"

"I said, how may people are there in—"

"About twenty-seven!"

We curved away from the mountain, curved back.

The Gila Monster flashed below, was gone behind rocks. The mountain turned, opened a rocky gash.

At the back of the gorge, vaulting the stream that plummeted the mountain's groin, someone had erected a mansion. It was a dated concrete and glass monstrosity of the late twentieth century (pre-power lines). Four terraced stories were cantilevered into the rock. Much of the glass was broken. Places that had once been garden had gone wild with vine and brush. A spectacular metal stairway wound from the artificial pool by the end of the roadway that was probably the same one we'd ridden with the chameleon, from porch to porch, rust-blotched like a snake's back.

The house still had much stolid grandure. Racked against a brick balustrade were maybe twenty pteracycles (what better launch than the concrete overhang, railing torn away). One cycle was off the rack. A guy was on his knees before it, the motor in pieces around him. A second, fists on hips, was giving advice.

A third guy shielded his eyes to watch us. A couple of others stopped by the edge of the pool. One was the girl, Pitt, who had been down with Roger before.

"High Haven?"

"What?" Pteracycles are loud.

"Is that High Haven?"

"Yeah!" We glided between the rocks, skimmed foaming boulders, rose toward glass and concrete. Cement rasped beneath the runners and we jounced to a stop.

A couple of guys stepped from a broken window. A couple more came up the steps. Someone looking from the upper porch disappeared, to return a moment later with five others, another girl among them.

There was a lot of dirt, a lot of hair, a number of earrings (I counted four more torn ears; I'd avoid fights if I were going to wear my jewelry that permanent) a kid with much red hair—couldn't quite make a beard yet— straddled the cycle rack. He pushed back the flap of his leather jacket to scratch his bare belly with black nails. The dragon on his chest beat its wings about the twisted cross.

I got off the cycle left, Roger right.

Someone said: "Who's that?"

A few of the guys glanced over their shoulders, then stepped aside so we could see.

She stood by the dawn-splashed hem of glass at the side of the broken wall-window.

"He's from the Global Power Commission." Roger shoved a thumb at me. "They're parked down the mountain."

"You can tell him to go back to hell where he came from."

She wasn't young. She was beautiful though.

"We don't need anything he's selling.'

The others mumbled, shuffled.

"Shut it," Roger said. "He's not selling anything."

I stood there feeling uncomfortably silver, but wondering that I'd managed to win over Roger.

"That's Fidessa," he said.

She stepped through the window.

Wide, high facial bones, a dark mouth and darker eyes. I want to describe her hair as amber, but it was an amber so dark only direct sunlight caught its reds. The morning fell full on it; it spread her shoulders. Her hands were floured, and she smeared white on her hips as she came toward me.

"Fidessa?" All right. I'm not opposed to reality imitating art if it doesn't get in the way.

"He's okay," Roger said in response to her look.

"Yeah?"

"Yeah. Get out of the way." He shoved her. She nearly collided with one of the men, who just stepped out of the way in time. She still gave the poor guy a withering *noli me tangere* stare. Kept her stuff, too.

"You want to see the place?" Roger said and started in. I followed.

Someone who looked like he was used to it picked up Roger's cycle and walked it to the rack.

Fidessa came up beside us as we stepped into the house.

"How long has this bunch been here?" I asked.

"There's been angels on High for forty years. They come; they go. Most of this bunch has been here all summer."

We crossed a room where vandals, time, and fire had left ravage marks. The backs of the rooms had been cut into the rock. One wall, wood-paneled, had become a palimpsest of scratched names and obscenities: old motors and motor parts, a pile of firewood, rags, and chains.

"We don't want power up here," Fidessa said. "We don't need it." Her voice was belligerent and intense.

"How do you survive?"

"We hunt," Roger said as the three of us turned down a stone stairwell. The walls at the bottom flickered. "There's Hainesville about ten miles from here. Some of us go over there and work when we have to."

"Work it over a little too?" (Roger's mouth tightened.) "When you have to?"

"When we have to."

I could smell meat cooking. And bread.

I glanced at Fidessa's powdered hips. They rocked with her walking: I didn't look away.

"Look." I stopped three steps from the doorway. "About the power installation here." Light over my uniform deviled the bottom of my vision.

Roger and Fidessa looked.

"You've got over two dozen people here, and you say there have been people here for forty years? How do you cook? What do you do for heat in winter? Suppose you have medical emergencies? Forget the law. It's made for you; not us."

"Go to hell," Fidessa said and started to turn away. Roger pulled her back by the shoulder.

"I don't care how you live up here," I said because at least Roger was listening. "But you've got winter sitting on your doorstop. You use liquid fuel for your broomsticks. You could have them converted to battery and run them off of rechargeable cells for a third of the cost."

"Storage cells still give you about a hundred and fifty miles less than a full liquid tank."

Fidessa looked disgusted and started downstairs again. I think Roger was losing patience because he turned after her. I followed again.

The lower room was filled with fire.

Chains and pulley apparatus hung from the ceiling. Two furnaces were going. Two pit fires had been dug into the floor. The ceiling was licked across with inky tongues. Hot air brushed back and forth across my face; the third brush left it sweaty.

I looked for food.

"This is our forge." Roger picked up a small sledge and rattled it against a sheet of corrugated iron leaning on the wall. "Danny, come out here!"

Barefoot, soot-smeared, the smears varnished with sweat: bellows and hammers had pulled the muscles taut, chiseled and defined them, so that each sat on his frame apart. Haircut and bath, admitted, he would have been a fine-looking kid—twenty, twenty-five? He came forward knuckling his left eye. The right was that strange blue-gray that always seems to be exploding when it turns up (so rarely) in swarthy types like him.

"Hey there! What you doing?" Roger grimaced at me. "He's nearly deaf."

Danny dropped his fist from his face and motioned us into the back.

And I caught my breath.

What he'd been rubbing wasn't an eye at all. Scarred, crusted, then the crust broken and drooling; below his left eyebrow was only a leaking sore.

We followed Danny between the fires and anvils to a worktable at the back. Piles of throwing blades (I touched the one in my belt) were at varied stages of completion. On the pitted boards among small hammers, punches, and knives, were some lumps of gold, a small pile of gems, and three small ingots of silver. About the jeweler's anvil lay earrings, and a buckle with none of the gems set.

"This is what you're working on now?" Roger picked up the buckle in greasy fingers already weighted with gold.

I bent to see, then pointed from the buckle to Roger's ring, and looked curious. (Why are we always quiet or shouting before the deaf?) Roger nodded.

"Danny does a lot of stuff for us. He's a good machinist, too. We're all pretty good turbo mechanics, but Danny here can do real fine stuff. Sometimes we fly him over to Hainesville and he works there."

"Another source of income?"

"Right."

Just then Pitt came between the flames. She held half a loaf of bread. "Hey, Danny!" in a voice for the deaf, "I brought you some—" saw us and stopped.

Dan looked up, grinned, and circled the girl's shoulder with one arm, took the bread in the other hand, and bit. His smile reflected on Pitt's.

The elastic fear loosened on her face as she watched the one-eyed smith chewing crust. She was very close to pretty then.

I was glad of that.

Dan turned back to the bench, Pitt's shoulder still tucked under his arm. He fingered the rings, found a small one for her, and she pulled forward with, "Oh . . ." and the gold flickered in her palm. The smile moved about her face like flame. (The throwing blades clinked on her hip.) Silent Dan had the rapt look of somebody whose mind was bouncing off the delight he could give others.

Fidessa said. "Have they got all of the first batch out of the ovens?" She looked at the bread and actually snarled. Then she sucked her teeth, turned, and marched away.

"Say," I asked Pitt, "do you like it up here?"

She dropped the ring, looked at me; then all the little lines of fear snapped back.

I guess Dan hadn't heard me, but he registered Pitt's discomfort. As he looked between us, his expression moved toward bewildered anger.

"Come on." Roger surprised me with a cuff on the shoulder. "Leave the kids alone. Get out of here." I was going to object to being pushed, but I guess Roger just pushed people. We left.

"Hey," Roger said, watching his feet as he walked, "I want to explain something to you." We left the fires. "We don't want any power up here."

"That has come across." I tried to sound as sincere as he did. "But there is the law." Sincerity is my favorite form of belligerence.

Roger stopped in front of the window (unbroken here), put his hands in his back pockets, and watched the stream spit down the gorge.

It was, I realized, the same stream the Gila Monster was parked across a mile below.

"You know I'm new at this job, Blacky," he said after a while. "I've just been archangel a couple of weeks. The only reason I took over the show is because I had some ideas on how to do it better than the guy before me. One of my ideas was to run it with as little trouble as possible."

"Who was running it before?"

"Sam was archangel before I was, and Fidessa was head cherub. They ran the business up here, and they ran it hard."

"Sam?"

"Take a whole lot of mean and pour it into a hide about three times as ugly as mine: Sam. He put out Danny's eye. When we get hold of a couple of cases of liquor, we have some pretty wild times up here. Sam came down to the forge to fool around. He heated up one end of a pipe and started swinging it at people. He liked to see them jump and holler. That's the kind of mean he was. Danny doesn't like people fooling around with his tools and things anyway. Sam got after Pitt, and Danny rushed him. So Sam stuck the hot pipe into Danny's head." Roger flexed his thumbs. "When I saw that, I realized I was going to have to do something. We rumbled about two weeks ago." He laughed and dropped his hands. "There was a battle in Haven that day!"

"What happened?"

He looked at the water. "You know the top porch of Haven? I threw him off the top porch onto the second. Then I came down and threw him off onto the bottom one." He pointed out the window. "Then I came down and threw him into the river. He hung around until I finally told the guys to run him down the rocks where I couldn't see him no more." Behind his back now he twisted his ring. "I can't see him. Maybe he made it to Hainesville."

"Did . . . eh, Fidessa go along with the promotion?"

"Yeah." He brought his hands before him. Light struck and struck in the irregularities of metal. "I don't think I would have tried for the job if she hadn't. She's a lot of woman."

"Kill the king and take the queen."

"I took Fidessa first. Then I had to . . . kill the king. That's the way things go in Haven."

"Roger?"

He didn't look at me.

"Look, you've got a kid back there at the anvil who needs a doctor. You say he's a good part of your bread and butter. And you let him walk around with a face like that? What *are* you trying to do?"

"Sam used to say we were trying to live long enough to show the bastards how mean we could be. I say we're just trying to live."

"Suppose Danny's eye infection decides to spread? I'm not casting moral aspersions just to gum up the works. I'm asking if you're even doing what you want to."

He played with his ring.

"So you've avenged Danny; you won the fair damsel. What about that infection—"

Roger turned on me. His scar twisted on his cheek and lines of anger webbed his forehead. "You really think we didn't try to get him to a doctor? We took him to Hainesville, then we took him to Kingston, then back to Hainesville and finally out to Edgeware. We carried that poor screaming half-wit all over the night." He pointed back among the fires. "Danny grew up in an institute, and you get him anywhere near a city when he's scared, and he'll try to run away. We couldn't get him in to a doctor."

"He didn't run away from here when his eye was burned."

"He lives here. He's got a place to do the few things he can do well. He's got a woman. He's got food and people to take care of him. The business with Sam, I don't even think he understood what happened. When you're walking through a forest and a tree falls on you and breaks your leg, you don't run away from the forest. Danny didn't understand that he was more important in Haven than big Sam with all his orders and bluster and beat-you-to-a-pulp if you look at him wrong: that's why Sam had to hurt him. But you try to explain that to Danny." He gestured at the fire. "I understood though." As he gestured, his eye caught on the points and blades of the ring. Again he stopped to twist it. "Danny made this for Sam. I took it off him on the bottom porch."

"I still want to know what's going to happen to Danny."

Roger frowned. "When we couldn't get him into a doctor's office in Edgeware, we finally went into town, woke up the doctor there at two in the morning, made him come outside the town and look at him there. The doc gave him a couple of shots of antibiotics and some salve to put on it, and Pitt makes sure he puts it on every day, too. The doc said not to bandage it because it heals better in the air. We're bringing him back to check it next week. What the hell do you think we are?" He didn't sound like he wanted an answer. "You said you wanted to look around. Look. When you're finished, I'll take you back down, and you tell them we don't want no power lines up here." He shook his finger at me with the last six words.

I walked around Haven awhile (pondering as I climbed the flickering stair that even angels in Haven have their own spot of hell), trying to pretend I was enjoying the sun and the breeze, looking over the shoulders of the guys working on their cycles. People stopped talking when I passed. Whenever I turned, somebody looked away. Whenever I looked at one of the upper porches, somebody moved away.

I had been walking twenty long minutes when I finally came into a room to find Fidessa, smiling.

"Hungry?"

She held an apple in one hand and in the other half a loaf of that brown bread, steaming.

"Yeah." I came and sat beside her on the split-log bench.

"Honey?" in a can rusted around the edge with a kitchen knife stuck in it.

"Thanks." I spread some on the bread and it went running and melting into all those little air bubbles like something in Danny's jewelry furnace. And I hadn't had breakfast. The apple was so crisp and cold it hurt my teeth. And the bread was warm.

"You're being very nice."

"It's too much of a waste of time the other way. You've come up here to look around. All right. What have you seen?"

"Fidessa," I said, after a silent while in which I tried to fit her smile with her last direct communication with me ("Go to hell," it was?) and couldn't. "I am *not* dense. I do *not* disapprove of you people coming up here to live away from the rest of the world. The chains and leather bit is not exactly my thing, but I haven't seen anybody here under sixteen, so you're all old enough to vote: in my book that means run your own lives. I could even say this way of life opens pathways to the more mythic and elemental hooey of mankind. I have heard Roger, and I have been impressed, yea, even moved, by how closely his sense of responsibility resembles my own. I too am new at my job. I still don't understand this furor over half a dozen power outlets. We come peacefully; we'll be out in a couple of hours. Leave us the key, go make a lot of noise over some quiet hamlet, and shake up the locals. We'll lock up when we go and stick it under the door mat. You won't even know we've been here."

"Listen, line-demon. . . ."

An eighty-seven-year-old granny of mine, who had taken part in the Detroit race riots in nineteen sixty-nine, must have used that same tone to a bright-eyed civil rights worker in the middle of the gunfire who, three years later, became my grandfather: "Listen, white-boy. . . ." Now I understood what granny had been trying to get across with her anecdote.

". . . you don't know what's going on up here. You've wandered around for half an hour and nobody but me and Roger have said a thing to you. What is it you think you do understand?"

"Please, not demon. Devil."

"All you've seen is a cross-section of a process. Do you have any idea what was here five, or fifteen years ago? Do you know what will be here five years from now? When I came here for the first time, almost ten years back—"

"You and Sam?"

Four thoughts passed behind her face, none of which she articulated.

"When Sam and me first got here, there were as many as a hundred and fifty angels at a time roosting here. Now there's twenty-one."

"Roger said twenty-seven."

"Six left after Sam and Roger rumbled. Roger thinks they're going to come back. Yoggy might. But not the others."

"And in five years?"

She shook her head. "Don't you understand? You don't have to kill us off. We're dying."

"We're not trying to kill you."

"You are."

"When I get down from here, I'm going to do quite a bit of proselytizing. Devil often speak with—" I took another bite of bread "—honeyed tongue. Might as well use it on Mabel." I brushed crumbs from my shining lap.

She shook her head, smiling sadly. "No." I wish women wouldn't smile sadly at me. "You are kind, handsome, perhaps even good." They always bring that up too. "And you are out to kill us."

I made frustrated noises.

She held up the apple.

I bit; she laughed.

She stopped laughing.

I looked up.

There in the doorway Roger looked a mite puzzled. I stood. "You want to run me back down the mountain?" I asked with brusque ingenuousness. "I can't promise you anything. But I'm going to see if I can't get Mabel to sort of forget this job and take her silver-plated juggernaut somewhere else."

"You just do . . . this thing," Roger said. "Come on."

While Roger was cutting his pteracycle out from the herd, I glanced over the edge.

At the pool, Pitt had coaxed Danny in over his knees. It couldn't have been sixty-five degrees out. But they were splashing and laughing like happy mud puppies from, oh, some warmer clime.

IV

A Gila Monster rampant?

Watch:

Six hydraulic lifts with cylinders thick as oil drums adjust the suspension up another five feet to allow room for blade work. From the "head" the "plow," slightly larger than the skull of a Triceratops, chuckles down into the dirt, digs down into the dirt. What chuckled before, roars. Plates on the side slide back.

Then Mabel, with most of her office, emerges on a telescoping lift to peer over the demons' shoulders with telephoto television.

The silver crew itself scatters across the pine needles like polished bearings. The monster hunkers backward, dragging the plow (angled and positioned by one of the finest contemporary poets of the French language): a trough two dozen feet wide and deep is opened upon the land. Two mandibles extend now, with six-foot wire brushes that rattle around down there, clearing off the top of the ribbed housing of a sixteen-foot cable. Two demons (Ronny and Ann) guide the brushes, staking worn ribs, metering for shorts in the higher frequency levels. When the silver worm has been bared a hundred feet, side cabinets open and from over the port treads the crane swings out magnetic grapples.

One of the straightest roads in the world runs from Leningrad to Moscow. The particular czar involved, when asked for his suggestion as to just where the road should run, surprised architects and chancellors by taking a rule and scribing a single line between the cities. "There," he said, or its Russian equivalent. What with Russia being what it was in the mid-nineteenth century, there the road was built.

Except in some of the deeper Pacific trenches and certain annoying Himalayan passes, the major cables and most of the minor ones were laid out much the same way. The only time a cable ever bends sharp enough to see is when a joint is put in. We were putting in a joint.

Inside, demons (Julia, Bill, Frank, Dimitri) are readying the clip, a U of cable fifteen feet from bend to end. On those ends are very complicated couplings. They check those couplings very carefully, because the clip carries all that juice around the gap while the joint is being inserted.

The cranes start to squeal as, up in her tower, Mabel presses the proper button. The clip rises from the monster's guts, swings over the gleaming rib with Scott hanging onto the rope and riding the clip like some infernal surfer.

Frank and Dimitri come barreling from between the tread rollers to join Sue outside, so that the half-circle clips slip over the cable right on the chalk mark. Then Scott slides down to dance on the line, with a ratchet. Sue with another. On each end of the clip they drive down the contacts that sink to various depths in the cable.

Frank: "She uses that thing pretty well."

Dimitri: "Maybe they're teaching them something in the academy after all these years?"

Frank: "She's just showing off because she's new, hey, Sue? Do you think she'd go after a neck tourniquet if we sent her?"

The eight-foot prong goes down to center core. Sixty thousand volts there. The seven-foot six-inch goes to the stepper ground. That's a return for a three-wire high voltage line that boosts you up from the central core to well over three hundred thousand volts. Between those two, you can run all the utilities for a city of a couple or six million. Next prong takes you down to general high-frequency utility power. Then low-frequency same. There's a layer of communications circuits next that lets you plug into a worldwide computer system, I mean if you ever need a worldwide computer. Then the local antennae for radio and TV broadcasts. Then all the check circuits to make sure that all the inner circuits are functioning. Then smaller antennae that broadcast directly to Gila

Monster and sibling the findings of the check circuits. And so forth. And so on. For sixteen feet.

Scott's ratchet clicks on the bolt of the final prong (he let Sue beat him—he will say—by one connection), and somebody waves up at Mabel, who has discovered they're a minute and half behind schedule and worries about these things.

Another crane is lowering the double blade. Teeth ratch, and sparks whiten their uniforms. Demons squint and move back.

Dimitri and Scott are already rolling the connecting disk on the sledge to the rim of the trough ("Hey, Sue! Watch it, honey. This thing only weighs about three hundred pounds!"

"I bet she don't make a hundred and ten.")

A moment later the blade pulls away, and the section of cable is lifted and tracked down the monster, and the whole business slips into the used-blade compartment.

The joint, which has the connections to take taps from the major cable so we can string the lines of power to Haven itself, is rolled and jimmied into place. Ratchets again. This time the whole crew screws the lugs to the housing.

And Mabel sighs and wipes her pale, moist brow, having gotten through the operation without a major blackout anywhere, in the civilized world—nothing shorted, casualties nil, injuries same. All that is left is for the U to be removed so that things start flowing again. And there's hardly anything that can go wrong now.

Roger got me back just as they were removing the U. I came jogging down the rocks, waved to people, bopped on up the stairs and played through the arteries of the beast. I came out on the monster's back, shielding my eyes against the noon.

The shadow of Mabel's office swung over me. I started up the ladder on the side of the lift, and moments later poked my head through the trapdoor.

"Hey, Mabel! Guess what's up on High Haven."

I don't think she was expecting me. She jumped a little. "What?"

"A covey of pteracycle angels, straight from the turn of the century. Tattoos, earrings, leather jackets and all—actually I don't think most of them can afford jackets. They're pretty scroungy."

Mabel frowned. "That's nice."

I hoisted to sitting position. "Theyre not really bad sorts. Eccentric, yes. I know you just got through connecting things up. But what say we roll up all our extension cords and go someplace else?"

"You are out of your mind." Her frown deepened.

"Naw. Look, they're just trying to do their thing. Let's get out of here."

"Nope."

"They look on this whole business as an attempt to wipe them—why not?"

"Because I want to wipe them out."

"Huh? Now don't tell me you were buzzed by angels when you were a little girl and you've carried feud fodder ever since."

"Told you we were going to argue, Blacky." She turned around in her chair. "The last time I had a conversion, it was a vegetarian cult that had taken refuge in the Rockies. Ate meat only once a year on the eve of the autumnal equinox. I will never forget the look on that kid's face. The first arrow pinned his shirt to the trunk of an oak—"

"Happy Halloween, St. Sebastian. *Ehhh!* But these aren't cannibals," I said, "Mabel."

"The conversion before that was a group of utopian socialists who had set up camp in the Swiss Alps. I don't think I could ever trace a killing directly to them—I'm sorry, I'm not counting the three of my men who got it when the whole business broke out into open fighting. But they made the vegetarians look healthy: at least they got it out of their systems. The one before that——"

"Mabel—"

"I assume you're interrupting me because you've gotten my point."

"You were talking about ways of life before. Hasn't it occurred to you that there is more than one way of life possible?"

"That is too asinine for me even to bother answering. Get up off the floor."

I got up.

"If we are going to begin our argument with obvious banalities, consider these: hard work does not hurt the human machine. That's what it is made for. But to work hard simply to remain undernourished, or to have to work harder than you're able so that someone else can live well while you starve, or to have no work at all and have to watch yourself and others starve—this is disastrous to

the human machine. Subject any statistically meaningful
sample of people to these situations, and after a couple of
generations you will have wars, civil and sovereign, along
with all the neuroses that such a *Weltenshauung* produces."

"You get A for obviousness."

"The world being the interrelated mesh that it is, two
hundred million people starving in Asia had an incalculable
effect on the psychology and sociology of the two hundred
million overfed, overleisured North Americans during
the time of our grandparents."

"B for banality."

"Conclusion——"

"For which you automatically get a C."

"——there has not been a war in forty years. There were
only six murders in New York City last year. Nine in
Tokyo. The world has a ninety-seven percent literacy
rate. Eighty-four percent of the world population is at
least bilingual. Of all the political and technological
machinations that have taken place in the last century
to cause this, Global Power Lines were probably the biggest
single factor. Because suddenly people did not have to work
to starve. That problem was alleviated, and the present
situation has come about in the time it takes a child to
become a grandparent. The generation alive when Global
Power began was given the time to raise an interesting
bunch of neurotics for a second generation, and they had
the intelligence and detachment to raise their bunch
healthy enough to produce us."

"We've gone about as far as we can go?"

"Don't be snide. My point is simply that in a world
where millions were being murdered by wars and hundreds
of thousands by less efficient means, there was *perhaps*
some justification for saying about any given injustice,
'What can I do?' But that's not this world. Perhaps we
know too much about our grandparents' world so that we
expect things to be like that. But when the statistics are
what they are today, one boy shot full of arrows to a tree
is a very different matter."

"What I saw up there——"

"——bespoke violence, brutality, unwarranted cruelty
from one person to another, and if not murder, the
potential for murder at every turn. Am I right?"

"But it's a life they've chosen! They have their own
sense of honor and responsibility. You wouldn't go see,
Mabel. I did. It's not going to harm——"

"Look, teak-head! Somebody tried to kill *me* this

morning with that thing you've still got in your belt!"
"Mabel—!" which exclamation had nothing to do with
our argument.

She snatched up the microphone, flicked the button.
"Scott, what the hell are you doing!" Her voice, magnified
by the loudspeakers, rolled over the plates and cropped
among the demons.

What Scott Had Done:

He'd climbed on the U to ride it back up into the
monster. With most of the prongs ratcheted out, he had
taken a connector line (probably saying to Sue first, "Hey,
I bet you never seen this before!") and tapped the high
voltage and stuck it against the metal housing. There's
only a fraction of an ampere there, so it wasn't likely to
hurt anything. The high voltage effect in the housing
causes a brush discharge the length of the exposed cable.
Very impressive. Three-foot sparks crackling all over, and
Scott grinning, and all his hair standing up on end.

A hedge of platinum—

A river of diamonds—

A jeweled snake—

What is dangerous about it and why Mabel was upset
is, (One) if something does go wrong with that much
voltage, it is going to be more than serious. (Two) The U
clip's connected to the (Bow!) gig-crane; the gig-crane's
connected to the (Poo!) crane-house; the crane-house is
anchored to the (Bip!) main chassis itself, and hence the
possibility of all sorts of damage.

"Goddamn it, Scott—!"

The least dangerous thing that could have gone wrong
would have been a random buildup of energies right
where Scott had stuck the wire against the housing.
Which I guess is what happened because he kept reaching
for it and jerking his hand away, like he was being tickled.

Mable got at the controls and pulled the arm of the
rheostat slowly down. She has a blanket ban on all current,
and could walk it down to nothing. (All the voltage in
the world won't do a thing if there're no amps behind it.)
"They know damned well I don't like to waste power!"
she snapped. "All right, you silver-plated idiots," she
rumbled about the mountain, "get inside. That's enough
for today."

She was mad. I didn't pursue the conversation.

Born out of time, I walked eye-deep in Gila droppings.
Then I sat for a while. Then I paced some more. I was

supposed to be filling out forms in the navigation office, but most of the time I was wondering if I wouldn't be happier shucking silver for denim to go steel wool the clouds. Why grub about the world with dirty demons when I could be brandishing my resentments against the night winds, beating my broomstick (as it were) across the evening; only all my resentments were at Mabel.

A break on the balcony from figure flicking.

And leaning on the rail, this, over-looked and -heard:

Sue and Pitt stood together on the rim of the trough. "Well, I'll tell you," Sue was saying, "I like working here. Two years in the Academy after high school and you learn all about Power Engineering and stuff. It's nice 'cause you do a lot of traveling," Sue went on, rather like the introduction to the Academy Course of Study brochure. Well, it's a good introduction. "By the way," she finished, and by the way she finished I knew she'd been wondering awhile, "what happened to your friend's eye?"

Pitt hoofed at the dirt. "Aw, he got in a fight and got it hurt real bad."

"Yeah," Sue said. "That's sort of obvious." The two girls looked off into the woods. "He could really come out here. Nobody's going to bother him."

"He's shy," Pitt said. "And he doesn't hear good."

"It's all right if he wants to stay back there."

"It would be nice to travel around in a healer monster," Pitt said. "I'd like that."

"You want to go inside—?"

"Oh, no! Hey I gotta get back up on High Haven." And Pitt (maybe she'd seen me on the balcony) turned and ran into the trees.

"Good-bye!" Sue called. "Thank your friend for riding me all around the mountain. That was fun." And above the trees I saw a broomstick break small branches.

I went back into the office. Mabel had come in and was sitting on my desk, looking over the forms in which I'd been filling.

I sorted through various subjects I might bring up to avoid arguing with the boss.

"It takes too much energy to sort out something we won't argue about," Mabel said. "Shall we finish up?"

"Fine. Only I haven't had a chance to argue."

"Go on."

"You go on. The only way I'll ever get you is to let you have enough cable to strangle yourself."

She put the forms down. "Take you up on that last

bit of obvious banality for the day: suppose we put the outlets and lines in? They certainly don't have to use them if they don't like."

"Oh, Mabel! The whole thing is a matter of principle!"

"I'm not strangling yet."

"Look. You *are* the boss. I've said we do it your way. Okay. I mean it. Good night!" Feeling frustrated, but clean and silver, I stalked out.

Frank Faltaux told me that the French phrase for it is *l'esprit d'escalier*—the spirit of the backstairs. You think of what you *should* have said after you're on the way down. I lay in the hammock in my new room fairly blistering the varnish on the banister.

Evening shuffled leaves outside my window and slid gold poker chips across the pane. After much restlessness, I got up and went outside to kibitz the game.

On the stream bank I toed stones into the water, watched the water sweep out the hollow, ambled beside the current, the sound of the falls ahead of me; behind, laughing demons sat on the treads drinking beer.

Then somebody called the demons inside, so there was only the evening and water.

And laughter above me . . .

I looked up the falls.

Fidessa sat there, swinging her sneaker heels against the rock.

"Hello?" I asked.

She nodded and looked like a woman with a secret. She jumped down and started over the rocks.

"Hey, watch it. Don't slip in the—"

She didn't.

"Blacky!"

"Eh . . . what can I do for you?"

"Nothing!" with her bright brown eyes. "Do you want to come to a party?"

"Huh?"

"Up on High Haven."

Thought: that the cables had not gone up there this afternoon had been mistaken for a victory on my part.

"You know I haven't won any battles down here yet." Oh, equivocatious "yet."

I scratched my neck and did other things that project indecision. "It's very nice of you and Roger to ask me."

"Actually, I'm asking you. In fact!" conspiratorial look, "why don't you bring one of your girls along?" For a whole

second I thought it was a non-ulterior invitation. "Roger
might be a little peeved if he thought I just came down to
drag you up to an angel blast."

Tall, very dark, and handsome, I've had a fair amount
of this kind of treatment at the hands of various ladies
even in this enlightened age.

So it doesn't bother me at all. "Sure. Love to come."

My ulterior was a chance to drag Mabel out to see my
side (as devils stalked the angels' porches . . . I slew
the thought).

Then again, I was still feeling pretty belligerent. Hell,
who wants to take your debate rival to a party.

I looked back at the monster. Sue sat at the top of the
step, reading.

"Hey!"

She looked up. I made come-here motions. She put
down the book and came.

"What's Scott doing?"

"Sleeping."

One of the reasons Scott will never be a devil is that
he can sleep anywhere, anytime. A devil must be able
to worry all night, then be unable to sleep because he's
so excited about the solution that arrived with the dawn.

"Want to go to a party?"

"Sure."

"Fidessa's invited us up to High Haven. You'll have a
chance to see your friend Pitt again."

She came into the scope of my arm and settled her head
on my shoulder, frowning. "Pitt's a funny kid." The passing wrinkles on a seventeen-year-old girl's face are charming. "But I like her." She looked up, took hold of my
thumb, and asked. "When are we going?"

"Now," Fidessa said.

We climbed.

"Ever fly a broomstick?" Fidessa asked.

"I used to fly my wife back and forth to classes when I
was at the academy," I admitted. (Interesting I've managed
to put that fact out of this telling so long. Contemplate
that awhile.) "Want me to drive?"

With me at the steering shaft, Sue behind me chinning
my scapula, and Fidessa behind her, we did a mildly
clumsy takeoff, then a lovely spiral—"Over there," Fidessa
called—around the mountain's backbone and swung up
toward the gorge.

"Oh, I love riding these things!" Sue was saying. "It's
like a roller coaster. Only more so!"

That was *not* a comment on my flying. We fell into the rocky mouth. (One doesn't forget how to ride a bicycle, either.) Our landing on the high porch was better than Roger's.

I found out where they did the cooking I'd smelled that morning. Fidessa led us up through the trees above the house. (Roast meat . . .) Coming through the brush, hand in hand with Sue, I saw our late cadet wrinkle her nose, frown: "Barbecued pork?"

They had dug a shallow pit. On the crusted, gleaming grill a pig, splayed over coals, looked up cross-eyed. His ears were charred. The lips curled back from tooth and gap-tooth. He smelled great.

"Hey," Roger called across the pit. "You come up here this evening? Good!" He saluted with a beer can. "You come for the party?"

"I guess so."

Someone came scrabbling up the rock carrying a cardboard crate. It was the red-headed kid with the dragon on his chest. "Hey, Roger, you need some lemons? I was over in Hainesville and I swiped this whole goddamn box of lemons . . . !"

Someone grabbed him by the collar of his leather jacket with both hands and yanked it down over his shoulders; he staggered. The crate hit the edge of the pit. Lemons bounced and rolled.

"God damnit, cut that out—"

Half a dozen fell through the grate. Somebody kicked the carton and another half dozen rolled down the slope.

"Hey—"

Half a minute into a free-for-all, two cans of beer came across. I caught them, and looked up to see Roger, by the cooler, laughing. I twisted the tops off (there was a time, I believe, when such a toss would have wreaked havoc with the beer—progress), handed one to Sue, saluted.

Fidessa had maneuvered behind Roger. And was laughing too.

Sue drank, scowled. "Say, where is Pitt?"

"Down at the house."

She flashed bright teeth at me. I nodded.

"Call me when food's on." She pulled away, skirting tussling angels, and hopped down the rocks.

Where does the mountain go when it goes higher than Haven?

Not knowing, I left the revelers and mounted among the bush and boulders. Wind snagged on pines and reached me limping. I looked down the gorge, surveyed the crowded roofs of Haven, sat for a while on a log, and was peaceful. I heard feet on leaves behind, but didn't look. Fingers on my eyes and Fidessa laughing. I caught one wrist and pulled her around. The laugh stilled on her face. She, amused, and I curious, watched each other watch each other.

"Why," I asked, "have you become so friendly?"

Her high-cheeked face grew pensive. "Maybe it's because I know a better thing when I see it."

"Better?"

"Comparative of *good*." She sat beside me. "I've never understood how power is meted out in this world. When two people clash, the more powerful wins. I was very young when I met Sam. I stayed with him because I thought he was powerful. Does that sound naïve?"

"At first, yes. Not when you think about it."

"He insisted on living in a way totally at odds with society. That takes . . . power."

I nodded.

"I still don't know whether he lost it at the end. Maybe Roger simply had more. But I made my decision before they rumbled. And I ended up on the right side."

"You're not stupid."

"No, I'm not. But there's another clash coming. I think I know who will win."

"I don't."

She looked at her lap. "Also I'm not so young. I'm tired of being on the side of the angels. My world is falling apart, Blacky. I've got Roger; I understand why Sam lost, but I don't understand why Roger won. In the coming battle, you'll win and Roger will lose. That I don't understand at all."

"Is this a request for me in my silver long-johns to take you away from all this?"

She frowned. "Go back down to Haven. Talk to Roger."

"On the eve of the war, the opposing generals meet together. They explain how war would be the worst thing for all concerned. Yet all creation knows they'll go to war."

Her eyes inquired.

"I'm quoting."

"Go down and talk to Roger."

I got up and walked back through the woods. I had been walking five minutes when:

"Blacky?"

I stopped by an oak whose roots clutched a great rock.

When trees get too big in terrain like this, there is very little for them to hold, and they eventually fall.

"I thought I saw you wander off up here."

"Roger," I said, "things don't look so good down at the Gila Monster."

He fell into step beside me. "You can't stop the lines from coming up here?" He twisted the great ring on his scarred finger.

"The law says that a certain amount of power must be available for a given number of people. Look. Even if we put the lines up, why do you have to use them? I don't understand why this business is so threatening to you."

"You don't?"

"Like I said, I sympathize . . ."

His hands went into his pockets. It was dark enough here among the trees so that, though light flaked above the leaves, I couldn't see his expression.

His tone of voice surprised me: "You don't understand what's going on up here, do you? Fidessa said you didn't." It was fatigue. "I thought you . . ." and then his mind went somewhere else. "These power lines. Do you know what holds these guys here? I don't. I do know it's weaker than you think."

"Fidessa says they've been drifting away."

"I'm not out to make any man do what he don't want. Neither was Sam. That's the power he had and I have. You put them lines up and they'll use them. Maybe not at first. But they will. You beat us long enough, and we go down!"

Beyond the trees I could see the barbecue pit. "Maybe you're just going to have to let it go."

He shook his shadowed face. "I haven't had it long, so it shouldn't be so hard to lose it. But no."

"Roger, you're not losing anything. When the lines go up here, just ignore—"

"I'm talking about power. *My* power."

"How?"

"They know what's going on." He motioned to include the rest of the angels in Haven. "They know it's a contest. I am going to lose. Would it be better if I came on like Sam? He'd have tried to break your head. Then he'd have tried to bust your tinfoil eggcrate apart with broomsticks. Probably got himself and most of the rest of us in the hoosegow."

"He would have."

"Have you ever lost something important to you, something so important you couldn't start to tell anybody else how important it was? It went. You watched it go. And then it was all gone."

"Yes."

"Yeah? What?"

"Wife of mine."

"She leave you for somebody else?"

"She was burned to death on an exposed power cable, one night, in Tibet. I watched. And then she was . . . gone."

"You and me," Roger said after a moment, "we're a lot alike, you know?" I saw his head drop. "I wonder what it would be like to lose Fidessa . . . too."

"Why do you ask?"

Broad shoulders shrugged. "Sometimes the way a woman acts, you get to feel . . . Sam knew. But it's stupid, huh? You think that's stupid, Blacky?"

Leaves crashed under feet behind us. We turned.

"Fidessa . . . ?" Roger said.

She stopped in the half-dark. I knew she was surprised to overtake us.

Roger looked at me. He looked at her. "What were you doing up there?"

"Just sitting," she said before I did.

We stood a moment more in the darkness above Haven. Then Roger turned, beat back branches, and strode into the clearing. I followed.

The pig had been cut. Most of one ham had been sliced. But Roger yanked up the bone and turned to me. "This is a party, hey, Blacky!" His scarred face broke on laughter. "Here! Have some party!" He thrust the hot bone into my hands. It burned me.

But Roger, arm around somebody's shoulder, lurched through the carousers. Someone pushed a beer at me. The hock, where I'd dropped it on pine needles, blackened beneath the boots of angels.

I did get food after a fashion. And a good deal to drink.

I remember stopping on the upper porch of Haven, leaning on what was left of the rail.

Sue was sitting down by the pool. Stooped but glistening from the heat of the forge, Danny stood beside her.

Then behind me:

"You gonna fly? You gonna fly the moon off the sky? I can see three stars up there! Who's gonna put them out?" Roger balanced on the cycle rack, feet wide, fist shaking at the night. "I'm gonna fly! Fly till my stick pokes a hole

in the night! Gods, you hear that? We're coming at you!
We're gonna beat you to death with broomsticks and roar
the meteors down before we're done. . . ."

They shouted around him. A cycle coughed. Two more.

Roger leaped down as the first broomstick pulled from
the rack, and everybody fell back. It swerved across the
porch, launched over the edge, rose against the branches,
above the branches, spreading dark wings.

"You gonna fly with me?"

I began a shrug.

His hand hit my neck and stopped it. "There are gods
up there we gotta look at. You gonna stare 'em down with
me?"

Smoke and pills had been going around as well as beer.

"Gods are nothing but low blood sugar," I said.
"St. Augustine, Peyote Indians . . . you know how it
works—"

He turned his hand so the back was against my neck.
"Fly!" and if he'd taken his hand away fast, that ring
would have hooked out an inch of jugular.

Three more broomsticks took off.

"Okay, why not?"

He turned to swing his cycle from the rack.

I mounted behind him. Concrete rasped. We went over
the edge, and the bottom fell out of my belly again.
Branches clawed at us, branches missed.

Higher than Haven.

Higher than the mountain that is higher than Haven.

Wind pushed my head back, and I stared up at the
night. Angels passed overhead.

"Hey!" Roger bellowed, turning half around so I could
hear. "You ever done any sky-sweeping?"

"No!" I insisted.

Roger nodded for me to look.

Maybe a hundred yards ahead and up, an angel turned
wings over the moon, aimed down, and—his elbows jerked
sharply in as he twisted the throttle rings—turned off
both turbos.

The broomstick swept down the night.

And down.

And down.

Finally I thought I would lose him in the carpet of
green-black over the mountain. And for a while he was
lost. Then:

A tiny flame, and tiny wings, momentarily illuminated,
pulled from the tortuous dive. As small as he was, I could

see the wings bend from the strain. He was close enough
to the treetops so that for a moment the texture of the
leaves was visible in a speeding pool of light. (How many
angels *can* dance on the head of a pin?) He was so
tiny. . . .

"What the hell is our altitude anyway?" I called to Roger.

Roger leaned back on the shaft, and we were going
up again.

"Where are we going?"

"High enough to get a good sweep on."

"With two people on the cycle?" I demanded.

And we went up.

And there were no angels above us any more.

And the only thing higher than us was the moon.

There is a man in the moon.

And he leers.

We reached the top of our arc. Then Roger's elbows
struck his sides.

My tummy again. Odd feeling: the vibrations on your
seat and on your foot stirrups aren't there. Neither is
the roar of the turbos.

It is a very quiet trip down.

Even the sound of the wind on the wings behind you
is carried away too fast to count. There is only the
mountain in front of you. Which is down.

And down.

And down.

Finally I grabbed Roger's shoulder, leaned forward,
and yelled in his year, "I hope you're having fun!"

Two broomsticks zoomed apart to let us through.

Roger looked back at me. "Hey, what were you and my
woman doing up in the woods?" With the turbos off you
don't have to yell.

"Picking mushrooms."

"When there's a power struggle, I don't like to lose."

"You like mushrooms?" I asked. "I'll give you a whole
goddamn basket just as soon as we set runners on Haven."

"I wouldn't joke if I was sitting as far from the throttle
ring as you are."

"Roger—"

"You can tell things from the way a woman acts,
Blacky. I've done a lot of looking, at you, at Fidessa, even
at that little girl you brought up to Haven this evening.
Take her and Pitt. I bet they're about the same age. Pitt
don't stand up too well against her. I don't mean looks
either. I'm talking about the chance of surviving they'd

have if you just stuck them down someplace. I'm thirty-three years old, Blacky. You?"

"Eh . . . thirty-one."

"We don't check out too well either."

"How about giving it a chance?"

"You're hurting my shoulder."

My hand snapped back to the grip. There was a palm print in sweat on the denim.

Roger shook his head. "I'd dig to see you spread all over that mountain."

"If you don't pull out, you'll never get the opportunity."

"Shit," Roger said. His elbows went out from his side. The broomstick vibrated.

Branches stopped coming at us quite so fast. (I could see separate branches!) The force of the turn almost tore me off. I told you before, you could see the wings bend? You can hear them too. Things squeaked and creaked in the roar.

Then, at last, we were rising gently once more. I looked up. I breathed. The night was loud and cool and wonderful.

Miniature above us now, another angel swept down across the moon. He plummeted toward us as we rode up the wind.

Roger noticed before I did.

"Hey, the kid's in trouble!"

Instead of holding his arm hugged to his sides, the kid worked them in and out as though he were trying to twist something loose.

"His rings are frozen!" Roger exclaimed.

Others had realized the trouble and circled in to follow him down. He came fast and wobbling; passed us!

His face was all teeth and eyes as he fought the stick. The dragon writhed on his naked chest. It was the redhead.

The flock swooped to follow.

The kid was below us. Roger gunned his cycle straight down to catch up, wrenched out again, and the kid passed us once more.

The kid had partial control of one wing. It didn't help because whenever he'd shift the free aileron, he'd just bank off in another direction at the same slope.

Branches again. . . .

Then something unfroze in the rogue cycle. His slope suddenly leveled and there was fire from the turbos.

For three seconds I thought he was going to make it.

Fire raked the treetops for thirty feet; we swooped over a widening path of flame. And nothing at the end of it.

A minute later we found a clearing. Angels settled like mad leaves. We started running through the trees.

He wasn't dead.

He was screaming.

He'd been flung twenty feet from his broomstick through small branches and twigs, both legs and one arm broken. Most of his clothes had been torn off. A lot of skin too.

Roger forgot me, got very efficient, got Red into a stretcher between two broomsticks, and got to Hainesville, fast. Red was only crying when the doctor finally put him to sleep.

We took off from the leafy suburban streets and rose toward the porches of Haven.

The gorge was a serpent of silver.

The moon glazed the windows of Haven.

Somebody had already come back to bring the news.

"You want a beer?" Roger asked.

"No thanks. Have you seen the little girl who came up here with me? I think it's about time we got back."

But he had already started away. There was *still* a party going on.

I went into the house, up some stairs, didn't find Sue, so went down some others. I was halfway down the flickering stairs to the forge when I heard a shriek.

Then Sue flashed through the doorway, ran up the steps, and crashed into me. I caught her just as one-eyed Danny swung round the door jamb. Then Pitt was behind him, scrabbling past him in the narrow well, the throwing blade in her hand halfway through a swing.

And stopping.

"Why doesn't someone tell me what the hell is going on?" I proposed. "You put yours away, and I'll put away mine." Remember that throwing blade I had tucked under my belt? It was in my hand now. Pitt and I lowered our arms together.

"Oh, Blacky, let's get *out* of here!" Sue whispered.

"Okay," I said.

We backed up the steps. Then we ducked from the door and came out on the porch. Sue still leaned on my shoulder. When she got her breath back, she said, "They're nuts!"

"What happened?"

"I don't know, I mean. . . ." She stood up now. "Dan

was talking to me and showing me around the forge. And
he makes all that beautiful jewelry. He was trying to fool
around, but I mean, really—with that eye? And I was
trying to cool him anyway, when Pitt came in. . . ." She
looked at the porch. "That boy who fell . . . they got
him to the doctor?"

I nodded.

"It was the red-headed one, wasn't it? I hope he's all
right." Sue shook her head. "He gave me a lemon."

Fidessa appeared at my shoulder. "You want to get
down?"

"Yeah."

"Take that cycle. The owner's passed out inside. Somebody'll bring him down tomorrow to pick it up."

"Thanks."

Glass shattered. Somebody had thrown something through
one of Haven's windows.

The party was getting out of hand at the far end of the
porch. Still point in the wheeling throng, Roger watched
us.

Fidessa looked a moment, then pushed my shoulder.
"Go on." We dropped over white water, careening down
the gorge.

Scott opened an eye and frowned a freckled frown
over the edge of his hammock. "Where . . . (obscured by
yawn) . . . been?"

"To a party. Don't worry. I brought her back safe and
sound."

Scott scrubbed his nose with his fist. "Fun?"

"Sociologically fascinating, I'm sure."

"Yeah?" He pushed up on his elbow. "Whyn't you wake
me?" He looked back at Sue who sat quietly on her hammock.

"We shook you for fifteen minutes, but you kept trying
to punch me."

"I did?" He rubbed his nose again. "I did not!"

"Don't worry about it. Go to sleep. G'night, Sue."

In my room I drifted off to the *whirr* of broomsticks
remembered.

Then—was it half an hour later?—I came awake to a
real turbo. A cycle came near the Monster's roof.

Runners . . .

Correction: landed on.

I donned silver and went outside on the long terrace.
I looked to my left up at the roof.

Thuds down the terrace to the right—

Danny recovered from his leap. His good eye blinked
rapidly. The other was a wet fistful of shadow.

"What are you doing here?" I asked too quietly for him
to have heard. Then I looked up the curved wall. Fidessa
slid down. Danny steadied her.

"Would you mind telling me what brings you here this
hour of the morning?"

After five silent seconds I thought she was playing a
joke. I spent another paranoid three thinking I was about
to be victim to a cunning nefariousness.

But she was terrified.

"Blacky—"

"Hey, what's the matter, girl?"

"I . . ." She shook her head. "Roger . . ." Shook it
again.

"Come inside and sit down."

She took Danny's arm. "Go in! Go in, Danny . . .
please!" She looked about the sky.

Stolid and uncomprehending, Danny went forward. Inside he sat on the hammock, left fist wrapped in his right
hand.

Fidessa stood, turned, walked, stopped.

"What's the matter? What happened on High Haven?"

"We're leaving." She watched for my reaction.

"Tell me what happened."

She put her hands in her pockets, took them out again.
"Roger tried to get at Danny."

"What?"

We regarded the silent smith. He blinked and smiled.

"Roger got crazy after you left."

"Drunk?"

"Crazy! He took everybody down to the forge and they
started to break up the place. . . . He made them stop
after a little while. But then he talked about killing Danny.
He said that Sam was right. And then he told me he was
going to kill me."

"It sounds like a bad joke."

"It wasn't. . . ." I watched her struggle to find words
to tell me what it was.

"So you two got scared and left?"

"I wasn't scared then." Her voice retreated to shortness.
She glanced up. "I'm scared now."

Swaying gently, Danny put one foot on top of the other and meshed his toes.

"How come you brought Danny along?"

"He was running away. After the fracas down in the forge, he was taking off into the woods. I told him to come with me."

"Clever of you to come here."

She looked angry, then anger lost focus and became fear again. "We didn't know anywhere else to go." Her hands closed and broke like moths. "I came here first because I . . . wanted to warn you."

"Of what?"

"Roger—I think him and the rest of the angels are going to try and rumble with you here."

"What . . . ?"

She nodded.

"This has suddenly gotten serious. Let's go talk to Boss Lady." I opened the door to the corridor. "You too."

Danny looked up surprised, unfolded his hands and feet.

"Yeah, you!"

Mabel was exercising her devilish talents:

Ashtray filled with the detritus of a pack of cigarettes, papers all over everything; she had one pencil behind her ear and was chewing on another. It was three in the morning.

We filed into the office, me first, Fidessa, then Danny.

"Blacky? Oh, hello—good *Lord!*" (That was Danny's eye.)

"Hi, Mabel. How's the midnight oil?"

"If you strain it through white bread, reduce it over a slow Bunsen, and recondense the fumes in a copper coil, I hear you have something that can get you high." She frowned at Danny, realized she was frowning, smiled. "What happened to that boy's face?"

"Meet Fidessa and Danny, from High Haven. They've just run away and stopped off to tell us that we may be under attack shortly by angels who are none too happy about the lines and outlets we're putting up tomorrow."

Mabel looked over the apex of her fingertips. "This has gotten serious," she echoed. Mabel looked tired. "The Gila Monster is a traveling maintenance station, not a mobile fortress. How have your goodwill efforts been going?"

I was going to throw up my hands—

"If Blacky hadn't been up there," Fidessa said, "talking

with Roger like he did, they'd have been down here yesterday morning instead."

I projected her an astral kiss.

"What about him?" She nodded at Danny. "What
happened too—"

"Where the hell," Scott demanded, swinging through
the door like a dappled griffon, "did you take that poor
kid, anyway?"

"What kid?"

"Sue! You said you went to a party. That's not what
I'd call it!"

"What are you talking about?"

"She's got two bruises on her leg as big as my hand
and one on her shoulder even bigger. She said some one-
eyed bastard tried to rape——"

Then he frowned at Danny, who smiled back quizzically.

"She told me," I said, "that he tried to get fresh with
her—"

"With a foot and a half of two-by-four? She told *me*
she didn't want to tell *you*," his mottled finger swung at
me, "what really happened, so you wouldn't be too hard
on them!"

"Look, I haven't been trying to gloss over anything I
saw on——"

At which point Mabel stood.

Silence.

You-know-what were passing.

Something clanged on the skylight: cracks shot the
pane, though it didn't shatter. We jumped, and Scott hic-
coughed. Lying on the glass was a four-pronged blade.

I reached over Mabel's desk and threw a switch by
her thumb.

Fidessa: "What . . . ?"

"Floodlights," I said. "They can see us, lights or no.
This way we can see them—if they get within fifty meters." We used the lights for night work. "I'm going to
take us up where we can look at what's going on," I
told Mabel.

She stepped back so I could take the controls.

When the cabin jerked, Danny's smile gave out. Fidessa
patted his arm.

The cabin rose.

"I hope you know what you're . . ." Scott began.

Mabel told him to shut up with a very small movement
of the chin.

Outside the window, broomsticks scratched like matches behind the trees.

Water whispered white down the falls. The near leaves shook neon scales. And the cable arched the dark like a flayed rib.

Wingforms fell and swept the rocks, shadowed the water. I saw three land.

"That's Roger!"

At the window Fidessa stood at my left, Mabel at my right.

Roger's broomstick played along the cable, came down in a diminishing pool of shadow directly on the line. I heard runners scrape the housing. Half a dozen more angels had landed on either side of the trough.

Roger, at the far end of the exposed line up near the rocks, dismounted and let his broomstick fall on its side. He started slowly to walk the ribbing.

"What do they want?" Scott asked.

"I'm going to go out and see," I said. Mabel turned sharply. "You've got peeper-mikes in here." The better to overhear scheming demons; if they'd been on, Mabel would have been able to foresee Scott's little prank of the afternoon. "Hey! You remember Scott's little prank of the afternoon? You can duplicate it from here, can't you?"

"A high voltage brush discharged from the housing? Sure I can—"

"It'll look so much more impressive at night! I'm going out there to talk to Roger on the cable. If anything goes wrong, I'll yell. You start the sparks. Nobody will get hurt, but it should scare enough hell out of them to give me a chance to get out of harm's way." I flipped on the peeper-mike and started for the trapdoor. An introductory burst of static cleared to angel mumblings.

Mabel stopped me with a hand on my shoulder. "Blacky, I can make a brush discharge from in here. I can also burn anybody on that line—"

I looked at her. I breathed deeply. Then I pulled away and dropped through to the Gila Monster's roof. I sprinted over the plated hull, reached the "head" between two of the floods, and gazed down. "Roger!"

He stopped and squinted up into the light. "—Blacky?"

"What are you doing here?"

Before he answered, I kicked the latch of the crane housing and climbed down onto the two-foot grapple. I was going to yell back at Mabel but she was watching.

The crane began to hum, and swung forward with me riding, out and down.

When I came close to the cable, I dropped (floodlights splashing my shoulders); I got my balance on the curved ribbing. "Roger?"

"Yeah?"

"What are you doing down here?"

On the dirt piled beside the cable the other angels stood. I walked forward.

"What are you doing? Come on; it's the third time I've asked you." When the wire is sixteen feet in diameter, a tightrope act isn't that hard. Still . . .

Roger took a step and I stopped. "You're not going to put up those cables, Blacky."

He looked awful. Since I'd seen him last he'd been in a fight. I couldn't tell if he'd won or lost.

"Roger, go back up on High Haven."

His shoulders sagged; he kept swallowing. Throwing blades clinked at his belt.

"You think you've won, Blacky."

"Roger—"

"You haven't. We won't let you. We won't. He looked at the angels around us. "IS THAT RIGHT!" I started at his bellow.

They were silent. He turned back and whispered. "We won't. . . ."

My shadow reached his feet. His lay out behind him on the ribbing.

"You came down here to make trouble, Roger. What's it going to get you?"

"A chance to see you squirm."

"You've done that once this evening."

"That was before . . ." He looked down at his belt. My stomach tightened. ". . . Fidessa left. She ran away from me." Hung on his cheek scar, confusion curtained his features.

"I know." I glanced over my shoulder where the office swayed above the monster. In the window were four silhouettes: two women and two men.

"She's up . . . ?" The curtain pulled back to reveal rage. "She came down here to you?"

"To us. Have you got that distinction through your bony head?"

"Who's up there with her?" He squinted beyond the floodlights. "Danny?"

"That's right."

"Why?"

"She said he was running away anyway."

"I don't have to ask you. I know why."

"They're listening to us. You can ask them if you want."

Roger scowled, threw back his head. "Danny! What you running away from me for?"

No answer.

"You gonna leave Haven and Pitt and everything?"

No answer.

"Fidessa!"

Yes . . . Roger?

Her voice, so firm in person, was almost lost in the electronic welter.

"Danny really wants to run down here with the devils?"

He . . . does, Roger.

"Danny!"

No answer.

"I know you can hear me! You make him hear me, Fidessa! Don't you remember, Danny . . . ?"

No answer.

"Danny, you come out of there if you want and go on back with me."

As Roger's discomfort grew to fill the silence, the kindest thing I could think was that, just as Danny had been unable to comprehend Sam's brutalities, so he could ignore Roger's generosities.

"Fidessa?"

Roger?

"You coming back up to High Haven with me." Neither question mark nor exclamation point defines that timbre.

No, Roger.

When Roger turned back to me, it looked like the bones in his head had all broken and were just tossed in a bag of his face.

"And you . . . you're putting up them cables tomorrow?"

"That's right."

Roger's hand went out from his side; started forward. Things came apart. He struck at me.

"Mabel, *now!*"

When he hit at me again, he hit through fire.

The line grew white stars. We crashed, crackling. I staggered, lost my balance, found it again.

Beyond the glitter I saw the angels draw back. The discharge was scaring everybody but Roger.

We grappled. Sparks tangled his lank hair, flickered in

his eyes, on his teeth; we locked in the fire. He tried to force me off the cable. "I'm gonna . . . break . . . you!"

We broke.

I ducked by, whirled to face him. Even though the other angels had scattered, Roger had realized the fireworks were show.

He pulled at his belt.

"I'll stop you!"

The blade was a glinting cross above his shoulder.

"Roger, even if you do, that's not going to stop—"

"I'll kill you!"

The blade spun down the line.

I ducked and it missed.

"Roger, stop it! Put that blade—" I ducked again, but the next one caught my forearm. Blood ran inside my sleeve . . . "Roger! You'll get burned!"

"You better hurry!" The third blade spun out with the last word.

I leaped to the side of the trough, rolled over on my back—saw him crouch with the force of the next blade, now dug into the dirt where my belly had been.

I had already worked the blade from my own belt. As I flung it (I knew it was going wild, but it would make Roger pause), I shrieked with all rage and frustration playing my voice: *"Burn* him!"

The next blade was above his head.

Off balance on my back, there was no way I could have avoided it. Then:

The sparks fell back into the housing.

From the corner of my eye, I'd seen Mabel, in the office window, move to the rheostat.

Roger stiffened.

He waved back; snapped up screaming. His arm flailed the blade around his head.

Then the scream was exhausted.

The first flame flickered on his denims.

His ankle chain flared cherry and smoked against the skin.

The blade burned in his hand.

Broomsticks growled over the sky as angels beat retreat. I rolled to my stomach, coughing with rage, and tried to crawl up (the smell of roast meat . . .), but I only got halfway to the top before my arm gave. I went flat and started to slide down toward the line. My mouth was full of dirt. I tried to swim up the slope, but kept slipping down. Then my feet struck the ribbing.

I just curled up against the cable, shaking, and the only thing going through my mind: "Mabel doesn't like to waste power."

V

Gules, azure, sable—
(Working bottom to top.)
"You sure you feel all right?"

I touched the bandage beneath torn silver. "Mabel, your concern is sweet. Don't overdo it."

She looked across the chill falls.

"You want to check out Haven before we go to work?"

Her eyes were red from fatigue. "Yeah."

"Okay. There's still a broomstick—aw, come on."

Just then the chameleon swung up the roadway with Scott, properly uniformed now, driving. He leaned out, "Hey, I got Danny down to town. Doctor looked at his eye." He shrugged.

"Put it away and go to bed."

"For twenty minutes?"

"More like a half an hour."

"Better than nothing." Scott scratched his head. "I had a good talk with Danny. No, don't worry. He's still alive."

"What did you say?"

"Just rest assured I said it. And he heard it." He swung the door closed, grinned through it, and drove off toward the hub.

A way of life.

Mabel and I went up on the monster's roof. Fidessa and Danny had left it there. Mabel hesitated again before climbing on.

"You can't get the chameleon up the road," I told her.

The turbos hummed and we rose above the trees.

We circled the mountain twice. As Haven came into view, I said: "Power, Mabel. How do you delegate it so that it works for you? How do you set it up so that it doesn't turn against itself and cause chaos?"

"You just watch where you're flying."

High Haven was empty of angels. The rack was overturned and there were no broomsticks about. In the forge the fires were out. We walked up the metal stairway through beer cans and broken glass. At the barbecue pit I kicked a lemon from the ashes.

"The devils gain Haven only to find the angels fled."

"Sure as hell looks like it."

On the top porch Mabel said, "Let's go back down to the Gila Monster."

"You figure out where you're going to put in your outlets?"

"Everyone seems to have decided the place is too hot and split." She looked at her bright toe. "So if there's nobody living up here, there's no reason to run power up here—by law. Maybe Roger's won after all."

"Now wait a minute—"

"I've been doing a lot of thinking this morning, Blacky."

"So have I."

"Then give a lady the benefit of your ponderings."

"We've just killed somebody. And with the world statistics being what they are . . ."

Mabel brushed back white hair. "Self-defense and all that. I still wonder whether I like myself as much this morning as I did yesterday."

"You're not putting lines up?"

"I am not."

"Now wait a minute. Just because—"

"Not because of that. Because of nothing to do with angels. Because of what angels have taught me about me. There's nobody up here any more. I go by the books."

"All right. Let's go back then."

I didn't feel particularly good. But I understood: you have to respect somebody who forces you to accept his values. And in that situation, the less you agree, the more you have to respect.

We flew back down the mountain.

I landed a little clumsily fifty yards up the stream.

"You liked that?"

Mabel just sighed deeply, and grinned at me a little. "I guess I'm just not made for that sort of thing. Coming back?"

I squinted. "You go on. I'll be down in a few minutes."

She cocked her silver brows high as though she understood something I didn't, but grinned again. Then she started away.

What I really wanted to do was take another ride. I also wanted to get the whole thing out of my mind: well, there were a lot more forms to be filled. Big choice, but if fixed me squarely at the brink of indecision. I stood there toeing stones into the water.

Sound behind me in the leaves made me turn.

Fidessa, tugging at the pteracycle, one leg over the

seat, cringed when she saw me. "It's mine!" she insisted with all the hostility of the first time we'd met.

I'd already jerked my hand back, when I realized she meant the broomstick. "Oh," I said. "Yeah, sure. You go on and take it. I've done my high-flying for the week."

But she was looking at me strangely. She opened her mouth, closed it. Suddenly she hissed, "You're a monster! You're a monster, Blacky, and the terrible thing is you'll never understand why!"

My reflex was to put my hand behind me again. But that was silly, so I didn't. "You think I'm some sort of ghoul? I'm not trying to steal anything that isn't mine. I tried to give it back to Danny, but he wouldn't take—" I reached down to pull it off my finger.

Then I saw Fidessa's eyes drop and realized with guilt and astonishment that she hadn't even seen the ring—till now.

I opened my mouth. Excuses and apologies and expressions of chagrin blundered together on my tongue. Nothing came out.

"Monster!" she whispered once more. And the smile of triumph with the whisper made the backs of my thighs and shoulders erupt in gooseflesh.

Fidessa laughed and threw about her black-red hair. Laughing, she twisted at the rings. The laugh became a growl. The growl became a roar. She jerked back on the rod, and the broomstick leaped, like a raging thing. Bits of the forest swirled up thirty feet. She leaned (I thought) dangerously to the side, spun around, and lifted off. Her high wing sliced branch ends and showered me with twigs and more torn green.

I brushed at my face and stepped back as, beyond the leaves, she rose and rose and rose, like Old Meg, like ageless Mab, like an airborne witch of Endor.

Some history here:

I was transferred at the end of the week to Iguana. Six months later word came over the line that Mabel had retired. So Global Power lost another good devil. Iguana lumbers and clanks mainly about Drake's Passage, sniffing around in Antarctica and Cape Horn. Often I sit late in the office, remembering, while the cold south winds scour the skylight—

So I forgot something:

When I went to look at Roger's body.

He had fallen by the line. We were going to let the

Gila Monster bury him when it covered up the cable.

I'd thought the ring might have melted. But that hand had hardly blistered.

I took it off him and climbed out of the trough. As I came over the mound, between the brush and the tree trunks, something moved.

"Pitt?"

She darted forward, changed her mind, and ducked back.

"Do you . . . want to take this back to Danny?" I held it out.

She started forward again, saw what I held. A gasp, she turned, fled into the woods.

I put it on.

Just then Sue, all sleepy-eyed and smiling, stepped onto the balcony and yawned, "Hello, Blacky."

"Hi. How do you feel?"

"Fine. Isn't it a perfectly—?" She flexed her arm. "Sore shoulder." (I frowned.) "Nothing so bad I can't [sigh] work."

"That's good."

"Blacky, what was the commotion last night? I woke up a couple of times, saw lights on. Did Mabel send everybody back to work?"

"It wasn't anything, honey. You just stay away from the trough until we cover it up. We had some trouble there last night."

"Why? *Isn't* it a perfectly—?"

"That's an order."

"Oh. Yes, sir."

She looked surprised but didn't question. I went inside to get Mabel to get things ready to leave.

I kept it.

I didn't take if off.

I wore it.

For years.

I still do.

And often, almost as often as I think about that winter in Tibet, I recall the October mountains near the Canadian border where the sun sings cantos of mutability and angels fear to tread now; where still, today, the wind unwinds, the trees re-leave themselves in spring, and the foaming gorge disgorges.

THICKENING THE PLOT

by Samuel R. Delany

I DISTRUST the term "plot," and most of the other terms that head the sections of this book, in discussions of *writing*: It, and they, refer to effects a story produces in the *reading*. But writing is an internal process the writer goes through (or puts himself through) in front of a blank paper that leaves a detritus of words there. The truth is, practically nothing is known about it. Talking about plot, or character, or setting, to a beginning writer is like giving the last three years' movie reviews from the Sunday *Times* to a novice film-maker. A camera manual, a few pamphlets on matched action, viable cutting points, and perhaps one on lighting (in the finished film, the viewer hardly ever sees the light sources, so the reviewer can hardly discuss them; but their placement is essential to everything from mood to plain visibility) would be more help. In short, a vocabulary that has grown from a discussion of effects is only of limited use in a discussion of causes.

A few general things, however, can be noted through introspection. Here is an admittedly simplified description of how writing strikes me. When I am writing I am trying to allow/construct an image of what I want to write about in my mind's sensory theater. Then I describe it as accurately as I can. The most interesting point I've noticed is that the *writing-down* of words about my imagined vision (or at least the choosing/arranging of words to write down) causes the *quality* of the vision to change.

Here are two of the several ways it changes:

First—the vision becomes clearer. Sudden lights are thrown on areas of the mental diorama dark before. Other areas, seen dimly, are revised into much more specific and sharper versions. (What was vaguely imagined as a green dress, while I fix my description of the light bulb hanging from its worn cord, becomes a patterned, turquoise print with a frayed hem.) The notation causes the imagination to resolve focus.

Second—to the extent that the initial imagining contains an action, the notating process tends to propel that action forward (or sometimes backward) in time. (As I describe how Susan, both hands locked, side-punched Frank,

I see Frank grab his belly in surprise and stagger back against the banister—which will be the next thing I look at closely to describe.) Notating accurately what happens *now* is a good way to prompt a vague vision of what happens *next*.

Let me try to indicate some of the details of this process.

I decide, with very little mental concretizing, that I want to write about a vague George who comes into a vague room and finds a vague Janice. . . .

. . . picture George outside the door. Look at his face; no, look closer. He seems worried . . . ? Concerned . . . ? No. Look even closer and write down just what you see: *The lines across his forehead deepened.* Which immediately starts him moving. What does he do . . . ? *He reached for the* . . . doorknob? No. Be more specific . . . *brass doorknob. It turned* . . . easily? No, the word "brass" has cleared the whole knob-and-lock mechanism. Look harder and describe how it's actually turning . . . *loosely in its collar.* While he was turning the knob, something more happened in his face. Look at it; describe it: *He pressed his lips together—* No, cross that line out: not accurate enough. Describe it more specifically: *The corners of his mouth tightened.* Closer. And the movement of the mouth evokes another movement: He's pressing his other hand against the door to open it. (Does "press" possibly come from the discarded version of the previous sentence? Or did wrong use of it there anticipate proper use here? No matter; what does matter is that you look again to make sure it's the accurate word for what he's doing.) *He pressed his palm against the door* . . . And look again; that balk between the two versions of the sentence suggests a balk in his next movement . . . , *twice, to open it.* As the door opens, I hear the wood give: *You could hear the jamb split* – No, cross out "split," that isn't right . . . *crack—* No, cross that out too; it's even less accurate. Go back to "split" and see what you can do; listen harder . . . *split a little more.* Yes, that's closer. He's got the door open, now. What do you see? *The paint—* No, that's not paint on the wall. Look harder: *The wallpaper was some color between green and gray.* Why can't you see it more clearly? Look around the rest of the room. Oh, yes: *The tan shade was drawn.* What about Janice? She was one of the first things you saw when the door opened. Describe her as you saw her: *Janice sat on the bed* . . . no, more accurately . . . *the unmade bed.* No, you haven't got it yet. . . . *Janice sat at the edge of the bed on a spot of bare mattress ticking.* No, no, let's back up a little and go through that again for a precise description of the picture you see: *Janice sat on the bare mattress ticking, the bedding piled loosely around her.* Pretty good, but the bedding is not really in "piles" . . . *the bedding loose around her.* Closer. Now say what you have been aware of all the time you were wrestling to get that description right: *Light from the shade-edge went up her shoulder and cheek like tape.* Listen: George is about to speak: *"What are you doing here . . . ?"* No, come on! That's not it. Banal as they are, they may be the words he says, but watch him more closely while he says them. *"What . . . ?" He paused, as though to shake his head. But the only movement in his face was a shifting—* Try again: . . . *a tightening* . . . Almost; but once more . . . *a deepening of the lines, a loosening of the lips; " . . . are you doing here?"* Having gotten his expression more accurately, now you can hear a vocal inflection you missed before: *". . . are you* doing *here?"* There, that's much closer to what you really saw and heard. What has Janice just done? *She uncrossed her legs but did not look at him.* Ordinary grammar rules say that because the sentence's two clauses have one subject, you don't need any comma. But her uncrossing her leg and not looking up go at a much slower pace than proper grammar indicates. Let's make it: *She uncrossed her legs, but did not look at him* . . .

Now let's review the residue of all that, the admittedly undistinguished, if vaguely Chandleresque bit of prose the reader will have:

The lines across his forehead deepened. He reached for the brass doorknob. It turned loosely in its collar. The corners of his mouth tightened. He pressed his palm against the door, twice, to open it. You could hear the jamb split a little more.

The wallpaper was some color between green and gray. The tan shade was drawn. Janice sat on the bare mattress ticking, the bedding loose around her. Light from the shade-edge went up her shoulder and cheek like tape.

"What . . . ?" He paused, as though to shake his head. But the only movement in his face was a deepening of the lines, a loosening of the lips; ". . . are you *doing* here?"

She uncrossed her legs, but did not look at him.

And if you, the writer, want to know what happens next, you must take your seat again in the theater of imagination and observe closely till you see George's next motion, Janice's first response; hear George's next words, and Janice's eventual reply.

A reader, asked to tell the "plot" of even this much of the story, might say: "Well, this man comes looking for this woman named Janice in her room; he finds the door open and goes in, only she doesn't talk at first."

That's a fair description of the reading experience. But what *we* started with, to *write*, was simple: George goes into a room and finds Janice. (George, notice, at this point in the story hasn't even been named.) The rest came through the actual envisioning/notating process, from the interaction of the words and the vision. Most of the implied judgments that the reader picks up—the man is looking *for* Janice; it is *Janice's* room—are simply over-heard (or, more accurately, overseen) suppositions yielded by the process itself. Let's call this continuous, developing interchange between imagination and notation, the *story process*. With Dr. Wilson's indulgence, I will make that my subject, rather that "plot."

A last point to make about our example before a general point about the story process itself: By the time we have gone as far as we have with our "story," all this close observation has given us a good deal more information than we've actually used. Though I didn't when I began (to momentarily drop my editorial stance), I now have a very clear picture of George's and Janice's clothing. I've also picked up a good deal about the building they are in. As well, I've formed some ideas about the relationship between them. And all of this would be re-scrutinized as I came to it, via the story process, were I writing a real story.

The general point: The story process keeps the vision clear and the action moving. But if we do not notate the vision accurately, if we accept some phrase we should have discarded, if we allow to stand some sentence that is not as sharp as we can make it, then the vision is not changed in the same way it would have been otherwise: the new sections of the vision will not light up quite so clearly, perhaps not at all. As well, the movement of the vision—its action—will not develop in the same way if we put down a different phrase. And though the inaccurate employment of the story process may still get you to the end of the tale, the progress of the story process, which eventually registers in the reader's mind as "the plot," is going to be off: An inaccuracy in either of the two story process elements, the envisioning or the notating, automatically detracts from the other. When they go off enough, the progress of the story-process will appear unclear, or clumsy, or just illogical.

It has been said enough times so that most readers have it by rote: A synopsis cannot replace a story. Nor can any analysis of the symbolic structure replace the reading experience that exposes us to those symbols in their structural place. Even so, talking to would-be or beginning writers, I find many of them working under the general assumption that the writer, somehow, must begin with such a synopsis (whether written down or no) and/or such an analysis.

This, for what it's worth, does not parallel my experience. At the beginning of a story, I am likely to have one or more images in my mind, some clearer than others (like the strip of light up Janice's arm), that, when I examine them, suggest relations to one another. Using the story process—envisioning and notating, envisioning and notating—I try to move from one of these images to the next, lighting and focusing, step by step, the dark areas between. As I move along, other areas well ahead in the tale will suddenly come vaguely into light; when I actually reach the writing of them, I use the story process to bring them into still sharper focus.

As likely as not, some of the initial images will suggest obvious synopses of the material between (one image of a man on his knees before a safe; another of the same man fleeing across a rooftop while gunshots ring out behind; a third of the same man, marched between two policemen into a van) that the story process, when finished, will turn out to have followed pretty closely. But it is the process, not the synopsis, that produces the story.

The writer is always grappling with two problems: He must make his story interesting (to himself, if no one else), yet keep it believable (because, somehow, when it ceases to be believable on some level, it ceases to be interesting).

Keeping things interesting seems to be primarily the province of the conscious mind (which, from the literature available, we know far less about than the unconscious), while believability is something that is supplied, in the images it throws up into the mind's theater, primarily by the unconscious. One thing we know about the unconscious is that it contains an incredibly complete "reality model," against which we are comparing our daily experiences moment to moment, every moment. This model lets us know that the thing over there is a garbage can while the thing over there is a gardenia bush, without our having to repeat the learning process of sticking our noses in them each time we pass. It also tells us that, though the thing over there *looks* like a gardenia bush, from a certain regularity in the leaves, an evenness in its coloring, and the tiny mold lines along the stem, it is really a plastic model of a gardenia bush and, should we sniff, will not smell at all. The story process puts us closer to the material stored in our reality model than anything we do besides dream. This material is what yielded us the splitting door jamb, the strip of light, the mattress ticking. This model is highly syncretic: Reality is always presenting us with new experiences that are combinations of old ones. Therefore, even if we want to describe some Horatian impossibility " . . . with the body of a lion and the head of an eagle . . . ," our model will give us, as we stare at the back of the creature's neck, the tawny hairs over the muscled shoulders, in which nestle the first, orange-edged pinfeathers. Come to it honestly, and it will never lie: Search as you want, it will not yield you the height of *pi,* the smell of the number seven, the sound of green, nor, heft hard as you can in palm of your mind, the weight of the note D-flat. (This is not to suggest that such mysterious marvels aren't the province of fiction [especially speculative fiction]; only that they are mysterious and marvelous constructions of the equally mysterious and marvelous *conscious* mind. That is where you must go to find out about *them.*)

When writers get (from readers or from themselves) criticism in the form: "The story would be more believable if such and such happened," or "The story would be more interesting if such and such . . . " *and* they agree, to make use of the criticism, they must translate it: "Is there any point in the story process I can go back to, and, by examining my visualization more closely, catch something I missed before, which, when I notate it, will move the visualization/notation process forward again in this new way?" In other words, can the writers convince themselves that on some ideal level the story actually did happen (as opposed to "should have happened") in the new way, and that it was their inaccuracy as a story-process practitioner that got it going on the wrong track at some given point? If you don't do this, the corrections are going to clunk a bit and leave a patch-as-patch-can feel with the reader.

Writers work with the story process in different ways. Some writers like to work through a short story at a single, intense sitting, to interrupt as little as possible the energy that propels the process along, to keep the imagined visualization clearly and constantly in mind.

Other writers must pause, pace, and sometimes spend days between each few phrases, abandoning and returning to the the visualization a dozen times a page. I think this is done as a sort of test, to make sure only the strongest and most vitally clear elements—the ones that cling tenaciously to the underside of the memory—are retained.

Masterpieces have been written with both methods. Both methods have produced drivel.

To a novice writer one might suggest: Try both. But I also note most writers I've talked to seem to have settled very early on one, the other, or their own particular alternation pattern. One of their clues that their work is not going well, often, is finding this pattern broken; the writer who customarily works slowly, a sentence at a time, may criticize his own story: "I knew it wasn't working; it was coming too quickly," while a writer who usually works at an intense, concentrated pace, may say of her tale: "I thought something was off. It didn't flow."

Sometimes a writer will consciously construct a George-goes-in-and-finds-Janice outline for his entire story before actually beginning the story process. If, here and there, the outline leads to an image which can get the process going, all well and good. Perhaps the constructed outline will be a guide to other images or scenes that will work very well. Far more frequently, however, the finished story will be congruent with the constructed superstructure in only a few places. The writer has to be ready for the story process, again and again, to leave the synopsis, especially if it is to material more interesting and/or more believable. If the finished story bears any relation at all to the outline—perhaps in some element of the initial situation, peripeteia, or denouement—the writer should be content. In a very real way, one writes a story to find out what happens in it. Before it is written it sits in the mind like a piece of overheard gossip or a bit of intriguing tattle. The story process is like taking up such a piece of gossip, hunting down the people actually involved, questioning them, finding out what really occurred, and visiting the pertinent locations. As with gossip, you can't be too surprised if important things turn up that were left out of the first-heard version entirely; or if points initially made much of turn out to have been distorted, or simply not to have happened at all.

Among those stories which strike us as perfectly plotted, with those astonishing endings both a complete surprise and a total satisfaction, it is amazing how many of their writers will confess that the marvelous resolution was as much of a surprise for them as it was for the reader, coming, in imagination and through the story process, only a page or a paragraph or a word before its actual notation.

On the other hand, those stories which make us say, "Well, that's clever, I *suppose* . . . " but with a certain dissatisfied frown (the dissatisfaction itself, impossible to analyze), are often those stories worked out carefully in advance to be, precisely, clever.

One reason it is so hard to discuss the story process, even with introspection, is that it is something of a self-destruct process as well. The notation changes the imagination; it also distorts the writer's memory of the story's creation. The new, intensified visualization (which, depending on the success of the story process, and sometimes in spite of it, may or may not have anything to do with the reader's concept of the story) comes to replace the memory of the story process itself.

The writer cannot make any objective statement on what he was trying to do, or even how he did it, because— as the only residue of the story process the reader has is the writer's words on the page—the only residue of the story process in the writer's mind is the clarified vision, which like the synopsis, is not the story, but the story's result.

With this apology, I turn to the next thing we have been asked to cover in these essays: "Discuss in terms of the subject assigned, your own story in the collection."

I have never read any writer seriously discussing the creation of his own work, be it Mann or Borges, Yeats or Valéry, who did not, at least for the duration of the discussion, seem a slightly smaller person; and the work under discussion, at least momentarily, a slightly smaller work. Looking at my own modest entry here, I am simply afraid that, with any diminution at all, it might vanish. On these grounds, then, I ask to be excused.

CHARACTER:
The Determinant of Incident

*What is character but the determination
of incident?
What is incident but the illustration of
character?*

HENRY JAMES's felicitous phrases underscore the futility of
considering aspects of fiction separately. All—plot, character, point of view, setting, theme, and a dozen others—
are interrelated and mutually dependent in the gestalt of
the story; no two more so than plot and character. To
paraphrase James: every story has its unique characters;
every character has his own story.

Functioning characters are not stock items, carefully labeled and stored on shelves in the writer's mind until he
needs them. Instead, they are meticulously constructed
within the framework of their stories, imagined in a depth
and detail that usually surpasses the demands of the drama
they act out. They are, of course, modeled after life; a
writer has no other source for his knowledge of behavior
and motivation. They are presented in accord with two
judgments the writer must make: the *quantity* of information about the character the reader must have and the
function of the character in the story. The quantitative
decision is particularly important in short fiction, where
every word must count, and the writer—who is as interested in his creations as any fond parent—must struggle
against prolixity. The functional decision helps to determine the quantitative one by distinguishing between important and unimportant characters. But even here, the
writer who plots by the "plant some characters in a situation and see what grows" method is likely to see some unimportant little sprout suddenly develop great leaves and
strong tentacles and strangle the rest of the tale.

Again from the drama, we borrow some useful terms
for the functions of characters. There are, of course, the
protagonist and *antagonist* (or *hero* and *villain*), who must

be understood to be not just good guys and bad guys but the two parties to the central dramatic conflict of the story. They may be people or animals or natural forces or social movements or odd bits of machinery or even opposing views within one person—just so long as they are, in some way or another, personified. George R. Stewart managed to make a *Fire* and a *Storm* the central characters in the two novels with those titles, and perhaps "central character" is a better term than "hero" or "villain," avoiding the value judgments they imply.

Other character functions are the *foil*, the person whose character contrasts with that of the central character, thus making it more perceptible; the *confidante*, the person to whom the central character may speak with some honesty, revealing himself to the reader or delivering necessary expository information in the process; the *narrator*, the person who tells the story (and more on this in the section on point of view); and a host of nonspecific spear carriers who deliver important telegrams, pour drinks behind the bar, arrest the villain, or act as nameless persons from Porlock who are important simply through their presence.

The writer characterizes through two basic methods, the *explicit* and the *dramatic*. The choice between the two seems to follow a kind of faddish cycle, with James's reaction to the explicit techniques of the nineteenth-century novel expressed in his exhortation to "Dramatize! Dramatize!" now appearing as "Show, don't tell!" But the pendulum seems to be swinging back, and if the explicit method is not yet in vogue, it is holding its own. The writer who chooses the explicit method of characterization has limited his choice of point of view (he requires omniscience or a third-person narrator), but he has two powerful tools: the *essay method*, concentrated expository character portraits, and the *method of progressive analysis*, running commentary on the actions and motivations of the character.

The dramatic (or implicit) method of characterization requires that the character be revealed through the opinions of other characters, through his interactions with his environment, and through his acted-out attitudes toward others. Specifically, the implicit method requires great attention to the character's appearance, speech, mannerisms, possessions, and reactions to others. It is one thing to characterize George as a mean man, another to describe him kicking a cup of pencils out of a blind man's hand, yet another to describe the scene and tell the reader why

George did it and what was going through his mind at the time—obviously a combination of the explicit and dramatic methods.

One last revelation: writers construct characters partly from their observations of others, partly from their understanding of certain general principles of human behavior, but mostly from their analyses of themselves. Good writers develop introspection into a high art, become professional schizoids, experiment dangerously in the laboratories of their own souls, and sometimes drink too much.

CRAZY MARO

by Daniel Keyes

THE WAY some people hunt for antiques or old books, searching through second-hand stores, rummage shops, or musty auction rooms for the priceless articles that unknowing people have discarded—in that same way I trace unusual children. Being a lawyer, I have access to the good hunting spots: The Children's Shelter, Warwick, The Paige School for Emotionally Disturbed Adolescents, and —of course—the Juvenile Court.

I've made some finds, and I've been well paid for some rare items. Fifty thousand dollars for a blonde thirteen-year-old delinquent who had spent six months in a Georgia reformatory, and my fee could have been doubled if I'd wanted to haggle with them. She was the first real telepath they'd ever found.

There was the case of the four-month-old mongoloid idiot with the squashed nose and jaw. I got to the unwed mother in time to stop her from smothering it. The tests, provided by my clients, proved beyond doubt that the child was indeed a para-genuis—one they were really interested in. I netted twenty thousand after paying the mother five thousand to sign the adoption papers.

But the strangest one I ever went after, a tall, eighteen-year-old Negro boy with a wild look in his rolling eyes, changed my life. He was called Crazy Maro, and they had offered me a half a million clear if I could get him to sign the waiver and agree to be transported into the future.

The first time I saw Maro there were three boys after him. He was too fast for them and when one of them had him cornered, Maro turned and with the grace of an antelope, darted out of reach.

"Crazy Maro!" one of them taunted.

The others took up the chant. "Crazy Maro! Crazy Maro! . . ."

He stood there on the corner, just fifty yards from them, hands on his hips, sweating and panting for breath. He dared them to come after him, but they had given up the chase.

He saw me watching him, or—as I had been informed —he smelled me or heard me or felt me, or all of these at once. He perceived with all his senses that I was there. I'd been told he could *smell the colors* beyond the visible spectrum as easily as he could smell the colors of a girl's pink and blue summer dress; he could *see the sound* of high-frequency radio waves as sharply as he could see the barking of a dog; he could *hear the odor* of radioactive carbon as clearly as he could hear whisky on a bum's breath.

Although the records of the Juvenile Court showed that he'd been up before the court three times since the age of nine for petty theft and violent behavior, he was needed in the year 2752 to do a job that no one else born before or since could do. That is why they commissioned me to get him. I'd been wandering around this neighborhood between St. Nicholas and Eighth Avenues, commonly referred to by its inhabitants as "the pit," for more than a month with not much data to go on, but now I was certain he was the one they wanted.

Free of his tormenters, he sauntered across the street to where I was standing, his hands deep in the pockets of his patched, wash-pale dungarees. He looked me up and down and cocked his head to one side like a bird or a dog who has heard high-pitched vibrations.

"You *cool* man?"

"No," I said. "I'm quite comfortable."

He snapped his fingers. "Don't bug *me*, mister. You ain't square. You dig me all right. You're cool and deep and rough. Gritty and smooth like worn-out sandpaper." He winked and glared at me out of one eye, as if through a jeweler's glass. "Give me a dollar."

"Why?"

"Cause I'm tough. You get away all in one piece if you pay me. Otherwise . . ." He shrugged to indicate the hopelessness of my case if I didn't pay up.

"Why do they call you Crazy Maro?"

He stared at the sidewalk and it made his eyelids flutter. "Cause I am. Why else? Man, you smell green and paper —like money. Now it's gonna cost you two dollars."

"Why do you expect me to give you money you haven't earned?"

When his head came up, there were only the whites of his eyes against the dark lids. He stood there swaying back and forth to a silent rhythm, snapping his fingers and clapping his hands to a beat he seemed to hear from within. He came out of it frowning.

"You a cop?"

"No," I said, "I'm a lawyer." I fished a card out of my vest pocket and handed it to him. "As you see, it says Eugene—"

"I can read," he snapped. He studied the card and read the words slowly. "Eugene H. Denis . . . attorney-at-law . . ." He studied me and then put the card in his pocket. "It says you're a lawyer. So what do you want with me?"

"Well, er . . . if you would come to my office we could talk privately."

"We can talk right here."

He was touchy and I had to be careful. "Well, if you prefer. My clients have heard about you. They know about your—er—special talents, and they've authorized me to contact you about an important position. The only thing is that I'm not permitted to divulge—I mean tell you— the details unless you agree to go. You would be getting out of this neighborhood permanently, and—"

He was watching me curiously, and then before I knew what was happening, he grabbed my arm. I tried to pull away. "What are you doing? What's the matter?"

He laughed and slapped his thigh with his big hand. "You're scared to death of me. You're afraid I'm gonna hurt you." There was meanness in his eyes suddenly. "Well, I am. I'm going to knock your teeth down your throat."

Somehow I knew he was going to do it. "Why?" I said, still trying to get free of him. "I'm not trying to fool you. This is a great opportunity. You can trust me—"

His long left hand snapped out before I could avoid it and caught me on the mouth. Then a knee came up and hit my groin. I doubled forward and fell to the side-

walk. "What—what's the matter with you?" I choked,
trying to catch my breath. "You nuts? I've come to help
you."

He stood over me and watched me. And then he gagged
and made a sour face as if he tasted and felt the blood
that trickled from the corner of my mouth.

"Salty-sick," he sputtered. "Stop grinding on my teeth."

"Don't hit me," I begged him. "I'm your friend." I was
afraid of the fury in his rolling eyes, and yet I was afraid
I'd lose him.

"Friend, hell!" He kicked my side. "You smell scared
of me. You don't trust me, and you don't like me, and it
smells like a file grinding on my teeth."

"I'm not scared of you, Maro." I tried to control my
agony. "I like you. I came here looking for you. They need
you, and you need them—"

Another kick.

"Don't lie. You're scared of me. Well, you can have
another—"

Out of the corner of his eye he must have caught the
glimpse of the blue uniform, or maybe he smelled it or
heard it or felt it at the end of his long fingertips. "Oh,
crap, man," he sighed. "Cops again."

He drew up tight like a frightened deer caught in the
bright glare of headlights.

"Wait, Maro!" I shouted. "Don't go. I won't press
charges."

He fled.

I shouted after him. "The address on the card! Come
and see me! It's important to you!"

He looked back for an instant as he sprinted across the
street. I saw the big white smile of his teeth, broad and
mocking, against the dark skin. The only fear I had now
was that he would not come to me. He might think I was
setting a trap for him. It had taken me nearly two months
to find him, and in less than half an hour I had driven him
off by botching the whole thing. I had made the mistake
of being afraid of him.

For the next three days I stayed close to my Park Avenue
apartment. All I could think of was that dark glistening
face and the white mocking smile. Would he come? And
if he did, would he agree to be transported into the future?

In the past, the others I had sent had been easy to handle. They hadn't asked embarrassing questions and it hadn't
been necessary for me to explain that I could tell them
nothing about the time, the place, or the job to which they

were going. But Maro, wild as he was, was an intelligent adolescent. Would he accept the fact that he was trading a life and society in which he was a mistake and a misfit for one in which he was right and desperately needed? How in the world was I going to get him to trust me with his life?

The third night the tapping on the window woke me. My radio-clock said 3:45. I started to reach for my .32 automatic in the night-table drawer, but I rejected the idea. Maro would smell danger the same way he had smelled fear and it would make him violent. I couldn't pretend with him. I had to show him I trusted him, or he would resent it. I got out of bed and unlocked the window before turning on the light.

He drew back, lost for an instant in the shadows. I heard him sniffing.

"Come on in, Maro. There's no one else here. I've been waiting for you."

He edged closer to the window, alert to everything in the room behind me. I backed away from the window. He leaped over the sill and landed on the floor without a sound.

It was the first time that I got a close, unhurried look at him. He was tall and sinewy with his hair shaved close to his skull. His fingernails were bitten down beyond the quick and his arms bore long shiny scars. He trembled expectantly as he waited for me to speak. I started to work on him.

"I understand you now, Maro. At least, I know about you and accept you for what you are. To many people who don't appreciate your special gifts, you're frightening. People hate what they don't understand, which is why you have to hide and pretend—"

He laughed and dropped into my easy chair.

"Am I wrong?"

"You're so wrong it stinks. Maybe—if you were in my place—you'd hide. I can smell it in you. You're afraid of your own goddam shadow. Right now you're feeling around for the right words like a man trying to climb up out of a slippery bowl. Man, don't you know yet that I can *feel* it? You're looking at me, Mr. Denis, but you don't see me. You're acting. And if there's one thing that gets me sick inside and mad enough to kill, it's when people don't trust me."

His voice, intense and angry, had so absorbed me that only when he stopped to glare at me, was I shocked to realize that his speech and manner had changed completely. There was no trace of the drawling, slurring dialect, no trace of the wild "bop talk" he had used the first time we met. His eyes were starting to roll again and I saw him kneading his fists. I thought of the gun in the drawer. He quivered and leaned forward with his body tensed to the danger in the air. In that second, I realized that I was handling the whole thing wrong. I decided on the ultimate gamble—telling the truth.

"Hold it," I snapped. "Okay, you're right. I'm afraid of you, and you know it. There's no sense in my trying to fool you. I have a gun in that drawer, and for a second I was thinking I needed it to protect myself."

As I said it, he relaxed. He leaned his head back on the chair and rolled it to massage the muscles in his neck. "Thanks," he sighed. "I didn't know what it was, or where, but I knew it was something. When anyone lies to me or puts it on for me, I feel it hurt deep inside my guts. That's one of the things Dr. Landmeer thinks he can cure. He says I've got to accept people lying and pretending all the time, and when I learn to live with it, I'll be normal."

The court records had mentioned the fact that Maro was to be referred for psychiatric examination, but I had no idea that he would be undergoing treatment. "This Dr. Landmeer... have you been seeing him long?"

"Eight months. The judge sent me to the psycho-clinic, and they sent me to Dr. Landmeer. He's a phoney like all the rest. Even though I know he thinks he's helping me, there are times I want to grab him by the throat and make him stop. He lies and pretends he trusts me, and he thinks I don't see through him. Costs me half a buck a visit. Hey, you know some people pay him fifteen, twenty bucks an hour?"

"Some of them get more," I mused. "Fifty or sixty an hour."

He squinted at me. "You ever been analyzed?"

"No. When I was a kid my father took me to five different psychoanalysts. He finally gave up."

He laughed and slapped me on the back as if he enjoyed the idea. "My old man's just the opposite. He's a minister and he figures it's more important to save my soul. Anyway, I can't take it much longer. That couch of Landmeer's stinks from the talk of so many people. There's a green touch that hammers away so I can hardly hear myself thinking. But he don't hear anything at all, so how can he make me normal? You think I'm crazy, Mr. Denis?"

"No, I don't."

He snickered. "Yes you do. You're crapping me."

"Look," I said, making no effort to hide my annoyance, "You're needed in the future the way you are. If this doctor changes you, you're no good to them."

"The future?" His eyes opened wide.

"That's the deal. There's not much I can tell you except that there is an agency operating out of the future to pick up special children who are born in a time when their talents aren't understood. Kids like you are isolated, or scorned, or even destroyed in their own time. This way they live useful happy lives in a time that needs them."

He gave a long low whistle and dropped back into the chair.

"Wow!" he said. "Dr. Landmeer wants to make me normal. My old man wants to save my soul. Delia wants to make a he-man out of me. And now you come along and tell me I'm okay the way I am, but I'm just living in the wrong time."

I nodded. "That's the size of it."

He got up and paced back and forth, sniffing the air and rubbing it between his fingers. "And you?" he asked, "I can't figure your angle."

I hesitated for a moment and then decided to stay with the truth. "If I get you to agree to go and to sign a waiver of your right to return, I get a half a million dollars."

He sniffed again and then shook his head. "There's something else you're looking for. It's not only the money. You want something out of this more than the money."

"There's nothing else." I insisted. His nostrils trembled in anger as he tightened up all over. "Nothing else that I *know of*, Maro. I swear, if there's anything else, I don't know what it is."

He relaxed again and smiled, studying me through fluttering lids. "How did you get mixed up in this racket, Mr. Denis? I thought you were a lawyer."

Under the pressure of trying to get him to relax with me and trust me, I spoke freely about my becoming a criminal lawyer when I got out of Harvard Law School instead of joining my father and older brother in the firm of *Denis & Denis*, corporation lawyers. I explained how in the eyes of the upper-crust of the legal profession this made me a social outcast, and how my father disinherited me because of it, and how I felt free for the first time in my life, not having to depend on him for anything.

"You meet all kinds of people when you work in the criminal courts," I said. "You're probably too young to remember the case that was on the front pages about six years ago—about the kid who was in a wheelchair, paralyzed from the neck down. He was accused of a dozen thefts from jewelry stores."

Maro leaned forward. "What? That's crazy."

"Well, they never found out how it was done, but he was there every time it happened, and the police found the missing articles in his room. I took the case, and I got him off. I didn't know at the time that he was really guilty."

"But how—?"

"That's what no one else could figure out either. But the story made the front pages for a week. A few months later, after it all died down, they got in touch with me from the future. *They* figured out how he did it, and they wanted him badly. When I confronted the kid with it, he admitted everything. Sure he'd been born paralyzed from the neck down. Sure his muscles were withered away. But there had been a compensation. He was a telekinetic. It was amazing to see how that kid could move and manipulate things around by just using his mind."

"Did he agree to go?"

"Well, at first he was frightened. I didn't blame him. I was suspicious too. I thought that maybe they were crackpots or criminals out to do him some harm. But they sent a man down to see me. He was a lawyer too, and he proved to me beyond doubt that it was okay. When the boy found out that he could really be useful to the world, he was crazy to go. I could hardly hold him back.

"After that first contact with my clients, they got in touch with me from time to time when their researchers found hints or clues about someone special they wanted to move up. I find what they want, get the person's agreement to be transported, and they take care of the rest. The money is always deposited to my account. I've closed nine deals with them in the past five years, and there's not much more that I know."

Maro had been sitting hunched over, never moving his eyes from my face. "And did all the others go without knowing where to or what they were to be used for?"

I nodded. "That's part of the deal. The one thing my clients insist upon. Otherwise it can't be done legally. You've got to trust them."

"And you—I've got to trust you. I don't know anything about them but what you tell me. I've got to put my life into your hands." He looked at the carpet and drew lines in the nap with the edge of his shoe. "Tell me, Mr.

Denis, would you trust me that far? Would you put *your* life into *my* hands?"

The question startled me. My first reaction was to reassure him, but he would know it wasn't true. "No," I said. "No sense in lying. You're like a wild animal to me. How could I trust you that way?"

"Then why are you really doing this, Mr. Denis?"

"I told you. For the money."

"That's crap."

"Is it?" I shouted. "Well believe it, if you want to, or not. I don't give a damn any more." I was angry, and since there was no sense in trying to hide it, I let myself go. "You can walk out of here right now if you want to, and we'll forget about the whole thing."

"What are you looking for, Mr. Denis?"

"It's the money, Maro! The money! The money!" I shouted at him. I was furious at him for making me lose control of myself. He stood there trembling and shaking as I screamed at him, and I felt my insides heaving too. My hands and armpits were clammy.

It was a bursting within me as I had never known before, a flow of anger and resentment so that I wanted to call him filthy names. I wanted to hit him. I wanted to hurt him. His teeth were chattering and his palms were up as he trembled. I hated him. I was sick inside with something waiting to rip loose and smash his face with everything I had.

And suddenly I hit him.

He made no effort to defend himself. I hit him in the face again and again and again, and he smiled as he took it. His eyes rolled up showing two white balls against the dark flesh. I grabbed his throat and I screamed at him. "Look at me! Look at me when I hit you, you bastard! Look at me when I hit you!"

And then, as suddenly as the wave came, it left. I was heavy and limp and soggy and I fell back into the chair. My arms and legs were wet and I was trembling. We sat in silence for a while. Then in a soft voice, not to shatter the silence, he said, "I could trust you a little now, Mr. Denis."

"Why? I haven't changed."

"You have. A little. Enough for me to trust you a bit."

"That's no good," I said. "You've got to trust me completely."

He shook his head. "I trust you for as much as you've changed. Not completely yet. But once you turn on the juice, you're with it. Ever see a man hanging on the end of a live wire? He can't let go. That was what you were like there for a few minutes. Maybe you turned it on just to impress me, but once it's on—that's it. I know, man. I live with the juice turned on and way up all the time."

"Sounds like hell."

"Hell and heaven both. It's a short circuit for me because I'm lying across both wires. But about this putting myself into your hands and signing those papers—that'll take time."

"But how long?"

"You don't understand, Mr. Denis. That's up to you. Whenever you're ready to trust *me*."

I thought about it for a long time. He was right. It was that simple, that logical, that terrifying. He was ready now. I was the one who had to change. He would trust me when I was capable of trusting him. From his point of view it was only fair.

"I don't know if I can do what you ask, Maro. I'd like to, but I don't think I can. I've never been one to trust people. Do you know I stopped going to confession when I was thirteen? People tried to convince me that the priests never revealed anything that was told to them. But my father used to give large donations to the parish, and do you know to this very day I believe that he used to have weekly conferences with Father Moran about my confessions. Even though I know he could have found that book under my mattress without being told by Father Moran, I still can't get it into my head that I could have put complete faith in the priest.

"I can't let myself go that way, Maro. It's not just you. It's all people. I'm the kind of guy who always checks to make sure his wallet is there no matter who bumps into him. Last week I was talking to a judge that I know. He brushed up against me on the way out of the room, and before I knew it I had put my hand to my pocket. He didn't notice it, but I was embarrassed just the same. So how can you ask me to trust you completely?"

He smiled and then shrugged. "One of us will have to give in first, and you're the one who wants this thing. You need me more than I need you—and I'm sure it's not only for the money—so you'll have to prove yourself to me first. That's the only way it can be."

I sat there and looked at him as he examined my apartment. "Quite a place you've got here. Must cost a fortune." He sniffed and cocked his head to listen. "No women up here, huh? You're not married either."

I sighed. "I almost was—about twenty years ago—when I was twenty-three. We broke up a week before the wedding."

"You figured she was after your family's dough?"

"No. She had wealth of her own—a rich old Connecticut family. But I didn't believe she really loved me. Down deep I was sure that she was seeing other men. She broke it off when she discovered I was spying on her. Just as well—it would never have worked out. I guess I'm just the bachelor type."

He stood there and studied me for a long time. "Well, Mr. Denis. I'm sorry about all that. But as far as I'm concerned, what I said still goes. I guess it's about time in your life you really trusted somebody. And it might as well be me."

It was dawn when he left, and I sat staring at the walls for a long time. The more I thought about it the lousier I felt. How did I go about trusting completely a kid like that—me? It was such a crazy thing to think about that it took three shots of bourbon before I could tell myself in the mirror:

"You've got to *show* him that you trust him. You've got to *really* trust him. You've got to *put your life into his hands.*"

That required another drink, and another, and the mirror started talking back to me . . .

The dreams I had were messes, of course. Variations of putting my life into Maro's hands, and each time backing out before the real test came. Finally, when they started setting fire to the half-million dollars, I found the courage. I handed him a cutlass and put my head on the chopping block. And the louse chopped it off. Only the face changed at the end of the dream. It wasn't Maro; it was my father.

It was a vivid session. I awoke at noon with a hangover— a very wobbly head—and I sat at the edge of the bed for a long time feeling sorry for myself and cursing myself for not being able to trust people. But this was getting me nowhere. I had to trust Maro, and if I wanted to be young enough to enjoy the money, I had to be damned quick about it.

The first step in the process of getting to trust him, I decided, was to get to know him as completely as possible. The names of the three people who knew him best came to me clearly: Dr. Landmeer, Reverend Tyler, and a girl by the name of Delia.

Through one of my contacts at the Municipal Mental Health Clinic, I learned that Dr. Landmeer had set aside six hours a week from his private practice to work with three cases assigned to him by the clinic. I learned also that his pet interest was research in adolescent psychotherapy.

In order to get him to talk to me freely, I had my friend at the clinic introduce me first to the directors as an attorney for one of the large philanthropic foundations handled by the firm of *Denis & Denis*, corporation lawyers. Our client, I hinted, was considering substantial donations to be made to worthwhile research projects.

An appointment was made for me to see Dr. Landmeer the following day.

Dr. Landmeer reminded me very much of one of the analysts my father had sent me to when I was a boy. He was short and stubby with thick glasses that distorted his brown eyes into curlicues like knots in a pine board. He ushered me into his consulting room—most enthusiastically.

"Mr. Williams, our director, tells me you're interested in adolescent psychotherapy, Mr. Denis."

"I have been told," I said, "that it is an important field for psychiatric research. I'd like to know a bit about the work that is being done by men like yourself."

"I have always felt," he said, settling in his leather chair and lighting his huge meerschaum pipe, "that techniques of working with adolescents have been neglected too much. It is in this period between childhood and adulthood that study is needed. I know how important it is because I suffered through many of the things that these kids are suffering through now, and if not for the help of one man who cared enough for me, I— Well, no need to go into that. All I can say is that I really feel close to these children who feel afraid and unwanted. There is no reason for the fantastic number of young people who are mentally crippled or destroyed each year. It's a crime."

"That's exactly why I'm here," I said. "Now, if you would tell me something about the cases that have been referred to you by the clinic. Without mentioning any names of course. Just what was wrong with them and how they're coming along."

He described his three clinic cases in detail. I pretended to be interested in the young violinist who had become paralyzed in both hands shortly after his father left his mother, and I asked provocative questions about the brilliant young girl who at the age of sixteen developed the compulsion to disrobe in public. Finally, he came to the young Negro boy who had delusions of persecution.

"A very intelligent boy," he said, "but disturbed. He feels that people are always lying to him. When he first came to me, he pretended to have all of the behavior and speech patterns that prejudiced people have associated with Negroes—the deep drawl, the shuffling walk, dullness . . ."

I nodded, recalling that first day I had seen Maro on the street. ". . . Now of course," Landmeer continued, "he drops the pose when he is with me. The Negro stereotype is his way of protecting himself in his dealings with non-Negroes. You see, he's clever and sensitive enough to know that most people *expect* him to behave that way, so they're easily fooled."

As Landmeer went on to describe him, it became evident that Maro had come here for nearly eight months without revealing his multi-sensory perception. I knew that Landmeer in his desire to impress me with the importance of his work would have mentioned that strange talent if he had known of it. It was clear that although Maro trusted the doctor enough to discard certain traits, he did not trust him enough to reveal himself in any important way.

That was a warning to me. Now, in a sense, it was a race between the doctor and myself. If Maro ever gave himself over completely to Landmeer, he was lost to me and the future that needed him.

"Tell me, Dr. Landmeer, is it true, as I've heard about cases like this, that people who feel they're being plotted against are capable of violence?"

Landmeer pulled at his pipe. "You've got to understand that this patient of mine is emotionally unstable. He has deep-rooted hostilities. At the age of nine his father—a minister—revealed to him that he had been abandoned by his real parents when he was a newborn infant. The minister had heard an infant's cry and traced it to a cardboard box on top of a garbage heap. When he opened the box, he discovered that there was also a rat in it. An emergency transfusion saved the baby's life, but he bears scars on his arms and body to this very day."

"My God! Why was he told about it? Why tell a child of nine something like that?"

"According to the boy, his foster-father told him in a moment of anger. He wanted to prove to the boy that Providence had directed him to the spot where the box lay. I think we can understand some of the reasons for the patient's bitterness towards the world."

"Who wouldn't be bitter with a knowledge like that?"

The doctor nodded. "So to answer your question. With fear and hostility so deeply rooted, a patient like this would probably have no compunctions about violence. However, let me point out that in this case, I feel very confident. The boy is improving. I'm sure that eventually he will be able to adjust to society."

"I can see," I said, getting up to leave, "that your work with young people is extremely important. It should not be allowed to suffer for lack of funds."

The warmth and gratitude in his face was overwhelming, and I decided then and there that if my own little project with Maro ever succeeded I was going to donate a small portion of my fee to Dr. Landmeer's research.

None the less, I left Dr. Landmeer's office more confused and disturbed than when I went in. Throughout the conversation, I had the feeling that something was missing. The picture he gave me of Maro did not fit with the pieces of the boy's personality that I already had. Something was wrong . . .

At the home of Reverend Tyler, I discovered another facet of Maro's character. Mr. Tyler made a great display of cooperation when I told him that I was making a survey for the Child Welfare Bureau—a survey of adopted children who became habitual delinquents.

"I've had a time with that boy, sir." The reverend thumped the table to punctuate his remarks. "It's been a struggle to bring that boy into the flock. He was cast away, and with the Lord's guidance, I snatched him out of the Devil's jaws. He's got the mark of Cain on him, he has. But we're going to save his soul."

"What we at the Bureau are interested in, Reverend, is what he's really like. There might be a clue that would help us with other children on our case list."

He shook his head. "He was always a very emotional child. No matter what you wanted him to do, he did the opposite. I'm a mild man, Mr. Denis. But there were times . . . Do you know that when he was only nine years old, he got into a fight with a boy. He had one hand round the boy's throat and a knife in the other. I came upon them unexpectedly. If I hadn't been sent to intervene by the All-Mighty, he'd have killed that child."

"How do you know he'd have killed the boy? Maybe he was just trying to frighten him. Maybe he knew you were nearby and would stop him."

The minister glared. "Indeed! You don't know Maro. He has always been violent. Up to a few years ago, try as I would, it was impossible to teach him a fear of the All-Mighty. Between that knife and the other boy's heart, there was nothing to stop the deed but my hand directed by Providence. After all, Mr. Denis—what is it that keeps people from destroying each other but fear of Divine Wrath?"

"A faith in mankind . . . " I mumbled absently, thinking of what Maro would have said to that.

"I beg your pardon?"

"Nothing," I said, "just thinking aloud."

"Well, I can tell you it took a great deal of personal pain and inspired guidance to put the fear of Hell into that boy. But thank Heaven I am succeeding. Maro has lately shown a turn to religion that gives me great hope. Wouldn't it be glorious if he were called to the ministry?"

I agreed that it would, and took my leave of Reverend Tyler. The religious aspect didn't fit Maro at all. And neither did the incident with the knife. If Maro had really intended to stab the boy, then he was certainly too fast and clever to be stopped by the reverend. He would have seen or heard or smelled him coming. The real question was: "Why *didn't* he kill the boy?" I had no answer yet. Instead of understanding him, I was unraveling a nature more complex and shifting than any I had ever known.

There was only one person left to see—the one who probably knew him more intimately than anyone else. Would she be able to provide me with the key to Maro's nature?

Delia Brown lived in a tenement on 127th Street and Lenox Avenue. She wouldn't let me into the apartment at first.

"I'm not a cop, Delia. Look, you don't have to tell me where Maro is. I've already seen him, and I've spoken to Dr. Landmeer and the Reverend Tyler. It's you I want to talk to—"

She opened the door a little wider, but in her hand she held an ice-pick. "What about?"

I decided to gamble on the truth. "About trusting Maro. He wants me to trust him, and I've got to know about him first. I would think, Delia, that if you're really his kind of girl, you wouldn't need that thing."

My words stung her. She glared at me and then at the ice-pick in her hand. Then she set it on the table and moved away from the door. She sank into a chair as I pushed the door open.

"So you know him," she said. "Well, I can't be like him. He's a fool. You can tell him that if you want to."

"Then Maro does trust people. He's not afraid of them."

She shrugged. "He's not afraid of anything or anyone in the world. He's too simple and trusting to fear anyone. He's such a child."

"Then why does he pretend to be afraid? Why is he so wild and violent?"

"Wild and violent? Maro?" Her eyes opened wide and she laughed. "Oh, my. I thought you knew what he was really like, the way you talked. Why he's the most peaceful, most gentle soul on this earth. He wouldn't harm a living thing."

The description didn't come any closer to the Maro I knew. It didn't fit the picture of the boy who had smashed a fist into my face and kicked me in the ribs the first time we'd met. I began to feel more and more like a fool. Each time I reached out to grab his image, it slipped away from me like a cake of wet soap. She didn't know him either.

In fact, none of the people who were close to him really knew him. He had kept from each of them his multi-sensory perception, and I began to suspect he had carefully shielded those qualities of his character which disagreed with their different pictures of him.

". . . He's a helpless child," she was saying. "I have to protect him from himself. He'd let people walk all over him and take advantage of his good nature if I didn't scold him for it all the time. Last week he gave a stranger his last dollar. Can you imagine that? A perfect stranger. Maro needs me to take care of him and look after him. But he's getting better. I've convinced him to keep away from bad company . . . other boys influencing him to do bad things. He's such a trusting fool."

She grabbed my sleeve. "Not that I mind, really. He could become something special with the right kind of woman giving him the right kind of love. And he's changing. He's getting common sense. And if there's one thing in this world that a man needs it's common sense. I don't know what kind of a job it is you've got for him, but you could trust that boy with anything." She laughed wearily. "Mr. Denis, that boy doesn't know enough about life to be dishonest. No one ever told him the truth about Santa Claus."

Listening to Delia talk, as I saw our reflection in the clouded mirror over her dressing table, I became aware of the secret of Maro. Everything fell into place. Maro, with his unusual ability to perceive, could detect a person's feelings and know instantly what that person thought of him. He simply reflected the kind of character that person thought him to be. Protective coloration.

Maro was a mirror.

To Dr. Landmeer, he was a neurotic, not to be trusted because that was what the doctor believed him to be; and as the doctor thought he was curing Maro, Maro was getting well. To Reverend Tyler, Maro had been a lost soul; and as the reverend believed he was saving Maro, Maro was becoming religious. To Delia, who saw in Maro a simple youth needing her care and protection, Maro was childlike; and as she saw herself strengthening him against the world, Maro was growing up.

Maro was all of these thing, and none of them. He gave to each person that part of him that was needed. To me he had been a wild, strange, violent creature, and so he was wild, strange and violent. I didn't trust him, and he reflected that. Now I feared that he was capable of murdering me. And so . . .

All the way back to my apartment, I pondered over what I'd learned. Whether or not Maro's strange talents had been created in the upheaval of genetic mutation, there was little doubt in my mind that the unusual events of his infancy had contributed to the development of his shifting senses. For just that reason he was important to *them*—he was an accident of heredity compounded by a special hostile environment, a combination that might never happen again. They needed him, and so he had to go. It was up to me to arrange it.

It was a strange cycle I found here. Maro could be trusted . . . I could have complete faith in him . . . *if I honestly believed I could.* And I could not pretend to believe. He would know pretense, and that would be fatal. I had to put my life into his hands . . . or else forget about the whole thing.

Maro was the mirror. I was the one who had to change.

He was, as I had expected, waiting for me in my apartment. He was smoking my cigarettes and drinking my whiskey, his feet propped up on the coffee table, a clear reflection of the cocky youth I had judged him to be.

I stood there quietly looking at him, not thinking, just letting myself relax and be open in his presence. Knowing what he was really like, I was no longer afraid of him, and he sensed it.

He laughed. Then, seeing the look on my face, he put down the cigarette and stood up frowning. "Hey," he said, "what gives?" He sniffed the air and rubbed it between his fingers. His eyes rolled up and closed and he swayed back and forth as he had done the first time I saw him.

"You've changed," he whispered. There was awe in his voice. "Your breathing—it's like cold water right down to the bottom, and you smell smooth and clear like glass." He was confused. "I've never seen anyone change like that before." His expression shifted from bitterness to scorn to fear to anger to amusement to pleading to childlike simplicity and then, finally, went blank. It was as if he were trying on all the masks in his repertory, shifting back and forth to find out what it was I expected of him, trying to find out what I believed he was like, which of the Maros I wanted him to be. But as he said, I had become smooth, cold water and clear glass.

He dropped back into the chair, and waited. He sensed that I knew him and he was waiting to see what I would do. The cold water, the clear glass that he saw in me had to become a mirror. For the first time in his life, someone was going to be what Maro wanted. Someone was going to reflect *his* need. And what Maro had needed more than anything else in the years of his growing up was to be trusted.

I caught the movement of his eyes to the night-table drawer. He knew that I kept my gun there. It was as if he could sense my readiness to trust him, and he was showing me how to prove it. It was clear what I had to do. I had to try to kill myself, trusting that he would interfere to save me.

My inner self rebelled. What if I was wrong? What if Maro wasn't at all what I believed him to be? What if he didn't stop me? It was stupid—utterly ridiculous to trust anyone that much. A man couldn't even trust his own . . .

A picture flashed across my mind—a memory from my childhood. *My father standing at the foot of the staircase. Myself five or six steps up. He reaches out and calls to me to jump into his arms. He'll catch me. I'm afraid. He*

coaxes . . . assures me daddy won't let me fall. I jump. He
moves away and I scream as I fall to the floor. Hurt and
angry. Why did you lie to me? Why? . . . Why . . .
And the laughter and the words and the voice of my father,
never forgotten. "That's to teach you never to trust anyone
—not even your own father."

Was that why I had never married, or loved, or believed in anyone? Was that the fear that had impris-
oned me all these years behind the safe, hard shell of
suspicion? It was clear to me that at this moment my
decision was as important to me as it was to Maro. If I
backed away now, I would never in my life be able to trust
anyone.

He was watching me. He was wanting me to believe in
him.

Without speaking, I went to the drawer, opened it and
removed the gun. I checked it to make sure it was loaded,
and then I faced him. He showed no emotion, made no
sign.

"I trust you, Maro," I said. "You need proof of my faith
in you. Well, then, so do I. Let's both see if I'm capable
of giving it . . . if I can pull this trigger . . ."

I put the muzzle of the gun to my right temple. "I'm
going to count to three. I want to believe that you'll stop
me before I kill myself."

He smiled. "Will you really do it? Maybe I won't stop
me. Maybe I'll be too slow. Maybe—"

"One."

"You're a fool, Mr. Denis. It's not worth half a million
dollars to take a chance like this. Or isn't it the money
after all? What is it you expect to prove?"

"Two." *Would my finger react to the command? Was*
I capable of doing it? Then, almost as if our minds
touched for an instant, I knew that I would do it . . . as
clearly as I knew that he would save me. Nothing else was
worth knowing. It felt good.

The smile left his face. He breathed deeply and clenched
his fists. His eyes were wide.

"Three."

I squeezed the trigger without closing my eyes.

In that instant between me and eternity, Maro sprang.
His hand lashed out and whipped the gun aside. The
bullet grazed my forehead and crashed into the wall beside us. The white explosion burnt my face and I fainted.

When I came to, I felt him hovering over me. He had

put a wet towel across my face. "You'll be okay," he said. "Powder burns. I've called for a doctor."

"That was close," I said.

"You're a fool!" He moved back and forth restlessly, hitting his fists. "A damned fool. You shouldn't have done it."

"You wanted me to. I'm glad I did. It was as much for myself as for you."

He was overexcited now. I heard him stalking back and forth. A hassock was in his way and he kicked it aside. "I shouldn't have waited so long. I didn't think you were really going to do it. I didn't know. No one ever believed in me that way before. I think that all my life I've been waiting for someone who really would trust me. I didn't think it would be you."

I nodded. "I didn't think so either. I never trusted anyone like that since I was a small child. I've found something deep inside myself that I thought had been destroyed. It was worth it."

"Mr. Denis . . . " He moved back and sniffed the air.

"What's the matter?"

"There's something out there. Far away and yet close by. Music, but not real music. Faint violet and burnt-yellow ribbons of sound winding around me and dissolving. It's here and now and yet it's far off in the future."

"That's the place and time for you, Maro. They need you there—for what you are, the way you are. And you need them. You've got to trust them."

"I trust you, Mr. Denis. If you say it's all right, I'll go."

"It's all right. I'm not saying it for the money, you know that. I'm giving my fee to the clinic. I have more than enough for myself. I'm retiring. This will be my last job for them."

"You'll figure out something to tell Dr. Landmeer and my old man and Delia for me?"

"I will."

I told him how to call the telephone answering service to let them know that he was ready to leave. They would tell him where to wait and they would send someone to pick him up. He took my hand and clasped it for a long time.

"Mr. Denis, I thought you might like to know. That music . . . I saw and felt . . . you were right. It was from them. It was a hint about what they need me for."

"Can you tell me?"

"It's not clear, Mr. Denis. But I saw a picture of a great

gathering of people. They can't understand each other at all, and nobody knows what the others want. Words seem to have lost all meaning. Like . . . like what happened in the Old Testament when they built the Tower of Babel. There's a lot of confusion. I think they need me to help them talk to each other, and trust each other—and make peace."

"I'm glad you told me, Maro. It makes me feel better."

"So long, Mr. Denis."

"So long."

I waited until I heard the front door slam shut, and then I took the towel off my face and rolled over to sit on the edge of the bed. I felt around in my pockets for my cigarette lighter. I flipped it on, holding it up in front of my face. There was searing heat and the crackle and pungent odor of burning hair as I singed my eyebrows. But no light.

And then I knew what it was like to be totally blind.

I lay back in the bed, and from somewhere there flowed in through my window the sound of music. For a fleeting moment, I thought I heard it the way Maro had heard it —faint violet and burnt-yellow ribbons of sound winding about me and dissolving. But then the multiple image was gone, and I heard the muted strains of the melody as I have heard all sounds and music ever since.

In darkness . . .

HOW MUCH DOES A CHARACTER COST?

by Daniel Keyes

I USED to think that characters were free. Now I know better. I've paid the price.

Maro first appeared to me as an image, a black youth who lived across the street. I had seen him one day, standing in the middle of the street, tall, alert, haughty, and suddenly running faster than anyone I had ever seen. One day, years later, casting about for a story to write, I remembered him.

I knew the story would be about race and racism, about his strategies for survival in a world in which fear and hostility block understanding. I don't mean to imply that the character and events were planned to express this as a theme. It was the other way. Once I began to invent the fictions of Maro's life and background, I realized I would have to speak of the risks we have to take, the price we all have to pay. I guess you could say the image of the character came first, and then the concept, and finally out of the mixture came the story.

Writing, it has been said, is an act of discovery; to me that usually means the discovery of people. So I had to find a narrator who could search for Maro, unraveling the mystery of the character as he went along, becoming aware of his own feelings toward the black youth and toward his own unthinking acceptance of racial stereotypes, while at the same time surmounting the barriers he had erected to protect himself against the terrors— real or imagined—of trusting others.

Eugene Denis began as a narrator and foil, but as he became individualized, with his own memories, attitudes and fears, the story changed from Maro's to one of a relationship between Maro and Denis, based on self-awareness and risk-taking. Denis had to know himself before he could make demands on Maro (in the writing of the story, as well as in the fiction itself). Maro had to drop his mask and reveal himself to me and to Denis, and trust us both before he could fulfill his own destiny.

The story line now turned on the hinge of their encounter. To become involved with Maro without pretense, Denis had to know himself as well as he tried to know Maro. Maro did not really have to change much; Denis was the one who had been deceiving himself all these years. In his search for the true, inner Maro, Denis discovered that the young black man had to play many roles to reflect the expectations of others. Denis also discovered the lies and fears in his own make-up. Thus, the story became as much Denis's as Maro's, and was no longer about race and racism but about humanity and inhumanism.

When I am developing characters, I try to keep in mind the way we all get to know people. Visualize yourself at a party, noticing someone across the room. First, the overall impressions: size, shape, color—creating a frame of reference. Then, any unusual or attention-getting detail (if there is one, not forcing it) that will distinguish the character, showing how he differs from other people in his own group or type. Much like the simple act of definition. Indeed, at this point I am defining my charac-ter.

The character set in motion begins to individualize him-self. I learn about him by seeing what he does under different situations (including stress), and what he leaves undone. I pay attention to what he says about himself, as well as to what others say about him. Often, I discover that the minor figures have a limited knowledge of the main character. How the pieces fit to make a coherent whole often becomes part of the story development.

Among the discoveries we make is background; social and personal history gives our character a dimension of time. The reader, discovering a past as well as a present, begins to project the line that leads into the future. Add thoughts, hopes, fears, dreams, and the reader may sus-pend disbelief and cross over with us into the world of our fictional character. This is standard procedure. When I've done as many of these things as the story will bear, I've succeeded in creating a very lifelike puppet, a me-chanical doll. To bring it to life—the dream of every writer—requires something more.

This last ingredient went into "Crazy Maro"—into both characters—in the form of a memory of my youth when I was caught alone one night in a strange neighborhood and badly beaten by several older boys. When the time came to write of the first encounter between Denis and Maro, I recalled that experience, and the emotion of my memory was discharged into Denis's fear and Maro's an-ger. When I finished writing that scene, and the later scene in which Denis returns the beating, the memory of what really happened that night began to fade. Although I had recalled that experience, and the feelings connected to it, often before I wrote it, now I can say that I no longer remember what really happened that night. It seems I gave away a part of myself, a memory, an ex-perience, an emotion, to both Maro and Denis.

Not that I'm able to hit that level of feeling very often, but when a character begins to move, and I discover something in myself that he can use, I give it to him. Then it no longer belongs to me. It belongs to the char-acter and gives him a deeply felt experience rather than a contrived one. If I'm lucky, the puppet, the mechanical doll, will come alive and remain in the mind of the reader as something with the feeling of life. That's why creating characters is like raising children—you give each one a little bit of yourself, and you don't begrudge it.

The making of every living character thus extracts payment from the writer. Nothing from nothing. F. Scott Fitzgerald thought of it as a creative bank account: the more he drew out of it, the less he had. That's one way of looking at it. I don't know how many other writers have had this experience. But I suspect there is something at work like the laws of conservation of mass and of energy. The experiences and memories we give to our characters to bring them to life, we no longer have for ourselves. Not a bad exchange. A better bargain than Faust got. I'd say he sold his soul for less.

PRETTY MAGGIE MONEYEYES

by Harlan Ellison

WITH AN eight hole-card and a queen showing, with the dealer showing a four up, Kostner decided to let the house do the work. So he stood, and the dealer turned up. Six.

The dealer looked like something out of a 1935 George Raft film: Arctic diamond-chip eyes, manicured fingers long as a brain surgeon's, straight black hair slicked flat away from the pale forehead. He did not look up as he peeled them off. A three. Another three. Bam. A five. Bam. Twenty-one, and Kostner saw his last thirty dollars —six five-dollar chips—scraped on the edge of the cards, into the dealer's chip racks. Busted. Flat. Down and out in Las Vegas, Nevada. Playground of the Western World.

He slid off the comfortable stool-chair and turned his back on the blackjack table. The action was already starting again, like waves closing over a drowned man. He had been there, was gone, and no one had noticed. No one had seen a man blow the last tie with salvation. Kostner now had his choice: he could bum his way into Los Angeles and try to find something that resembled a new life . . . or he could go blow his brains out through the back of his head.

Neither choice showed much light or sense.

He thrust his hands deep into the pockets of his worn and dirty chinos, and started away down the line of slot machines clanging and rattling on the other side of the aisle between blackjack tables.

He stopped. He felt something in his pocket. Beside him, but all-engrossed, a fiftyish matron in electric lavender capris, high heels and Ship n' Shore blouse was working two slots, loading and pulling one while waiting for the other to clock down. She was dumping quarters in a seemingly inexhaustible supply from a Dixie cup held in her left hand. There was a surrealistic presence to the woman. She was almost automated, not a flicker of expression on her face, the eyes fixed and unwavering. Only when the gong rang, someone down the line had pulled a jackpot, did she look up. And at that moment Kostner knew what was wrong and immoral and deadly about Vegas, about legalized gambling, about setting the traps all baited and open in front of the average human. The woman's face was gray with hatred, envy, lust and dedication to the game—in that timeless instant when she heard another drugged soul down the line winning a minuscule jackpot. A jackpot that would only lull the player with words like *luck* and *ahead of the game*. The jackpot lure; the sparkling, bobbling many-colored wiggler in a sea of poor fish.

The thing in Kostner's pocket was a silver dollar.

He brought it out and looked at it.

The eagle was hysterical.

But Kostner pulled to an abrupt halt, only one half-footstep from the sign indicating the limits of Tap City. He was still with it. What the high-rollers called the edge, the *vigerish*, the fine hole-card. One buck. One cartwheel. Pulled out of the pocket not half as deep as the pit into which Kostner had just been about to plunge.

What the hell, he thought, and turned to the row of slot machines.

He had thought they'd all been pulled out of service, the silver dollar slots. A shortage of coinage, said the United States Mint. But right there, side by side with the nickel and quarter bandits, was one cartwheel machine. Two thousand dollar jackpot. Kostner grinned foolishly. If you're gonna go out, go out like a champ.

He thumbed the silver dollar into the coin slot and grabbed the heavy, oiled handle. Shining cast aluminum and pressed steel. Big black plastic ball, angled for arm-ease, pull it all day and you won't get weary.

Without a prayer in the universe, Kostner pulled the handle.

She had been born in Tucson, mother full-blooded

Cherokee, father a bindlestiff on his way through. Mother had been working a truckers' stop, father had popped for spencer steak and sides. Mother had just gotten over a bad scene, indeterminate origins, unsatisfactory culminations. Mother had popped for bed. And sides. Margaret Annie Jessie had come nine months later; black of hair, fair of face, and born into a life of poverty. Twenty-three years later, a determined product of Miss Clairol and Berlitz, a dream-image formed by Vogue *and intimate association with the rat race, Margaret Annie Jessie had become a contraction.*

Maggie.

Long legs, trim and coltish; hips a trifle large, the kind that promote that specific thought in men, about getting their hands around it; belly flat, isometrics; waist cut to the bone, a waist that works in any style from dirndl to disco-slacks; no breasts—all nipple, but no breast, like an expensive whore   (the way O'Hara pinned it)—and no padding . . . forget the cans, baby, there's other, more important action; smooth, Michelangelo-sculpted neck, a pillar, proud; and all that face.

Outthrust chin, perhaps a tot too much belligerence, but if you'd walloped as many gropers, you too, sweetheart; narrow mouth, petulant lower lip, nice to chew on, a lower lip as though filled with honey, bursting, ready for things to happen; a nose that threw the right sort of shadow, flaring nostrils, the acceptable words—aquiline, patrician, classic, allathat; cheekbones as stark and promontory as a spit of land after ten years of open ocean; cheekbones holding darkness like narrow shadows, sooty beneath the taut-fleshed bone-structure; amazing cheekbones, the whole face, really; simple uptilted eyes, the touch of the Cherokee, eyes that looked out at you, as you looked in at them, like someone peering out of the keyhole as you peered in; actually, dirty eyes, they said you can get it.

Blonde hair, a great deal of it, wound and rolled and smoothed and flowing, in the old style, the Gibson Girl thing men always admire; no tight little cap of slicked plastic; no ratted and teased Anapurna of bizarre coiffure; no ironed-flat discothèque hair like number 3 flat noodles. Hair, the way a man wants it, so he can dig his hands in at the base of the neck and pull all that face very close.

An operable woman, a working mechanism, a rigged and sudden machinery of softness and motivation.

Twenty-three, and determined as hell never to abide

in that vale of poverty her mother had called purgatory for her entire life; snuffed out in a grease fire in the last trailer, somewhere in Arizona, thank God no more pleas for a little money from babygirl Maggie hustling drinks in a Los Angeles topless joint. (There ought to be some remorse in there somewhere, for a Mommy gone where all the good grease fire victims go. Look around, you'll find it.)

Maggie.

Genetic freak. Mommy's Cherokee uptilted eye-shape, and Polack quickscrewing Daddy WithoutaName's blue as innocence color.

Blue-eyed Maggie, dyed blonde, alla that face, alla that leg, fifty bucks a night can get it and it sounds like it's having a climax.

Irish-innocent blue-eyed innocent French-legged innocent Maggie. Polack. Cherokee. Irish. All-woman and going on the market for this month's rent on the stucco pad, eighty bucks' worth of groceries, a couple months' worth for a Mustang, three appointments with the specialist in Beverly Hills about that shortness of breath after a night on the Bugalu.

Maggie, Maggie, Maggie, pretty Maggie Moneyeyes, who came from Tucson and trailers and rheumatic fever and a surge to live that was all kaleidoscope frenzy of clawing scrabbling no-nonsense. If it took laying on one's back and making sounds like a panther in the desert, then one did it, because nothing, but nothing was as bad as being dirt-poor, itchy-skinned, soiled-underwear, scuff-toed, hairy and ashamed lousy with the no-gots. Nothing!

Maggie. Hooker. Hustler. Grabber. Swinger. If there's a buck in it, there's rhythm and the onomatopoeia is Maggie Maggie Maggie.

She who puts out. For a price, whatever that might be.

Maggie was dating Nuncio. He was Sicilian. He had dark eyes and an alligator-grain wallet with slip-in pockets for credit cards. He was a spender, a sport, a high-roller. They went to Vegas.

Maggie and the Sicilian. Her blue eyes and his slip-in pockets. But mostly her blue eyes.

The spinning reels behind the three long glass windows blurred, and Kostner knew there wasn't a chance. Two thousand dollar jackpot. Round and round, whirring. Three bells or two bells and a jackpot bar, get 18; three plums or two plums and a jackpot bar, get 14; three oranges or two oranges and a jac—

Ten, five, two bucks for a single cherry cluster in first position. Something . . . I'm drowning . . . something . . .

The whirring . . .

Round and round . . .

As something happened that was not considered in the pit-boss manual.

The reels whipped and snapped to a stop, clank clank clank, tight in place.

Three bars looked up at Kostner. But they did not say JACKPOT. They were three bars on which stared three blue eyes. Very blue, very immediate, very JACKPOT!!!!

Twenty silver dollars clattered into the payoff trough at the bottom of the machine. An orange light flickered on in the Casino Cashier's cage, bright orange on the jackpot board. And the gong began clanging overhead.

The Slot Machine Floor Manager nodded once to the Pit Boss, who pursed his lips and started toward the seedy-looking man still standing with his hand on the slot's handle.

The token payment—twenty silver dollars—lay untouched in the payoff trough. The balance of the jackpot —one thousand nine hundred and eighty dollars—would be paid manually by the Casino Cashier. And Kostner stood dumbly, as the three blue eyes stared up at him.

There was a moment of idiotic disorientation, as Kostner stared back at the three blue eyes; a moment in which the slot machine's mechanisms registered to themselves; and the gong was clanging furiously.

All through the hotel's Casino people turned from their games to stare. At the roulette tables the white-on-white players from Detroit and Cleveland pulled their watery eyes away from the clattering ball and stared down the line for a second, at the ratty-looking guy in front of the slot machine. From where they sat, they could not tell it was a two grand pot, and their rheumy eyes went back into billows of cigar smoke, and that little ball.

The blackjack hustlers turned momentarily, screwing around in their seats, and smiled. They were closer to the slot-players in temperament, but they knew the slots were a dodge to keep the old ladies busy, while the players worked toward their endless twenty-ones.

And the old dealer, who could no longer cut it at the fast-action boards, who had been put out to pasture by a grateful management, standing at the Wheel of Fortune near the entrance to the Casino, even he paused in h.s zombie-murmuring ("Annnnother winner onna Wheel of Forchun!") to no one at all, and looked toward Kostner and that incredible gong-clanging. Then, in a moment, still with no players, he called *another* nonexistent winner.

Kostner heard the gong from far away. It had to mean he had won two thousand dollars, but that was impossible. He checked the payoff chart on the face of the machine. Three bars labeled JACKPOT meant JACKPOT. Two thousand dollars.

But these three bars did not say JACKPOT. They were three gray bars, rectangular in shape, with three blue eyes directly in the center of each bar.

Blue eyes?

Somewhere, a connection was made, and electricity, a billion volts of electricity, were shot through Kostner. His hair stood on end, his fingertips bled raw, his eyes turned to jelly, and every fiber in his musculature became radioactive. Somewhere, out there, in a place that was not this *place, Kostner had been inextricably bound to—to* someone. Blue eyes?

The gong had faded out of his head, the constant noise level of the Casino, chips chittering, people mumbling, dealers calling plays, it had all gone, and he was embedded in silence.

Tied to that someone else, out there somewhere, through those three blue eyes.

Then in an instant, it had passed, and he was alone again, as though released by a giant hand, the breath crushed out of him. He staggered up against the slot machine.

"You all right, fellah?"

A hand gripped him by the arm, steadied him. The gong was still clanging overhead somewhere, and he was breathless from a journey he had just taken. His eyes focused and he found himself looking at the stocky Pit Boss who had been on duty while he had been playing blackjack.

"Yeah . . . I'm okay, just a little dizzy is all."

"Sounds like you got yourself a big jackpot, fellah," the Pit Boss grinned. It was a leathery grin; something composed of stretched muscles and conditioned reflexes, totally mirthless.

"Yeah . . . great . . ." Kostner tried to grin back. But he was still shaking from that electrical absorption that had kidnaped him.

"Let me check it out," the Pit Boss was saying, edging

around Kostner, and staring at the face of the slot machine. "Yeah, three jackpot bars, all right. You're a winner."

Then it dawned on Kostner! Two thousand dollars! He looked down at the slot machine and saw—

Three bars with the word JACKPOT on them. No blue eyes, just words that meant money. Kostner looked around frantically, was he losing his mind? *From somewhere, not in the Casino room, he heard a tinkle of rhodium-plated laughter.*

He scooped up the twenty silver dollars, and the Pit Boss dropped another cartwheel into the Chief, and pulled the jackpot off. Then the Pit Boss walked him to the rear of the Casino, talking to him in a muted, extremely polite tone of voice. At the Cashier's window, the Pit Boss nodded to a weary-looking man at a huge Rolodex card-file, checking credit ratings.

"Barney, jackpot on the cartwheel Chief; slot five-oh-oh-one-five." He grinned at Kostner, who tried to smile back. It was difficult. He felt stunned.

The Cashier checked a payoff book for the correct amount to be drawn and leaned over the counter toward Kostner. "Check or cash, sir?"

Kostner felt buoyancy coming back to him. "Is the Casino's check good?" They all three laughed at that. "A check's fine," Kostner said. The check was drawn, and the Check-Riter punched out the little bumps that said two thousand. "The twenty cartwheels are a gift," the Cashier said, sliding the check through to Kostner.

He held it, looked at it, and still found it difficult to believe. Two grand, back on the golden road.

As he walked back through the Casino with the Pit Boss, the stocky man asked pleasantly, "Well, what are you going to do with it?" Kostner had to think a moment. He didn't really have any plans. But then the sudden realization came to him: "I'm going to play that slot machine again." The Pit Boss smiled: a congenital sucker. He would put all twenty of those silver dollars back into the Chief, and then turn to the other games. Blackjack, roulette, faro, baccarat . . . in a few hours he would have redeposited the two grand with the hotel Casino. It always happened.

He walked Kostner back to the slot machine, and patted him on the shoulder. "Lotsa luck, fellah."

As he turned away, Kostner slipped a silver dollar into the machine, and pulled the handle.

The Pit Boss had only taken five steps when he heard

the incredible sound of the reels clicking to a stop, the clash of twenty token silver dollars hitting the payoff trough, and that goddammed gong went out of its mind again.

She had known that sonofabitch Nuncio was a perverted swine. A walking filth. A dungheap between his ears. Some kind of monster in nylon undershorts. There weren't many kinds of games Maggie hadn't played, but what that Sicilian De Sade wanted to do was outright vomity!

She nearly fainted when he suggested it. Her heart— which the Beverly Hills specialist had said she should not tax—began whumping frantically. "You pig!" she screamed. "You filthy dirty ugly pig you, Nuncio you pig!" She had bounded out of the bed and started to throw on clothes. She didn't even bother with a brassiere, pulling the cable-knit sweater on over her thin breasts, still crimson with the touches and love-bites Nuncio had showered on them.

He sat up in the bed, a pathetic-looking little man, gray hair at the temples and no hair atall on top, and his eyes were moist. He was porcine, was indeed the swine she called him, but he was helpless before her. He was in love with his hooker, with the tart whom he was supporting. It had been the first time for the swine Nuncio, and he was helpless. Back in Detroit, had it been a floozy, a chippy broad, he would have gotten out of the double bed and rapped her around pretty good. But this Maggie, she tied him in knots. He had suggested . . . that, what they should do together . . . because he was so consumed with her. But she was furious with him. It wasn't that bizarre an idea!

"Gimme a chanct'a talk t'ya, honey . . . Maggie . . ."

"You filthy pig, Nuncio! Give me some money, I'm going down to the Casino, and I don't want to see your filthy pig face for the rest of the day, remember that!"

And she had gone in his wallet and pants, and taken eight hundred and sixteen dollars, while he watched. He was helpless before her. She was something stolen from a world he knew only as "class" and she could do what she wanted with him.

Genetic freak Maggie, blue-eyed posing mannequin Maggie, pretty Maggie Moneyeyes, who was one-half Cherokee and one-half a buncha other things, had absorbed her lessons well. She was the very model of a "class broad."

"Not for the rest of the day, do you understand?"
she snapped at him, and went downstairs, furious, to fret
and gamble and wonder about nothing but years of her-
self.

Men stared after her as she walked. She carried herself
like a challenge, the way a squire carried a pennant, the
way a prize bitch carried herself in the judge's ring. Born
to the blue. The wonders of mimicry and desire.

Maggie had no desire for gambling, none whatever. She
merely wanted to taste the fury of her relationship with
the swine Sicilian, her need for solidarity in a life built
on the edge of the slide area, the senselessness of being
here in Las Vegás when she could be back in Beverly Hills.
She grew angrier and more ill at the thought of Nuncio
upstairs in the room, taking another shower. She bathed
three times a day. But it was different with him. He knew
she resented his smell; he had the soft odor of wet fur
sometimes, and she had told him about it. Now he bathed
constantly, and hated it. He was a foreigner to the bath.
His life had been marked by various kinds of filths, and
baths for him now were more of an obscenity than dirt
could ever have been. For her, bathing was different. It
was a necessity. She had to keep the patina of the world
off her, had to remain clean and smooth and white. A
presentation, not an object of flesh and hair. A chro-
mium instrument, something never pitted by rust and
corrosion.

When she was touched by them, by any one of them,
by the men, by all the Nuncios, they left little pit holes of
bloody rust on her white permanent flesh; cobwebs, sooty
stains. She had to bathe. Often.

She strolled down between the tables and the slots, car-
rying eight hundred and sixteen dollars. Eight one hun-
dred dollar bills and sixteen dollars in ones.

At the change booth she got cartwheels for the sixteen
ones. The Chief waited. It was her baby. She played it to
infuriate the Sicilian. He had told her to play the nickel
slots, the quarter or dime slots, but she always infuriated
him by blowing fifty or a hundred dollars in ten minutes,
one coin after another, in the big Chief.

She faced the machine squarely, and put in the first
silver dollar. She pulled the handle that swine Nuncio.
Another dollar, pulled the handle how long does this go
on? The reels cycled and spun and whirled and whipped
in a blurringspinning metalhumming overandoverandover
as Maggie blue-eyed Maggie hated and hated and thought

*of hate and all the days and nights of swine behind her
and ahead of her and if only she had all the money in
this room in this Casino in this hotel in this town right
now this very instant just an instant this instant it would
be enough of whirring and humming and spinning and
overandoverandoverandover and she would be free free
free and all the world would never touch her body again
the swine would never touch her white flesh again and
then suddenly as dollarafterdollarafterdollar went arounda-
roundaround hummmmming in reels of cherries and bells
and bars and plums and oranges there was suddenly
painpainpain a SHARP pain!pain!pain! in her chest, her
heart, her center, a needle, a lancet, a burning, a pillar
of flame that was purest pure purer PAIN!*

*Maggie, pretty Maggie Moneyeyes, who wanted all that
money in that cartwheel Chief slot machine, Maggie who
had come from filth and rheumatic fever, who had come
all the way to three baths a day and a specialist in Very
Expensive Beverly Hills, that Maggie suddenly had a seizure, a flutter, a slam of a coronary thrombosis and fell
instantly dead on the floor of the Casino. Dead.*

*One instant she had been holding the handle of the slot
machine, willing her entire being, all that hatred for all
the swine she had ever rolled with, willing every fiber of
every cell of every chromosome into that machine, wanting to suck out every silver vapor within its belly, and the
next instant—so close they might have been the same—
her heart exploded and killed her and she slipped to
the floor . . . still touching the Chief.*

On the floor.
Dead.
Struck dead.
Liar. All the lies that were her life.
Dead on a floor.

[A moment out of time ■ lights whirling and spinning in a cotton candy universe ■ down a bottomless funnel roundly sectioned like a goat's horn ■ a cornucopia that rose up cuculiform smooth and slick as a worm belly ■ endless nights that pealed ebony funeral bells ■ out of fog ■ out of weightlessness ■ suddenly total cellular knowledge ■ memory running backward ■ gibbering spastic blindness ■ a soundless owl of frenzy trapped in a cave of prisms ■ sand endlessly draining down ■ billows of forever ■ edges of the world as they splintered ■ foam rising drowning from inside ■ the smell of rust ■ rough green corners that burn ■ memory the gibbering spastic blind memory ■ seven rushing vacuums of nothing ■ yellow ■ pinpoints cast in amber straining and elongating running like live wax ■ chill fevers ■ overhead the odor of stop ■ this is the stopover before hell or heaven ■ this is limbo ■ trapped and doomed alone in a mist-eaten nowhere ■ a soundless screaming a soundless whirring a soundless spinning spinning spinning ■ spinning spinning ■ spinning ■ spinning ■ spinninggggggggggg]

> Maggie had wanted all the silver in the machine. She had died, willing herself into the machine. Now looking out from within, from inside the limbo that had become her own purgatory, Maggie was trapped, in the oiled and anodized interior of the silver dollar slot machine. The prison of her final desires, where she had wanted to be, completely trapped in that last instant of life between life/death. Maggie, all soul now, trapped for all eternity in the soul of the soulless machine. Limbo. Trapped.

"I hope you don't mind if I call over one of the slot men," the Slot Machine Floor Manager was saying, from a far distance. He was in his late fifties, a velvet-voiced man whose eyes held nothing of light and certainly nothing of kindness. He had stopped the Pit Boss as the stocky man had turned in mid-step to return to Kostner and the jackpotted machine; he had taken the walk himself. "We have to make sure, you know how it is, somebody didn't fool with the slot, you know, maybe it's outta whack or something, you know."

He lifted his left hand and there was a clicker in it, the kind children use at Halloween. He clicked half a dozen times, like a rabid cricket, and there was a scurrying in the pit between the tables.

Kostner was only faintly aware of what was happening.

Instead of being totally awake, feeling the surge of adrenaline through his veins, the feeling any gambler gets when he is ahead of the game, a kind of desperate urgency when he has hit it for a boodle, he was numb, partaking of the action around him only as much as a drinking glass involves itself in the alcoholic's drunken binge.

All color and sound had been leached out of him.

A tired-looking, resigned-weary man wearing a gray porter's jacket, as gray as his hair, as gray as his indoor skin, came to them, carrying a leather wrap-up of tools. The slot repairman studied the machine, turning the pressed steel body around on its stand, studying the back. He used a key on the back door and for an instant Kostner had a view of gears, springs, armatures and the clock that ran the slot mechanism. The repairman nodded silently over it, closed and relocked it, turned it around again and studied the face of the machine.

"Nobody's been spooning it," he said, and went away.

Kostner stared at the Floor Manager.

"Gaffing. That's what he meant. Spooning's another word for it. Some guys use a little piece of plastic, or a wire, shove it down through the escalator, it kicks the machine. Nobody thought that's what happened here, but you know, we have to make sure, two grand is a big payoff, and twice . . . well, you know, I'm sure you'll understand. If a guy was doing it with a boomerang—"

Kostner raised an eyebrow.

"—uh, yeah, a boomerang, it's another way to spoon the machine. But we just wanted to make a little check, and now everybody's satisfied, so if you'll come back to the Casino Cashier with me—"

And they paid him off again.

So he went back to the slot machine, and stood before it for a long time, staring at it. The change girls and the dealers going off-duty, the little old ladies with their canvas work gloves worn to avoid calluses when pulling the slot handles, the men's room attendant on his way up front to get more matchbooks, the floral tourists, the idle observers, the hard drinkers, the sweepers, the busboys, the gamblers with poached-egg eyes who had been up all night, the showgirls with massive breasts and diminutive sugar daddies, all of them conjectured mentally about the beat-up walker who was staring at the silver dollar Chief. He did not move, merely stared at the machine . . . and they wondered.

The machine was staring back at Kostner.

Three blue eyes.

The electric current had sparked through him again, as the machine had clocked down and the eyes turned up a second time, as he had *won* a second time. But this time he knew there was something more than luck involved, for no one else had seen those three blue eyes.

So now he stood before the machine, waiting. It spoke to him. Inside his skull, where no one had ever lived but himself, now someone else moved and spoke to him. A girl. A beautiful girl. Her name was Maggie, and she spoke to him:

I've been waiting for you. A long time, I've been waiting for you, Kostner. Why do you think you hit the jackpot? Because I've been waiting for you, and I want you. You'll win all the jackpots. Because I want you, I need you. Love me, I'm Maggie, I'm so alone, love me.

Kostner had been staring at the slot machine for a very long time, and his weary brown eyes had seemed to be locked to the blue eyes on the jackpot bars. But he knew no one else could see the blue eyes, and no one else could hear the voice, and no one else knew about Maggie.

He was the universe to her. Everything to her.

He thumbed in another silver dollar, and the Pit Boss watched, the slot machine repairman watched, the Slot Machine Floor Manager watched, three change girls watched, and a pack of unidentified players watched, some from their seats.

The reels whirled, the handle snapped back, and in a second they flipped down to a halt, twenty silver dollars tokened themselves into the payoff trough and a woman at one of the crap tables belched a fragment of hysterical laughter.

And the gong went insane again.

The Floor Manager came over and said, very softly, "Mr. Kostner, it'll take us about fifteen minutes to pull this machine and check it out. I'm sure you understand." As two slot repairmen came out of the back, hauled the Chief off its stand, and took it into the repair room at the rear of the Casino.

While they waited, the Floor Manager regaled Kostner with stories of spooners who had used intricate magnets inside their clothes, of boomerang men who had attached their plastic implements under their sleeves so they could be extended on spring-loaded clips, of cheaters who had come equipped with tiny electric drills in their hands and wires that slipped into the tiny drilled holes. And he kept saying he knew Kostner would understand.

But Kostner knew the Floor Manager would not understand.

When they brought the Chief back, the repairmen nodded assuredly. "Nothing wrong with it. Works perfectly. Nobody's been boomin' it."

But the blue eyes were gone on the jackpot bars.

Kostner knew they would return.

They paid him off again.

He returned and played again. And again. And again. They put a "spotter" on him. He won again. And again. And again. The crowd had grown to massive proportions. Word had spread like the silent communications of the telegraph vine, up and down the Strip, all the way to downtown Vegas and the sidewalk casinos where they played night and day every day of the year, and the crowd moved toward the hotel, and the Casino, and the seedy-looking walker with his weary brown eyes. The crowd moved to him inexorably, drawn like lemmings by the odor of the luck that rose from him like musky electrical cracklings. And he won. Again and again. Thirty-eight thousand dollars. And the three blue eyes continued to stare up at him. Her lover was winning. Maggie and her Money-eyes.

Finally, the Casino decided to speak to Kostner. They pulled the Chief for fifteen minutes, for a supplemental check by experts from the slot machine company in downtown Vegas, and while they were checking it, they asked Kostner to come to the main office of the hotel.

The owner was there. His face seemed faintly familiar to Kostner. Had he seen it on television? The newspapers?

"Mr. Kostner, my name is Jules Hartshorn."

"I'm pleased to meet you."

"Quite a string of luck you're having out there."

"It's been a long time coming."

"You realize, this sort of luck is impossible."

"I'm compelled to believe it, Mr. Hartshorn."

"Um. As am I. It's happening to my Casino. But we're thoroughly convinced of one of two possibilities, Mr. Kostner: one, either the machine is inoperable in a way we can't detect, or two, you are the cleverest spooner we've ever had in here."

"I'm not cheating."

"As you can see, Mr. Kostner, I'm smiling. The reason

I'm smiling is at your naiveté in believing I would take
your word for it. I'm perfectly happy to nod politely and
say of course you aren't cheating. But no one can win
thirty-eight thousand dollars on nineteen straight jackpots
off one slot machine; it doesn't even have mathematical
odds against its happening, Mr. Kostner. It's on a cosmic
scale of improbability with three dark planets crashing
into our sun within the next twenty minutes. It's on a par
with the Pentagon, Peking and the Kremlin all three
pushing the red button at the same microsecond. It's an
impossibility, Mr. Kostner. An impossibility that's happening to me."

"I'm sorry."

"Not really."

"No, not really. I can use the money."

"For what, exactly, Mr. Kostner?"

"I hadn't thought about it, really."

"I see. Well, Mr. Kostner, let's look at it this way. I
can't stop you from playing, and if you continue to win,
I'll be required to pay off. And no stubble-chinned thugs
will be waiting in an alley to jackroll you and take the
money. The checks will all be honored. The best I can
hope for, Mr. Kostner, is the attendant publicity. Right
now, every player in Vegas is in that Casino, waiting for
you to drop cartwheels into that machine. It won't make
up for what I'm losing, if you continue the way you've
been, but it will help. Every high-roller in town likes to
rub up next to luck. All I ask is that you cooperate a
little."

"The least I can do, considering your generosity."

"An attempt at humor."

"I'm sorry. What is it you'd like me to do?"

"Get about ten hours' sleep."

"While you pull the slot and have it worked over
thoroughly?"

"Yes."

"If I wanted to keep winning, that might be a pretty
stupid move on my part. You might change the hicka-
majig inside so I couldn't win if I put back every dollar
of that thirty-eight grand."

"We're licensed by the state of Nevada, Mr. Kostner."

"I come from a good family, too, and take a look at me.
I'm a bum with thirty-eight thousand dollars in my pocket."

"Nothing will be done to that slot machine, Kostner."

"Then why pull it for ten hours?"

"To work it over thoroughly in the shop. If something

as undetectable as metal fatigue or a worn escalator tooth or—we want to make sure this doesn't happen with other machines. And the extra time will get the word around town; we can use the crowd. Some of those tourists will stick to our fingers, and it'll help defray the expense of having you break the bank at this Casino—on a slot machine."

"I have to take your word."

"This hotel will be in business long after you're gone, Kostner."

"Not if I keep winning."

Hartshorn's smile was a stricture. "A good point."

"So it isn't much of an argument."

"It's the only one I have. If you want to get back out on that floor, I can't stop you."

"No Mafia hoods ventilate me later?"

"I beg your pardon?"

"I said: no Maf—"

"You have a picturesque manner of speaking. In point of fact, I haven't the faintest idea what you're talking about."

"I'm sure you haven't."

"You've got to stop reading *The National Enquirer.* This is a legally run business. I'm merely asking a favor."

"Okay, Mr. Hartshorn, I've been three days without any sleep. Ten hours will do me a world of good."

"I'll have the desk clerk find you a quiet room on the top floor. And thank you, Mr. Kostner."

"Think nothing of it."

"I'm afraid that will be impossible."

"A lot of impossible things are happening lately."

He turned to go, as Hartshorn lit a cigarette.

"Oh, by the way, Mr. Kostner?"

Kostner stopped and half-turned. "Yes?"

His eyes were getting difficult to focus. There was a ringing in his ears. Hartshorn seemed to waver at the edge of his vision like heat lightning across a prairie. Like memories of things Kostner had come across the country to forget. Like the whimpering and pleading that kept tugging at the cells of his brain. The voice of Maggie. Still back in there, saying . . . things . . .

They'll try to keep you from me.

All he could think about was the ten hours of sleep he had been promised. Suddenly it was more important than the money, than forgetting, than anything. Hartshorn was talking, was saying things, but Kostner could not hear him. It was as if he had turned off the sound and saw only the silent rubbery movement of Hartshorn's lips. He shook his head trying to clear it.

There were half a dozen Hartshorns all melting into and out of one another. And the voice of Maggie.

I'm warm here, and alone. I could be good to you, if you can come to me. Please come, please hurry.

"Mr. Kostner?"

Hartshorn's voice came draining down through silt as thick as velvet flocking. Kostner tried to focus again. His extremely weary brown eyes began to track.

"Did you know about that slot machine?" Hartshorn was saying. "A peculiar thing happened with it about six weeks ago."

"What was that?"

"A girl died playing it. She had a heart attack, a seizure while she was pulling the handle, and died right out there on the floor."

Kostner was silent for a moment. He wanted desperately to ask Hartshorn what color the dead girl's eyes had been, but he was afraid the owner would say blue.

He paused with his hand on the office door. "Seems as though you've had nothing but a streak of bad luck on that machine."

Hartshorn smiled an enigmatic smile. "It might not change for a while, either."

Kostner felt his jaw muscles tighten. "Meaning I might die, too, and wouldn't *that* be bad luck."

Hartshorn's smile became hieroglyphic, permanent, a silent song stamped in stone. "Sleep tight, Mr. Kostner."

In a dream, she came to him. Long, smooth thighs and soft golden down on her arms; blue eyes deep as the past, misted with a fine scintillance like lavender spiderwebs; taut body that was the only body Woman had ever had, from the very first. Maggie came to him.

Hello, I've been traveling a long time.

"Who are you?" Kostner asked, wonderingly. He was standing on a chilly plain, or was it a plateau? The wind curled around them both, or was it only around him? She was exquisite, and he saw her clearly, or was it through a mist? Her voice was deep and resonant, or was it light and warm as night-blooming jasmine?

I'm Maggie. I love you. I've waited for you.

"You have blue eyes."

Yes. With love.

"You're very beautiful."

Thank you. *With female amusement.*

"But why me? Why let it happen to me? Are you the girl who—are you the one that was sick—the one who—?"

I'm Maggie. And you, I picked you, because you need me. You've needed someone for a long long time.

Then it unrolled for Kostner. The past unrolled and he saw who he was. He saw himself alone. Always alone. As a child, born to kind and warm parents who hadn't the vaguest notion of who he was, what he wanted to be, where his talents lay. So he had run off, when he was in his teens, and alone always alone on the road. For years and months and days and hours, with no one. Casual friendships, based on food, or sex, or artificial similarities. But no one to whom he could cleave, and cling, and belong. It was that way till Susie, and with her he had found light. He had discovered the scents and aromas of a spring that was eternally one day away. He had laughed, really laughed, and known with her it would at last be all right. So he had poured all of himself into her, giving her everything; all his hopes, his secret thoughts, his tender dreams; and she had taken them, taken him, all of him, and he had known for the first time what it was to have a place to live, to have a home in someone's heart. It was all the silly and gentle things he laughed at in other people, but for him it was breathing deeply of wonder.

He had stayed with her for a long time, and had supported her, supported her son from the first marriage; the marriage Susie never talked about. And then one day, he had come back, as Susie had always known he would. He was a dark creature of ruthless habits and vicious nature, but she had been his woman all along, and Kostner realized he had been used as a stop-gap, as a bill-payer till her wandering terror came home to nest. Then she had asked him to leave. Broke, and tapped out in all the silent inner ways a man can be drained, he had left, without even a fight, for all the fight had been drained out of him. He had left, and wandered West, and finally come to Las Vegas, where he had hit bottom. And found Maggie. In a dream, with blue eyes, he had found Maggie.

I want you to belong to me. I love you. *Her truth was vibrant in Kostner's mind. She was his, at last someone who was special, was his.*

"Can I trust you? I've never been able to trust anyone

*before. Women, never. But I need someone. I really need
someone."*

It's me, always. Forever. You can trust me.

*And she came to him, fully. Her body was a declaration
of truth and trust such as no other Kostner had ever
known before. She met him on a windswept plain of
thought, and he made love to her more completely than
he had known any passion before. She joined with him,
entered him, mingled with his blood and his thought and
his frustration, and he came away clean, filled with glory.*

Yes, I can trust you, I want you, I'm yours," he
whispered to her, when they lay side by side in a dream
nowhere of mist and soundlessness. *"I'm yours."*

*She smiled, a woman's smile of belief in her man; a
smile of trust and deliverance. And Kostner woke up.*

The Chief was back on its stand, and the crowd had
been penned back by velvet ropes. Several people had
played the machine, but there had been no jackpots.

Now Kostner came into the Casino, and the "spotters"
got themselves ready. While Kostner had slept, they had
gone through his clothes, searching for wires, for gaffs, for
spoons or boomerangs. Nothing.

Now he walked straight to the Chief, and stared at it.

Hartshorn was there. "You look tired," he said gently
to Kostner, studying the man's weary brown eyes.

"I am, a little." Kostner tried a smile, which didn't work.
"I had a funny dream."

"Oh?"

"Yeah . . . about a girl . . ." he let it die off.

Hartshorn's smile was understanding. Pitying, empathic
and understanding. "There are lots of girls in this town.
You shouldn't have any trouble finding one with your
winnings."

Kostner nodded, and slipped his first silver dollar into
the slot. He pulled the handle. The reels spun with a
ferocity Kostner had not heard before and suddenly
everything went whipping slantwise as he felt a wrenching
of pure flame in his stomach, as his head was snapped
on its spindly neck, as the lining behind his eyes was
burned out. There was a terrible shriek, of tortured
metal, of an express train ripping the air with its passage,
of a hundred small animals being gutted and torn to
shreds, of incredible pain, of night winds that tore the
tops off mountains of lava. And a keening whine of a

voice that wailed and wailed and wailed as it went away from there in blinding light—

Free! Free! Heaven or Hell it doesn't matter! Free! The sound of a soul released from an eternal prison, a genie freed from a dark bottle. And in that instant of damp soundless nothingness, Kostner saw the reels snap and clock down for the final time:

One, two, three. Blue eyes.

But he would never cash his checks.

The crowd screamed through one voice as he fell sidewise and lay on his face. The final loneliness . . .

The Chief was pulled. Bad luck. Too many gamblers resented its very presence in the Casino. So it was pulled. And returned to the company, with explicit instructions it was to be melted down to slag. And not till it was in the hands of the ladle foreman, who was ready to dump it into the slag furnace, did anyone remark on the final tally the Chief had clocked.

"Look at that, ain't that weird," said the ladle foreman to his bucket man. He pointed to the three glass windows.

"Never saw jackpot bars like that before," the bucket man agreed. "Three eyes. Must be an old machine."

"Yeah, some of these old games go way back," the foreman said, hoisting the slot machine onto the conveyor track leading to the slag furnace.

"Three eyes, huh. How about that. Three brown eyes." And he threw the knife-switch that sent the Chief down the track, to puddle, in the roaring inferno of the furnace.

Three brown eyes.

Three brown eyes that looked very very weary. That looked very very trapped. That looked very very betrayed.

Some of these old games go way back.

THE WHORE WITH A HEART OF IRON PYRITES;
OR,
WHERE DOES A WRITER GO TO FIND A MAGGIE?
by Harlan Ellison

So THERE was a screening of a new Clint Eastwood film (that turned out to be a genuine off-the-wall downer) and I didn't feel like going alone, so I called Lynda and asked her if she wanted to go and she said yes, and I drove out to Sepulveda (where there were just a *gang* of Wallace stickers everywhere, which made me more than a little twitchy, may I tell you) to pick her up, and her cousin Lane answered the door and let me in and told me Lynda was getting ready, so we sat and chatted till she put herself together. "I, uh, understand you write science fiction," he said. I nodded. "How, uh, how do you get into that?"

Fascinating question. There is no intelligent answer beyond pointless smalltalk, of course. Because it's a dumb question. It's like having someone ask you, how do you get into sex? Obviously, the response is: you just start doing it. Modifying the answer slightly to apply to writing— as opposed to sex, which even the inept can get into— the best you can offer is, "If you have talent, you just start doing it."

Setting aside flippancy, however, one might say you "get into" writing by being incredibly perceptive about people, by observing everything, the smallest details of how people speak and think, how they carry themselves, how they dress, how they compromise themselves, what they think of themselves and others, and how they react in company, how they pursue their goals, how they screw themselves up, what they do to make themselves feel good and in what special ways they unconsciously set about destroying themselves, what effect criticism has on them, how they react to love, what portion of their days is spent in revenge and what portion spent in adjustment to the world around them. . . .

In short, what you say is get to know people, and from your store of amassed knowledge will spring ideas for stories. Because *that* is the answer to the other dumb question asked of writers (usually by people in lecture audiences or by suburban housewives and orthodontists at cocktail parties): "Where do you get your ideas?"

And if you intend to be a writer, you'd better face the fact that you will have these two questions asked of you a million times before they put you down the hole. Because almost *everyone* thinks he can be a writer; most would stop short before they assumed they could be nuclear physicists or concert violinists, but *everyone* thinks he has a great novel in him, if only he had the time to sit down and do the writing. Nonsense, of course; but could you only be a fly on the wall and hear how many nits come up to writers and say, "I've had just a terrific life, really super-interesting, and why don't you write my life, and

I'll split all the money with you fifty-fifty," you'd know the core truth of that sad experience.

Because, at bottom, no matter how many sensational ideas you have for stories, you'll never be a writer unless you know people, and you'll never be a writer unless the people in your stories come to life. The best plot-line in the world is merely a series of incidents without living, breathing people scurrying along that line; but conversely, a dud of a story can be arresting if the people are compelling.

Ideally, a writer with talent will meld both into a story that makes you believe and care because the people are real and interesting, and what happens to them is different and fascinating. But if I were denied one or the other, I'd opt for the people over the plot, because it's as William Faulkner said in his Nobel Prize acceptance speech (December 10, 1950): ". . . the problems of the human heart in conflict with itself which alone can make good writing because only that is worth writing about, worth the agony and the sweat."

What I might have said to Lane is, go and live a lot of days and nights, and observe like crazy, and store up a vast knowledge of people, and then simply sit down and start spending *more* days and nights all alone with your typewriter, putting those people down on paper in fresh and fascinating ways. But how do you say that to someone who asked you the question in the first place? If he asked it, chances are good he never will be a writer. It's one of those things a writer knows intuitively. To ask it means the intuition isn't there.

Yet if I'd answered Lane with the secret formula offered above, would he not have followed up with the next stage question: "Where do you find the people you write about?" And that's the same question as "Where do you get your ideas?"

Well, it would take an essay easily as long as this one to *approach* an answer to Lane's other question, but since I'm here, and you're here, why not take a shot at it.

For instance, where did Maggie come from?

Parts of her came from a female named Shawn (who, when I laid a copy of the published story on her and told her she was the model for Maggie, looked at me as though I'd just come up through a trapdoor under a mushroom; she couldn't see herself in the character; which is precisely the way it *should* be; Maggie was born out of Shawn, but Shawn ain't Maggie; nor is Maggie Shawn, if you get what

I mean; there are points of similarity, and the general ambience *for me as a creator* is the same, but a creature of my own devising could never be taken from life stick for stick and stone for stone).

But *how* Maggie came to be born maybe possibly perhaps sorta kinda answers the question where stories and characters come from. So I'll tell you how it happened.

I met Shawn in 1963, here in Los Angeles. She was, and is, an extraordinarily beautiful woman with a commanding manner and a sense of self that projects her presence even when she walks into a crowded room. I have seen entire parties of wild revelers fall silent and stare when Shawn enters the room. She dresses elegantly, she's tall, her face is as I described it in the story, and taken in sum she is one of those women whose like you will not encounter twice in ten years.

I have no idea what Shawn *really* does for a living; I am certain she isn't a hooker or a call girl, yet I'm equally as certain she is the sort of woman who would use her uncommon femininity and sensuality to snare a wealthy man, and ride his life for as much, for as long as it was necessary to come away with handfuls of value. But she clearly treasures herself enough not to sell too cheaply. She is the sort of woman—as I see her—about whom Lautrec was speaking when he said, "Women never give their love, they lease it . . . at the very highest rates of interest." Please note the distinction I try to make here: *not* a chippy or a whore, but a woman who uses sex as merely another utensil to achieve her life-goals. The distinction is important, because it goes to the heart of Maggie's characterization. In the story, Maggie is *with* Nuncio, but as she makes perfectly clear to her paramour, she doesn't *belong* to him; she is still her own property. Had I made her one-dimensionally a tart, a piece of meat, I don't think the story would have squeezed the heart of the theme as I believe it now does. These often subtle and tonal distinctions in characterization can make all the difference between drawing a fresh character and merely setting out another cartoon. . . . In this case it would have been a whore with a heart of gold, that stale cliché of 1930s tearjerkers and cheap novels by writers more concerned with establishing their *machismo* than turning the mirror of life in a new way.

But, I wander from my story. To return . . .

I had a physical attraction for Shawn, but it was held in check by a gut reaction to her that I always seem to get in the face of whitewater, whirlpools, and fast currents. We never got down, as they say in the street. And in a strange sort of way we became friends; Shawn as one of those alien totems each of us keep in our world to show us how well-adjusted and "normal" we are; myself as something of a knowledgeable elf who made bright conversation at dull dinners, someone who wakes up alert at any wee hour of the night when the desperate phone calls are made.

One night we got back to her little house and she was pretty well drunk. I carried her into her bedroom, and it was a bedroom precisely like the one I describe in the story, even though I never described it in the story.

(Now what the hell does *that* mean?! Either he described it in the story, or he didn't. You can't have it both ways.

(Wrong. You *can* have it both ways; in fact, you've got to have it both ways if you want your characterization to work, if you want your people to have the semblance of life. Because—and here's the essence of it—what a writer must strive for is not the journalistic re-creation of life, but verisimilitude, an altered and heightened perception of life that *seems* to be real. In this way a writer can select those elements that work best, seem strongest, make the point most precisely. And in a writer's tool kit the best implement to attain that verisimilitude is a familiarity with the background of the characters. All the unspoken things, all the minute details that need never show up on the printed page but nonetheless live there in shadows, behind the words.

(Shawn's bedroom had flocked wallpaper, blood red and black. A huge bed with an ornate wrought iron headboard. There was sensuality everywhere, in each individual item she had chosen to place in that room. The bathroom was an extension of the bedroom, down to the gold dolphin spigots on the sink and bathtub. In its way it was a toney echo of a posh New Orleans pleasure house, and though there was nothing concrete on which one could fasten to make the comparison, the *totality* was one of . . . of . . . how can I phrase it . . . of *Maggie-ness*. The room was an extension of her needs, her drives, her past, her hopes for the future, her style, and her *façade*.

(I didn't happen to write in a scene that took place in Shawn's bedroom, but that bedroom was there, informing every line of description about Maggie. For me, the physical presence of that bedroom capped my feelings about who Shawn was, and the memory of it hung over

me as I wrote the story. And so, without writing in that
element of Maggie's backstory, it was *there*, not merely as
data but as a pivotal element.)

We could have made it that night, but the wariness I
noted earlier led me to cover her with a blanket and to
quietly let myself out.

I didn't see Shawn again for two years.

On Thursday, October 7, 1965, I was in Las Vegas and
we met again. I'd written (and been rewritten horribly) a
film called *The Oscar* for Joseph E. Levine's Embassy
Pictures. Though I'd written it for Steve McQueen and
Peter Falk, they cast Stephen Boyd and Tony Bennett and
to promote Bennett's first (and as it turned out, last) film
role, Levine flew the entire cast and crew, as well as publicity cadres, from Hollywood to Vegas, for Bennett's opening at the Riviera Hotel.

Now, a brief digression that is no digression at all.
People function in the context of their environment; that's
such an obvious remark I shouldn't have to make it, but
frequently even I am surprised at the *naïveté* of those who
want to be writers but ask questions like "Where do you
get your ideas," so I'll state it here.

Understanding that statement, you will understand that
characterization can be established in terms of setting.
That is, one kind of person finds emotional sustenance
living in a rural area, another finds it in big cities. A
writer can flesh out a character by relating him or her to
the scene in which the character functions. It takes a particular kind of person, it seems to me, to prowl successfully
in Las Vegas. The Country Mouse couldn't make it, and
even the City Rat has some trouble. Because Vegas is
neither a city nor a town. It is a cultural artificiality, an
unnatural lump in the middle of a desert. A thing that
could never have flourished had it not been for greed and
shallow dreams and a condition of need in the American
Character that demands fulfillment in Disneylands of all
sorts. The ambience of Vegas is somehow Lovecraftian to
me; dark and evil and glittering with a Borgia smile under
that innocent Nevada sun while it leaches all joy and hope
from the souls of the world's losers—guys like Kostner,
for instance. (As an aside to an aside, maybe it takes the
mind of a fantasist to see those qualitites in Vegas; I know
dozens of people who *live* in Vegas and they tell me of
the churches and schools and good living, but I get the
creeps every time I get near the place and it took another
fantasist, Richard Matheson, to perceive what I perceived

in the town, when he wrote the screenplay for *The Night-
Stalker;* thereby reassuring me that I wasn't the lone soul
who sensed nightmare behind the neon.) And it occurs
to me, relating to "characterization," that a highly effective technique for building original characters *vis-à-vis*
the special setting in which the character operates, must
draw on these subcutaneous vibes given off by the place,
whether it be a Harlem tenement or an antebellum mansion in a Louisiana backwash or a gambling casino in Las
Vegas. Again, the *intuitions* of the writer must be called
into play. You see, it wasn't such a digression, after all.

So. Las Vegas. A special place with a special feeling all
its own. A throb of illicit sex, a tension, an undercurrent
of danger and excitement, a special sound in the air.

I'd attended Bennett's performance at the Riviera—
black tie and tuxedo, lots of lovelies and lots of glitter—
and afterward my producers and the rest of the company
from *The Oscar* had gone off to do their individual numbers. Some to hustle the showgirls, some to sleep, some to
gamble. I was wide awake, though it was after midnight, and so I plonked myself down at a blackjack table
and started playing.

Perhaps a half hour had gone by, when I felt a hand
on my shoulder. I turned around from the dealer and there
was Shawn, looking extravagantly luscious, and suddenly
—click!—fitting into the scene so perfectly I realized
without even having to think about it, that Shawn was born
for Las Vegas and, contrariwise, Vegas had been born
for Shawn. According to the old saw, had Las Vegas or
Shawn not existed, in fact, they would have had to be invented for one another.

I cashed in my chips. (As a personal note, the character
of Kostner is not the Author. Often a motivating force in
a character comes from the writer's own personality, but
in the case of Kostner, who is a *loser*—in all the deepest
life-meanings of that word—I was drawing from other
sources. In the story, Kostner loses and loses at the tables.
In real life I win constantly. That's what's called, in writing, playing against the Portnoy Syndrome.) We took a
walk out to the parking lot. Shawn told me she was
working in the line at one of the casinos. Which struck me
as odd. She'd never indicated she even knew how to dance,
and to dance in one of the chorus lines at the big Vegas
hotels, a woman had to be *good*. There are, of course, what
they call "statue nudes," who just stand around looking
elegant, but I had a niggling feeling Shawn wasn't telling

me the truth. She may have been into some convoluted
hustle and didn't want me to know. It doesn't matter,
really. She told me she was living in Vegas, and why
didn't I come home with her.

That was probably the only moment in our relationship
during which we might have wound up in bed. And I
must confess I was about to say yes. But something was
gnawing at the back of my mind; something about Shawn,
and Las Vegas, and the night, and its electrical immediacy.
I said no, and she got into her car and took off; we'd
exchanged the usual vacuous promises to keep in touch.

I stood in the parking lot, trying to let that thought
feeding on the back of my brain chew its way to the
top. Understand: I was becoming detached from my own
reality at that moment. If there is a moment a writer can
point to, in an effort to isolate the instant of creativity
when a story takes form in his or her head, the moment
philosophers have tried to isolate since before the dawn of
recorded history, it *must* be moments such as the one I
lived through in the parking lot of the Riviera Hotel in
Las Vegas. Because *something* was bubbling up, all the
unconscious relays were being closed, all the computations
were being made, all the file cards of stored data were
being processed.

I walked back into the casino, and sat down at the
blackjack table. But I didn't bet. I was thinking, and I'd
returned, instinctively, to the territory where the dream had
been born. The dealer grew annoyed at my taking up space,
but he worked around me.

Sounds. It was an amalgam of *sounds* that finally triggered the dream into my conscious mind. The sounds of
slot machines clicking, clicking, turning and paying off
. . . the sounds of people betting their futures hoping to
escape their presents . . . the wheel of fortune . . . the
voices of the croupiers and dealers . . .

And it all fitted together.

Shawn. Las Vegas. The insidiousness of gambling machines. The worship of a modern deity personified by
chance and the despair brought by the death of luck.

I bolted away from the blackjack table and rushed upstairs.

It is a peculiarity of mine that I travel with my typewriter. Wherever I go, the machine is with me, because
I've found there is no predicting when the dreams will
hit. The typewriter was waiting, and I tossed off my
clothes and started writing. (It is endemic to understanding

what follows, to appreciate that frequently I write in the nude. It's no big artistic trip, it's simply a matter of convenience. When I write I frequently pace around and get very physical as the story unfolds. Sometimes I act out the parts and carry on conversations with the characters. So: I was naked and writing, in a Vegas hotel room where the air conditioning was Arctic.)

I've found the hardest part of any story is building the character properly. Usually it has to be done from the kernel out. The kernel being that particular function the character will serve in the plot-line. If it's necessary for a character to perform heavy action, for instance, it would be suicidal to make the physical characteristics inadequate: a cripple, a tubercular, a very short person, an adolescent . . .

If it's necessary for a character to grasp some abstract idea or arrive at some deep philosophical or moral decision, then it would be self-defeating to make the character a lout, or amoral, or so debased that the decisions seem inconsistent with the basic nature of the character . . .

These are rules-of-thumb, naturally. One can achieve fine counterpoint by presenting a cripple with a situation in which he or she must overcome the infirmity to save the day, or, similarly, one can strike a note of humanity if one takes a character who has never had to make fine ethical distinctions and show him or her grappling with the need. But in the main, the rules hold up.

It is also troublesome, sometimes, deciding whether a pivot character should be male or female.

Traditionally in fiction, men have been the viewpoint characters, the saviors, the heroes. I chalk much of that up to male chauvinism. Unconscious sexism.

In the case of "Pretty Maggie Moneyeyes" the problem was even more complex. The viewpoint character could not be Maggie, because of the style and format I'd decided to use, but Maggie had to be the protagonist, the strongest figure in the story. Kostner, to do what he had to do, had to be a loser, a weak man. Such do not make sympathetic viewpoint characters. So I split the viewpoint, integrating Kostner as present time and Maggie as flashback (merging them only in the dream-sequence where Maggie "possesses" Kostner's manhood); but I left wisps of Maggie's character lying about, swirling through Kostner's scenes, so her presence was always center stage.

As I wrote the story, all through that night and into the next day, I became obsessed with Maggie. She was one of

the most compelling characters I'd ever created. Actually,
it is to laugh: *I* didn't create Maggie, she created *herself*.
Which is why I think this is my best story. Because she is
so right, so fully-fleshed, she speaks to Faulkner's admoni-
tion about the only real reason for writing, and she brings
to fruition the holiest effort of writing: she becomes a real
person. For consider, the greatest books are those in which
a single character emerges with that aura of verisimilitude
so you never forget him or her. Pip, Huck Finn, Quasi-
modo, Captain Ahab, Robert Jordon, Jay Gatsby, Ben
Reich, Lady MacBeth, Prince Myshkin, Sherlock Holmes,
Winston Smith, Tuan Jim, Rima the bird-girl, Sister Carrie,
they all burn in the memory, they live on after the book is
closed. Long past the time when a reader remembers the
intricacies of plot or the niceties of writing style, the
character stays fixed in the mind. It is as if they lived,
they *really* lived, and for the gift of having been brought
into contact with a special person like that, there is no
fortune a reader can offer the writer in repayment.

But beyond the life I tried to pour into Maggie, there
was an energy *she* poured into my writing, forcing me to
set her down just so. Thus, again, as many times in the
past, I found a character taking over the story. And it
seems to me that if a writer is working fine, if the writer
is in control of the material, even though he or she may
not know in what direction the story is going, the lead
character will take charge and help. The stronger a character is fixed in the mind of the creator, the more that character will demand his or her story be told correctly, leading
the writer away from one area and into another, taking the
plot in directions the writer might never have suspected
were inherent in the plot. It is at once a miraculous and a
frightening experience.

So strong was Maggie that I wrote and wrote, without
conception of time or place or even the needs of the body.
And in her way, Maggie did *me* in as well as Kostner.
Sitting in that frigid hotel room, I came down with a cold
that became acute pneumonia and finally dropped into
pleurisy. As best I recall what happened, I collapsed during
the second day of writing, was flown back to Los Angeles where I was admitted to a hospital, and woke some-
time later yelling for my typewriter so I could complete the
story.

The fascinating upshot of what happened is that I do
not recall having written whole stretches of the story. The
two typographically variant sections immediately after

Maggie's heart attack and death were apparently written while I was going into a coma. They are very peculiar sections, indeed: one seems to attempt to describe the moment of death and the other—in the original manuscript—was handwritten in a tiny cribbed hand, the letters printed so small I had to retype the section before it could be submitted to an editor. I think I was trying in my semi-lucid way to describe what it felt like to be a disembodied soul trapped in a slot machine. And if *that* ain't berserk, Spiro Agnew is the Second Coming.

What it all proves, at least to me, is that Maggie is so forceful a personality that in some magic way she wrote her own story. This isn't an isolated happening, incidentally. Almost every good writer I've talked to has told me a similar story; at one or another time in the progress of a certain piece, a character has taken hold and refused to do what the writer thought the character should do. Some have refused to fall in love when ordered, others have refused to die, still others demanded *their* lives were more important than those of the characters the writer had chosen as main viewpoint protagonists. It happens.

Algis Budrys, a writer who used to write some of the best sf ever, told me once, when I was just getting started in the profession, you can't delineate a character by saying he looked just like Cary Grant except he had bigger ears. I remember a story Ayjay wrote, a long time ago, in which the heavy was a bureaucrat who munched candy bars all through a difficult interview with the protagonist. It was a key to the man's nature . . . I don't remember how . . . it's been over sixteen years since I read it . . . but that aspect of the character has stuck with me all this time, though I've forgotten the story it came from. What Ayjay meant about Cary Grant's ears, of course, is that there are no shortcuts to building a character. You have to dig and probe and live some, until you find the elements of humanity necessary to build a specific person to fit a specific story.

Further, you can't *tell* what a character is like; you have to *show* it. The way a character speaks of him- or herself and the truth or lies that reveal themselves when compared against what the character *does;* the way other characters speak of him or her; the way others react to the character—these are the ways in which we come to *see* the personality reveal itself, rather than being *told* this is the way it is, by an omniscient author.

The speech cadences of characters, the way they dress,

repeated mannerisms, their smells and the way they carry themselves . . . these are all parts of a fully developed sketch, bearing in mind one should tell no more about a character than is necessary for an understanding and identification pursuant to the importance of the character. Chekhov once said, "If, in act one, you display a pistol hanging on the wall, you had better fire it by the end of act two." In other words, don't lard in a glop of irrelevant personality facts if they aren't necessary to the plot or the furtherance of establishing the character as lifelike.

Remember: characters don't exist in a vacuum. They live in context with their era, their place, their past, and the reactions other characters produce in them. They must have an interior consistency. Kate Smith would never get busted smuggling dope. It simply wouldn't play. No one would buy it. Abbie Hoffman would never have a book published by Rod McKuen's Stanyan Press. That's illogical, and a writer has a hard enough time getting readers to suspend disbelief long enough to buy the basic premise of a story—especially an sf story—without throwing an illogical character, operating out of context, into the stew.

I ran into Shawn a couple of months ago at The Farmers' Market. She was looking great. A touch older, perhaps, but tanned and svelte. She was wearing a big eggshell-gray hat that swept down over one eye, and she had just come back from Guatemala or Uruguay or somesuch place.

I told her I was going to write this. She laughed and kissed me on the cheek. "I hope you're not still trying to convince people I'm the model for that terrible person," she said. "No one would believe it!"

Maybe not. But I've got a hunch that somewhere in Guatemala or Uruguay or somesuch place, at this very moment, is a wealthy man who's just a little less wealthy for having run alongside Maggie for a few weeks, and *he* would believe it.

SETTING:
A Local Habitation and a Name

. . . as imagination bodies forth
The Forms of things unknown, the poet's pen
Turns them to shapes, and gives to airy
   nothing
A local habitation and a name.

IN DEALING with short fiction, analogies with the drama come too readily to mind, and they are dangerous. The worlds of the narrative writer and the playwright are really quite different, nowhere more so than in the furnishings of their respective "stages." "Setting" in short fiction is a far more comprehensive term than its analogue in the theater. It is the sum of all factors—tangible and intangible—which form a background for and interact with characters and their doings.

The setting of a short story performs three basic functions. Like theatrical scenery, it attempts to give a palpable and pictorial locus for the action. Unlike the flats and sets behind the proscenium, it can constitute an environmental force which influences character and affects plot. And, with far greater freedom and effect than anything short of the Grand Guignol, it is productive of that elusive quality called *atmosphere.*

Mood, ambience, atmosphere: All are terms descriptive of the larger affective context within which a story takes place and which is carefully designed to lend emotional force to characters and their actions. Setting is always productive of atmosphere, but unless it is carefully constructed it may be productive of the wrong atmosphere, one that fails to reinforce (or effectively contrast with) emotional qualities established by plot and character. Some settings are clichés: the dark and stormy nights and gloomy castles of the gothic novel, the sagebrush and big sky of the western, the intimate midwestern or southern or New England town, the ghetto, the inky, awesome blackness of interstellar space. Some settings push the reader's psychological buttons too hard and too frequently.

Snakes and spiders and heights and rats and nostalgia and sealed caves and food and money and even erotic paraphernalia of one kind or another can produce—if clumsily handled—so strong a reaction, so powerful an atmosphere, as to drown out everything else in the story. Here, as in every other aspect of artistic composition, the writer is above all selective, choosing just those elements of setting that will provide the precise emotional loading he wishes to give the incidents he relates.

Not everything a writer does is fully conscious or deliberate; setting is. Faced on one hand by the necessity of making every word count, and on the other by the desire to make his work as sensuous and emotionally gratifying as possible, the writer dives into his own memories for sense impressions (since they are at the heart of setting) which have been, for him, very strong and meaningful. He uses all five senses, although—for most writers—the visual predominates. He tests his memories against what he understands of others' reactions to similar stimuli, aware at all times that he runs the danger of becoming a closet writer, truly effective to no one but himself. And he continues, consciously, to increase his stock of impressions, observing what goes on around him, looking for events and characters and elements of setting which are powerful and hold some promise of universality. Writers are seldom bored in waiting rooms.

Above all, the writer remembers that setting is a means to an end, not an end in itself.

Setting is particularly important in science fiction. Indeed, one might argue that science fiction is a fiction which varies from others only in setting. After all, one can imagine that people will fall in love or kill each other or be frustrated or successful in very much the same manner in 2073 or on the moon or in some parallel world as they do today, here. If they do not, they are not people, as we understand the term, and if they are alien, we will personify them and try to understand them in our own terms. Unlike the writer of more traditional forms of fiction, the science fiction writer cannot entirely depend upon his own learning or store of sense impressions; he must extrapolate from them, decide upon some increment of change, and carefully relate his wonders to our familiar world or he will lose us. To do this deftly, unobtrusively, requires great skill, but it is part of the fascination of science fiction.

THE MAN WHO COULD NOT SEE DEVILS

by Joanna Russ

MY FATHER, who saw devils at noonday, cursed me for a misbegotten abortion because I did not see them. But I saw nothing. Incubi, succubi, fiends, demons, werewolves, evil creatures of all sorts might do what they pleased for all of me; I could not eavesdrop on them and holy water turned to only water in my hands, though I have seen the victims carried in, bloodless, the next day, and indeed I carried one home myself, a boy with his throat cut from ear to ear, and that was the only time I got gratitude out of the pack of them. And for nothing.

My neighbors, I mean. "There! There! Don't you see?" they'd cry, the girls tumbling to get away from the hearth, the houselady fainting. "Don't you *see?*" But I saw nothing. Cats were possessed, strange shapes hovered in the air; in broad daylight one head turned, and then another, and then another, as I tried in vain, always in vain. "Don't you *see?*" Until I was twelve I lived terrified that I might bump into something some broad morning, out of sheer ignorance, and was never let abroad by myself. Then, when I was twelve and a half (if I had not been an only son, they might have let me alone, but I was too precious) a neighborhood conjuror tried to de-hex me of what he assured my parents was a particularly virulent curse—and failed—and I spent a night alone, by pure mistake, in a haunted ravine, trembling at every sound but emerging whole, and then repeating the experiment with a growing conviction that if I could not see the devils, perhaps it was because they could not see me.

When I told my father, he beat me.

"Those who cannot see devils, cannot see angels!" he roared.

I replied in a desperate fury that I should be glad enough to see some human beings, and when he reached for the poker I asked him, with mad inspiration, if he would like to spend the night in the ravine with me.

He turned pale. He said I was probably crazy and ought to be put to bed.

I said he would have to chain me up; but he could not do that every night; and as soon as I was free I would spend every night out in the woods and tell him about it in the daytime.

He said suicide was a sin.

I said I did not care.

"My poor boy," he said, trembling, "my poor boy, don't you see? Satan is deceiving you and giving you a false sense of security. Some day—"

"Show me Satan," I said.

"A ghost passed through this room three nights ago," he said, getting down on his knees, his beard wagging. "A ghost shaped like the body of a drowned girl, shining with a green light and we all saw it."

"I saw *you*," I said. "And pretty fools you looked too, let me tell you, gaping at nothing."

"And it was wearing a white dress covered with sea-weed," he went on in a singsong, "that shone in the darkness, and it passed through the candles and one by one they went out" (I had not seen that either) "and when it passed them they sprang up again and we saw each other's faces and we were all pale, all, all, except you" and to my amazement he burst into tears.

"I can't help that," I said, feeling uncomfortable.

"Didn't you see anything?" he said.

"Nothing."

"Anything?"

"Nothing."

I had never seen my father cry before, or since; in fact, this incident is my one even vaguely pleasant recollection of him, for the next day he was altogether himself. He thrashed me, thoroughly and formally, for no particular reason, and began that monotonous series of cursings that I have mentioned before. The story of the ghost (a distant cousin of my mother's) went the rounds of the village but with improvements—she had hovered over me, calling me by name; she had passed right through me; she had apostrophized me as one deaf and blind—

In three days no one would speak to me.

When I was sixteen, I ran away, got caught, and was brought back. They could beat me as much as they liked in the daytime, I said furiously, but they knew what would happen at night.

When I was seventeen, I ran away again, this time compounding the offense by stealing six silver pennies which is no more than the price of one-quarter of a not very good horse. I had the money wrested out of my hot hand (actually it was tied up in a tree and someone found it) and was set hoeing beans as a penance.

At nineteen I ransacked the house in a long, leisurely

afternoon's search (by now they were terrified of me), locked one cousin securely in a closet (into which he had fled at the sight of me), pinned another to the wall with an old rapier I had found in the attic, stuffed the price of three farmhouse estates into the front of my shirt, and rode off humming to myself bitterly between my teeth. I had escaped for good—or so I thought.

It was the money, of course. It had to be the money. It was too much to lose, even with ten thousand imps clinging to each coin. I was thirty-five miles away, eating my soup like a peaceable citizen in a neighborhood inn, when I felt a hand descend on my shoulder and sprang to my feet to see—my uncle! the most tough-minded of the lot, who always said, "A good man need fear nothing," though in what his goodness consisted, his wife—God help her!— and his maidservants and his black-and-blue children did not seem quite able to tell. But here he was with twenty men with him, and a priest. It was the priest that made them so brave.

"Be careful," I said. "You don't know what may happen."

"My boy, my boy," he said, excessively kind, "we've had enough of this."

"Not half as much as you will have," I said while I tried to size them up and remembered bitterly that the money was still on me and so I was in a bad bargaining position—also there was no back door. "Not half as much," said I, "as—"

"You shall come home at once," said my uncle softly, "and we will find a way to cure you, my dear boy, oh we will."

"With my allies?" said I. He was moving closer.

"You have no allies, poor boy," said he, sweating visibly. "Poor boy; they are only the deceitful fancies of the—" But I, knowing them by now, made for the priest, and then there was a frightened row, with much cursing and screaming (though the money made them desperate) and in the end the poor holy man was sitting in a chair having his bleeding head bathed with vinegar and water, and there I was under a heap, or rather clump, of relatives. They found the money immediately and my father (who had hidden behind them in his fright) began sobbing and saying "Praise be to God" for his estate come back.

I told them fervently what would happen to them.

"Let him up, let him up," said my father, and they let

me scramble to my feet, each retreating a little as the heat of the fight wore off.

"Give me a tenth and let me go," I said, out of breath.

"A tenth is for the church," said the priest, uncommonly keen all of a sudden, "and it would be blasphemous to do anything of the kind."

"I'll break your neck," I said intently, looking from one man to the other, "I'll break your spine, I'll make you die in slow torments, I'll—"

"Give it him, give it him," said my father, shaking all over, and he began to fumble among the money which my uncle immediately snatched away from him with the stern reminder that some people were too weak-minded for their own good.

"There is only one way to deal with this," said my uncle importantly, "and that is to take the boy home and exorcise him" (here his eyes gleamed) "and thrash him" (he tucked the money up neatly and buttoned it into the inside of his coat) "and make sure—sure" (said my uncle, hitting one fist into the other with slow relish) "make sure—sure, mind you—that this spell or devil or whatever it is, is driven out. Driven out!" added my uncle, loudly, to everyone's approbation. "Driven out! If we let him go, heaven only knows what may become of us. We may die in our sleep. Othor." Here he pushed a reluctant kinsman forward. "Tie him up." And, seeing that I was not to get away, not even penniless—I drove my head into the nearest stomach and called down such imprecations on them that they begged the innkeeper for a blanket to throw over me, the way you'd bag a cat, for my prophesying and cursing (as I could do nothing else) became every moment more frightful to their ears, seeing that I cursed them in curses they had never even heard before—as indeed they never had for I was making them all up.

"My God!" cried my uncle, "shut the boy up before it all comes true!" and as the innkeeper refused to interfere, someone went outside and got a horse blanket and it was with that abominable smell in my nose and throat that I stumbled blindly outside where I threw myself forward, I cared not where, and struck somebody's boots—or strongbox—or wall.

And that was the end of that, for the time.

I woke up sitting bolt upright on a stool set in the center of a room that looked vaguely familiar—it was my uncle's small estate—with a vague memory of riding dizzily in, saying, "That's right, that's right, I'm only a servant"—and then a blur in one corner resolved itself into a small, redheaded cousin of mine, a brat so ugly and unpleasant that even his own mother disliked him, God help him.

"What?" I said stupidly. I saw the imp jump a little, and then settle back onto his feet. He was watching me suspiciously. He was hung all over with charms: bangles, crosses, hearts, lockets, medals, rings, bells, garlands, and staves, until he looked like a dirty, decorated Christmas tree; I suppose they had put him to guard because he was the most expendable member of the clan, for he was only thirteen and very scrawny.

"Well, they've got *you*," he said, with a certain satisfaction. "They're inside, deciding what to do with you." I shut my eyes for a few minutes, and when I opened them he was lounging against the wall, picking his teeth. He sprang to attention.

"What time is it?" I said, and he said, "Late," and then colored; I guessed that he was not supposed to talk to me. I had not thought I had slept when I shut my eyes and my head was still ringing; it occurred to me that I was perhaps still a little out of my mind, but that seemed quite all right at the time; I took out of my shirt one coin they had not found, a gold piece given me by my nurse when I was a child, and I held it up and turned it round so the candlelight made it twinkle. I could see my little cousin licking his lips in his corner.

"This could be yours," I said. He looked doubtful.

"Nyah," he said, and then he said, "Is it real?"

"It won't disappear," I said, "if that's what you mean. It's not bewitched."

"Don't believe it," he said, standing virtuously upright, on guard again.

"Then don't believe it," I said, and I tossed it on the floor in front of him. It rang on the stones and lay, winking.

After a short hesitation he picked it up. He whistled ecstatically.

"Say, you don't want this," he said.

"Yes I do; give it back," I said. He snorted.

"Nyah! Nyah! Feeble-mind!" he crowed. "Feeble-mind! Now I have it," and he tossed it up and caught it deftly backhand, as if to prove that it was real.

"You don't have it," I said.

He stuck out his tongue at me. I got off the stool and

was at him in two strides; I covered his mouth and plucked the coin out of his hand; then I put it back, went back to my stool, and sat down. He stared at me dumbfounded.

"Do you really think," I said, "that they would let you keep it, if I told them about it?" (He thrust it into his coat.) "And do you think I wouldn't tell, if I felt like it?" (He threw it on the floor.) "No, no, keep it," I said carelessly. "Keep it. For a favor."

"Wouldn't do you a favor," he muttered, patting his magical garlands that encircled each wrist in the manner of a sacrificial lamb. "Wouldn't be right."

"Bah! nonsense," said I.

"*I'm* safe." he said, shaking his garlands, and tinkling all over. "Pooh," he added. He began to recite under his breath, imitating his father's nasal twang to perfection, a poor persecuted man whose crops always failed, whose babies always had the croup, whose attic leaked—

I took the boy by the arms and shook him till his teeth rattled.

"He—he—hel—" he said.

"Listen," I said, shaking him, "you numb-headed, misinformed baboon! You've known me all of your wretched life, you beast!" He began to cry. He stood there in the rags and tatters of his charms, bawling.

"Oh for God's sake," I said in despair, "shut up." And I sat back down on my stool and put my head between my knees.

He stopped crying. I said nothing. Then, after a considerable silence, he said: "You stole all that money?"

I nodded.

"Boy!" he said. There was a further silence.

"Hey, you wanna get out?" he said. I shook my head. "Sure you do. You wanna give me that gold money and get out?"

I shook my head again.

"Ah, come on," he said, "sure you do." And he sidled up to me and stood there in friendly fashion, his bells and jingles bumping lightly against me.

"Ah, come on," he said. I held up my hand with the coin in it. He took it and sprinted to the door, clanging; he flung open the door with spirit.

"I'm going to tell a story," he said. "I'm going to lie down and pretend to be dead."

"Bully for you," said I.

"I'll carry on," he said. "It'll be smashing. Shall I tell it to you?"

"No," I said, "and for God's sake, lower your voice."

"But it's *so* nice," he wheedled, "and it's—" So partly to shut him up and partly in a sudden liking for him (he was smiling a kind of gap-toothed, ecstatic smile and his orange freckles were aglow) I pulled off my ring—a cheap thing but my own—and gave it him.

"Hide it," I said, and slipped out into the courtyard.

Now I had a rough idea of where I was, but only a rough idea; so I went to the stables by taking what proved to be the longest way, hugging the walls and stumbling now and again against household remnants left out to freeze or dry, with a noise that I thought must waken the dead. I even saw the council through a window, and stood horribly bewitched for a moment, as if at my own funeral, until the sight gave me the shivers and I crept on. At the deserted stable I slashed the reins of all the horses, searched through saddlebags with my heart knocking at my teeth, found a small moneybag (my uncle's, one-quarter of a sheep this time) and mounted, snatching a torch from the wall, spurring toward the farm gate, dashing at the two guarding it, and firing the thatch above their heads.

What a blaze in an instant! What an uproar! Behind me in the court the freed beasts dashed effectively back and forth, barring everyone from the gate and then (in the most sensible manner possible) streaming behind me, leaving their owners horseless and homebound until someone should round them up the next morning. No one— not even my little cousin—would go out *that* night! The picture pleased me. As I rode through the windy black, I imagined uncles and cousins and grandfathers huddling uncomfortably in the dark of their charred and roofless rooms, seeing specters with every moan of the wind. It was damned cold. I was in my shirt. I stopped and searched the saddlebags again and heaven provided me with a jacket, knit by a suffering aunt. I became hysterical. The horse was stepping warily in the dark (we seemed to be traversing rocks) and we went around in circles until he simply stood still. I roared and rocked in the saddle. When I came to my senses, I headed south by the stars (who else but I even knew the stars? who else had spent nights in the open?) and saw the beautiful sun come up on my left, over gravelly hills, found a stream, washed and drank, and went on very much improved. But heaven proved to be remarkably improvident in the matter of food, and it was the next midday before I found a farm, stopped at it, and asked the hired girl—

She was off like a shot. I took advantage of my infamy and the sudden terror it produced to rifle the kitchen and change horses, leaving my uncle's to be de-hexed, de-bewitched, have chants chanted over it and expensive charms hung upon it and finally (I hoped) adopted and fed. Very likely my uncle would have to pay to have it back. I rode on in better spirits, but miserably fed, and finally, my infamy running out and reduced from a werewolf to a beggar, I sold the horse, proceeded on foot, sold my clothes and bought others cheaper and lighter and found—to my distress—that I had no money. None at all. In the north, where there was no food, I could have lived half a winter on that little bag. In the south, where the ricks ran over, I starved.

I do not like to remember what happened to me then. It was the only time in my life I saw things in simple truth. It seemed to me that the country was feeding off me, for as I got sicker I walked farther south and the spring came, and I fancied the wild mallows and the roses got their color from my blood; I was very sick. If I had not walked into houses at night and stolen, I think I would have died; for the people of the south do not disbelieve in demons, despite their cultivation; oh no. They would watch me, trembling behind the wall, as I stared at their pantry shelves, stared at the loaf in my hand, even forgetting why I had come. Sometimes I would put it down like a sleepwalker; once I lay on the grass by the open highway and wept for no reason, looking up at the stars. Someone saw me then, at dawn; someone (once!) gave me good-day. It was as I walked up to the gates of my first city, low and gray in the wet dawn mist, that I knew I was going to die. As I went through the gates, they closed over me like the dull roar of water over one's head, and I lay down (as I thought) to quit this world.

But the world had other ideas.

I woke on a stone floor, with two faces bending over me, one thin, one fat; the fat man plump as a pig and oily, delighted, writhing, pious, all at once. I thought I had gone to heaven. Then he said, "My dear boy." He beamed. "My dear, poor boy, a treasure! A find! A find! What a find!"

"He needs some more," said the other face, laconically, and disappeared to fetch something. Somebody put a pillow under my head and I tried to sit up.

"No, no, no, no," said the fat face, serenely, twiddling a finger at me. "Lie down. That's good. Here" (to someone outside my field of vision), "here, help him up," and they propped me against a wall. "Dear boy" (someone drew a blanket over me), "dear foolish boy, you didn't even have the sense to beg," and began feeding me something I could not taste, smacking his lips as if I were a baby, and muttering to himself. I am seeing visions at last, I thought, and they are angels, and with this thought (which was rather distressing) I came bolt awake.

"Who the devil are you?" I croaked. Fat-face wreathed and writhed in delight and thin-face next to him put hands together and cast eyes piously upward. Then he scuttled out of my field of vision.

"Friends," said fat-face, beaming; "Orthgar, get me a napkin" (presumably to someone in the room, for I was lying on the floor of a kind of office, with ledgers open on a table and parchments and such gear all about the walls), and he began feeding me some more. Then he stopped and, ecstatically shutting his eyes, kissed me on the forehead.

"You," he said, "are going to make a lot of money."

"What?" said I. He patted my cheek, still beaming as if I were a prize pig.

"Later," he said. "Do you think you can sit up?" and I said possibly and they propped me in a chair where I could see (wonder of wonders!) a garden, and a gardener clipping fruit trees.

"My dear fellow," said fat-face, "you must tell me your name." And I did, and he said, "I am Rigg and this is Orthgar. Orthgar, get me a brandy." Orthgar disappeared. I stared up at my fat host in bewilderment (it grew no less in the next ten years!) and asked him—well, asked him— He put up one hand for silence.

"You mustn't talk," he said fondly, "you'll exhaust yourself. You sit there like a good little boy and I—" (he heaved himself ponderously off the table, where he had been perched like a great, fat finch) "and I will explain everything." He smiled. "I am a banker," he said, shutting his eyes and then, opening them, he added delicately, "but not a banker," and looked modestly at his hands, which were fastidiously picking up pages and turning them over.

"Well?" said I.

He looked beatific. "I," he said, squirming with modesty, "I—that is, we—all of us—we are Appropriators."

"What?" I said. He shrugged.

"Thieves," he said. "But that's a nasty name. Call me Rigg. Ah! the brandy," and he poured from his glass into another and gave the second to me.

"I am not a good thief at all," said I.

"You will be," he said. "You will be. Besides, my dear—" (and here he and Orthgar smirked at each other) "think of your great talent."

"Talent?" I said dully.

"Oh yes," he said, sliding off the seat and walking expansively around the room. "Orthgar found you at dawn in the city cemetery. Orthgar is protected by very strong charms. There you were, sleeping like a baby, obviously unharmed except for semistarvation, of course, perfectly oblivious to the danger you ran. That is, you didn't run. That's the point. It's a ghastly place; people go mad there, cut each other's throats, hang themselves on empty air, really dreadful."

"City ought to do something," interposed Orthgar.

"Certainly they ought," said my host emphatically. "But they won't. Who can? Only our friend here." He beamed. "And he won't, either. He'll be too busy. The present administration," said Rigg heatedly, "is rotten! Rotten! Luckily." He stopped. "Am I boring you?" he said.

"How can I be useful?" said I.

" 'The clever fellow reaches conclusions more quickly than the stupid one,' " said Rigg, scratching behind his right ear and looking very piglike. "You ask good questions. Very. You see, when Orthgar brought you here—dear, brave fellow, Orthgar! I owe him a great deal—when Orthgar brought you here, we gave you all sorts of tests to see if you were suited to the job. We spoke Awakening Spells over you. You snored. We conjured up your spirit. You snored. Finally I had Thring—Thring's a friend of ours, very useful fellow, Thring—go out and get a priest to exorcise you, cleanse you and anoint you. Nothing. Finally we put you to the ultimate test, pronounced a frightful malediction upon you, several frightful maledictions, in fact—"

"It was a strain to be in the room," said Orthgar.

"But nothing happened," said Rigg. "In fact, you opened your eyes and said something unprintable about your uncle."

"Yes," said I, thoughtfully.

"So then," continued Rigg excitedly, drinking his brandy and mine too, "so then we *knew!* My dear fellow, we *knew!* One man like you is worth a hundred of us! Do you know how many lockmakers there are in this city? Well, there are twice as many magicians. And there you have it." They clinked glasses. At this I laughed, and then I said that I wanted some brandy, too.

"You'll throw it up," said Rigg warningly, "it's too soon," but he gave me some anyway and keep it down I could not, and made a mess that the landlady had to clean up.

"Beggars," she said, and then she said, "You owe three weeks' rent."

"Madam," said my host with dignity, "I shall give you six. Do you see this paper?" and he showed her a page of a ledger.

"I can't read," said the landlady sullenly, going out the door with the slop basin. "But I can count," she said, putting her head in at the door, and then vanishing.

"I feel sick," I said, and Rigg took from a pocket a small green vial with a brass stopper.

"Here," he said, smiling shrewdly. "Oil of peppermint. Good for the stomach." He gave it to me. "Even yours," he said, with meaning. I drank some and closed my eyes. It burned and numbed my mouth and it made me feel a little better that there was medicine in the world for me, for me, yes, even me.

"Well?" he said.

"Well?"

"What share will you take?"

"One-quarter," I said.

"One-eighth," he said.

"One-quarter," I said. "You have to give me reasons for living."

He looked unhappy.

"One-sixth?" he said.

"Done."

"I told you," said Orthgar, and he cleared away the ledgers. "You'd best put them back on the shelves," he said. "They don't belong to us."

I laughed again.

"The unholy alliance," I said.

"Mm?" said Rigg, over his brandy.

"Nothing," I said.

"Well," said Rigg, "if you feel better, let's get you to bed. The proper soup and in three days you'll be on your feet."

"We'll have to travel," said Orthgar. "All six of us. His life won't be worth anything once they find out."

"Oh it'll take time," said Rigg serenely, his eyes sparkling. "It'll take time. They'll try spells first" (and he giggled) "and by then we'll be somewhere else." He looked out the window and sighed. "I hate the provinces," he said. He strolled over and helped Orthgar get me to bed. "Wait," he said, patting my cheek. "Drink soup. Think of wine, women, and song."

"I have never heard songs," I said, "and I hate women only a little less than men, I assure you." My foster father patted my cheek again.

"You'll like music," he said. "It shows in the shape of your ears." And waving gaily, he gathered up the brandy, bottle, glasses, tray and all, and strolled out. Orthgar stood at the door for a moment.

"He's not too bad," said Orthgar. "You can trust him." And then he too went out.

But I was not thinking of money. I was thinking rather of the oddness of the world and how strange it was that people bothered themselves with spells and counter-spells and did not investigate the really compelling questions, such as whether the sun's fire burned the same material as ordinary fires, for anyone can look into a wood fire, even a goldsmith's, but it is common knowledge that the sun dazzles the eyes for even a moment. And the moon must burn still another thing, for its fire in the daytime is pale white.

I remembered my nurse, when I was little, asking me whether when the sun rose I did not see a great company of the heavenly host all crying Holy Holy Holy and I had said no, I saw only a round, red disk about the size of a penny coin. And then I wondered, drifting off to sleep to the sound of the gardener's shears, whether it might not be an advantage not to see demons and angels, and if it was, whether my children might not inherit the trait and pass it on to their children; and perhaps eventually (here the garden and its blossoming fruit trees wavered in the undulations of drowsiness) everyone would be like me, and if you asked people about the afreets, the succubi, the vampires, the angels and the fiends (very vaguely, far away, I could see the gardener cry out and back away from something, yet I knew I was safe; it might put its teeth into me and rage and roar and stamp—all silently— but I could sleep on), they would say *Those creatures? Oh, they're just legends; they don't exist. . . .*

ON SETTING

by Joanna Russ

"THE MAN WHO" etc. is a very early story of mine, written some time in the early 1960s. It was my first attempt to get into that strange, archaic, barbaric-Hellenistic world of sword and sorcery; I like to call it Fritz Leiberland because my first (and favorite) revelation of it was in Leiber's Gray Mouser stories, a collection by Gnome Press called *Two Sought Adventure*. My real reason for writing "The Man Who" was to get into this world and romp around in it. I loved it. It later became the much more detailed setting for my Alyx stories (which have been published by Damon Knight in various issues of *Orbit*—"The Adventuress" of *Orbit 2* is the first). By the time I got Alyx to the novel, *Picnic on Paradise*, I was much more interested in her than in her world, which I had pretty much used up. The novel uses real, historical setting—i.e. the Phoenician cities of 1600 B.C., still under the Cretan hegemony, more flexible and modern than what we think of as Ancient Egypt but with that combination of the barbaric and the sophisticatedly decadent that seems to be the real pleasure of Sword-and-Sorceryland.

American S & S writers are in the Western European tradition, so they (and I) really reflect a kind of cultural ur-mind when they put together the Barbaric North (the homeland of Fafhrd, also Brak the Barbarian, Conan the Conqueror, Douglas the Dilettante, and all those other mighty-thewed persons) and the corrupt Southern urban culture to which the barbarian usually migrates. (Leiber's usual originality shows up well here—he uses one hero for *each* culture.) To us "North" really means the already idealized and heroicized Northern Europe of *Beowulf*. Such a place never existed. It certainly never coexisted with first-century-B.C. Hellenistic culture: not only is there a millennium's difference and a geographical separation, but the Mediterranean of 100 B.C. is much too genuinely modern in tone for the blazing, archaic, goldenly corrupt cities of S & S. But our culture has two origins—medieval Europe (Northern or Teutonic) and the earlier Latin culture of, say, Southern France—these coexisting right now, with us. So we recklessly shift time and place and—lo! North and South again.

I did the same thing myself, without even thinking about it. What surprises me now, a decade after the story, is how much I used indirect description and how few visual details there really are. My story is an sf story, not an S & S one, and as in so much sf (and I guess S & S, too) *the setting itself is the antagonist*—and therefore quite as important as the protagonist, who is a character. My protagonist's quarrel is not with his family only, but with a whole world in which he is a genuine, biological misfit. So that, in part, his embroilment with the setting in itself describes the setting—which is very economical!

Somebody once said that Tolstoy made the Battle of Moscow out of a few aristrocrats (all cousins) and a handful of snow. Fritz makes up his settings partly out of descriptive detail, partly out of outrageously transplanted terrestrial words (e.g."Mingols"), and partly out of his attitude toward the whole business, a sort of wry wit. I find that I unthinkingly adopted the wit—for I can't stomach serious S & S, which I find too great a strain on the risibilities—but piloted round my own incapacity to imagine a whole world by one very simple and unconscious principle: *the setting is important only as it impinges upon the protagonist*. After all, the setting is his antagonist, his enemy. When somebody is trying to shoot you, you don't have much interest in the exact shade of his hair. It is much more important to shoot him back, or get behind a rock, or run away.

Thus, with my story. The first-person point of view made it possible constantly to mediate the setting through the protagonist's intentions, his likes, his dislikes (i.e. his character)—a lucky break that spared me the necessity of creating a whole, self-consistent fantasy world. I was not ready to do that, although I did it later for the Alyx stories (which, by the way, are written in the third person, one of them even in the *omniscient* third person!). When I wrote "Man Who" I was explicity aware of the problem only in two places. One is that "Christmas tree" simile, which is not only much too modern (Christmas trees are nineteenth-century English inventions) but has all the wrong associations. The other is my hero's entrance into the Southern city. I could see that city but I could not describe it—though I tried and tried—so finally I threw up my hands in despair and decided I would confine myself to describing one room in it; after all, he was sick, wasn't he? He was delirious, wasn't he? So I neatly circumvented the undescribable city by having my hero

faint before he could get well into it, and having him
come to inside a room. I find interiors much easier to
suggest (let alone describe) than scenery. The interior,
in fact, is barely there; among other things, he spends
his time flat on his back and preoccupied with other
things. The only exterior detail is a scene through a
window: a "garden" outside with a "gardener" clipping
"fruit trees."

I also find that I had visualized the Northern scene
much more fully than I could write it. But again, what
matters (especially in a short story) is what matters to
the protagonist, *especially* when the story is told in the
first person. He is not likely to describe what he is familiar with, what he is indifferent to, what bores him,
or what he hates (although he might describe this last).
The only scene visually elaborated in the first part of the
story is the last captivity with that kid cousin, whom I
modeled on a kid cousin of my own and whom I find
charming. There is a lot there indirectly, all of it Northern
medieval-European: holy water, some kind of religion,
tithing, charms, leather, wool, stone, thatch, attics, stables,
horses, knitting (!), hoeing beans, a tree, an inn, a coat,
a jacket, a blanket, a wooden stool, and so forth. I tried
for an effect of prosperous but provincial and very stingy
rich farmers—rather like the villagers in a 1930s Pagnol
movie. In the transition, where the hero grows ill, you
will find that the flinty and hilly countryside (with its
"ravine," its "windy black night") begins to sprout flowers
and grass, and finally real weather. We walk up to our
first Southern city "low and gray in the wet dawn mist"
(wasn't I clever, I didn't even have to describe the
gates). The Northern bareness and clarity gives way to
Southern plenty, softness, flowers, and blurriness.

I notice with astonishment that people do not have
names in the North (the protagonist is concerned only
with family relationships) but only in the South. Of
course—civilization! We contrast a country inn with a
"landlady"—how sophisticated, to actually rent out a
whole house! There are: brandy, oil of peppermint, irony,
intelligence, magic, thievery, money, banking, lock-picking,
ledgers, music, beggary, "a small green vial with a brass
stopper," reading, numbers, deception, and glasses and
a bottle on a tray—in short, we are in the civilized world.
I had especial fun with Rigg, who is modeled on the
Krushchev-pig in Pogo and who comes out with a proverb,
a not-very-good proverb, that suits both his model and

himself (I thought): "The clever fellow reaches conclusions more quickly than the stupid one." I think the
South manifests itself most through Rigg's personality:
his writhing, his emotionalism, his "tasting" his own clever-
ness, his little asides, his self-dramatization. I am still proud
of Orthgar's dour comment that the city really ought to
do something about that haunted cemetery, just as if he
were talking about the traffic problem. This is Leiberland
technique: you plump down some outrageously modern
detail right into the middle of your ancient society—but
the detail has to be organic and not an anachronism; the
pleasure is in recognizing that the wit is justified wit.
The magic/archaic is so similar to ourselves. We also
learn indirectly that this is a small city; Rigg says, "I
hate the provinces." I think one of the temptations to use
talky, self-dramatizing characters is the chance they offer
to get exposition in painlessly.

The protagonist *notices* the Southern environment
because it is strange to him, just as he does not really
notice the Northern one because it is familiar (ditto for
the people). In the North he acts and is concerned with
acts; in the South he observes and describes.

First-person narrative gives one extraordinary flex-
ibility in the way one can approach setting; one of the
best (and hardest) effects in sf is the description of a
strange world through the eyes of characters *to whom it
is familiar*—so that we gradually learn what it is that
we are looking at. Robert Heinlein's story "All You Zom-
bies" is a masterpiece of just such exposition. The exposition is entirely through action (or seems to be) yet everything is strange—*to us*. The clearing up of the exposition is
exactly simultaneous with the climax in the story's plot.

My story is not that sophisticated until (I like to think)
the very end—the protagonist's reverie as he falls asleep.
Here I had to convey that he is 1) the ancestor of
modern humanity, by natural selection, and 2) that the
world of the supernatural still exists, invisible to us, because we are immune to it. I also wanted to indicate
that with his immunity to the supernatural goes a
rational or "scientific" turn of mind. Thus I tried to think
what questions a logical but untrained person might ask
about the world; hence the conjecture about the sun's
fire, a question not properly asked until the mid-nineteenth
century and not answered until the twentieth. Monday
morning quarterbacking of this kind is great fun in sf—
read James Blish's marvelous novel *Doctor Mirabilis.*

Implicit setting:

> I was *thirty-five miles away,** eating my *soup* like a
> *peaceable citizen in a neighborhood inn,* when I felt
> a hand descend on my shoulder . . . my uncle! the
> most *tough-minded* of the lot . . . with *twenty men*
> . . . *and a priest. It was the priest that made them*
> *so brave.* (*2 days by horse)
> > "The Man Who Could Not See Devils"

Explicit setting:

> At night *Ourdh* is a suburb of the Pit . . . though
> the *lights of the city* never show *fairer* than then.
> At night *the rich wake up* and *the poor sink into a*
> *distressed sleep,* and everyone takes to the *flat, white-*
> *washed roofs.* Under the *light of gold lamps* the
> *wealthy converse, sliding* across one another, *silky but*
> *never vulgar* . . . all ascend the *broad, white steps*
> to someone's *roof.*
> > *Orbit 2,* "The Adventuress"

There is also what I like to call Fused Setting, a kind
of unity between the camera-eye objectivity of direct
description (above) and the off-handed telegraphy that
tells you as much about the describer as about the
described. Here the objective and subjective mix together,
so that perception becomes action and action perception;
the impression of what the scene is, *is* its description, yet
its description is objectively accurate; states of mind,
intentions, possibilities, action, environment, all become
one. Example:

> she . . . melted into the blackness not two feet away,
> moving swiftly along the corridor wall. Her fingers
> brushed lightly alongside her, like a creeping animal:
> stone, stone, a gap, warm air rising . . . In the dark
> she felt wolfish, her lips skinned back over her teeth;
> like another species she made her way with hands and
> ears. Through them the villa sighed and rustled in its
> sleep . . . They crossed an empty space where two
> halls met; they retreated noiselessly into a room where
> a sleeper lay breathing against a dimly lit window,
> while someone passed in the corridor outside . . . past
> ghostly staircases that opened up in vast wells of dark-
> ness, breathing a faint, far updraft, their steps rustling
> and creaking—
> > *Orbit 3,* "The Barbarian"

The setting here is also mediated through a character's perceptions, but what Robin calls the auctorial voice has gotten in there also, with its strange metaphors, its "ghostly" staircases and "vast wells of darkness," which do not belong precisely to the protagonist but rather to the reader's experience of the protagonist's experience, or to mine. It is not Alyx who thinks of herself as "like another species" but I; yet the simile expresses Alyx's *experience* of nighttime burglary, even though she would never put it in those words. You are not listening to someone talk (as in "The Man Who") or seeing things as in a movie, but are right inside the experience itself— I hope.

"The Man Who" has as its theme, I suppose, the misfit mutation, the superman (?) or what-not; but I wrote it, as Thurber once said, just to run amok in a Setting. In his introduction to the first edition of *The Thirteen Clocks* Thurber describes how he kept tinkering with the manuscript and how it was finally taken away from him by his friends on the grounds that he wasn't rewriting, just having fun running up and down secret staircases and rescuing beautiful enchanted Princesses.

He adds, "They had me there."

SUNDANCE

by Robert Silverberg

TODAY YOU liquidated about 50,000 Eaters in Sector A, and now you are spending an uneasy night. You and Herndon flew east at dawn, with the green-gold sunrise at your backs, and sprayed the neural pellets over a thousand hectares along the Forked River. You flew on into the prairie beyond the river, where the Eaters have already been wiped out, and had lunch sprawled on that thick, soft carpet of grass where the first settlement is expected to rise. Herndon picked some juiceflowers, and you enjoyed half an hour of mild hallucinations. Then, as you headed toward the copter to begin an afternoon of further pellet-spraying, he said suddenly, "Tom, how would you feel about this if it turned out that the Eaters weren't just animal pests?

That they were *people,* say, with a language and rites and a history and all?"
You thought of how it had been for your own people.
"They aren't," you said.
"Suppose they were. Suppose the Eaters—"
"They aren't. Drop it."
Herndon has this streak of cruelty in him that leads him to ask such questions. He goes for the vulnerabilities; it amuses him. All night now his casual remark has echoed in your mind. Suppose the Eaters . . . Suppose the Eaters . . . Suppose . . . Suppose . .
You sleep for a while, and dream, and in your dreams you swim through rivers of blood
Foolishness. A feverish fantasy. You know how important it is to exterminate the Eaters fast, before the settlers get here. They're just animals, and not even harmless animals at that; ecology-wreckers is what they are, devourers of oxygen-liberating plants, and they have to go. A few have been saved for zoological study. The rest must be destroyed. Ritual extirpation of undesirable beings, the old, old story. But let's not complicate our job with moral qualms, you tell yourself. Let's not dream of rivers of blood.
The Eaters don't even *have* blood, none that could flow in rivers, anyway. What they have is, well, a kind of lymph that permeates every tissue and transmits nourishment along the interfaces. Waste products go out the same way, osmotically. In terms of process, it's structurally analogous to your own kind of circulatory system, except there's no network of blood vessels hooked to a master pump. The life-stuff just oozes through their bodies, as though they were amoebas or sponges or some other low-phylum form. Yet they're definitely high-phylum in nervous system, digestive setup, limb-and-organ template, etc. Odd, you think. The thing about aliens is that they're alien, you tell yourself, not for the first time.
The beauty of their biology for you and your companions is that it lets you exterminate them so neatly.
You fly over the grazing grounds and drop the neural pellets. The Eaters find and ingest them. Within an hour the poison has reached all sectors of the body. Life ceases; a rapid breakdown of cellular matter follows, the Eater literally falling apart molecule by molecule the instant that nutrition is cut off; the lymph-like stuff works like acid; a universal lysis occurs; flesh and even the bones, which are cartilaginous, dissolve. In two hours, a puddle

on the ground. In four, nothing at all left. Considering
how many millions of Eaters you've scheduled for extermination here, it's sweet of the bodies to be self-disposing.
Otherwise what a charnel-house this world would become!

Suppose the Eaters . . .

Damn Herndon. You almost feel like getting a memory-
editing in the morning. Scrape his stupid speculations
out of your head. If you dared. If you dared.

In the morning he does not dare. Memory-editing
frightens him; he will try to shake free of his new-found
guilt without it. The Eaters, he explains to himself, are
mindless herbivores, the unfortunate victims of human ex-
pansionism, but not really deserving of passionate defense.
Their extermination is not tragic; it's just too bad. If Earthmen are to have this world, the Eaters must relinquish it.
There's a difference, he tells himself, between the elimina-
tion of the Plains Indians from the American prairie in
the nineteenth century and the destruction of the bison
on that same prairie. One feels a little wistful about the
slaughter of the thundering herds; one regrets the butcher-
ing of millions of the noble brown woolly beasts, yes. But
one feels outrage, not mere wistful regret, at what was
done to the Sioux. There's a difference. Reserve your
passions for the proper cause.

He walks from his bubble at the edge of the camp toward the center of things. The flagstone path is moist and
glistening. The morning fog has not yet lifted, and every
tree is bowed, the long, notched leaves heavy with drop-
lets of water. He pauses, crouching, to observe a spider-
analog spinning its asymmetrical web. As he watches, a
small amphibian, delicately shaded turquoise, glides as in-
conspicuously as possible over the mossy ground. Not in-
conspicuously enough; he gently lifts the little creature
and puts it on the back of his hand. The gills flutter in
anguish, and the amphibian's sides quiver. Slowly, cun-
ningly, its color changes until it matches the coppery
tone of the hand. The camouflage is excellent. He lowers
his hand and the amphibian scurries into a puddle. He
walks on.

He is forty years old, shorter than most of the other
members of the expedition, with wide shoulders, a heavy
chest, dark glossy hair, a blunt, spreading nose. He is a
biologist. This is his third career, for he has failed as an
anthropologist and as a developer of real estate. His name

is Tom Two Ribbons. He has been married twice but has had no children. His great-grandfather died of alcoholism; his grandfather was addicted to hallucinogens; his father had compulsively visited cheap memory-editing parlors. Tom Two Ribbons is conscious that he is failing a family tradition, but he has not yet found his own mode of self-destruction.

In the main building he discovers Herndon, Julia, Ellen, Schwartz, Chang, Michaelson, and Nichols. They are eating breakfast; the others are already at work. Ellen rises and comes to him and kisses him. Her short soft yellow hair tickles his cheeks. "I love you," she whispers. She has spent the night in Michaelson's bubble. "I love you," he tells her, and draws a quick vertical line of affection between her small pale breasts. He winks at Michaelson, who nods, touches the tops of two fingers to his lips, and blows them a kiss. We are all good friends here, Tom Two Ribbons thinks.

"Who drops pellets today?" he asks.

"Mike and Chang," says Julia. "Sector C."

Schwartz says, "Eleven more days and we ought to have the whole peninsula clear. Then we can move inland."

"If our pellet supply holds up," Chang points out.

Herndon says, "Did you sleep well, Tom?"

"No," says Tom. He sits down and taps out his breakfast requisition. In the west, the fog is beginning to burn off the mountains. Something throbs in the back of his neck. He has been on this world nine weeks now, and in that time it has undergone its only change of season, shading from dry weather to foggy. The mists will remain for many months. Before the plains parch again, the Eaters will be gone and the settlers will begin to arrive. His food slides down the chute and he seizes it. Ellen sits beside him. She is a little more than half his age; this is her first voyage; she is their keeper of records, but she is also skilled at editing. "You look troubled," Ellen tells him. "Can I help you?"

"No. Thank you."

"I hate it when you get gloomy."

"It's a racial trait," says Tom Two Ribbons.

"I doubt that very much."

"The truth is that maybe my personality reconstruct is wearing thin. The trauma level was so close to the surface. I'm just a walking veneer, you know."

Ellen laughs prettily. She wears only a sprayon half-wrap. Her skin looks damp; she and Michaelson have had a swim at dawn. Tom Two Ribbons is thinking of asking her to marry him, when this job is over. He has not been married since the collapse of the real estate business. The therapist suggested divorce as part of the reconstruct. He sometimes wonders where Terry has gone and whom she lives with now. Ellen says, "You seem pretty stable to me, Tom."

"Thank you," he says. She is young. She does not know.

"If it's just a passing gloom I can edit it out in one quick snip."

"Thank you," he says. "No."

"I forgot. You don't like editing."

"My father—"

"Yes?"

"In fifty years he pared himself down to a thread," Tom Two Ribbons says. "He had his ancestors edited away, his whole heritage, his religion, his wife, his sons, finally his name. Then he sat and smiled all day. Thank you, no editing."

"Where are you working today?" Ellen asks.

"In the compound, running tests."

"Want company? I'm off all morning."

"Thank you, no," he says, too quickly. She looks hurt. He tries to remedy his unintended cruelty by touching her arm lightly and saying. "Maybe this afternoon, all right? I need to commune a while. Yes?"

"Yes," she says, and smiles, and shapes a kiss with her lips.

After breakfast he goes to the compound. It covers a thousand hectares east of the base; they have bordered it with neural-field projectors at intervals of eighty meters, and this is a sufficient fence to keep the captive population of two hundred Eaters from straying. When all the others have been exterminated, this study group will remain. At the southwest corner of the compound stands a lab bubble from which the experiments are run: metabolic, psychological, physiological, ecological. A stream crosses the compound diagonally. There is a low ridge of grassy hills at its eastern edge. Five distinct copses of tightly clustered knifeblade trees are separated by patches of dense savanna. Sheltered beneath the grass are the oxygen-plants, almost completely hidden except for the photosynthetic spikes that jut to heights of three or four meters at regular intervals, and for the lemon-colored respiratory bodies, chest high, that make the grassland sweet and dizzying with exhaled gases. Through the fields move the Eaters in a straggling herd, nibbling delicately at the respiratory bodies.

Tom Two Ribbons spies the herd beside the stream and goes toward it. He stumbles over an oxygen-plant hidden in the grass but deftly recovers his balance and, seizing the puckered orifice of the respiratory body, inhales deeply. His despair lifts. He approaches the Eaters. They are spherical, bulky, slow-moving creatures, covered by masses of coarse orange fur. Saucer-like eyes protrude above narrow rubbery lips. Their legs are thin and scaly, like a chicken's, and their arms are short and held close to their bodies. They regard him with bland lack of curiosity. "Good morning, brothers!" is the way he greets them this time, and he wonders why.

I noticed something strange today. Perhaps I simply sniffed too much oxygen in the fields; maybe I was succumbing to a suggestion Herndon planted; or possibly it's the family masochism cropping out. But while I was observing the Eaters in the compound, it seemed to me, for the first time, that they were behaving intelligently, that they were functioning in a ritualized way.

I followed them around for three hours. During that time they uncovered half a dozen outcroppings of oxygen-plants. In each case they went through a stylized pattern of action before starting to munch. They:

Formed a straggly circle around the plants.

Looked toward the sun.

Looked toward their neighbors on left and right around the circle.

Made fuzzy neighing sounds *only* after having done the foregoing.

Looked toward the sun again.

Moved in and ate.

If this wasn't a prayer of thanksgiving, a saying of grace, then what was it? And if they're advanced enough spiritually to say grace, are we not therefore committing genocide here? Do chimpanzees say grace? Christ, we wouldn't even wipe out chimps the way we're cleaning out the Eaters! Of course, chimps don't interfere with human crops, and some kind of coexistence would be possible, whereas Eaters and human agriculturalists simply can't function on the same planet. Nevertheless, there's a moral issue here. The liquidation effort is predicted on the assumption that the intelligence level of the Eaters is about on a par with that of oysters, or, at best, sheep. Our con-

sciences stay clear because our poison is quick and pain-
less and because the Eaters thoughtfully dissolve upon
dying, sparing us the mess of incinerating millions of
corpses. But if they pray—
   I won't say anything to the others just yet. I want more
evidence, hard, objective. Films, tapes, record cubes. Then
we'll see. What if I show that we're exterminating intelligent beings? My family knows a little about genocide,
after all, having been on the receiving end just a few centuries back. I doubt that I could halt what's going on here.
But at the very least I could withdraw from the operation.
Head back to Earth and stir up public outcries.
   I hope I'm imagining this.

   I'm not imagining a thing. They gather in circles; they
look to the sun; they neigh and pray. They're only balls
of jelly on chicken-legs, but they give thanks for their food.
Those big round eyes now seem to stare accusingly at me.
Our tame herd here knows what's going on: that we have
descended from the stars to eradicate their kind, and
that they alone will be spared. They have no way of fighting back or even of communicating their displeasure, but
they *know*. And hate us. Jesus, we have killed two million
of them since we got here, and in a metaphorical way
I'm stained with blood, and what will I do, what can I do?
   I must move very carefully, or I'll end up drugged and
edited.
   I can't let myself seem like a crank, a quack, an agita-
tor. I can't stand up and *denounce!* I have to find allies.
Herndon, first. He surely is on to the truth; he's the
one who nudged *me* to it, that day we dropped pellets. And I thought he was merely being vicious in his
usual way!
   I'll talk to him tonight.

   He says, "I've been thinking about that suggestion you
made. About the Eaters. Perhaps we haven't made suffi-
ciently close psychological studies. I mean, if they really
are intelligent—"
   Herndon blinks. He is a tall man with glossy dark hair,
a heavy beard, sharp cheekbones. "Who says they are,
Tom?"
   "You did. On the far side of the Forked River, you
said—"
   "It was just a speculative hypothesis. To make conversation."

"No, I think it was more than that. You really believed it."

Herndon looks troubled. "Tom, I don't know what you're trying to start, but don't start it. If I for a moment believed we were killing intelligent creatures, I'd run for an editor so fast I'd start an implosion wave."

"Why did you ask me that thing, then?" Tom Two Ribbons says.

"Idle chatter."

"Amusing yourself by kindling guilts in somebody else? You're a bastard, Herndon. I mean it."

"Well, look, Tom, if I had any idea that you'd get so worked up about a hypothetical suggestion—" Herndon shakes his head. "The Eaters aren't intelligent beings. Obviously. Otherwise we wouldn't be under orders to liquidate them."

"Obviously," says Tom Two Ribbons.

Ellen said, "No, I don't know what Tom's up to. But I'm pretty sure he needs a rest. It's only a year and a half since his personality reconstruct, and he had a pretty bad breakdown back then."

Michaelson consulted a chart. "He's refused three times in a row to make his pellet-dropping run. Claiming he can't take time away from his research. Hell, we can fill in for him, but it's the idea that he's ducking chores that bothers me."

"What kind of research is he doing?" Nichols wanted to know.

"Not biological," said Julia. "He's with the Eaters in the compound all the time, but I don't see him making any tests on them. He just watches them."

"And talks to them," Chang observed.

"And talks, yes," Julia said.

"Who knows?"

Everyone looked at Ellen. "You're closest to him," Michaelson said. "Can't you bring him out of it?"

"I've got to know what he's in, first," Ellen said. "He isn't saying a thing."

You know that you must be very careful, for they outnumber you, and their concern for your mental welfare can be deadly. Already they realize you are disturbed, and Ellen has begun to probe for the source of the disturbance. Last night you lay in her arms and she questioned you, obliquely, skillfully, and you knew what she is trying to find out. When the moons appeared she suggested that you and she stroll in the compound, among the sleeping Eaters. You declined, but she sees that you have become involved with the creatures.

You have done probing of your own—subtly, you hope. And you are aware that you can do nothing to save the Eaters. An irrevocable commitment has been made. It is 1876 all over again; these are the bison, these are the Sioux, and they must be destroyed, for the railroad is on its way. If you speak out here, your friends will calm you and pacify you and edit you, for they do not see what you see. If you return to Earth to agitate, you will be mocked and recommended for another reconstruct. You can do nothing. You can do nothing.

You cannot save, but perhaps you can record.

Go out into the prairie. Live with the Eaters; make yourself their friend; learn their ways. Set it down, a full account of their culture, so that at least that much will not be lost. You know the techniques of field anthropology. As was done for your people in the old days, do now for the Eaters.

He finds Michaelson. "Can you spare me for a few weeks?" he asks.

"Spare you, Tom? What do you mean?"

"I've got some field studies to do. I'd like to leave the base and work with Eaters in the wild."

"What's wrong with the ones in the compound?"

"It's the last chance with wild ones, Mike. I've got to go."

"Alone, or with Ellen?"

"Alone."

Michaelson nods slowly. "All right, Tom. Whatever you want. Go. I won't hold you here."

I dance in the prairie under the green-gold sun. About me the Eaters gather. I am stripped; sweat makes my skin glisten; my heart pounds. I talk to them with my feet, and they understand.

They understand.

They have a language of soft sounds. They have a god. They know love and awe and rapture. They have rites. They have names. They have a history. Of all this I am convinced.

I dance on thick grass.

How can I reach them? With my feet, with my hands,

with my grunts, with my sweat. They gather by the hundreds, by the thousands, and I dance. I must not stop. They cluster about me and make their sounds. I am a conduit for strange forces. My great-grandfather should see me now! Sitting on his porch in Wyoming, the firewater in his hand, his brain rotting—see me now, old one! See the dance of Tom Two Ribbons! I talk to these strange ones with my feet under a sun that is the wrong color. I dance. I dance.

"Listen to me," I say. "I am your friend, I alone, the only one you can trust. Trust me, talk to me, teach me. Let me preserve your ways, for soon the destruction will come."

I dance, and the sun climbs, and the Eaters murmur.

There is the chief. I dance toward him, back, toward, I bow, I point to the sun, I imagine the being that lives in that ball of flame, I imitate the sounds of these people, I kneel, I rise, I dance. Tom Two Ribbons dances for you.

I summon skills my ancestors forgot. I feel the power flowing in me. As they danced in the days of the bison, I dance now, beyond the Forked River.

I dance, and now the Eaters dance too. Slowly, uncertainly, they move toward me, they shift their weight, lift leg and leg, sway about. "Yes, like that!" I cry. "Dance!"

We dance together as the sun reaches noon height.

Now their eyes are no longer accusing. I see warmth and kinship. I am their brother, their redskinned tribesman, he who dances with them. No longer do they seem clumsy to me. There is a strange ponderous grace in their movements. They dance. They dance. They caper about me. Closer, closer, closer!

We move in holy frenzy.

They sing, now, a blurred hymn of joy. They throw forth their arms, unclench their little claws. In unison they shift weight, left foot forward, right, left, right. Dance, brothers, dance, dance, dance! They press against me. Their flesh quivers; their smell is a sweet one. They gently thrust me across the field, to a part of the meadow where the grass is deep and untrampled. Still dancing, we seek for the oxygen-plants, and find clumps of them beneath the grass, and they make their prayer and seize them with their awkward arms, separating the respiratory bodies from the photosynthetic spikes. The plants, in anguish, release floods of oxygen. My mind reels. I laugh and sing. The Eaters are nibbling the lemon-colored per-

forated globes, nibbling the stalks as well. They thrust
their plants at me. It is a religious ceremony, I see. Take
from us, eat with us, join with us, this is the body, this
is the blood, take, eat, join. I bend forward and put a
lemon-colored globe to my lips. I do not bite; I nibble,
as they do, my teeth slicing away the skin of the globe.
Juice spurts into my mouth, while oxygen drenches my
nostrils. The Eaters sing hosannas. I should be in full paint
for this, paint of my forefathers, feathers too, meeting
their religion in the regalia of what should have been
mine. Take, eat, join. The juice of the oxygen-plant flows
in my veins. I embrace my brothers. I sing, and as my
voice leaves my lips it becomes an arch that glistens like
new steel, and I pitch my song lower, and the arch turns
to tarnished silver. The Eaters crowd close. The scent of
their bodies is fiery red to me. Their soft cries are puffs
of steam. The sun is very warm; its rays are tiny jagged
pings of puckered sound, close to the top of my range of
hearing, plink! plink! plink! The thick grass hums to me,
deep and rich, and the wind hurls points of flame along
the prairie. I devour another oxygen-plant, and then a
third. My brothers laugh and shout. They tell me of their
gods, the god of warmth, the god of food, the god of
pleasure, the god of death, the god of holiness, the god of
wrongness, and the others. They recite for me the names
of their kings, and I hear their voices as splashes of green
mold on the clean sheet of the sky. They instruct me in
their holy rites. I must remember this, I tell myself, for
when it is gone it will never come again. I continue to
dance. They continue to dance. The color of the hills becomes rough and coarse, like abrasive gas. Take, eat,
join. Dance. They are so gentle!

I hear the drone of the copter, suddenly.

It hovers far overhead. I am unable to see who flies in
it. "No," I scream. "Not here! Not these people! Listen to
me! This is Tom Two Ribbons! Can't you hear me? I'm
doing a field study here! You have no right—!"

My voice makes spirals of blue moss edged with red
sparks. They drift upward and are scattered by the breeze.

I yell, I shout, I bellow. I dance and shake my fists.
From the wings of the copter the jointed arms of the
pellet-distributors unfold. The gleaming spigots extend
and whirl. The neural pellets rain down into the meadow,
each tracing a blazing track that lingers in the sky. The
sound of the copter becomes a furry carpet stretching to
the horizon, and my shrill voice is lost in it.

The Eaters drift away from me, seeking the pellets, scratching at the roots of the grass to find them. Still dancing, I leap into their midst, striking the pellets from their hands, hurling them into the stream, crushing them to powder. The Eaters growl black needles at me. They turn away and search for more pellets. The copter turns and flies off, leaving a trail of dense oily sound. My brothers are gobbling the pellets eagerly.

There is no way to prevent it.

Joy consumes them and they topple and lie still. Occasionally a limb twitches; then even this stops. They begin to dissolve. Thousands of them melt on the prairie, sinking into shapelessness, losing their spherical forms, flattening, ebbing into the ground. The bonds of the molecules will no longer hold. It is the twilight of protoplasm. They perish. They vanish. For hours I walk the prairie. Now I inhale oxygen; now I eat a lemon-colored globe. Sunset begins with the ringing of leaden chimes. Black clouds make brazen trumpet calls in the east and the deepening wind is a swirl of coaly bristles. Silence comes. Night falls. I dance. I am alone.

The copter comes again, and they find you, and you do not resist as they gather you in. You are beyond bitterness. Quietly you explain what you have done and what you have learned, and why it is wrong to exterminate these people. You describe the plant you have eaten and the way it affects your senses, and as you talk of the blessed synesthesia, the texture of the wind and the sound of the clouds and the timbre of the sunlight, they nod and smile and tell you not to worry, that everything will be all right soon, and they touch something cold to your forearm, so cold that it is a whir and a buzz and the deintoxicant sinks into your vein and soon the ecstasy drains away, leaving only the exhaustion and the grief.

He says, "We never learn a thing, do we? We export all our horrors to the stars. Wipe out the Armenians, wipe out the Jews, wipe out the Tasmanians, wipe out the Indians, wipe out everyone who's in the way, and then come out here and do the same damned murderous thing. You weren't with me out there. You didn't dance with them. You didn't see what a rich, complex culture the Eaters have. Let me tell you about their tribal structure. It's dense: seven levels of matrimonial relationships, to begin with, and an exogamy factor that requires—"

Softly Ellen says, "Tom, darling, nobody's going to harm the Eaters."

"And the religion," he goes on. "Nine gods, each one an aspect of *the* god. Holiness and wrongness both worshiped. They have hymns, prayers, a theology. And we, the emissaries of the god of wrongness—"

"We're not exterminating them," Michaelson says. "Won't you understand that, Tom? This is all a fantasy of yours. You've been under the influence of drugs, but now we're clearing you out. You'll be clean in a little while. You'll have perspective again."

"A fantasy?" he says bitterly. "A drug dream? I stood out in the prairie and saw you drop pellets. And I watched them die and melt away. I didn't dream that."

"How can we convince you?" Chang asks earnestly. "What will make you believe? Shall we fly over the Eater country with you and show you how many millions there are?"

"But how many millions have been destroyed?" he demands.

They insist that he is wrong. Ellen tells him again that no one has ever desired to harm the Eaters. "This is a scientific expedition, Tom. We're here to *study* them. It's a violation of all we stand for to injure intelligent life-forms."

"You admit that they're intelligent?"

"Of course. That's never been in doubt."

"Then why drop the pellets?" he asks. "Why slaughter them?"

"None of that has happened, Tom," Ellen says. She takes his hand between her cool palms. "Believe us. Believe us."

He says bitterly, "If you want me to believe you, why don't you do the job properly? Get out the editing machine and go to work on me. You can't simply *talk* me into rejecting the evidence of my own eyes."

"You were under drugs all the time," Michaelson says.

"I've never taken drugs! Except for what I ate in the meadow, when I danced—and that came after I had watched the massacre going on for weeks and weeks. Are you saying that it's a retroactive delusion?"

"No, Tom," Schwartz says. "You've had this delusion all along. It's part of your therapy, your reconstruct. You came here programmed with it."

"Impossible," he says.

Ellen kisses his fevered forehead. "It was done to recon-

cile you to mankind, you see. You had this terrible resentment of the displacement of your people in the nineteenth
century. You were unable to forgive the industrial society
for scattering the Sioux, and you were terribly full of hate.
Your therapist thought that if you could be made to
participate in an imaginary modern extermination, if you
could come to see it as a necessary operation, you'd be
purged of your resentment and able to take you place
in society as—"

He thrusts her away. "Don't talk idiocy! If you knew
the first thing about reconstruct therapy, you'd realize that
no reputable therapist could be so shallow. There are no
one-to-one correlations in reconstructs. No, don't touch
me. Keep away. Keep away."

He will not let them persuade him that this is merely
a drugborn dream. It is no fantasy, he tells himself, and
it is no therapy. He rises. He goes out. They do not follow
him. He takes a copter and seeks his brothers.

Again I dance. The sun is much hotter today. The
Eaters are more numerous. Today I wear paint, today I
wear feathers. My body shines with my sweat. They dance
with me, and they have a frenzy in them that I have never
seen before. We pound the trampled meadow with our
feet. We clutch for the sun with our hands. We sing, we
shout, we cry. We will dance until we fall.

This is no fantasy. These people are real, and they are
intelligent, and they are doomed. This I know.

We dance. Despite the doom, we dance.

My great-grandfather comes and dances with us. He
too is real. His nose is like a hawk's, not blunt like mine,
and he wears the big headdress, and his muscles are like
cords under his brown skin. He sings, he shouts, he cries.

Others of my family join us.

We eat the oxygen-plants together. We embrace the
Eaters. We know, all of us, what it is to be hunted.

The clouds make music and the wind takes on texture
and the sun's warmth has color.

We dance. We dance. Our limbs know no weariness.

The sun grows and fills the whole sky, and I see no
Eaters now, only my own people, my father's fathers
across the centuries, thousands of gleaming skins, thousands of hawk's noses, and we eat the plants, and we
find sharp sticks and thrust them into our flesh, and the
sweet blood flows and dries in the blaze of the sun, and
we dance, and we dance, and some of us fall from weari-

ness, and we dance, and the prairie is a sea of bobbing
headdresses, an ocean of feathers, and we dance, and my
heart makes thunder, and my knees become water, and
the sun's fire engulfs me, and I dance, and I fall, and I
dance, and I fall, and I fall, and I fall.

Again they find you and bring you back. They give you
the cool snout on your arm to take the oxygen-plant drug
from your veins, and then they give you something else
so you will rest. You rest and you are very calm. Ellen
kisses you and you stroke her soft skin, and then the others
come in and they talk to you, saying soothing things, but
you do not listen, for you are searching for realities. It
is not an easy search. It is like falling through many trap-
doors, looking for the one room whose floor is not hinged.
Everything that has happened on this planet is your
therapy, you tell yourself, designed to reconcile an em-
bittered aborigine to the white man's conquest; nothing is
really being exterminated here. You reject that and fall
through and realize that this must be the therapy of your
friends; they carry the weight of accumulated centuries
of guilts and have come here to shed that load, and you
are here to ease them of their burden, to draw their sins
into yourself and give them forgiveness. Again you fall
through, and see that the Eaters are mere animals who
threaten the ecology and must be removed; the culture
you imagined for them is your hallucination, kindled out
of old churnings. You try to withdraw your objections
to this necessary extermination, but you fall through again
and discover that there is no extermination except in your
mind, which is troubled and disordered by your obsession
with the crime against your ancestors, and you sit up, for
you wish to apologize to these friends of yours, these
innocent scientists whom you have called murderers. And
you fall through.

INTRODUCTION TO "SUNDANCE"
by Robert Silverberg

ON THE surface, there appears to be a transaction taking place between the artist and the audience, and that transaction has the form of an elementary quid-pro-quo deal: I make or do something for your pleasure, you look upon my work and are pleased, you pay me for the time I expended on your behalf. Almost any sort of "entertainment" involving doer and spectator can be viewed in terms of that transactional relationship: the roster of hirelings encompasses writers, actors, painters, football players, sculptors, composers, musical performers, stage and film directors, and a long list of others.

But the deeper we look into the psychology of the artist—or the psychology of the spectator—the more clearly we see that artistic effort is only coincidentally transactional in nature. Artist and audience are on separate trips, and the point at which they meet in order that the spectators may pay the price of admission is only one brief flashing intersection on two otherwise independent journeys. Consider the very different things that a short story "does" for the person who writes it and the one who reads it. These are some of the benefits the writer gets from the creative effort:

- Satisfaction of the shaping impulse, that seemingly universal human drive to reduce entropy, to bring order out of randomness, form out of chaos.
- Codification of the writer's own thinking in the cognitive sphere through the organization and development of the ideational substructure of the story—a factor typical of science fiction, in which conceptual rather than emotional material often lies at the story's heart.
- Emotional catharsis derived from transfer of some aspect of personal experience, perhaps painful, from recollection to artistic manifestation.
- Development of technical skills through exploration of form and possible extensions of the possibilities of form.

The reader, on the other hand, may obtain some or all of these benefits from a story:

- A moment of encapsulation in a "pocket universe" drawing him away from the problems of real-world existence: fiction as escape.
- Esthetic response to form and style: the pleasure of experiencing a well-made verbal object.
- Acquisition of vicarious experience: learning something from a story, perhaps of a technical nature (operations of the stock market, theories of linguistics, effects of psychedelic drugs, methods of sexual intercourse) or perhaps in some more general field of human relationships.
- Stimulation of thought: reflections evoked by the story, leading to conclusions not explicit in the text.

There is, of course, a good deal of overlapping in these two groups of categories, and neither writer nor reader ever separates them as neatly as I have done here. The point is merely that the satisfactions a writer gets from writing only occasionally intersect the satisfactions a reader gets from reading.

"Sundance," which I wrote in September, 1968, is a good example of this. It pleased me when I wrote it, and pleases me now: I think I like it best, out of my hundreds of short stories. After a slow start, it has come to please readers too: when awards were handed out for the best science fiction stories published in 1969, a different story of mine received a trophy, but since then "Sundance" has been reprinted eight or nine times, and its career as an anthology piece appears to be just beginning. I am the last person in the world who could tell you what values "Sundance" has to a reader, but I can tell you quite precisely what it achieved for its author in the way of esthetic and emotional satisfaction.

It did not, for instance, give me the special science-fictional delight of creating or developing ideas. One of science fiction's highest values for me as reader is its inventiveness: the putting forth of some new notion, or the recombination of old ideas into dramatically vivid new form. Heinlein achieved that for me in "Universe," the multi-generation-starship story; Clement did it in *Mission of Gravity* and Blish in "Surface Tension"; Asimov accomplished it in his robotics stories and novels. All of these are works that methodically exhaust all the implications of an unfamiliar concept. In my own writing I think I've come closest to achieving that in the urban monad stories collected under the title *The World Inside*.

But there are no unfamiliar concepts in "Sundance." The central action is the extermination of an abundant animal species by humans who have uses of their own for the territory where that species is dominant. Hardly an original notion: all I have done has been to transfer to another planet the extermination of the American bison in the nineteenth century. Merely using an alien setting does not, however, give the story much validity as science fiction, since there is nothing so alien about the setting I devised as to make it *fundamentally* different from Nebraska or North Dakota; only when I add the possibility that the beasts being slaughtered on that world may in fact be an intelligent species with a rich cultural heritage does the story begin to take on some speculative attributes. Even then I am offering nothing new. And when I make my protagonist an American Indian who is part of the slaughter operation, and thus is compelled to recapitulate the tragic experience of his own race, I provide only an extra level of irony, not any true conceptual insight.

So the material that generates the story is—to me— pretty unpromising stuff. I yoke together a transplanted Western (Buffalo Bill in the Zilch Galaxy) and some currently fashionable radical sentiments (We Sure Gave the Injuns a Raw Deal) to create—what? A tract proving that the expansionist imperialist United States is going to repeat in space all its crimes of the recent past? A little nugget of agitprop that gives the enlightened reader a quick hot flush of righteous indignation? Well, maybe. No doubt "Sundance" can be read, and has been, for its "relevant" political sentiments. No doubt my own anti-imperialist bias and sympathy for the fate of the Plains Indians (and the bison) gives the story thrust and intensity. But I see little value in writing tracts warning against crimes that already have been committed, or even crimes yet to come; my stories may occasionally have politico-ideological content, but never a primary political intent.

What was I up to, then, in "Sundance"? For one thing to get inside the mind and soul of a human being—Tom Two Ribbons—who is manifesting the long-term effects of the destruction of his ancestral culture and who is unable to escape the pain of that destruction even on another planet. But on another level I was after two main things:

- An exploration of ways to dramatize subjective, ambiguous perceptions of reality.

- An exploration of the feasibility of shifting grammatical person within a short story.

Those are both technical aims—matters of literary
carpentry. I wanted to see if it was possible for me to tell
a story in which the events-as-narrated do not necessarily
coincide with the events-as-they-really-happened, and in
which the events-as-they-really-happened are withheld as
irrelevant. I also wanted to see if I could shift from third
person to first, and even to second, without causing fatal
discontinuities of structure. The second aim would merely
have been a virtuoso stunt, self-contained and irrelevant
to the needs of most readers, if I had not integrated it with
the first, producing this more refined statement of technical
purpose:

- To dramatize a shifting, subjective perception of
reality by means of shifts in grammatical person.

Any situation might have let me do this. I chose the
bison-Indian parallel because the implied genocidal myth
carried its own built-in emotional charge, and a story
in which my goals were so abstract, so technical, needed
all the emotional intensity I could provide. Whether actual
genocide was taking place on that planet was unimportant
to me, indeed was outside the scope of the story: what
mattered was Tom Two Ribbons' perception, perhaps
inaccurate, that such a crime was being committed. A
careful reading of the story·shows that the action remains
ambiguous to the end: not only is the reader uncertain
that the aliens really do have intelligence of a human level,
but there is some doubt that an extermination is in fact
in progress. Since I was not writing an oh-the-horror-of-
it-all sermon, the "real" situation did not concern me.
What did was the presentation of Tom Two Ribbons'
fluctuating emotional states. To do this I set up these
structural propositions:

- First-person sections would describe Tom Two Ribbons' subjective perceptions of events.
- Second-person sections would allow the author to
speak directly to Tom, laying down basic narrative situations and providing the concluding statement
of ultimate ambiguity.
- Third-person sections would render the reality-
perceptions of other members of the expedition and
show Tom interrelating with those members. I

would use present tense when Tom is with them, to heighten the sense of ambiguity, and past tense when Tom is absent from the scene, since his absence removes the feeling of shifting, feverish uncertainty.

I did not always follow this somewhat mechanical scheme; some of the second-person passages, I now see, might well have been told in the first person, and some of the third-person material might have been shifted to second person; basically, though, I think I was consistent to my structural program and that it aided me in bringing off the effect of developing the disintegration of a personality. But a structural program would not have been enough. Having devised my framework, having conceived the character of Tom Two Ribbons, having worked out the basic situation of conflict involving the alien beings, I still had a big job ahead: orchestrating the story, giving it texture and density and color, providing the reader with sensory data to keep him reading on through shift after shift of perception.

Here a strong sense of setting was necessary to keep the story from becoming a mere abstraction, a series of empty postures. Placing the story on another planet gave me a good opportunity for this sort of exterior decoration; giving the aliens a ritual that included the ingestion of a hallucinogenic plant allowed me an even better way of making the story vivid.

One way to describe an alien planet is to drop into the matrix of the story a solid lump of specifications: "Planet X, the ninth of sixteen worlds orbiting the blue-white star Q, had an atmosphere composed of This and That, a diameter So Big, and a gravitational pull That Heavy. There were five continents, and the one on which our story is laid was located in the south temperate zone." Stuff like that gets published all the time. I've written my share of it. Such a passage has the virtue of giving the reader all the background data in one place, for quick reference. It has the drawback of turning that data into a disposable unit that can be excreted from memory before the page is turned. In "Sundance" I had no special intention of creating a novel and ingenious new planet, of the sort that Hal Clement or Larry Niven or Poul Anderson might dream up; that's a noble sport, but it would only interfere with the real business of this particular story. All I wanted was a sense of alienness. So in the first paragraph you encounter a "green-gold sunrise."

It isn't Earth. A few paragraphs on, I offer a life-form
with low-phylum bodily organization, high-phylum intelligence. More alienness, and, not incidentally, the
potential for some misunderstanding by the characters
of these creatures' true scope. Two pages farther on come
some small creatures—a "spider-analog spinning its
asymmetrical web" and a small turquoise amphibian,
and after another page comes a note on the weather
cycle, from dry weather to foggy. Bits of texture continue
to surface until a respectable feeling of density has been
achieved: the sun is hot, the grasslands are sweet with
gases exhaled by the towering photosynthetic spikes of
the oxygen-plants, there are streams and rivers, and yet—
and yet—how few words were needed to provide that
sense of density! A sensory jab here, a sensory nibble
there, a splash of color, a nip of fragrance—yet nowhere
in the story is there any information about the size and
mass of the planet, its periods of rotation or revolution, the
inclination of its orbit, the distribution of its continents.
Stories set on Earth, mundane stories about Indians and
bison, manage to achieve effects of density of setting
without telling you any of those things; why then do it
for that alien world, when repeated brief strokes can convey
the desired effects?

But there is one place where I pile on the effects, calling
on every weapon in the sensorium to make the setting
concrete. This is the passage beginning, "They sing now,
a blurred hymn of joy," in which Tom Two Ribbons
dances with the aliens (or thinks he does), eats their
sacred hallucinogenic plant, and experiences that confusion of the senses known as *synesthesia*. I appeal here
to taste, touch, smell, sight, and hearing, loading the story
with sensory data for 1400 words, more than a quarter
of its total length. This is the climax of the story, though
it comes in the middle, another technical experiment.
(There is a secondary climax, recapitulating the imagery
of the first and developing it by introducing members of
Tom's family, just before the story ends.) The sensory
overload of that 1400-word scene defines the psychological
setting of the story, just as another writer might use
overload techniques to define his geographical setting.
The place where "Sundance" unfolds is the interior of
Tom Two Ribbons' mind, and, although I was content to
outline the planetary geography with a minimum of data,
I provide a wealth of interior data, psychological data,
to make the climactic scene as immediate as I can. *And*

the sensory details are scrambled. Sunset is perceived as the ringing of leaden chimes, the wind is a swirl of coaly bristles, the scent of the aliens' bodies is fiery red. Setting reinforces the inner drama. Tom Two Ribbons' psychological disorientation surfaces as hallucinatory synesthesia at the moment of his communion with the alien beings whom he identifies with his own ancestors. (Do the aliens themselves experience synesthesia when they eat the plant? The story doesn't say.) What might have been mere decorative detail in another story is intrinsic to theme here. Which is why a writer's dry-as-dust experiment in jiggling with grammar turns out to be the story "Sundance" is. It was a difficult story to write. It was an exciting story to write.

THEME:
To Mean Intensely

*This world's no blot for us,
Nor blank; it means intensely, and means
good:
To find its meaning is my meat and drink.*

BROWNING'S FRA LIPPO LIPPI was clearly no existentialist, and although we live in an existential age, we still seek meaning—if not in the natural world, in mankind's relation to that world and what he has made of it. It may well be that the peculiar appeal of science fiction is that it so often seeks to mediate between human beings and the more and more hostile environment they have created, seeks to explain the ways of the god technology to man.

Put formally, *theme* is the writer's vision of life interpreted in terms of his own personality; it is a series of perceptions which the writer believes to be accurate and significant and which he communicates in the system of values and sentiments and incidents that is the story. It is the sum of plot, character, and setting.

Isolating *the* theme of a story—call it intellectual concept, message, meaning, intention, moral (as in Aesop) or ontology—is a slippery business. Good stories are likely to exhibit a family of related themes, no one of which is clearly delineated. Stories in which theme is unequivocal and immediately apparent are likely to result from the subservience of art to propaganda, or at least to didacticism. Theme-hunting can be a lot of fun, and an appreciation of the thematic content of a story is important, but no one should look for ready agreement on a statement of theme unless it is very broad, and no one should attempt to find meaning where none was intended, interpolating his own personality into the story instead of carefully analyzing that of the writer.

It is in the development of thematic material that the writer most fully reveals himself to the perceptive reader. The writer is bound to display certain beliefs and values which can be described as *judicial* and *preferential* attitudes. A pair of *judicial attitudes* are *optimism* and *pessimism,* reasoned convictions that life is essentially good or evil. Another pair are *sentimentalism* and *cynicism,* emotional judgments on the same issue. The two basic preferential attitudes are *realism* and *romanticism,* the one expressing the notion that truth is found through submission to fact, the other that truth is found in escape from fact. These terms are vast over-simplifications: in a given story, a writer may vary his attitudes, may equivocate, may, indeed, build his story to express his own uncertainties on the matter—itself a powerful and increasingly popular theme.

Relatively few writers begin a story with a clear and fixed concept of theme in mind (although propagandists invariably do so). More likely, a writer enters his story through some notion of plot or some fascination with a character. This is less true of science fiction, which is preeminently a literature of ideas, and which so often finds its genesis in questions such as "What would things be like if?" or "What would people do if thus-and-such should occur?" Here, Joanna Russ, who has suffered with students over the matter, suggests I include a caveat for the new writer: beware of the thematic approach to writing! It can swiftly lead you into the viscous toils of allegory, which is for most writers—trying to make a living from their work—a fate worse than debt.

But whether or not the writer begins with a firm thematic intention, theme will be there buried somewhere in the first draft. At this point, he is likely to see meanings that surpass his original intentions (if he had any), and he will go back in his revision to tinker and adjust, to clarify meaning and express it more artfully. In this effort one of the writer's principal tools is symbolism, the substitution of an idea or a thing for some other idea or thing less amenable to the kind of compressed expression demanded in short fiction. Good symbols are not merely decorative embellishment, are not (except at the linguistic level) stock devices with universal meanings, are frequently more or less ambiguous, and must so far as possible be interpreted solely within the little world of the story and in terms of the personality of the writer as revealed. It is there, and only there, that symbolic rhetoric can carry its greatest freight of meaning.

Freud, forgive me.

NINE LIVES

by Ursula K. Le Guin

SHE WAS alive inside, but dead outside, her face a black and dun net of wrinkles, tumors, cracks. She was bald and blind. The tremors that crossed Libra's face were mere quiverings of corruption: underneath, in the black corridors, the halls beneath the skin, there were crepitations in darkness, ferments, chemical nightmares that went on for centuries. "Oh the damned flatulent planet," Pugh murmured as the dome shook and a boil burst a kilometer to the southwest, spraying silver pus across the sunset. The sun had been setting for the last two days. "I'll be glad to see a human face."

"Thanks," said Martin.

"Your is human to be sure," said Pugh, "but I've seen it so long I can't see it."

Radvid signals cluttered the communicator which Martin was operating, faded, returned as face and voice. The face filled the screen, the nose of an Assyrian king, the eyes of a samurai, skin bronze, eyes the color of iron: young, magnificent. "Is that what human beings look like?" said Pugh with awe. "I'd forgotten."

"Shut up, Owen, we're on."

"Libra Exploratory Mission Base, come in please, this is *Passerine* launch."

"Libra here. Beam fixed. Come on down, launch."

"Expulsion in seven E-seconds. Hold on." The screen blanked and sparkled.

"Do they all look like that? Martin, you and I are uglier men than I thought."

"Shut up, Owen. . . ."

For twenty-two minutes Martin followed the landing-craft down by signal and then through the cleared dome they saw it, small star in the blood-colored east, sinking. It came down neat and quiet, Libra's thin atmosphere carrying little sound. Pugh and Martin closed the headpieces of their imsuits, zipped out of the dome airlocks, and ran with soaring strides, Nijinsky and Nureyev, toward the boat. Three equipment modules came floating down at four-minute intervals from each other and hundred-meter intervals east of the boat. "Come on out," Martin said on his suit radio, "we're waiting at the door."

"Come on in, the methane's fine," said Pugh.

The hatch opened. The young man they had seen on
the screen came out with one athletic twist and leaped
down onto the shaky dust and clinkers of Libra. Martin
shook his hand, but Pugh was staring at the hatch, from
which another young man emerged with the same neat
twist and jump, followed by a young woman who emerged
with the same neat twist, ornamented with a wriggle,
and a jump. They were all tall, with bronze skin, black
hair, high-bridged noses, epicanthic fold, the same face.
They all had the same face. The fourth was emerging from
the hatch with a neat twist and jump. "Martin bach," said
Pugh, "we've got a clone."

"Right," said one of them, "we're a tenclone. John
Chow's the name. You're Lieutenant Martin?"

"I'm Owen Pugh."

"Alvaro Guillen Martin," said Martin, formal, bowing
slightly. Another girl was out, the same beautiful face;
Martin stared at her and his eye rolled like a nervous
pony's. Evidently he had never given any thought to cloning, and was suffering technological shock. "Steady,"
Pugh said in the Argentine dialect, "it's only excess twins."
He stood close by Martin's elbow. He was glad himself of
the contact.

It is hard to meet a stranger. Even the greatest extravert
meeting even the meekest stranger knows a certain dread,
though he may not know he knows it. Will he make a fool
of me wreck my image of myself invade me destroy me
change me? Will he be different from me? Yes, that he
will. There's the terrible thing: the strangeness of the
stranger.

After two years on a dead planet, and the last half year
isolated as a team of two, oneself and one other, after that
it's even harder to meet a stranger, however welcome he
may be. You're out of the habit of difference, you've
lost the touch; and so the fear revives, the primitive anxiety, the old dread.

The clone, five males and five females, had got done in
a couple of minutes what a man might have got done in
twenty: greeted Pugh and Martin, had a glance at Libra,
unloaded the boat, made ready to go. They went, and the
dome filled with them, a hive of golden bees. They hummed
and buzzed quietly, filled up all silences, all spaces with
a honey-brown swarm of human presence. Martin looked
bewilderedly at the long-limbed girls, and they smiled at
him, three at once. Their smile was gentler than that of
the boys, but no less radiantly self-possessed.

"Self-possessed," Owen Pugh murmured to his friend, "that's it. Think of it, to be oneself ten times over. Nine seconds for every motion, nine ayes on every vote. It would be glorious!" But Martin was asleep. And the John Chows had all gone to sleep at once. The dome was filled with their quiet breathing. They were young, they didn't snore. Martin sighed and snored, his Hershey-bar-colored face relaxed in the dim afterglow of Libra's primary, set at last. Pugh had cleared the dome and stars looked in, Sol among them, a great company of lights, a clone of splendors. Pugh slept and dreamed of a one-eyed giant who chased him through the shaking halls of Hell.

From his sleeping-bag Pugh watched the clone's awakening. They all got up within one minute except for one pair, a boy and a girl, who lay snugly tangled and still sleeping in one bag. As Pugh saw this there was a shock like one of Libra's earthquakes inside him, a very deep tremor. He was not aware of this, and in fact thought he was pleased at the sight; there was no other such comfort on this dead hollow world; more power to them, who made love. One of the others stepped on the pair. They woke and the girl sat up flushed and sleepy, with bare golden breasts. One of her sisters murmured something to her; she shot a glance at Pugh and disappeared in the sleeping-bag, followed by a giant giggle, from another direction a fierce stare, from still another direction a voice: "Christ, we're used to having a room to ourselves. Hope you don't mind, Captain Pugh."

"It's a pleasure," Pugh said half-truthfully. He had to stand up then, wearing only the shorts he slept in, and he felt like a plucked rooster, all white scrawn and pimples. He had seldom envied Martin's compact brownness so much. The United Kingdom had come through the Great Famines well, losing less than half its population: a record achieved by rigorous food-control. Black-marketeers and hoarders had been executed. Crumbs had been shared. Where in richer lands most had died and a few had thriven, in Britain fewer died and none throve. They all got lean. Their sons were lean, their grandsons lean, small, brittle-boned, easily infected. When civilization became a matter of standing in lines, the British had kept queue, and so had replaced the survival of the fittest with the survival of the fair-minded. Owen Pugh was a scrawny little man. All the same, he was there.

At the moment he wished he wasn't.

At breakfast a John said, "Now if you'll brief us, Captain Pugh—"

"Owen, then."

"Owen, we can work out our schedule. Anything new on the mine since your last report to your Mission? We saw your reports when *Passerine* was orbiting Planet V, where they are now."

Martin did not answer, though the mine was his discovery and project, and Pugh had to do his best. It was hard to talk to them. The same faces, each with the same expression of intelligent interest, all leaned toward him across the table at almost the same angle. They all nodded together.

Over the Exploitation Corps insignia on their tunics each had a nameband, first name John and last name Chow of course, but the middle names different. The men were Aleph, Kaph, Yod, Gimel, and Samedh; the women Sadhe, Daleth, Zayin, Beth, and Resh. Pugh tried to use the names but gave it up at once; he could not even tell sometimes which one had spoken, for the voices were all alike.

Martin buttered and chewed his toast, and finally interrupted: "You're a team. Is that it?"

"Right," said two Johns.

"God, what a team! I hadn't seen the point. How much do you each know what the others are thinking?"

"Not at all, properly speaking," replied one of the girls, Zayin. The others watched her with the proprietary, approving look they had. "No ESP, nothing fancy. But we think alike. We have exactly the same equipment. Given the same stimulus, the same problem, we're likely to be coming up with the same reactions and solutions at the same time. Explanations are easy—don't even have to make them, usually. We seldom misunderstand each other. It does facilitate our working as a team."

"Christ yes," said Martin. "Pugh and I have spent seven hours out of ten for six months misunderstanding each other. Like most people. What about emergencies, are you as good at meeting the unexpected problem as a nor . . . an unrelated team?"

"Statistics so far indicate that we are," Zayin answered readily. Clones must be trained, Pugh thought, to meet questions, to reassure and reason. All they said had the slightly bland and stilted quality of answers furnished to the Public. "We can't brainstorm as singletons can, we as a team don't profit from the interplay of varied minds;

but we have a compensatory advantage. Clones are drawn from the best human material, individuals of IIQ 99th percentile, Genetic Constitution alpha double A, and so on. We have more to draw on than most individuals do."

"And it's multiplied by a factor of ten. Who is—who was John Chow?"

"A genuis surely," Pugh said politely. His interest in cloning was not so new and avid as Martin's.

"Leonardo Complex type," said Yod. "Biomath, also a cellist, and an undersea hunter, and interested in structural engineering problems, and so on. Died before he'd worked out his major theories."

"Then you each represent a different facet of his mind, his talents?"

"No," said Zayin, shaking her head in time with several others, "We share the basic equipment and tendencies, of course, but we're all engineers in Planetary Exploitation. A later clone can be trained to develop other aspects of the basic equipment. It's all training; the genetic substance is identical. We *are* John Chow. But we were differently trained."

Martin looked shell-shocked. "How old are you?"

"Twenty-three."

"You say he died young— Had they taken germ cells from him beforehand or something?"

Gimel took over: "He died at twenty-four in an aircar crash. They couldn't save the brain, so they took some intestinal cells and cultured them for cloning. Reproductive cells aren't used for cloning since they have only half the chromosomes. Intestinal cells happen to be easy to despecialize and reprogram for total growth."

"All chips off the old block," Martin said valiantly. "But how can . . . some of you be women . . . ?"

Beth took over: "It's easy to program half the clonal mass back to the female. Just delete the male gene from half the cells and they revert to the basic, that is, the female. It's trickier to go the other way, have to hook in artificial Y chromosomes. So they mostly clone from males, since clones function best bisexually."

Gimel again: "They've worked these matters of technique and function out carefully. The taxpayer wants the best for his money, and of course clones are expensive. With the cell-manipulations, and the incubation in Ngama Placentae, and the maintenance and training of the foster-parent groups, we end up costing about three million apiece."

"For your next generation," Martin said, still struggling, "I suppose you . . . you breed?"

"We females are sterile," said Beth with perfect equanimity; "you remember that the Y chromosome was deleted from our original cell. The males can interbreed with approved singletons, if they want to. But to get John Chow again as often as they want, they just reclone a cell from this clone."

Martin gave up the struggle. He nodded and chewed cold toast. "Well," said one of the Johns, and all changed mood, like a flock of starlings that change course in one wingflick, following a leader so fast that no eye can see which leads. They were ready to go. "How about a look at the mine? Then we'll unload the equipment. Some nice new models in the roboats; you'll want to see them. Right?" Had Pugh or Martin not agreed they might have found it hard to say so. The Johns were polite but unanimous; their decisions carried. Pugh, Commander of Libra Base 2, felt a qualm. Could he boss around this superman-woman-entity-of-ten? and a genius at that? He stuck close to Martin as they suited for outside. Neither said anything.

Four apiece in the three large jetsleds, they slipped off north from the dome, over Libra's dun rugose skin, in starlight.

"Desolate," one said.

It was a boy and girl with Pugh and Martin. Pugh wondered if these were the two that had shared a sleeping-bag last night. No doubt they wouldn't mind if he asked them. Sex must be as handy as breathing, to them. Did you two breathe last night?

"Yes," he said, "it is desolate."

"This is our first time Off, except training on Luna." The girl's voice was definitely a bit higher and softer.

"How did you take the big hop?"

"They doped us. I wanted to experience it." That was the boy; he sounded wistful. They seemed to have more personality, only two at a time. Did repetition of the individual negate individuality?

"Don't worry," said Martin, steering the sled, "you can't experience no-time because it isn't there."

"I'd just like to once," one of them said. "So we'd know."

The Mountains of Merioneth showed leprotic in starlight to the east, a plume of freezing gas trailed silvery from a vent-hole to the west, and the sled tilted groundward. The twins braced for the stop at one moment, each with a slight protective gesture to the other. Your skin is my skin, Pugh thought, but literally, no metaphor. What would it be like, then, to have someone as close to you as that? Always to be answered when you spoke, never to be in pain alone. Love your neighbor as you love yourself. . . . That hard old problem was solved. The neighbor was the self: the love was perfect.

And here was Hellmouth, the mine.

Pugh was the Exploratory Mission's ET geologist, and Martin his technician and cartographer; but when in the course of a local survey Martin had discovered the U-mine, Pugh had given him full credit, as well as the onus of prospecting the lode and planning the Exploitation Team's job. These kids had been sent out from Earth years before Martin's reports got there, and had not known what their job would be until they got here. The Exploitation Corps simply sent out teams regularly and blindly as a dandelion sends out its seeds, knowing there would be a job for them on Libra or the next planet out or one they hadn't even heard about yet. The Government wanted uranium too urgently to wait while reports drifted home across the light-years. The stuff was like gold, old-fashioned but essential, worth mining extraterrestrially and shipping interstellar. Worth its weight in people, Pugh thought sourly, watching the tall young men and women go one by one, glimmering in starlight, into the black hole Martin had named Hellmouth.

As they went in their homeostatic forehead-lamps brightened. Twelve nodding gleams ran along the moist, wrinkled walls. Pugh heard Martin's radiation counter peeping twenty to the dozen up ahead. "Here's the drop-off," said Martin's voice in the suit intercom, drowning out the peeping and the dead silence that was around them. "We're in a side-fissure; this is the main vertical vent in front of us." The black void gaped, its far side not visible in the headlamp beams. "Last vulcanism seems to have been a couple of thousand years ago. Nearest fault is twenty-eight kilos east, in the Trench. This region seems to be as safe seismically as anything in the area. The big basalt-flow overhead stabilizes all these substructures, so long as it remains stable itself. Your central lode is thirty-six meters down and runs in a series of five bubble-caverns northeast. It is a lode, a pipe of very high-grade ore. You saw the percentage figures, right? Extraction's going to be no problem. All you've got to do is get the bubbles topside."

"Take off the lid and let 'em float up." A chuckle. Voices began to talk, but they were all the same voice and the suit radio gave them no location in space. "Open the thing right up. —Safer that way. —But it's a solid basalt roof, how thick, ten meters here? —Three to twenty, the report said. —Blow good ore all over the lot. —Use this access we're in, straighten it a bit and run slider-rails for the robos. —Import burros. —Have we got enough propping material? —What's your estimate of total payload mass, Martin?"

"Say over five million kilos and under eight."

"Transport will be here in ten E-months. —It'll have to go pure. —No, they'll have the mass problem in NAFAL shipping licked by now; remember it's been sixteen years since we left Earth last Tuesday. —Right, they'll send the whole lot back and purify it in Earth orbit. —Shall we go down, Martin?"

"Go on. I've been down."

The first one—Aleph? (Heb., the ox, the leader)— swung onto the ladder and down; the rest followed. Pugh and Martin stood at the chasm's edge. Pugh set his intercom to exchange only with Martin's suit, and noticed Martin doing the same. It was a bit wearing, this listening to one person think aloud in ten voices, or was it one voice speaking the thoughts of ten minds?

"A great gut," Pugh said, looking down into the black pit, its veined and warted walls catching stray gleams of headlamps far below. "A cow's bowel. A bloody great constipated intestine."

Martin's counter peeped like a lost chicken. They stood inside the epileptic planet, breathing oxygen from tanks, wearing suits impermeable to corrosives and harmful radiations, resistant to a two-hundred-degree range of temperatures, tear-proof, and as shock-resistant as possible given the soft vulnerable stuff inside.

"Next hop," Martin said, "I'd like to find a planet that has nothing whatever to exploit."

"You found this."

"Keep me home next time."

Pugh was pleased. He had hoped Martin would want to go on working with him, but neither of them was used to talking much about their feelings, and he had hesitated to ask. "I'll try that," he said.

"I hate this place. I like caves, you know. It's why I came in here. Just spelunking. But this one's a bitch.

Mean. You can't ever let down in here. I guess this lot can handle it, though. They know their stuff."

"Wave of the future, whatever," said Pugh.

The wave of the future came swarming up the ladder, swept Martin to the entrance, gabbled at and around him: "Have we got enough material for supports? —If we convert one of the extractor-servos to anneal, yes. —Sufficient if we miniblast? —Kaph can calculate stress."

Pugh had switched his intercom back to receive them; he looked at them, so many thoughts jabbering in an eager mind, and at Martin standing silent among them, and at Hellmouth, and the wrinkled plain. "Settled! How does that strike you as a preliminary schedule, Martin?"

"It's your baby," Martin said.

Within five E-days, the Johns had all their material and equipment unloaded and operating, and were starting to open up the mine. They worked with total efficiency. Pugh was fascinated and frightened by their effectiveness, their confidence, their independence. He was no use to them at all. A clone, he thought, might indeed be the first truly stable, self-reliant human being. Once adult it would need nobody's help. It would be sufficient to itself physically, sexually, emotionally, intellectually. Whatever he did, any member of it would always receive the support and approval of his peers, his other selves. Nobody else was needed.

Two of the clone stayed in the dome doing calculations and paperwork, with frequent sled-trips to the mine for measurements and tests. They were the mathematicians of the clone, Zayin and Kaph. That is, as Zayin explained, all ten had had thorough mathematical training from age three to twenty-one, but from twenty-one to twenty-three she and Kaph had gone on with math while the others intensified other specialties, geology, mining engineering, electronic engineering, equipment robotics, applied atomics, and so on. "Kaph and I feel," she said, "that we're the element of the clone closest to what John Chow was in his singelton lifetime. But of course he was principally in biomath, and they didn't take us far in that."

"They needed us most in this field," Kaph said, with the patriotic priggishness they sometimes evinced.

Pugh and Martin soon could distinguish this pair from the others, Zayin by gestalt, Kaph only by a discolored left fourth fingernail, got from an ill-aimed hammer at the age of six. No doubt there were many such differences, physical and psychological, among them; nature might be identical, nurture could not be. But the differences were hard to find. And part of the difficulty was that they really never talked to Pugh and Martin. They joked with them, were polite, got along fine. They gave nothing. It was nothing one could complain about; they were very pleasant, they had the standardized American friendliness. "Do you come from Ireland, Owen?"

Nobody comes from Ireland, Zayin."

"There are lots of Irish-Americans."

"To be sure, but no more Irish. A couple of thousand in all the island, the last I knew. They didn't go in for birth-control, you know, so the food ran out. By the Third Famine there were no Irish left at all but the priesthood, and they were all celibate, or nearly all."

Zayin and Kalph smiled stiffly. They had no experience of either bigotry or irony. "What are you then, ethnically?" Kalph asked, and Pugh replied, "A Welshman."

"Is it Welsh that you and Martin speak together?"

None of your business, Pugh thought, but said, "No, it's his dialect, not mine: Argentinean. A descendent of Spanish."

"You learned it for private communication?"

"Whom had we here to be private from? It's just that sometimes a man likes to speak his native language."

"Ours is English," Kaph said unsympathetically. Why should they have sympathy? That's one of the things you give because you need it back.

"Is Wells quaint?" asked Zayin.

"Wells? Oh, Wales, it's called. Yes. Wales is quaint." Pugh switched on his rock-cutter, which prevented further conversation by a synapse-destroying whine, and while it whined he turned his back and said a profane word in Welsh.

That night he used the Argentine dialect for private communication. "Do they pair off in the same couples, or change every night?"

Martin looked surprised. A prudish expression, unsuited to his features, appeared for a moment. It faded. He too was curious. "I think it's random."

"Don't whisper, man, it sounds dirty. I think they rotate."

"On a schedule?"

"So nobody gets omitted."

Martin gave a vulgar laugh and smothered it. "What about us? Aren't we omitted?"

"That doesn't occur to them."

"What if I proposition one of the girls?"

"She'd tell the others and they'd decide as a group."

"I am not a bull," Martin said, his dark, heavy face heating up. "I will not be judged—"

"Down, down, *machismo*," said Pugh. "Do you mean to proposition one?"

Martin shrugged, sullen. "Let 'em have their incest."

"Incest is it, or masturbation?"

"I don't care, if they'd do it out of earshot!"

The clone's early attempts at modesty had soon worn off, unmotivated by any deep defensiveness of self or awareness of others. Pugh and Martin were daily deeper swamped under the intimacies of its constant emotional-sexual-mental interchange: swamped yet excluded.

"Two months to go," Martin said one evening.

"To what?" snapped Pugh. He was edgy lately and Martin's sullenness got on his nerves.

"To relief."

In sixty days the full crew of their Exploratory Mission were due back from their survey of the other planets of the system. Pugh was aware of this.

"Crossing off the days on your calendar?" he jeered.

"Pull yourself together, Owen."

"What do you mean?"

"What I say."

They parted in contempt and resentment.

Pugh came in after a day alone on the Pampas, a vast lava-plain the nearest edge of which was two hours south by jet. He was tired, but refreshed by solitude. They were not supposed to take long trips alone, but lately had often done so. Martin stooped under bright lights, drawing one of his elegant, masterly charts: this one was of the whole face of Libra, the cancerous face. The dome was otherwise empty, seeming dim and large as it had before the clone came. "Where's the golden horde?"

Martin grunted ignorance, crosshatching. He straightened his back to glance around at the sun, which squatted feebly like a great red toad on the eastern plain, and at the clock, which said 18:45. "Some big quakes today," he said, retruning to his map. "Feel them down there? Lots of crates were falling around. Take a look at the seismo."

The needle jigged and wavered on the roll. It never

stopped dancing here. The roll had recorded five quakes of major intensity back in mid-afternoon; twice the needle had hopped off the roll. The attached computer had been activated to emit a slip reading, "Epicenter 61' N by 4'24" E."

"Not in the Trench this time."

"I thought I felt a bit different from usual. Sharper."

"In Base One I used to lie awake all night feeling the ground jump. Queer how you get used to things."

"Go spla if you didn't. What's for dinner?"

"I thought you'd have cooked it."

"Waiting for the clone."

Feeling put upon, Pugh got out a dozen dinnerboxes, stuck two in the Instobake, pulled them out. "All right, here's dinner."

"Been thinking," Martin said, coming to the table. "What if some clone cloned itself? Illegally. Made a thousand duplicates—ten thousand. Whole army. They could make a tidy power-grab, couldn't they?"

"But how many millions did this lot cost to rear? Artificial placentae and all that. It would be hard to keep secret, unless they had a planet to themselves. . . . Back before the Famines when Earth had national governments, they talked about that: clone your best soldiers, have whole regiments of them. But the food ran out before they could play that game."

They talked amicably, as they used to do.

"Funny," Martin said, chewing. "They left early this morning, didn't they?"

"All but Kaph and Zayin. They thought they'd get the first payload aboveground today. What's up?"

"They weren't back for lunch."

"They won't starve, to be sure."

"They left at seven."

"So they did." Then Pugh saw it. The air-tanks held eight hours' supply.

"Kaph and Zayin carried out spare cans when they left. Or they've got a heap out there."

"They did, but they brought the whole lot in to recharge." Martin stood up, pointing to one of the stacks of stuff that cut the dome into rooms and alleys.

"There's an alarm signal on every imsuit."

"It's not automatic."

Pugh was tired and still hungry. "Sit down and eat, man. That lot can look after themselves."

Martin sat down, but did not eat. "There was a big

quake, Owen. The first one. Big enough, it scared me."

After a pause Pugh sighed and said, "All right."

Unenthusiastically, they got out the two-man sled that was always left for them, and headed it north. The long sunrise covered everything in poisonous red Jell-O. The horizontal light and shadow made it hard to see, raised walls of fake iron ahead of them through which they slid, turned the convex plain beyond Hellmouth into a great dimple full of bloody water. Around the tunnel entrance a wilderness of machinery stood, cranes and cables and servos and wheels and diggers and robocarts and sliders and control-huts, all slanting and bulking incoherently in the red light. Martin jumped from the sled, ran into the mine. He came out again, to Pugh. "Oh God, Owen, it's down," he said. Pugh went in and saw, five meters from the entrance, the shiny, moist, black wall that ended the tunnel. Newly exposed to air, it looked organic, like visceral tissue. The tunnel entrance, enlarged by blasting and double-tracked for robocarts, seemed unchanged until he noticed thousands of tiny spiderweb cracks in the walls. The floor was wet with some sluggish fluid.

"They were inside," Martin said.

"They may be still. They surely had extra air-cans—"

"Look, Owen, look at the basalt flow, at the roof; don't you see what the quake did, look at it."

The low hump of land that roofed the caves still had the unreal look of an optical illusion. It had reversed itself, sunk down, leaving a vast dimple or pit. When Pugh walked on it he saw that it too was cracked with many tiny fissures. From some a whitish gas was seeping, so that the sunlight on the surface of the gas-pool was shafted as if by the waters of a dim red lake.

"The mine's not on the fault. There's no fault here!"

Pugh came back to him quickly. "No, there's no fault, Martin. Look, they surely weren't all inside together."

Martin followed him and searched among the wrecked machines dully, then actively. He spotted the airsled. It had come down heading south, and struck at an angle in a pothole of colloidal dust. It had carried two riders. One was half sunk in the dust, but his suit-meters registered normal functioning; the other hung strapped onto the tilted sled. Her imsuit had burst open on the broken legs, and the body was frozen hard as any rock. That was all they found. As both regulation and custom demanded, they cremated the dead at once with the laser-guns they carried by regulation and had never used before. Pugh, knowing he was going to be sick, wrestled the survivor onto the two-man sled and sent Martin off to the dome with him. Then he vomited, and flushed the waste out of his suit, and finding one four-man sled undamaged followed after Martin, shaking as if the cold of Libra had got through to him.

The survivor was Kaph. He was in deep shock. They found a swelling on the occiput that might mean concussion, but no fracture was visible.

Pugh brought two glasses of food-concentrate and two chasers of aquavit. "Come on," he said. Martin obeyed, drinking off the tonic. They sat down on crates near the cot and sipped the aquavit.

Kaph lay immobile, face like beeswax, hair bright black to the shoulders, lips stiffly parted for faintly gasping breaths.

"It must have been the first shock, the big one," Martin said. "It must have slid the whole structure sideways. Till it fell in on itself. There must be gas layers in the lateral rocks, like those formations in the Thirty-first Quadrant. But there wasn't any sign—" As he spoke the world slid out from under them. Things leaped and clattered, hopped and jigged, shouted Ha! Ha! Ha! "It was like this at fourteen hours," said Reason shakily in Martin's voice, amidst the unfastening and ruin of the world. But Unreason sat up, as the tumult lessened and things ceased dancing, and screamed aloud.

Pugh leaped across his spilled aquavit and held Kaph down. The muscular body flailed him off. Martin pinned the shoulders down. Kaph screamed, struggled, choked; his face blackened. "Oxy," Pugh said, and his hand found the right needle in the medical kit as if by homing instinct; while Martin held the mask he stuck the needle home to the vagus nerve, restoring Kaph to life.

"Didn't know you knew that stunt," Martin said, breathing hard.

"The Lazarus Jab; my father was a doctor. It doesn't often work," Pugh said. "I want that drink I spilled. Is the quake over? I can't tell."

"Aftershocks. It's not just you shivering."

"Why did he suffocate?"

"I don't know, Owen. Look in the book."

Kaph was breathing normally and his color was restored, only his lips were still darkened. They poured a new shot of courage and sat down by him again with their medical guide. "Nothing about cyanosis or asphyxiation under 'shock' or 'concussion.' He can't have breathed in anything with his suit on. I don't know. We'd get as much good out of *Mother Mog's Home Herbalist*. . . .'Anal Hemorrhoids,' fy!" Pugh pitched the book to a crate-table. It fell short, because either Pugh or the table was still unsteady.

"Why didn't he signal?"

"Sorry?"

"The eight inside the mine never had time. But he and the girl must have been outside. Maybe she was in the entrance, and got hit by the first slide. He must have been outside, in the control-hut maybe. He ran in, pulled her out, strapped her onto the sled, started for the dome. And all that time never pushed the panic button in his imsuit. Why not?"

"Well, he'd had that whack on his head. I doubt he ever realized the girl was dead. He wasn't in his senses. But if he had been I don't know if he'd have thought to signal us. They looked to one another for help."

Martin's face was like an Indian mask, grooves at the mouth-corners, eyes of dull coal. "That's so. What must he have felt, then, when the quake came and he was outside, alone—"

In answer Kaph screamed.

He came up off the cot in the heaving convulsions of one suffocating, knocked Pugh right down with his flailing arm, staggered into a stack of crates and fell to the floor, lips blue, eyes white. Martin dragged him back onto the cot and gave him a whiff of oxygen, then knelt by Pugh, who was just sitting up, and wiped at his cut cheekbone. "Owen, are you all right, are you going to be all right, Owen?"

"I think I am," Pugh said. "Why are you rubbing that on my face?"

It was a short length of computer-tape, now spotted with Pugh's blood. Martin dropped it. "Thought it was a towel. You clipped your cheek on that box there."

"Is he out of it?"

"Seems to be."

They stared down at Kaph lying stiff, his teeth a white line inside dark parted lips.

"Like epilepsy. Brain damage maybe?"

"What about shooting him full of meprobamate?"

Pugh shook his head. "I don't know what's in that shot I already gave him for shock. Don't want to overdose him."

"Maybe he'll sleep it off now."

"I'd like to myself. Between him and the earthquake I can't seem to keep on my feet."

"You got a nasty crack there. Go on, I'll sit up a while."

Pugh cleaned his cut cheek and pulled off his shirt, then paused.

"Is there anything we ought to have done—have tried to do—"

"They're all dead," Martin said heavily, gently.

Pugh lay down on top of his sleeping-bag, and one instant later was wakened by a hideous, sucking, struggling noise. He staggered up, found the needle, tried three times to jab it in correctly and failed, began to massage over Kaph's heart. "Mouth-to-mouth," he said, and Martin obeyed. Presently Kaph drew a harsh breath, his heartbeat steadied, his rigid muscles began to relax.

"How long did I sleep?"

"Half an hour."

They stood up sweating. The ground shuddered, the fabric of the dome sagged and swayed. Libra was dancing her awful polka again, her Totentanz. The sun, though rising, seemed to have grown larger and redder; gas and dust must have been stirred up in the feeble atmosphere.

"What's wrong with him, Owen?"

"I think he's dying with them."

"Them— But they're dead, I tell you."

"Nine of them. They're all dead, they were crushed or suffocated. They were all him, he is all of them. They died, and now he's dying their deaths one by one."

"Oh pity of God," said Martin.

The next time was much the same. The fifth time was worse, for Kaph fought and raved, trying to speak but getting no words out, as if his mouth were stopped with rocks or clay. After that the attacks grew weaker, but so did he. The eighth seizure came at about four-thirty; Pugh and Martin worked till five-thirty doing all they could to keep life in the body that slid without protest into death. They kept him, but Martin said, "The next will finish him." And it did; but Pugh breathed his own breath into the inert lungs, until he himself passed out.

He woke. The dome was opaqued and no light on. He listened and heard the breathing of two sleeping men. He slept, and nothing woke him till hunger did.

The sun was well up over the dark plains, and the planet had stopped dancing. Kaph lay asleep. Pugh and Martin drank tea and looked at him with proprietary triumph.

When he woke Martin went to him: "How do you feel, old man?" There was no answer. Pugh took Martin's place and looked into the brown, dull eyes that gazed toward but not into his own. Like Martin he quickly turned away. He heated food-concentrate and brought it to Kaph. "Come on, drink."

He could see the muscles in Kaph's throat tighten. "Let me die," the young man said.

"You're not dying."

Kaph spoke with clarity and precision: "I am nine-tenths dead. There is not enough of me left alive."

That precision convinced Pugh, and he fought the conviction. "No," he said, peremptorily. "They are dead. The others. Your brothers and sisters. You're not them, you're alive. You are John Chow. Your life is in your own hands."

The young man lay still, looking into a darkness that was not there.

Martin and Pugh took turns taking the Exploitation hauler and a spare set of robos over to Hellmouth to salvage equipment and protect it from Libra's sinister atmosphere, for the value of the stuff was, literally, astronomical. It was slow work for one man at a time, but they were unwilling to leave Kaph by himself. The one left in the dome did paperwork, while Kaph sat or lay and stared into his darkness, and never spoke. The days went by silent.

The radio spat and spoke: the Mission calling from ship. "We'll be down on Libra in five weeks, Owen. Thirty-four E-days nine hours I make it as of now. How's tricks in the old dome?"

"Not good, chief. The Exploit team were killed, all but one of them, in the mine. Earthquake. Six days ago."

The radio crackled and sang starsong. Sixteen seconds lag each way; the ship was out around Planet 11 now. "Killed, all but one? You and Martin were unhurt?"

"We're all right, chief."

Thirty-two seconds.

"*Passerine* left an Exploit team out here with us. I may put them on the Hellmouth project then, instead of the Quadrant Seven project. We'll settle that when we come down. In any case you and Martin will be relieved at Dome Two. Hold tight. Anything else?"

"Nothing else."

Thirty-two seconds.

"Right then. So long, Owen."

Kaph had heard all this, and later on Pugh said to him, "The chief may ask you to stay here with the other Exploit team. You know the ropes here." Knowing the exigencies of Far Out Life, he wanted to warn the young man. Kaph made no answer. Since he had said. "There is not enough of me left alive," he had not spoken a word.

"Owen," Martin said on suit intercom, "he's spla. Insane. Psycho."

"He's doing very well for a man who's died nine times."

"Well? Like a turned-off android is well? The only emotion he has left is hate. Look at his eyes."

"That's not hate, Martin. Listen, it's true that he has, in a sense, been dead. I cannot imagine what he feels. But it's not hatred. He can't even see us. It's too dark."

"Throats have been cut in the dark. He hates us because we're not Aleph and Yod and Zayin."

"Maybe. But I think he's alone. He doesn't see us or hear us, that's the truth. He never had to see anyone else before. He never was alone before. He had himself to see, talk with, live with, nine other selves all his life. He doesn't know how you go it alone. He must learn. Give him time."

Martin shook his heavy head. "Spla," he said. "Just remember when you're alone with him that he could break your neck one-handed."

"He could do that," said Pugh, a short, soft-voiced man with a scarred cheekbone; he smiled. They were just outside the dome airlock, programming one of the servos to repair a damaged hauler. They could see Kaph sitting inside the great half-egg of the dome like a fly in amber.

"Hand me the insert pack there. What makes you think he'll get any better?

"He has a strong personality, to be sure."

"Strong? Crippled. Nine-tenths dead, as he put it."

"But he's not dead. He's a live man: John Kaph Chow. He had a jolly queer upbringing, but after all every boy has got to break free of his family. He will do it."

"I can't see it."

"Think a bit, Martin bach. What's this cloning for? To repair the human race. We're in a bad way. Look a me. My IIQ and GC are half this John Chow's. Yet they wanted me so badly for the Far Out Service that when I volunteered they took me and fitted me out with an artificial lung and corrected my myopia. Now if there were enough good sound lads about would they be taking one-lunged shortsighted Welshmen?"

"Didn't know you had an artificial lung."

"I do then. Not tin, you know. Human, grown in a tank from a bit of somebody; cloned, if you like. That's how they make replacement-organs, the same general idea as cloning, but bits and pieces instead of whole people. It's my own lung now, whatever. But what I am saying is this; there are too many like me these days and not enough like John Chow. They're trying to raise the level of the human genetic pool, which is a mucky little puddle since the population crash. So then if a man is cloned, he's a strong and clever man. It's only logic, to be sure."

Martin grunted; the servo began to hum.

Kaph had been eating little; he had trouble swallowing his food, choking on it, so that he would give up trying after a few bites. He had lost eight or ten kilos. After three weeks or so, however, his appetite began to pick up, and one day he began to look through the clone's possessions, the sleeping-bags, kits, papers which Pugh had stacked neatly in a far angle of a packing-crate alley. He sorted, destroyed a heap of papers and oddments, made a small packet of what remained, then relapsed into his walking coma.

Two days later he spoke. Pugh was trying to correct a flutter in the tape-player, and failing; Martin had the jet out, checking their maps of the Pampas. "Hell and damnation!" Pugh said, and Kaph said in a toneless voice, "Do you want me to do that?"

Pugh jumped, controlled himself, and gave the machine to Kaph. The young man took it apart, put it back together, and left it on the table.

"Put on a tape," Pugh said with careful casualness, busy at another table.

Kaph put on the topmost tape, a chorale. He lay down on his cot. The sound of a hundred human voices singing together filled the dome. He lay still, his face blank.

In the next days he took over several routine jobs, unasked. He undertook nothing that wanted initiative, and if asked to do anything he made no response at all.

"He's doing well," Pugh said in the dialect of Argentina.

"He's not. He's turning himself into a machine. Does what he's programmed to do, no reaction to anything else. He's worse off than when he didn't function at all. He's not human any more."

Pugh sighed. "Well, good night," he said in English. "Good night, Kaph."

"Good night," Martin said; Kaph did not.

Next morning at breakfast Kaph reached across Martin's plate for the toast. "Why don't you ask for it?" Martin said with the geniality of repressed exasperation. "I can pass it."

"I can reach it," Kaph said in his flat voice.

"Yes, but look. Asking to pass things, saying good night or hello, they're not important, but all the same when somebody says something a person ought to answer. . . ."

The young man looked indifferently in Martin's direction; his eyes still did not seem to see clear through to the person he looked toward. "Why should I answer?"

"Because somebody has said something to you."

"Why?"

Martin shrugged and laughed. Pugh jumped up and turned on the rock-cutter.

Later on he said, "Lay off that, please, Martin."

"Manners are essential in small isolated crews, some kind of manners, whatever you work out together. He's been taught that, everybody in Far Out knows it. Why does he deliberately flout it?"

"Do you tell yourself good night?"

"So?"

"Don't you see Kaph's never known anyone but himself?"

Martin brooded and then broke out, "Then by God this cloning business is all wrong. It won't do. What are a lot of duplicate geniuses going to do for us when they don't even know we exist?"

Pugh nodded. "It might be wiser to separate the clones and bring them up with others. But they make such a grand team this way."

"Do they? I don't know. If this lot had been ten average inefficient ET engineers, would they all have been in the same place at the same time? Would they all have got killed? What if, when the quake came and things started caving in, what if all those kids ran the same way, farther into the mine, maybe, to save the one that was farthest in? Even Kaph was outside and went in. . . . It's hypothetical. But I keep thinking, out of ten ordinary confused guys, more might have got out."

"I don't know. It's true that identical twins tend to die at about the same time, even when they have never seen each other. Identity and death, it is very strange. . . ."

The days went on, the red sun crawled across the dark sky, Kaph did not speak when spoken to, Pugh and Martin snapped at each other more frequently each day. Pugh complained of Martin's snoring. Offended, Martin moved his cot clear across the dome and also ceased speaking to Pugh for some while. Pugh whistled Welsh dirges until Martin complained, and then Pugh stopped speaking for a while.

The day before the Mission ship was due, Martin announced he was going over to Merioneth.

"I thought at least you'd be giving me a hand with the computer to finish the rock-analyses," Pugh said, aggrieved.

"Kaph can do that. I want one more look at the Trench. Have fun," Martin added in dialect, and laughed, and left.

"What is that language?"

"Argentinean. I told you that once, didn't I?"

"I don't know." After a while the young man added, "I have forgotten a lot of things, I think."

"It wasn't important, to be sure," Pugh said gently, realizing all at once how important this conversation was. "Will you give me a hand running the computer, Kaph?"

He nodded.

Pugh had left a lot of loose ends, and the job took them all day. Kaph was a good co-worker, quick and systematic, much more so than Pugh himself. His flat voice, now that he was talking again, got on the nerves; but it didn't matter, there was only this one day left to get through and then the ship would come, the old crew, comrades and friends.

During tea-break Kaph said, "What will happen if the Explorer ship crashes?"

"They'd be killed.'

"To you, I mean."

"To us? We'd radio SOS all signals, and live on half rations till the rescue cruiser from Area Three Base came. Four and half E-years away it is. We have life-support here for three men for, let's see maybe between four and five years. A bit tight, it would be."

"Would they send a cruiser for three men?"

"They would."

Kaph said no more.

"Enough cheerful speculations," Pugh said cheerfully, rising to get back to work. He slipped sideways and the chair avoided his hand; he did a sort of half-pirouette and fetched up hard against the dome-hide. "My goodness," he said, reverting to his native idiom, "what is it?"

"Quake," said Kaph.

The teacups bounced on the table with a plastic cackle, a litter of papers slid off a box, the skin of the dome swelled and sagged. Underfoot there was a huge noise, half sound half shaking, a subsonic boom.

Kaph sat unmoved. An earthquake does not frighten a man who died in an earthquake.

Pugh, white-faced, wiry black hair sticking out, a frightened man, said, "Martin is in the Trench."

"What trench?"

"The big fault line. The epicenter for the local quakes. Look at the seismograph." Pugh struggled with the stuck door of a still-jittering locker.

"Where are you going?"

"After him."

"Martin took the jet. Sleds aren't safe to use during quakes. They go out of control."

"For God's sake, man, shut up."

Kaph stood up, speaking in a flat voice as usual. "It's unnecessary to go out after him now. It's taking an unnecessary risk."

"If his alarm goes off, radio me," Pugh said, shut the headpiece of his suit, and ran to the lock. As he went out Libra picked up her ragged skirts and danced a bellydance from under his feet clear to the red horizon.

Inside the dome, Kaph saw the sled go up, tremble like a meteor in the dull red daylight, and vanish to the northeast. The hide of the dome quivered; the earth coughed. A vent south of the dome belched up a slow-flowing bile of black gas.

A bell shrilled and a red light flashed on the central control board. The sign under the light read Suit Two and scribbled under that, A.G.M. Kaph did not turn the signal off. He tried to radio Martin, then Pugh, but got no reply from either.

When the aftershocks decreased he went back to work, and finished up Pugh's job. It took him about two hours. Every half hour he tried to contact Suit One, and got no reply, then Suit Two and got no reply. The red light had stopped flashing after an hour.

It was dinnertime. Kaph cooked dinner for one, and ate it. He lay down on his cot.

The aftershocks had ceased except for faint rolling tremors at long intervals. The sun hung in the west, oblate,

pale-red, immense. It did not sink visibly. There was
no sound at all.

Kaph got up and began to walk about the messy, half-
packed-up, overcrowded, empty dome. The silence continued. He went to the player and put on the first tape
that came to hand. It was pure music, electronic, without
harmonies, without voices. It ended. The silence continued.

Pugh's uniform tunic, one button missing, hung over a
stack of rock-samples. Kaph stared at it a while.

The silence continued.

The child's dream: There is no one else alive in the
world but me. In all the world.

Low, north of the dome, a meteor flickered.

Kaph's mouth opened as if he were trying to say something, but no sound came. He went hastily to the north
wall and peered out into the gelatinous red light.

The little star came in and sank. Two figures blurred
the airlock. Kaph stood close beside the lock as they came
in. Martin's imsuit was covered with some kind of dust
so that he looked raddled and warty like the surface of
Libra. Pugh had him by the arm.

"Is he hurt?"

Pugh shucked his suit, helped Martin peel off his.
"Shaken up," he said, curt.

"A piece of cliff fell onto the jet," Martin said, sitting
down at the table and waving his arms. "Not while I was
in it, though. I was parked, see, and poking about that
carbon-dust area when I felt things humping. So I went
out onto a nice bit of early igneous I'd noticed from above,
good footing and out from under the cliffs. Then I saw
this bit of the planet fall off onto the flyer, quite a sight it
was, and after a while it occurred to me the spare aircans
were in the flyer, so I leaned on the panic button. But I
didn't get any radio reception, that's always happening
here during quakes, so I didn't know if the signal was
getting through either. And things went on jumping
around and pieces of the cliff coming off. Little rocks
flying around, and so dusty you couldn't see a meter ahead.
I was really beginning to wonder what I'd do for breathing
in the small hours, you know, when I saw old Owen
buzzing up the Trench in all that dust and junk like a big
ugly bat—"

"Want to eat?" said Pugh.

"Of course I want to eat. How'd you come through the
quake here, Kaph? No damage? It wasn't a big one
actually, was it, what's the seismo say? My trouble was

I was in the middle of it. Old Epicenter Alvaro. Felt
like Richter Fifteen there—total destruction of planet—"
"Sit down," Pugh said. "Eat."
After Martin had eaten a little his spate of talk ran dry.
He very soon went off to his cot, still in the remote angle
where he had removed it when Pugh complained of his
snoring. "Good night, you one-lunged Welshman," he said
across the dome.
"Good night."
There was no more out of Martin. Pugh opaqued the
dome, turned the lamp down to a yellow glow less than
a candle's light, and sat doing nothing, saying nothing,
withdrawn.
The silence continued.
"I finished the computations."
Pugh nodded thanks.
"The signal from Martin came through, but I couldn't
contact you or him."
Pugh said with effort, "I should not have gone. He had
two hours of air left even with only one can. He might have
been heading home when I left. This way we were all out
of touch with one another. I was scared."
The silence came back, punctuated now by Martin's
long, soft snores.
"Do you love Martin?"
Pugh looked up with angry eyes: "Martin is my friend.
We've worked together, he's a good man." He stopped.
After a while he said, "Yes, I love him. Why did you ask
that?"
Kaph said nothing, but he looked at the other man. His
face was changed, as if he were glimpsing something he
had not seen before; his voice too was changed. "How can
you . . . ? How do you . . .?"
But Pugh could not tell him. "I don't know," he said,
"it's practice, partly. I don't know. We're each of us alone,
to be sure. What can you do but hold your hand out in
the dark?"
Kaph's strange gaze dropped, burned out by its own
intensity.
"I'm tired," Pugh said. "That was ugly, looking for him
in all that black dust and muck, and mouths opening and
shutting in the ground. . . . I'm going to bed. The ship
will be transmitting to us by six or so." He stood up and
stretched.
"It's a clone," Kaph said. "The other Exploit team they're
bringing with them."

"Is it, then?"

"A twelveclone. They came out with us on the *Passerine*."

Kaph sat in the small yellow aura of the lamp seeming to look past it at what he feared: the new clone, the multiple self of which he was not part. A lost piece of a broken set, a fragment, inexpert at solitude, not knowing even how you go about giving love to another individual, now he must face the absolute, closed self-sufficiency of the clone of twelve; that was a lot to ask of the poor fellow, to be sure. Pugh put a hand on his shoulder in passing. "The chief won't ask you to stay here with a clone. You can go home. Or since you're Far Out maybe you'll come on farther out with us. We could use you. No hurry deciding. You'll make out all right."

Pugh's quiet voice trailed off. He stood unbuttoning his coat, stooped a little with fatigue. Kaph looked at him and saw the thing he had never seen before: saw him: Owen Pugh, the other, the stranger who held his hand out in the dark.

"Good night," Pugh mumbled, crawling into his sleeping-bag and half asleep already, so that he did not hear Kaph reply after a pause, repeating, across darkness, benediction.

ON THEME

by Ursula K. Le Guin

WRITERS of science fiction get asked a lot of funny questions, but the one we dread most, because it is asked most often, is, "Where do you get your ideas from?" At this most of us will either flinch and mumble, or say something snappy like "When did you stop beating your wife?" Because the question is unanswerable. It implies that there is a mysterious storeroom somewhere full of Strange Ideas, where sf writers go when they need one. Well, of course there is such a storeroom, but it is the writer's own head. And the ideas in it can come from anywhere. For example, I can trace the sources of the main general ideas of one novel of mine thus: they came from a) five years of reading (for pure pleasure) everything I could find about Antarctica, b) thirty-eight years of being of the feminine gender. But that isn't what the fellow asking the question *means*. Sometimes— especially if he is a scientist—he goes on, "But I mean, do you ever read any real science?" The only appropriate response to this is to strangle him and donate the body to the nearest anatomy laboratory. Yes, Virginia, sf writers do read science. In their own peculiar fashion.

After all, until you can read the lines, you can't read between the lines.

But every now and then one can say of a specific short story that it did begin with a single, specific idea, with a single, specific source. This is the case with "Nine Lives."

I had been reading *The Biological Time Bomb* by Gordon Rattray Taylor, a splendid book for biological ignoramuses, and had been intrigued by his chapter on the cloning process. I knew a little about cloning (the excitation of single cells in laboratory conditions to replicate themselves or the organism of which they were a part), but so little that I had not got past carrots, where it all started, to speculate about the notion of duplicating entire higher organisms, such as frogs, donkeys, or people. I did not have to read between the lines: Rattray Taylor did it for me. He pointed out that some biologists have been contemplating these more ambitious possibilities quite seriously (why don't people ever ask biologists where they get *their* ideas from?). In thinking about this possibility, I found it alarming. In wondering why I found it alarming, I began to see that the duplication of anything complex enough to have personality would involve the whole issue of what personality is—the question of individuality, of identity, of selfhood. Now that question is a hammer that rings the great bells of Love and Death.

The idea, then, came from the biologists' laboratories, via a book of popular biology. But in itself it was no more than an idea—a kind of hook to hang a story on, like the idea-for-an-ingenious-murder which most detective novels are hung (up) on. When I began to realize its implications concerning human identity, then it became a *theme*.

In other words, I don't think sf writers merely play with scientific or other ideas, merely speculate or extrapolate; I think—if they're doing their job—they get very involved with them. They take them personally, which is precisely what scientists must forbid themselves to do.

They try to hook them in with the rest of existence. A writer's ability to find a genuine theme (and the great writers' ability to develop profound and complex themes out of very simple materials) seems to be a function of his capacity to see implications, to make connections.

This description of the process is, of course, intellectualized after the fact. I'm trying to describe a synthetic process analytically, which is misleading. It all took place in the dark, in silence, by groping. I didn't say Oh! an idea!—Ah! a theme!— It just began to come together, in odd moments, out of odd corners of my mind. As well as I can recall (this was four years ago and in another country) it "came together," presented itself as a story to be written, rather suddenly: when it found itself expressed in, embodied in, a *situation*. There's this fellow— no, it's two people—working in isolation in a hostile environment, and then a clone of identical twins arrives as a team of assistants.

Together with this glimpse of the situation, the character of Owen Pugh presented itself, complete and unquestionable, and indeed, at that very point, pretty enigmatic. Having a character really is very like having a baby, sometimes, except that there's a lot less warning, and babies don't arrive full-grown. But one has the same sense of pleased bewilderment. For instance, why was this man short and thin? Why was he honest, disorderly, nervous, and warmhearted? Why on earth was he Welsh? I had no idea at the time. There he was. And his name was Owen Pugh, to be sure. It was up to me to do right by him. All he offered (just like a baby) was his existence. Any assurance that this highly individualized, peculiar, intransigent person really was somehow related to my theme had to be taken on trust. A writer must trust the unconscious, even when it produces unexpected Welshmen.

The setting offered itself as simply, as clearly, with as little conscious reasoning-out. It was to be "a hostile environment." In other words, a nasty place. A place where no human beings or animals or plants lived, or had lived, or ought to live. A place where one would feel lonely, threatened—where even a whole group of people would feel isolated, and where their need for one another, their interdependence, would always be stressed, and under stress. No need to look far for such a place; just think of any description of any actual planet we know about other than the Earth. . . . The dome in which they live only emphasizes their isolation and their enforced closeness. The cave, though, the cave where the mine is—why a cave? I don't know. After all it could perfectly well have been a surface mine. I know about the accepted symbolisms and implications of large dark caves; but none of them quite seems to fit. The planet is personalized in the very first sentence as "she," and the cave is described, both by me and by Pugh, in clearly physiological terms, as if it were somebody's innards. All the same, I don't see a symbolism either of rape, or of birth and rebirth; or rather I can see it, but it doesn't feel right. The cave may involve *inwardness* in a nonsexual, totally personal sense —the kind of fearful, compulsive consciousness of one's own body one may have when ill, a sense of being trapped "inside" something and unable to communicate—a pathological inwardness. Or the cave may *be* the unconscious. I really don't know.

Given a setting, a character, and a theme, it was now high time for the plot to develop itself. For me, this is the chancy part. This is where intellect enters in, where choices must be deliberately made. I have lost innumerable splendid people and fascinating places at this point. They are all there, but they won't interact. The scenery is scenic, the people run around and talk . . . but it doesn't add up. I have a huge, depressing collection of manuscripts of one page, or three, or ten, or twenty pages, which start out grand, and even seem to be going on just grand, and then stop, bang, in midair: where I realized that it wasn't coming together, it wasn't adding up. This is a wasteful way to work. But for some of us it's the only way. It's a kind of experimenting, testing. You have to see if your theme holds up, if it works. Sometimes by making such false starts you see what the right one might be: a change in the plot, a different point of view, a novel instead of a short story. Sometimes, most often, it's just a loss. But those who trust to the unconscious must expect a good deal of wasted effort. It's only when you write in obedience to external standards, or for a market, that you can turn out reams with never a false start; or when you're a plain genius, on the order of Shakespeare or Mozart.

As well as I can remember, I worked out a plot for this story pretty firmly in only a couple of hours' brooding and scribbling—probably a few sentences and fragments on one side of a notebook page. I have to actually write down the major events, usually in a few words, with a lot of underlinings and circles and fingers pointing, to keep it all straight in my head; because when I get to writing I have a tendency to skip the high points of the narrative, and dwell lovingly on all the dull bits in between. I'm not sure I knew precisely what the ending would be, at this point; but I knew there was an ending, and that I would come to it. That is, I knew the theme was imperative enough, strong enough, that it would find its narrative beginning, middle, and end quite surely.

Along with this planning or foreseeing of what "should happen," and during the actual writing, the other characters began to develop themselves. There are only two of them, of course: Martin, and the clone. And now the reasons for some of Owen's peculiarities became clear. He was the *opposite of something.* He was peculiar, because the clone were aggressively "normal." He was frail and sloppy because they were healthy, strong, and efficient. He was over thirty because they were young. He was an introvert because they were extraverted. He was Welsh because they were abstractly American—the marginal, defensive culture vs. the dominant, domineering one. Etc. Though conceived as something's opposite, he defined himself and took on substance first because he was a person, with all the limitations and irreducibilities of personality: whereas none of the clone-members was an independent person, and the group, the clone itself, was a kind of marvelously effective simulacrum of a human individual. The real precedes the imitation.

Martin is also defined by contrast with Owen, but the contrast is more superficial. I wanted the reader to be able to tell him apart from Owen. I wanted the reader to feel the reality of Owen's and Martin's friendship—asserting itself, as friendships do, against disparities and strains and irritations. So he came out dark, sturdy, cynical, Argentinean, etc. But on a deeper level, he is simply a reinforcement of Owen: a restatement of certain qualities which differentiate the individual from the group—independence, touchiness, humor, self-respect, self-doubt, compassion, anxiety, etc.

So the story was written, and revised, and re-revised. No revisions eliminated one glaring technical flaw in it. I am sure you will have noticed it; it concerns point of view. The story is mostly told in the "limited" mode, or a sort of comfortable compromise between that and the "omniscient" mode; if we see through anybody's eyes it is always Owen's, and there are several surreptitious slitherings directly into Owen's mind; in any case, Owen is always on stage. All this is conventional and I think painlessly acceptable. Then Owen goes off in a panic to try and rescue Martin, and Kaph is left alone in the dome— and instead of following Owen, we stay with Kaph. We don't get inside his mind yet, but in the sentence, "The child's dream. . . . " we're pretty close to it. Then, in the next to last paragraph, all pretense is dropped and we are in Kaph's mind, seeing with his eyes. This is a bit awkward. It strains the frame. It can be defended only on one ground, that it is stylistically significant. That is, up until the last three pages it was not possible to get inside Kaph's mind, because it was closed to all outsiders —all others but the clone—himself. That it is now done, that we now see through Kaph's eyes, implies (awkwardly and oversubtly) that it is now possible. We can reach Kaph. He is no longer self-sufficient.

Self-sufficient. There the hammer strikes the great bells. What does it mean, to be sufficient to yourself? What is a self? Can a self be sufficient to itself? If not, what is the role of the Other? Is the existence of a foreign self a threat or a necessity, or both? And what is the role of total otherness—of death? Can a being unaware of itself be aware of its own mortality, and conversely, can a being ignorant of its mortality be aware of itself—or of the Other?

I didn't answer any of these questions, of course. To get a question asked properly is all I hope to do, or at least to indicate that there are questions to be asked.

But now that sounds like a scientist talking, and I should quickly say that I pretend to no objectivity whatever. That's not my job. My interpretation of the effect of cloning, of replication, on human personality, is a subjective and biased one, exaggerated for dramatic purposes, not intended to be prophetic, not even fully descriptive of known facts. The only basis for it, outside my imagination, is a couple of books I had read some while before about identical twins (a subject of interest to psychologists and human biologists): a grounding in fact, yes, but used only as a take-off platform. As for personal experience, I had never even met a pair of identical twins, though as a kid I had had good friends who were fraternal (sororal) twins, different in physique and personality but more closely linked emotionally than most sisters. And that's all. It was guesswork, prejudice, and imagination, with no pretense of accuracy. The theme controlled the interpretation from beginning to end.

However, I did not misrepresent any fact that I knew to be accepted by science or by general personal experience. That would be lying.

A lot of people, especially of the businessman turn of mind, would laugh at that statement. It's all a pack of lies anyhow, isn't it? They see no distinction between fiction and lying; or they reverse the artist's evaluation, dismissing the aesthetic fiction because it is useless, and accepting the lie (in the form of advertising, business ethics, national security, etc.) because it is profitable. A fiction writer is unlike a businessman or politician, and more like a scientist, in that he will not lie if he can help it. But he is unlike any scientist (except to some extent the mathematicians) in that his guide, the thing to which his imagination is subordinated, is not fact, but the aesthetic imperative. To this he submits everything else freely and happily. That *is* his job. The theme of a story is more than its descriptive content, its intellectual concepts, or its moral assumptions; it is the coherence of these to form an aesthetically determined whole. And that "wholeness" (however complex, however subtle) is, in the end, the only standard by which it may be judged.

AN ANNOTATED "MASKS"

by Damon Knight

THEME, IF such a thing exists, is the spirit of a story, its ghost, which can be separated from the story only at the cost of the patient's life. What I think is much more interesting and useful is the idea of a story as *mechanism*. What is the story supposed to accomplish? What means are used? Do they work? Etc.

"Masks" was the result of a deliberate effort to make a story about what I call here a TP or "total prosthesis"

—a complete artificial body. I wanted to do this because it was topical, in the sense that there had been a lot of discussion of this kind of thing and a good deal of R&D on sophisticated artificial limbs. The subject was one which had a deep attraction for me; I had written about it in two early stories called "Ask Me Anything" and "Four in One," and again in a collaboration with James Blish, "Tiger Ride." And, finally, I wanted to do it because it seemed to me that most treatments of the subject in science fiction had been romantic failures, and that to do it realistically would be an achievement.

I read and thought about prosthetic problems until I was sure I knew how my protagonist's artificial body would be built and maintained. I realized that it would take a government-funded effort comparable to the Manhattan Project, so I couldn't put it in the corner of a lab somewhere: the background of the story grew out of this. The other characters were those who had to be there.

Glimpses of scenes and action came to me spontaneously: the first of these was the one which gave the story its title—the silvery mask worn by the protagonist. As I got deeper into the story, I became more and more convinced that the psychic effect of losing the whole body and having it replaced by a prosthetic system had been too casually shrugged off by previous writers, even C. L. Moore in her beautiful "No Woman Born."

The protagonist of my story is the ultimate eunuch: as another character remarks, "This man has had everything cut off." Such a catastrophic loss can be compensated for only by a massive mental tilt. The man in the story has lost the physiological basis of every human emotion, with one exception. He has no heart to accelerate its beat, no gonads, no sweat glands, no endocrines except the pineal: he can't feel love, fear, hate, affection. But he can and must accept his own clean smooth functioning as the norm. When he looks at the sweaty, oozing meat that other people are made of, his one possible emotion is disgust, brought to an intensity we cannot imagine.

Given this, and the fact that the man is intelligent, I saw that the conflict of the story must turn on his effort to conceal the truth about himself, because if it became known the project would be terminated and his life shortened. My problem in writing the story was to hold this back as a revelation, and at the same time to build the story logically, without leaving out anything essential.

The story is a mechanism designed to draw the reader

in, provoke his curiosity and interest, involve him in the argument, and give him a series of emotional experiences culminating (I hope) in a double view of the protagonist, from inside and outside, which will squeeze out of him a drop of sympathy and horror.

MASKS

by Damon Knight

This opening (not part of the early drafts) performs several functions—gets us promptly into the action of the story, describes part of the background, introduces minor characters, and so on. In a sense, the "mechanical lobster" is an image of the protagonist. The opening lacks elegance, but it is an effective brute-force solution to a difficult problem, and it satisfies a requirement of mine that wherever possible, the first sentence of a story should foreshadow everything that follows.

All this about the man's dreaming is meant to indicate that something is deeply wrong, and that the project managers don't know what it is. (I tried inserting the dream itself here where it falls in sequence, and found that it did not work.) The presence of the man from Washington makes it clear that the problem is serious and urgent.

THE EIGHT pens danced against the moving strip of paper, like the nervous claws of some mechanical lobster. Roberts, the technician, frowned over the tracings while the other two watched.

"Here's the wake-up impulse," he said, pointing with a skinny finger. "Then here, look, seventeen seconds more, still dreaming."

"Delayed response," said Babcock, the project director. His heavy face was flushed and he was sweating. "Nothing to worry about."

"OK, delayed response, but look at the difference in the tracings. Still dreaming, after the wake-up impulse, but the peaks are closer together. Not the same dream. More anxiety, more motor pulses."

"Why does he have to sleep at all?" asked Sinescu, the man from Washington. He was dark, narrow-faced. "You flush the fatigue poisons out, don't you? So what is it, something psychological?"

"He needs to dream," said Babcock. "It's true he has no physiological need for sleep, but he's got to dream. If he didn't, he'd start to hallucinate, maybe go psychotic."

"Psychotic," said Sinescu. "Well—that's the question, isn't it? How long has he been doing this?"

"About six months."

"In other words, about the time he got his new body— and started wearing a mask?"

"About that. Look, let me tell you something: he's rational. Every test—"

"Yes, OK, I know about tests. Well—so he's awake now?"

The technician glanced at the monitor board. "He's up. Sam and Irma are with him." He hunched his shoulders, staring at the EEG tracings again. "I don't know why it should bother me. It stands to reason, if he has dream needs of his own that we're not satisfying with the pro-

This much is prologue; now we make another entrance into the story. These successive delays are deliberate, used to increase the feeling of enigma or mystery about the protagonist.

Babcock is on the point of hallucinating with fatigue—another indicator of the seriousness of the problem, and also an echo of the protagonist's abnormal state of consciousness—a whiff of madness from the center of the story which we are now beginning to approach.

A false clue. The protagonist and I want you to think that his aberrant behavior is caused by nothing more than a fear of germs.

The masks of the title in their least important form. Others are the metal mask the protagonist wears, and the flesh masks that we all wear every day.

This alludes to another important fact about the protagonist's state of mind. The willingness to expose yourself to danger tends to decrease as life expectancy increases, grammed stuff, this is where he gets them in." His face hardened. "I don't know. Something about those peaks I don't like."

Sinescu raised his eyebrows. "You program his dreams?"

"Not program," said Babcock impatiently. "A routine suggestion to dream the sort of thing we tell him to. Somatic stuff, sex, exercise, sport."

"And whose idea was that?"

"Psych section. He was doing fine neurologically, every other way, but he was withdrawing. Psych decided he needed that somatic input in some form, we had to keep him in touch. He's alive, he's functioning, everything works. But don't forget, he spent forty-three years in a normal human body."

In the hush of the elevator, Sinescu said, "Washington."

Swaying, Babcock said, "I'm sorry; what?"

"You look a little rocky. Getting any sleep?"

"Not lately. What did you say before?"

"I said they're not happy with your reports in Washington."

"Goddamn it, I know that." The elevator door silently opened. A tiny foyer, green carpet, gray walls. There were three doors, one metal, two heavy glass. Cool, stale air. "This way."

Sinescu paused at the glass door, glanced through: a gray-carpeted living room, empty. "I don't see him."

"Around the el. Getting his morning checkup."

The door opened against slight pressure; a battery of ceiling lights went on as they entered. "Don't look up," said Babcock. "Ultraviolet." A faint hissing sound stopped when the door closed.

"And positive pressure in here? To keep out germs? Whose idea was that?"

"His." Babcock opened a chrome box on the wall and took out two surgical masks. "Here, put this on."

Voices came muffled from around the bend of the room. Sinescu looked with distaste at the white mask, then slowly put it over his head.

They stared at each other. "Germs," said Sinescu through the mask. "Is that rational?"

"All right, he can't catch a cold, or what have you, but think about it a minute. There are just two things now that could kill him. One is a prosthetic failure, and we guard against that; we've got five hundred people here, we check on the same principle that causes rich men to worry more about robbers than poor men do. You ride in airplanes although they sometimes crash; you cross busy intersections and breathe the air of big cities, because after all you can't live forever. But my protagonist *can.*

Some of this is needed to account for the mask. The drafting table will be used later.

Clues, not obvious enough to be interpreted correctly now, but I hope you will remember them later. *Fire* and *Storm* are novels without human protagonists. *The Wizard of Oz* is the first book in which the Tin Woodman appeared.

The plot turns on Irma, who could not be there unless she was Sam's wife. Like everybody else in the project, she is under intolerable pressure. She intuitively understands the protagonist's abnormality better than any of the others, and she can't bear it.

Rubbing your nose in something other writers have pretended not to notice: no prosthetic limb is ever going to look real enough to fool you.

Justifying the expense of the project as NASA often does. *Myoelectric* means controlled by nerve impulses, and *servo-controlled,* operated by motors which are part of feedback systems.

him out like an airplane. That leaves a cerebrospinal infection. Don't go in there with a closed mind."

The room was large, part living room, part library, part
workshop. Here was a cluster of Swedish-modern chairs,
a sofa, coffee table; here a workbench with a metal lathe,
electric crucible, drill press, parts bins, tools on wall-
boards; here a drafting table; here a free-standing wall of
bookshelves that Sinescu fingered curiously as they
passed. Bound volumes of project reports, technical jour-
nals, reference books; no fiction, except for *Fire* and
Storm by George Stewart and *The Wizard of Oz* in a worn
blue binding. Behind the bookshelves, set into a little al-
cove, was a glass door through which they glimpsed another living room, differently furnished: upholstered
chairs, a tall philodendron in a ceramic pot. "There's
Sam," Babcock said.

A man had appeared in the other room. He saw them,
turned to call to someone they could not see, then came
forward, smiling. He was bald and stocky, deeply tanned.
Behind him, a small pretty woman hurried up. She
crowded through after her husband, leaving the door open.
Neither of them wore a mask.

"Sam and Irma have the next suite," Babcock said.
"Company for him; he's got to have somebody around.
Sam is an old Air Force buddy of his and, besides, he's
got a tin arm."

The stocky man shook hands, grinning. His grip was
firm and warm. "Want to guess which one?" He wore
a flowered sport shirt. Both arms were brown, muscular
and hairy; but when Sinescu looked more closely, he saw
that the right one was a slightly different color, not
quite authentic.

Embarrassed, he said, "The left, I guess."

"Nope." Grinning wider, the stocky man pulled back
his right sleeve to show the straps.

"One of the spin-offs from the project," said Babcock. "Myoelectric, servo-controlled, weighs the same as
the other one. Sam, they about through in there?"

"Maybe so. Let's take a peek. Honey, you think you
could rustle up some coffee for the gentlemen?"

"Oh, why, sure." The little woman turned and darted
back through the open doorway.

The far wall was glass, covered by a translucent white
curtain. They turned the corner. The next bay was full of

All this background detail serves various subsidiary purposes, *e.g.* hinting at the protagonist's dislike of living things. Its main purpose, however, is just to give the characters a solid stage to walk around on.

medical and electronic equipment, some built into the walls, some in tall black cabinets on wheels. Four men in white coats were gathered around what looked like an astronaut's couch. Sinescue could see someone lying on it: feet in Mexican woven-leather shoes, dark socks, gray slacks. A mutter of voices.

"Not through yet," Babcock said. "Must have found something else they didn't like. Let's go out onto the patio a minute."

"Thought they checked him at night—when they exchange his blood, and so on . . . ?"

"They do," Babcock said. "And in the morning, too." He turned and pushed open the heavy glass door. Outside, the roof was paved with cut stone, enclosed by a green-plastic canopy and tinted-glass walls. Here and there were concrete basins, empty. "Idea was to have a roof garden out here, something green, but he didn't want it. We had to take all the plants out, glass the whole thing in."

Sam pulled out metal chairs around a white table and they all sat down. "How is he, Sam?" asked Babcock.

He grinned and ducked his head. "Mean in the mornings."

"Talk to you much? Play any chess?"

"Not too much. Works, mostly. Reads some, watches the box a little." His smile was forced; his heavy fingers were clasped together and Sinescu saw now that the fingertips of one hand had turned darker, the others not. He looked away.

"You're from Washington, that right?" Sam asked politely. "First time here? Hold on." He was out of his chair. Vague upright shapes were passing behind the curtained glass door. "Looks like they're through. If you gentlemen would just wait here a minute, till I see." He strode across the roof. The two men sat in silence. Babcock had pulled down his surgical mask; Sinescu noticed and did the same.

"Sam's wife is a problem," Babcock said, leaning nearer. "It seemed like a good idea at the time, but she's lonely here, doesn't like it—no kids—"

The door opened again and Sam appeared. He had a mask on, but it was hanging under his chin. "If you gentlemen would come in now."

In the living area, the little woman, also with a mask hanging around her neck, was pouring coffee from a flowered ceramic jug. She was smiling brightly but looked

I borrowed this device (periods instead of question marks) from Anthony Boucher's "The Quest For Saint Aquin." *Playboy*'s editors put the question marks back in.

unhappy. Opposite her sat someone tall, in gray shirt and slacks, leaning back, legs out, arms on the arms of his chair, motionless. Something was wrong with his face.

"Well, now," said Sam heartily. His wife looked up at him with an agonized smile.

The tall figure turned its head and Sinescu saw with an icy shock that its face was silver, a mask of metal with oblong slits for eyes, no nose or mouth, only curves that were faired into each other. "Project," said an inhuman voice.

Sinescu found himself half bent over a chair. He sat down. They were all looking at him. The voice resumed. "I said, are you here to pull the plug on the project." It was unaccented, indifferent.

"Have some coffee." The woman pushed a cup toward him.

Sinescu reached for it, but his hand was trembling and he drew it back. "Just a fact-finding expedition," he said.

"Bull. Who sent you—Senator Hinkel."

"That's right."

"Bull. He's been here himself; why send you. If you are going to pull the plug, might as well tell me." The face behind the mask did not move when he spoke, the voice did not seem to come from it.

"He's just looking around, Jim," said Babcock.

"Two hundred million a year," said the voice, "to keep one man alive. Doesn't make much sense, does it. Go on, drink your coffee."

Sinescu realized that Sam and his wife had already finished theirs and that they had pulled up their masks. He reached for his cup hastily.

"Hundred percent disability in my grade is thirty thousand a year. I could get along on that easy. For almost an hour and a half."

"There's no intention of terminating the project," Sinescu said.

"Phasing it out, though. Would you say phasing it out."

"Manners, Jim," said Babcock.

"OK. My worst fault. What do you want to know."

Sinescu sipped his coffee. His hands were still trembling. "That mask you're wearing," he started.

"Not for discussion. No comment, no comment. Sorry about that; don't mean to be rude; a personal matter. Ask me something—" Without warning, he stood up, blaring, "Get that damn thing out of here!" Sam's wife's cup

The puppy represents life in one of the forms we ordinarily find most appealing. See this in double vision, now or when you have finished the story—the puppy's furriness, liquid eye, wet tongue, etc., as we perceive them and as they appear to the protagonist.

I won't call attention to this every time, but notice now how the background has been distributed through the story.

The whole complex of mask, death, rebirth, embryo, and fetus can be observed in connection with the Latin *larva.* The Latin *lār, lāris,* mostly in the plural

smashed, coffee brown across the table. A fawn-colored
puppy was sitting in the middle of the carpet, cocking its
head, bright-eyed, tongue out.

The table tipped, Sam's wife struggled up behind it. Her
face was pink, dripping with tears. She scooped up the
puppy without pausing and ran out. "I better go with her,"
Sam said, getting up.

"Go on; and, Sam, take a holiday. Drive her into
Winnemucca, see a movie."

"Yeah, guess I will." He disappeared behind the book-
shelf wall.

The tall figure sat down again, moving like a man; it
leaned back in the same posture, arms on the arms of the
chair. It was still. The hands gripping the wood were
shapely and perfect but unreal: there was something wrong
about the fingernails. The brown, well-combed hair
above the mask was a wig; the ears were wax. Sinescu
nervously fumbled his surgical mask over his mouth and
nose. "Might as well get along," he said, and stood up.

"That's right, I want to take you over to Engineering
and R and D," said Babcock. "Jim, I'll be back in a little
while. Want to talk to you."

"Sure," said the motionless figure.

Babcock had had a shower, but sweat was soaking
through the armpits of his shirt again. The silent elevator,
the green carpet, a little blurred. The air cool, stale. Seven
years, blood and money, five hundred good men. Psych
section, Cosmetic, Engineering, R & D, Medical, Immu-
nology, Supply, Serology, Administration. The glass doors.
Sam's apartment empty, gone to Winnemucca with Irma.
Psych. Good men, but were they the best? Three of the
best had turned it down. Buried in the files. *Not like an
ordinary amputation, this man has had everything cut
off.*

The tall figure had not moved. Babcock sat down. The
silver mask looked back at him.

"Jim, let's level with each other."

"Bad, huh."

"Sure it's bad. I left him in his room with a bottle.
I'll see him again before he leaves, but God knows what
he'll say in Washington. Listen, do me a favor, take that
thing off."

"Sure." The hand rose, plucked at the edge of the silver
mask, lifted it away. Under it, the tan-pink face,
sculptured nose and lips, eyebrows, eyelashes, not hand-

lāres, "tutelar deities," is a personification of ancestral spirits. . . . The derivative of this name is *larva, larua,* "a ghost, specter," also "a mask, skeleton." . . . This word, *larva,* however, came to denote in our language, "the earliest stage of certain insects emerging wormlike from the egg, until they become pupae or chrysalises." In the Latin *pūpa* means "little girl, doll, puppet." The *larva* refers thus to the prenatal embryonic and fetal state. The ancestral ghost appears first as a frightening ghost, then as a mask, and finally reaches the stage of rebirth as a new being.

—Theodore Thass-Thienemann,
The Subconscious Language

The protagonist has to lie to Babcock, but I could not use him to lie to the reader. I solved the problem by having the protagonist tell Babcock plainly that he is going to lie, and the reason for it, knowing Babcock will dismiss and forget it.

some but good-looking, normal-looking. Only the eyes wrong, pupils too big. And the lips that did not open or move when it spoke. "I can take anything off. What does that prove."

"Jim, Cosmetic spent eight and half months on that model and the first thing you do is slap a mask over it. We've asked you what's wrong, offered to make any changes you want."

"No comment."

"You talked about phasing out the project. Did you think you were kidding?"

A pause. "Not kidding."

"All right, then open up, Jim, tell me; I have to know. They won't shut the project down; they'll keep you alive but that's all. There are seven hundred on the volunteer list, including two U.S. Senators. Suppose one of them gets pulled out of an auto wreck tomorrow. We can't wait till then to decide; we've got to know now. Whether to let the next one die or put him into a TP body like yours. So talk to me."

"Suppose I tell you something, but it isn't the truth."

"Why would you lie?"

"Why do you lie to a cancer patient."

"I don't get it. Come on, Jim."

"OK, try this. Do I look like a man to you."

"Sure."

"Bull. Look at this face." Calm and perfect. Beyond the fake irises, a wink of metal. "Suppose we had all the other problems solved and I could go into Winnemucca tomorrow; can you see me walking down the street—going into a bar—taking a taxi."

"Is that all it is?" Babcock drew a deep breath. "Jim, sure there's a difference, but for Christ's sake, it's like any other prosthesis—people get used to it. Like that arm of Sam's. You see it, but after a while you forget it, you don't notice."

"Bull. You pretend not to notice. Because it would embarrass the cripple."

Babcock looked down at his clasped hands. "Sorry for yourself?"

"Don't give me that," the voice blared. The tall figure was standing. The hands slowly came up, the fists clenched. "I'm in this thing, I've been in it for two years. I'm in it when I go to sleep, and when I wake up, I'm still in it."

Babcock looked up at him. "What do you want, facial mobility? Give us twenty years, maybe ten, we'll lick it."

From the cover of the July, 1931, *Astounding Stories*, illustrating Jack Williamson's "The Doom From Planet 4." Writers are magpies.

From Henry Kuttner's "Camouflage," and later on Larry Niven's "Becalmed in Hell"; but would you ride in a cyborg-controlled ship? *Cf.* also Kubrick's *2001*.

A little joke: without thinking, Babcock started to say, "Keep your pecker up."

"I want you to close down Cosmetic."

"But that's—"

"Just listen. The first model looked like a tailor's dummy, so you spent eight months and came up with this one, and it looks like a corpse. The whole idea was to make me look like a man, the first model pretty good, the second model better, until you've got something that can smoke cigars and joke with women and go bowling and nobody will know the difference. You can't do it, and if you could what for."

"I don't— Let me think about this. What do you mean, a metal—"

"Metal, sure, but what difference does that make. I'm talking about shape. Function. Wait a minute." The tall figure stode across the room unlocked a cabinet, came back with rolled sheets of paper. "Look at this."

The drawing showed an oblong metal box on four jointed legs. From one end protruded a tiny mushroom-shaped head on a jointed stem and a cluster of arms ending in probes, drills, grapples. "For moon prospecting."

"Too many limbs," said Babcock after a moment. "How would you—"

"With the facial nerves. Plenty of them left over. Or here." Another drawing. "A module plugged into the control system of a spaceship. That's where I belong, in space. Sterile environment, low grav, I can go where a man can't go and do what a man can't do. I can be an asset, not a goddamn billion-dollar liability."

Babcock rubbed his eyes. "Why didn't you say anything before?

"You were all hipped on prosthetics. You would have told me to tend my knitting."

Babcock's hands were shaking as he rolled up the drawings.

"Well, by God, this just may do it. It just might." He stood up and turned toward the door. "Keep your—" He cleared his throat. "I mean hang tight, Jim."

"I'll do that."

When he was alone, he put on his mask again and stood motionless a moment, eye shutters closed. Inside, he was running clean and cool; he could feel the faint reassuring hum of pumps, click of valves and relays. They had given him that: cleaned out all the offal, replaced it with machinery that did not bleed, ooze or suppurate. He thought of the lie he had told Babcock. *Why do you lie*

Now dig it. You are made of plastic and metal, running clean and cool. The others, the flesh people, are bags of decaying meat; they have pimples, their skin is shiny with grease, there's food stuck between their teeth, they're crawling with microbes, scaly with dandruff, they ooze and they stink.

to a cancer patient? But they would never get it, never understand.

He sat down at the drafting table, clipped a sheet of paper to it and with a pencil began to sketch a rendering of the moon-prospector design. When he had blocked in the prospector itself, he began to draw the background of craters. His pencil moved more slowly and stopped; he put it down with a click.

No more adrenal glands to pump adrenaline into his blood, so he could not feel fright or rage. They had released him from all that—love, hate, the whole sloppy mess—but they had forgotten there was still one emotion he could feel.

Sinescu, with the black bristles of his beard sprouting through his oily skin. A whitehead ripe in the crease beside his nostril.

Moon landscape, clean and cold. He picked up the pencil again.

Babcock, with his broad pink nose shining with grease, crusts of white matter in the corners of his eyes. Food mortar between his teeth.

Sam's wife, with raspberry-colored paste on her mouth. Face smeared with tears, a bright bubble in one nostril. And the damn dog, shiny nose, wet eyes . . .

He turned. The dog was there, sitting on the carpet, wet red tongue out *left the door open again* dripping, wagged its tail twice, then started to get up. He reached for the metal T square, leaned back, swinging it like an ax, and the dog yelped once as metal sheared bone, one eye spouting red, writhing on its back, dark stain of piss across the carpet and he hit it again, hit it again.

The body lay twisted on the carpet, fouled with blood, ragged black lips drawn back from teeth. He wiped off the T square with a paper towel, then scrubbed it in the sink with soap and steel wool, dried it and hung it up. He got a sheet of drafting paper, laid it on the floor, rolled the body over onto it without spilling any blood on the carpet. He lifted the body in the paper, carried it out onto the patio, then onto the unroofed section, opening the doors with his shoulder. He looked over the wall. Two stories down, concrete roof, vents sticking out of it, nobody watching. He held the dog out, let it slide off the paper, twisting as it fell. It struck one of the vents, bounced, a red smear. He carried the paper back inside, poured the blood down the drain, then put the paper into the incinerator chute.

Splashes of blood were on the carpet, the feet of the

The story is circular: now we come back to the dream, which explains everything. And if I have been successful, I've made you feel like my protagonist for a moment, and learn what it's like to be an enemy of life.

Now I maintain that "theme" is an academic shibboleth, an imaginary entity that is read into a work by the teacher in order that the student may be required to read it out. If my story has a theme, what is it? "The tragedy of inadequate communications"? That is certainly a part of the story, and it is certainly a part of *Othello*, too, but is that all that *Othello* means? Be damned if it is.

In the academic sense, viz., *the meaning of a work of art reduced to a single phrase or sentence,* the theme of "Masks" or of any work of art is: "Life is like this." But to expand the meaning of "this" requires the whole story. It is easy to see that "Masks" makes use of a number of ideas and relationships of the kind that are usually called "thematic." I might instance the recurring appearance of amputations in my work, or the several levels of meaning in the word "masks." But to extract these little nuggets of meaning and dismiss the rest as vehicle is to falsify the story. A story is not a kiddy-car containing a message. A story is a formal structure which the author builds around you; in the process you learn to see some portion of the world in a new way and you experience certain esthetic responses and certain emotions. At the end you come away purged with pity and terror. That's all. It's enough.

drafting table, the cabinet, his trouser legs. He sponged them all up with paper towels and warm water. He took off his clothing, examined it minutely, scrubbed it in the sink, then put in in the washer. He washed the sink, rubbed himself down with disinfectant and dressed again. He walked through into Sam's silent apartment, closing the glass door behind him. Past the potted philodendron, overstuffed furniture, red-and-yellow painting on the wall, out onto the roof, leaving the door ajar. Then back through the patio, closing doors.

Too bad. How about some goldfish.

He sat down at the drafting table. He was running clean and cool. The dream this morning came back to his mind, the last one, as he was struggling up out of sleep: *slithery kidneys burst gray lungs blood and hair ropes of guts covered with yellow fat oozing and sliding and oh god the stink like the breath of an outmouth no sound nowhere he was putting a yellow stream down the slide of the dunghole and*

He began to ink in the drawing, first with a fine steel pen, then with a nylon brush. *his heel slid and he was falling could not stop himself falling into slimy bulging softness higher than his chin, higher and he could not move paralyzed and he tried to scream tried to scream tried to scream*

The prospector was climbing a crater slope with its handling members retracted and its head tilted up. Behind it the distant ringwall and the horizon, the black sky, the pinpoint stars. And he was there, and it was not far enough, not yet, for the Earth hung overhead like a rotten fruit, blue with mold, crawling, wrinkling, purulent and alive.

POINT OF VIEW:
Who's Minding the Store?

*". . . and in the final, shattering
explosion, we all died."*

THE STUDENT who ended his story with the phrase above
has posed his reader a rather obvious logical question, one
that exists less obviously in all works of fiction: who's
telling the story? The author, of course, creates the story,
but in the complex transaction between author and reader,
between manufacturer and consumer, it is reasonable to
ask, Who's minding the store?

The "who" in these questions may be one or several
persons variously referred to as *narrator, persona, mask,
center of consciousness, auctorial presence,* or *implied author;* whatever he is, whatever term used to describe him,
he is not to be confused with the living creator, the person who pays taxes and raises a family and hassles
with editors and finds himself, someday, the subject of
doctoral dissertations on his life and times.

For the moment, call him *narrator,* recognize that he
can be either inside or outside the story, and term his
relationship to the story *point of view. Internal point of
view* is written in the first person as though by a partici-
pant in the action or—at least—a witness to it. Here the
"I" of the story may be a principal character, a minor
character, or a group of characters (*composite point of
view*). Stories written from the point of view of the principal character are the most limiting; only one mind is
revealed, and the revelation is perforce subjective. A minor
character who tells a story can be somewhat more detached, can speculate about the actions of the principal
character and provide a running gloss on those actions
that would be implausible if attributed to the principal
character himself. Still less limiting is the composite point
of view such as that employed in the Japanese film

Roshomon or Wilkie Collins's *The Moonstone* or Browning's *The Ring and the Book*. It is typical of the epistolary story and frequently used in tales of crime and mystery, perhaps in the form of court transcripts or tape recordings.

The *external point of view*, written in the third person, gives the author far more scope, particularly in characterization. If he employs an *omniscient* point of view, his knowledge of the events in the story and of the minds of his characters is all-inclusive. He may move where he will, see what he wishes, understand all, even predict the future within the little world of the story. He is, in that little world, God. But gods tend to be remote, and an author may wish to sacrifice some power to gain greater immediacy or deeper reader identification with a principal character. To do so, he arbitrarily limits his omniscience. The *limited point of view* confines the author's knowledge to one character; knowledge of other characters comes only through their interaction with the focal character; events unknown to him remain unknown to the reader. Strether in James's *The Ambassadors* is such a focal character.

Even more constrictive is the *detached point of view*, in which the author reports, without comment or analysis, what might be seen or heard by a detached observer. The narrator is a camera and tape recorder and a series of olfactory and tactile sensors, free to move into implausible places but otherwise incapable of reporting more than the sensors indicate. This is Hemingway in "The Killers," the technique of the pseudo-documentary, Lawrence Sanders's *The Anderson Tapes*.

A final and dreadfully complex aspect of point of view: However we define "narrator," there is likely to be yet another personality involved in the creative transaction. This *auctorial presence* may correspond precisely with the narrator (either within or outside the story), in which case it is lost in him and will not trouble us. In other cases, the auctorial presence seems to haunt the narrator, injecting in subtle ways the personality of the artist. When it is perceptible, the auctorial presence occupies a mediating position between author, characters, and reader. The distance between this presence and the other parties to the writer-reader-story transaction varies along scales of moral, philosophical, or even physical values. The gullible Gulliver is far away from the perceptive Dean Swift but close to the reader, his closeness fostered by his ingenuous first-person narrative. The Houyhnhnms are close, at least philosophically, to the Dean, enormously far away from him physically and geographically, and totally divorced from the Yahoos, the race to which the reader is forced to admit he belongs. And somewhere within the circle of Dean and Gulliver and Yahoo and Houyhnhnm and reader is the *auctorial presence,* mediating, making us aware of closeness and distance, of our identification with Yahoo and longing for Houyhnhnm, so that at the end we feel the pathos of Gulliver's departure and then laugh wryly at ourselves for being affected by: ". . . I took a second leave of my Master: But as I was going to prostrate myself to kiss his Hoof, he did me the honour to raise it gently to my Mouth. I am not ignorant how much I have been censured for mentioning this last Particular. Detractors are pleased to think it improbable, that so illustrious a Person should descend to give so great a Mark of Distinction to a Creature so inferior as I."

THE PLANNERS

by Kate Wilhelm

RAE STOPPED before the one-way glass, stooped and peered at the gibbon infant in the cage. Darin watched her bitterly. She straightened after a moment, hands in smock pockets, face innocent of any expression what-so-goddam-ever, and continued to saunter toward him through the aisle between the cages.

"You still think it is cruel, and worthless?"

"Do you, Dr. Darin?"

"Why do you always do that? Answer my question with one of your own?"

"Does it infuriate you?"

He shrugged and turned away. His lab coat was on the chair where he had tossed it. He pulled it on over his sky-blue sport shirt.

"How is the Driscoll boy?" Rae asked.

He stiffened, then relaxed again. Still not facing her, he said, "Same as last week, last year. Same as he'll be until he dies."

The hall door opened and a very large, very homely face appeared. Stu Evers looked past Darin, down the aisle. "You alone? Thought I heard voices."

"Talking to myself," Darin said. "The committee ready yet?"

"Just about. Dr. Jacobsen is stalling with his nose-throat spray routine, as usual." He hesitated a moment, glancing again down the row of cages, then at Darin. "Wouldn't you think a guy allergic to monkeys would find some other line of research?"

Darin looked, but Rae was gone. What had it been this time: the Driscoll boy, the trend of the project itself? He wondered if she had a life of her own when she was away. "I'll be out at the compound," he said. He passed Stu in the doorway and headed toward the livid greenery of Florida forests.

The cacophony hit him at the door. There were four hundred sixty-nine monkeys on the thirty-six acres of wooded ground the research department was using. Each monkey was screeching, howling, singing, cursing, or otherwise making its presence known. Darin grunted and headed toward the compound. The Happiest Monkeys in the World, a newspaper article had called them. Singing Monkeys, a subhead announced. MONKEYS GIVEN SMART-NESS PILLS, the most enterprising paper had proclaimed. *Cruelty Charged*, added another in subdued, sorrowful tones.

The compound was three acres of carefully planned and maintained wilderness, completely enclosed with thirty-foot-high, smooth plastic walls. A transparent dome covered the area. There were one-way windows at intervals along the wall. A small group stood before one of the windows: the committee.

Darin stopped and gazed over the interior of the compound through one of the windows. He saw Heloise and Skitter contentedly picking nonexistent fleas from one another. Adam was munching on a banana; Homer was lying on his back idly touching his feet to his nose. A couple of the chimps were at the water fountain, not drinking, merely pressing the pedal and watching the fountain, now and then immersing a head or hand in the bowl of cold water. Dr. Jacobsen appeared and Darin joined the group.

"Good morning, Mrs. Bellbottom," Darin said politely. "Did you know your skirt has fallen off?" He turned from her to Major Dormouse. "Ah, Major, and how many of the enemy have you swatted to death today with your pretty little yellow rag?" He smiled pleasantly at a pimply young man with a camera. "Major, you've brought a professional peeping tom. More stories in the paper, with pictures this time?" The pimply young man shifted his position, fidgeted with the camera. The major was fiery; Mrs. Bellbottom was on her knees peering under a bush, looking for her skirt. Darin blinked. None of them had on any clothing. He turned toward the window. The chimps were drawing up a table, laden with tea things, silver, china, tiny finger sandwiches. The chimps were all wearing flowered shirts and dresses. Hortense had on a ridiculous flop-brimmed sun hat of pale green straw. Darin leaned against the fence to control his laughter.

"Soluble ribonucleic acid," Dr. Jacobsen was saying when Darin recovered, "sRNA for short. So from the gross beginnings when entire worms were trained and fed to other worms that seemed to benefit from the original training, we have come to these more refined methods. We now extract the sRNA molecule from the trained animals and feed it, the sRNA molecules in solution, to untrained specimens and observe the results."

The young man was snapping pictures as Jacobsen talked. Mrs. Whoosis was making notes, her mouth a lipless line, the sun hat tinging her skin with green. The sun on her patterned red and yellow dress made it appear to jiggle, giving her fleshy hips a constant rippling motion. Darin watched, fascinated. She was about sixty.

". . . my colleague, who proposed this line of experimentation, Dr. Darin," Jacobsen said finally, and Darin bowed slightly. He wondered what Jacobsen had said about him, decided to wait for any questions before he said anything.

"Dr. Darin, is it true that you also extract this substance from people?"

"Every time you scratch yourself, you lose this substance," Darin said. "Every time you lose a drop of blood, you lose it. It is in every cell of your body. Sometimes we take a sample of human blood for study, yes."

"And inject it into those animals?"

"Sometimes we do that," Darin said. He waited for the next, the inevitable question, wondering how he would answer it. Jacobsen had briefed them on what to answer, but he couldn't remember what Jacobsen had said. The question didn't come. Mrs. Whoosis stepped forward, staring at the window.

Darin turned his attention to her; she averted her eyes,

quickly fixed her stare again on the chimps in the compound. "Yes, Mrs. uh . . . Ma'am?" Darin prompted her. She didn't look at him.

"Why? What is the purpose of all this?" she asked. Her voice sounded strangled. The pimpled young man was inching toward the next window.

"Well," Darin said, "our theory is simple. We believe that learning ability can be improved drastically in nearly every species. The learning curve is the normal, expected bell-shaped curve, with a few at one end who have the ability to learn quite rapidly, with the majority in the center who learn at an average rate, and a few at the other end who learn quite slowly. With our experiments we are able to increase the ability of those in the broad middle, as well as those in the deficient end of the curve so that their learning abilities match those of the fastest learners of any given group. . . ."

No one was listening to him. It didn't matter. They would be given the press release he had prepared for them, written in simple language, no polysyllables, no complicated sentences. They were all watching the chimps through the windows. He said, "So we gabbled the gazooka three times wretchedly until the spirit of camping fired the girls." One of the committee members glanced at him. "Whether intravenously or orally, it seems to be equally effective," Darin said, and the perspiring man turned again to the window. "Injections every morning . . . rejections, planned diet, planned parenthood, planned plans planning plans." Jacobsen eyes him suspiciously. Darin stopped talking and lighted a cigarette. The woman with the unquiet hips turned from the window, her face very red. "I've seen enough," she said. "This sun is too hot out here. May we see the inside laboratories now?"

Darin turned them over to Stu Evers inside the building. He walked back slowly to the compound. There was a grin on his lips when he spotted Adam on the far side, swaggering triumphantly, paying no attention to Hortense who was rocking back and forth on her haunches, looking very dazed. Darin saluted Adam, then, whistling, returned to his office. Mrs. Driscoll was due with Sonny at 1 P.M.

Sonny Driscoll was fourteen. He was five feet nine inches, weighed one hundred sixty pounds. His male nurse was six feet two inches and weighed two hundred twenty-seven pounds. Sonny had broken his mother's arm when he was twelve; he had broken his father's arm and leg when he was thirteen. So far the male nurse was intact. Every morning Mrs. Driscoll lovingly washed and bathed her baby, fed him, walked him in the yard, spoke happily to him of plans for the coming months, or sang nursery songs to him. He never seemed to see her. The male nurse, Johnny, was never farther than three feet from his charge when he was on duty.

Mrs. Driscoll refused to think of the day when she would have to turn her child over to an institution. Instead she placed her faith and hope in Darin.

They arrived at two-fifteen, earlier than he had expected them, later than they had planned to be there.

"The kid kept taking his clothes off," Johnny said morosely. The kid was taking them off again in the office. Johnny started toward him, but Darin shook his head. It didn't matter. Darin got his blood sample from one of the muscular arms, shot the injection into the other one. Sonny didn't seem to notice what he was doing. He never seemed to notice. Sonny refused to be tested. They got him to the chair and table, but he sat staring at nothing, ignoring the blocks, the bright balls, the crayons, the candy. Nothing Darin did or said had any discernible effect. Finally the time was up. Mrs. Driscoll and Johnny got him dressed once more and left. Mrs. Driscoll thanked Darin for helping her boy.

Stu and Darin held class from four to five daily. Kelly O'Grady had the monkeys tagged and ready for them when they showed up at the schoolroom. Kelly was very tall, very slender and red-haired. Stu shivered if she accidentally brushed him in passing; Darin hoped one day Stu would pull an Adam on her. She sat primly on her high stool with her notebook on her knee, unaware of the change that came over Stu during school hours, or, if aware, uncaring. Darin wondered if she was really a Barbie doll fully programmed to perform laboratory duties, and nothing else.

He thought of the Finishing School for Barbies where long-legged, high-breasted, stomachless girls went to get shaved clean, get their toenails painted pink, their nipples removed, and all body openings sewn shut, except for their mouths, which curved in perpetual smiles and led nowhere.

The class consisted of six black spider-monkeys who had not been fed yet. They had to do six tasks in order: 1) pull a rope; 2) cross the cage and get a stick that was released by the rope; 3) pull the rope again; 4) get the second stick that would fit into the first; 5) join the sticks together; 6) using the lengthened stick, pull a bunch of bananas close enough to the bars of the cage to reach them and take them inside where they could eat them. At five the monkeys were returned to Kelly, who wheeled them away one by one back to the stockroom. None of them had performed all the tasks, although two had gone through part of them before the time ran out.

Waiting for the last of the monkeys to be taken back to its quarters, Stu asked, "What did you do to that bunch of idiots this morning? By the time I got them, they all acted dazed."

Darin told him about Adam's performance; they were both laughing when Kelly returned. Stu's laugh turned to something that sounded almost like a sob. Darin wanted to tell him about the school Kelly must have attended, thought better of it, and walked away instead.

His drive home was through the darkening forests of interior Florida for sixteen miles on a narrow straight road.

"Of course, I don't mind living here," Lea had said once, nine years ago when the Florida appointment had come through. And she didn't mind. The house was air-conditioned; the family car, Lea's car, was air-conditioned; the back yard had a swimming pool big enough to float the Queen Mary. A frightened, large-eyed Florida girl did the housework, and Lea gained weight and painted sporadically, wrote sporadically—poetry—and entertained faculty wives regularly. Darin suspected that sometimes she entertained faculty husbands also.

"Oh, Professor Dimples, one hour this evening? That will be fifteen dollars, you know." He jotted down the appointment and turned to Lea. "Just two more today and you will have your car payment. How about that!" She twined slinky arms about his neck, pressing tight high breasts hard against him. She had to tilt her head slightly for his kiss. "Then your turn, darling. For free." He tried to kiss her; something stopped his tongue, and he realized that the smile was on the outside only, that the opening didn't really exist at all.

He parked next to an MG, not Lea's, and went inside the house where the martinis were always snapping cold.

"Darling, you remember Greta, don't you? She is going to give me lessons twice a week. Isn't that exciting?"

"But you already graduated," Darin murmured. Greta was not tall and not long-legged. She was a little bit of a thing. He thought probably he did remember her from somewhere or other, vaguely. Her hand was cool in his.

"Greta has moved in; she is going to lecture on modern art for the spring semester. I asked her for private lessons and she said yes."

"Greta Farrel," Darin said, still holding her small hand. They moved away from Lea and wandered through the open windows to the patio where the scent of orange blossoms was heavy in the air.

"Greta thinks it must be heavenly to be married to a psychologist." Lea's voice followed them. "Where are you two?"

"What makes you say a thing like that?" Darin asked.

"Oh, when I think of how you must understand a woman, know her moods and the reasons for them. You must know just what to do and when, and when to do something else . . . Yes, just like that."

His hands on her body were hot, her skin was cool. Lea's petulant voice drew closer. He held Greta in his arms and stepped into the pool where they sank to the bottom, still together. She hadn't gone to the Barbie School. His hands learned her body; then his body learned hers. After they made love, Greta drew back from him regretfully.

"I do have to go now. You are a lucky man, Dr. Darin. No doubts about yourself, complete understanding of what makes you tick."

He lay back on the leather couch staring at the ceiling. "It's always that way, Doctor. Fantasies, dreams, illusions. I know it is because this investigation is hanging over us right now, but even when things are going relatively well, I still go off on a tangent like that for no real reason." He stopped talking.

In his chair Darin stirred slightly, his fingers drumming softly on the arm, his gaze on the clock whose hands were stuck. He said, "Before this recent pressure, did you have such intense fantasies?"

"I don't think so," Darin said thoughtfully, trying to remember.

The other didn't give him time. He asked, "And can you break out of them now when you have to, or want to?"

"Oh, sure," Darin said.

Laughing, he got out of his car, patted the MG, and walked into his house. He could hear voices from the living room and he remembered that on Thursdays Lea really did have her painting lesson.

Dr. Lacey left five minutes after Darin arrived. Lacey

said vague things about Lea's great promise and untapped talent, and Darin nodded sober agreement. If she had talent, it certainly was untapped so far. He didn't say so.

Lea was wearing a hostess suit, flowing sheer panels of pale blue net over a skin-tight leotard that was midnight blue. Darin wondered if she realized that she had gained weight in the past few years. He thought not.

"Oh, that man is getting impossible," she said when the MG blasted away from their house. "Two years now, and he still doesn't want to put my things on show."

Looking at her, Darin wondered how much more her things could be on show.

"Don't dawdle too long with your martini," she said. "We're due at the Ritters' at seven for clams."

The telephone rang for him while he was showering. It was Stu Evers. Darin stood dripping water while he listened.

"Have you seen the evening paper yet? That broad made the statement that conditions are extreme at the station, that our animals are made to suffer unnecessarily."

Darin groaned softly. Stu went on, "She is bringing her entire women's group out tomorrow to show proof of her claims. She's a bigwig in the SPCA, or something."

Darin began to laugh then. Mrs. Whoosis had her face pressed against one of the windows, other fat women in flowered dresses had their faces against the rest. None of them breathed or moved. Inside the compound Adam laid Hortense, then moved on to Esmeralda, to Hilda . . .

"God damn it, Darin, it isn't funny!" Stu said.

"But it is. It is."

Clams at the Ritters' were delicious. Clams, hammers, buckets of butter, a mountainous salad, beer, and finally coffee liberally laced with brandy. Darin felt cheerful and contented when the evening was over. Ritter was in Med. Eng. Lit. but he didn't talk about it, which was merciful. He was sympathetic about the stink with the SPCA. He thought scientists had no imagination. Darin agreed with him and soon he and Lea were on their way home.

"I am so glad that you didn't decide to stay late," Lea said, passing over the yellow line with a blast of the horn. "There is a movie on tonight that I am dying to see."

She talked, but he didn't listen, training of twelve years drawing out an occasional grunt at what must have been appropriate times. "Ritter is such a bore," she said. They were nearly home. "As if you had anything to do with that incredible statement in tonight's paper."

"What statement?"

"Didn't you even read the article? For heaven's sake, why not? Everyone will be talking about it . . ." She sighed theatrically. "Someone quoted a reliable source who said that within the foreseeable future, simply by developing the leads you now have, you will be able to produce monkeys that are as smart as normal human beings." She laughed, a brittle meaningless sound.

"I'll read the article when we get home," he said. She didn't ask about the statement, didn't care if it was true or false, if he had made it or not. He read the article while she settled down before the television. Then he went for a swim. The water was warm, the breeze cool on his skin. Mosquitoes found him as soon as he got out of the pool, so he sat behind the screening of the verandah. The bluish light from the living room went off after a time and there was only the dark night. Lea didn't call him when she went to bed. He knew she went very softly, closing the door with care so that the click of the latch wouldn't disturb him if he was dozing on the verandah.

He knew why he didn't break it off. Pity. The most corrosive emotion endogenous to man. She was the product of the doll school that taught that the trip down the aisle was the end, the fulfillment of a maiden's dreams; shocked and horrified to learn that it was another beginning, some of them never recovered. Lea never had. Never would. At sixty she would purse her lips at the sexual display of uncivilized animals, whether human or not, and she would be disgusted and help formulate laws to ban such activities. Long ago he had hoped a child would be the answer, but the school did something to them on the inside too. They didn't conceive, or if conception took place, they didn't carry the fruit, and if they carried it, the birth was of a stillborn thing. The ones that did live were usually the ones to be pitied more than those who fought and were defeated *in utero*.

A bat swooped low over the quiet pool and was gone again against the black of the azaleas. Soon the moon would appear, and the chimps would stir restlessly for a while, then return to deep untroubled slumber. The chimps slept companionably close to one another, without thought of sex. Only the nocturnal creatures, and the human creatures, performed coitus in the dark. He wondered if Adam remembered his human captors. The colony in the compound had been started almost twenty years ago, and since then none of the chimps had seen a human being. When it was necessary to enter the grounds, the chimps were fed narcotics in the evening to insure against their waking. Props were changed then, new obstacles added to the old conquered ones. Now and then a chimp was removed for study, usually ending up in dissection. But not Adam. He was father of the world. Darin grinned in the darkness.

Adam took his bride aside from the other beasts and knew that she was lovely. She was his own true bride, created for him, intelligence to match his own burning intelligence. Together they scaled the smooth walls and glimpsed the great world that lay beyond their garden. Together they found the opening that led to the world that was to be theirs, and they left behind them the lesser beings. And the god searched for them and finding them not, cursed them and sealed the opening so that none of the others could follow. So it was that Adam and his bride became the first man and woman and from them flowed the progeny that was to inhabit the entire world. And one day Adam said, for shame woman, seest thou that thou art naked? And the woman answered, so are you, big boy, so are you. So they covered their nakedness with leaves from the trees, and thereafter they performed their sexual act in the dark of night so that man could not look on his woman, nor she on him. And they were thus cleansed of shame. Forever and ever. Amen. Hallelujah.

Darin shivered. He had drowsed after all, and the night wind had grown chill. He went to bed. Lea drew away from him in her sleep. She felt hot to his touch. He turned to his left side, his back to her, and he slept.

"There is potential x," Darin said to Lea the next morning at breakfast. "We don't know where x is actually. It represents the highest intellectual achievement possible for the monkeys, for example. We test each new batch of monkeys that we get and sort them—x-1, x-2, x-3, suppose, and then we breed for more x-1's. Also we feed the other two groups the sRNA that we extract from the original x-1's. Eventually we get a monkey that is higher than our original x-1, and we reclassify right down the line and start over, using his sRNA to bring the others up to his level. We make constant checks to make sure we aren't allowing inferior strains to mingle with our highest achievers, and we keep control groups that are given the same training, the same food, the same sorting process, but no sRNA. We test them against each other."

Lea was watching his face with some interest as he talked. He thought he had got through, until she said, "Did you realize that your hair is almost solid white at the temples? All at once it is turning white."

Carefully he put his cup back on the saucer. He smiled at her and got up. "See you tonight," he said.

They also had two separate compounds of chimps that had started out identically. Neither had received any training whatever through the years; they had been kept isolated from each other and from man. Adam's group had been fed sRNA daily from the most intelligent chimps they had found. The control group had been fed none. The control-group chimps had yet to master the intricacies of the fountain with its ice-cold water; they used the small stream that flowed through the compound. The control group had yet to learn that fruit on the high, fragile branches could be had, if one used the telescoping sticks to knock them down. The control group huddled without protection, or under the scant cover of palm-trees when it rained and the dome was opened. Adam long ago had led his group in the construction of a rude but functional hut where they gathered when it rained.

Darin saw the women's committee filing past the compound when he parked his car. He went straight to the console in his office, flicked on a switch and manipulated buttons and dials, leading the group through the paths, opening one, closing another to them, until he led them to the newest of the compounds, where he opened the gate and let them inside. Quickly he closed the gate again and watched their frantic efforts to get out. Later he turned the chimps loose on them, and his grin grew broader as he watched the new-men ravage the old women. Some of the offspring were black and hairy, others pink and hairless, some intermediate. They grew rapidly, lined up with arms extended to receive their daily doses, stood before a machine that tested them instantaneously, and were sorted. Some of them went into a disintegration room, others out into the world.

A car horn blasted in his ears. He switched off his ignition and he got out as Stu Evers parked next to his car. "I see the old bats got here," Stu said. He walked toward the lab with Darin. "How's the Driscoll kid coming along?"

"Negative," Darin said. Stu knew they had tried using human sRNA on the boy, and failed consistently. It was too big a step for his body to cope with. "So far he has shown total intolerance to A-127. Throws it off almost instantly."

Stuart was sympathetic and noncommital. No one else had any faith whatever in Darin's own experiment. A-127 might be too great a step upward, Darin thought. The *Ateles* spider monkey from Brazil was too bright.

He called Kelly from his office and asked about the newly arrived spider monkeys they had tested the day before. Blood had been processed; a sample was available. He looked over his notes and chose one that had shown interest in the tasks without finishing any of them. Kelly promised him the prepared syringe by 1 P.M.

What no one connected with the project could any longer doubt was that those simians, and the men that had been injected with sRNA from the Driscoll boy, had actually had their learning capacities inhibited, some of them apparently permanently.

Darin didn't want to think about Mrs. Driscoll's reaction if ever she learned how they had been using her boy. Rae sat at the corner of his desk and drawled insolently, "I might tell her myself, Dr. Darin. I'll say, Sorry, Ma'am, you'll have to keep your idiot out of here; you're damaging the brains of our monkeys with his polluted blood. Okay, Darin?"

"My God, what are you doing back again?"

"Testing," she said. "That's all, just testing."

Stu called him to observe the latest challenge to Adam's group, to take place in forty minutes. Darin had forgotten that he was to be present. During the night a tree had been felled in each compound, its trunk crossing the small stream, damming it. At eleven the water fountains were to be turned off for the rest of the day. The tree had been felled at the far end of the compound, close to the wall where the stream entered, so that the trickle of water that flowed past the hut was cut off. Already the group not taking sRNA was showing signs of thirst. Adam's group was unaware of the interrupted flow.

Darin met Stu and they walked together to the far side where they would have a good view of the entire compound. The women had left by then. "It was too quiet for them this morning," Stu said. "Adam was making his rounds; he squatted on the felled tree for nearly an hour before he left it and went back to the others."

They could see the spreading pool of water. It was muddy, uninviting looking. At eleven-ten it was generally known within the compound that the water supply had failed. Some of the old chimps tried the fountain; Adam tried it several times. He hit it with a stick and tried it again. Then he sat on his haunches and stared at it. One of the young chimps whimpered pitiably. He wasn't thirsty yet, merely puzzled and perhaps frightened. Adam scowled at him. The chimp cowered behind Hortense, who bared her fangs at Adam. He waved menacingly at her, and she began picking fleas from her offspring. When he whimpered again, she cuffed him. The young chimp looked from her to Adam, stuck his forefinger in his mouth and ambled away. Adam continued to stare at the useless fountain. An hour passed. At last Adam rose and wandered nonchalantly toward the drying stream. Here and there a shrinking pool of muddy water steamed in the sun. The other chimps followed Adam. He followed the stream through the compound toward the wall that was its source. When he came to the pool he squatted again. One of the young chimps circled the pool cautiously reached down and touched the dirty water, drew back, reached for it again, and then drank. Several of the others drank also. Adam continued to squat. At twelve-forty Adam moved again. Grunting and gesturing to several younger males, he approached the tree-trunk. With much noise and meaningless gestures, they shifted the trunk. They strained, shifted it again. The water was released and poured over the heaving chimps. Two of them dropped the trunk and ran. Adam and the other two held. The two returned.

They were still working when Darin had to leave, to keep his appointment with Mrs. Driscoll and Sonny. They arrived at one-ten. Kelly had left the syringe with the new formula in Darin's small refrigerator. He injected Sonny, took his sample, and started the tests. Sometimes Sonny cooperated to the extent of lifting one of the articles from the table and throwing it. Today he cleaned the table within ten minutes. Darin put a piece of candy in his hand; Sonny threw it from him. Patiently Darin put another piece in the boy's hand. He managed to keep the eighth piece in the clenched hand long enough to guide the hand to Sonny's mouth. When it was gone, Sonny opened his mouth for more. His hands lay idly on the table. He didn't seem to relate the hands to the candy with the pleasant taste. Darin tried to guide a second to his mouth, but Sonny refused to hold a piece a second time.

When the hour was over and Sonny was showing definite signs of fatigue, Mrs. Driscoll clutched Darin's hands in hers. Tears stood in her eyes. "You actually got him to feed himself a little bit," she said brokenly. "God bless you, Dr. Darin. God bless you!" She kissed his hand and turned away as the tears started to spill down her cheeks.

Kelly was waiting for him when the group left. She collected the new sample of blood to be processed. "Did you hear about the excitement down at the compound? Adam's building a dam of his own."

Darin stared at her for a moment. The breakthrough? He ran back to the compound. The near side this time was where the windows were being used. It seemed that the entire staff was there, watching silently. He saw Stu and edged in by him. The stream twisted and curved through the compound, less than ten inches deep, not over two feet anywhere. At one spot stones lay under it; elsewhere the bottom was of hard-packed sand. Adam and his crew were piling up stones at the one suitable place for their dam, very near their hut. The dam they were building was two feet thick. It was less than five feet from the wall, fifteen feet from where Darin and Stu shared the window. When the dam was completed, Adam looked along the wall. Darin thought the chimp's eyes paused momentarily on his own. Later he heard that nearly every other person watching felt the same momentary pause as those black, intelligent eyes sought out and held other intelligence.

". . . next thunderstorm. Adam and the flood . . ."

". . . eventually seeds instead of food . . ."

". . . his brain. Convolutions as complex as any man's."

Darin walked away from them, snatches of future plans in his ears. There was a memo on his desk. Jacobsen was turning over the SPCA investigatory committee to him. He was to meet with the university representatives, the local SPCA group, and the legal representatives of all concerned on Monday next at 10 A.M. He wrote out his daily report on Sonny Driscoll. Sonny had been on too good behavior for too long. Would this last injection give him just the spark of determination he needed to go on a rampage? Darin had alerted Johnny, the bodyguard, whoops, male nurse, for just such a possibility, but he knew Johnny didn't think there was any danger from the kid. He hoped Sonny wouldn't kill Johnny, then turn on his mother and father. He'd probably rape his mother, if that much goal-directedness ever flowed through him. And the three men who had volunteered for the injections from Sonny's blood? He didn't want to think of them at all, therefore couldn't get them out of his mind as he sat at his desk staring at nothing. Three convicts. That's all, just convicts hoping to get a parole for helping science along. He laughed abruptly. They weren't planning anything now. Not that trio. Not planning for a thing. Sitting, waiting for something to happen, not thinking about what it might be, or when, or how they would be affected. Not thinking. Period.

"But you can always console yourself that your motives were pure, that it was all for Science, can't you, Dr. Darin?" Rae asked mockingly.

He looked at her. "Go to hell," he said.

It was late when he turned off his light. Kelly met him in the corridor that led to the main entrance. "Hard day, Dr. Darin?"

He nodded. Her hand lingered momentarily on his arm. "Good night," she said, turning in to her own office. He stared at the door for a long time before he let himself out and started toward his car. Lea would be furious with him for not calling. Probably she wouldn't speak at all until nearly bedtime, when she would explode into tears and accusations. He could see the time when her tears and accusations would strike home, when Kelly's body would be a tangible memory, her words lingering in his ears. And he would lie to Lea, not because he would care actually if she knew, but because it would be expected. She wouldn't know how to cope with the truth. It would entangle her to the point where she would have to try an abortive suicide, a screaming-for-attention attempt that would ultimately tie him in tear-soaked knots that would never be loosened. No, he would lie, and she would know he was lying, and they would get by. He started the car, aimed down the long sixteen miles that lay before him. He wondered where Kelly lived. What it would do to Stu when he realized. What it would do to his job if Kelly should get nasty, eventually. He shrugged. Barbie dolls never got nasty. It wasn't built in.

Lea met him at the door, dressed only in a sheer gown, her hair loose and unsprayed. Her body flowed into his so that he didn't need Kelly at all. And he was best man when Stu and Kelly were married. He called to Rae, "Would that satisfy you?" but she didn't answer. Maybe she was gone for good this time. He parked the car outside his darkened house and leaned his head on the steering wheel for a moment before getting out. If not gone for

good, at least for a long time. He hoped she would stay
away for a long time.

ON POINT OF VIEW
by Kate Wilhelm

THERE ARE so many ways for a story to go wrong that it
is discouraging to start to think about them, but the surest
and quickest way to lose a good story is to tell it from
the wrong point of view. Each story is defined by the
narrator and the point of view adopted for it; it is the
viewpoint that determines the effect that the story will
have on the reader. When it is wrong the characters are
stillborn, the story lies inert. And there is no way to fix it,
not through rewriting the end, or adding a paragraph at
the beginning, or making word changes. The story has to
be rewritten from the first word.

Assuming certain facts, A,B,C, . . . , there are three
different stories if those facts are seen through the eyes
of three different characters. Suppose a story about the
Manhattan Project, and the same facts, A,B,C, . . . , are
examined by the janitor, by a physicist's wife, and by
one of the physicists. Three stories. This is the easy part
of the viewpoint problem, knowing whose story it really
is. The hard part is deciding how to handle the viewpoint.
With each change in viewpoint the story changes, although the facts remain the same, and the narrator is the
same one in each instance.

What the writer always wants is to involve the reader
with the characters and incidents he has created. Most
amateur writing is done in the first person because in-
experienced writers automatically assume that is the most
effective way to involve everyone. They are the I-nar-
rators, and they expect the readers to be willing to assume
this role also. In fact the I-narrator-protagonist is probably the most difficult of all to do well. The difficulty
rises as the story becomes tragic or comic. Few people
want to be laughed at, and fewer want to become tragic
figures and suffer hurt, even vicariously. Even when the
I-narrator-protagonist story does not involve tragedy or

comedy, too often the reader becomes rebellious simply because he knows he would not behave in the way the fictional I is behaving; he would not speak that way, react like that, and so on. His skepticism forces him out of the story instead of more deeply into it.

Too often the writer is afraid that his message is not coming through, and if he does not use the first person, he turns to the limited omniscient point of view and explains, and explains, and explains through the thoughts of his character. The character questions himself and answers his own questions endlessly. If the character is a tragic one, then it is very hard to avoid self-pity.

There are some viewpoints that are automatically excluded by the material. The camera eye can't work when fantasy is an integral part of the story. What is seen is a person going about his business or sitting with a blank look, and neither is very informative.

What becomes clear is that every point of view has its built-in limitations, and the author must work around these as best he can. If the author fails to consider the limitations, he sometimes finds himself nearing the end of the story with a viewpoint that can no longer be used. He must then make an abrupt shift to someone else's point of view. This rarely works; almost always it jars the reader and reduces the effect of the story, if it doesn't destroy it completely.

At first glance it seems that the omniscient author approach is foolproof, but even this is not a safe assumption. There isn't room in a short story to tell everything, but if an omniscient viewpoint leaves out vital information, the story becomes gimmicky. The reader feels that he's been had. A short story is essentially a climactic incident in the life of a single character, or the revelation of a character through a series of incidents. It needs a single, sharp focus, usually one character.

When I started to write "The Planners" the first time, I was using an internal viewpoint, and the story didn't come to life. I know why I tried to do it that way. I had to deal with fantasy and reality in equal parts, and it seemed that the only way was to internalize everything. Years later when I actually wrote the story, I found that it would work if I used a third-person external viewpoint. I worked around the limitations by objectifying the fantasy and writing it as if it were external reality. From a position immediately behind Darin's eyes we see the real world, then the spotlight is turned inward to focus on his fantasy world.

There is an inherent danger in dealing with a story made up of equal parts of fantasy and reality. If the author chooses the interior viewpoint, he must be wary of the madman syndrome. There is a thin line between insanity and fantasy in fiction, and a madman is not as interesting as a man with a fantastic imagination. This is because the fantasy is directly linked to the reality of the world that the reader can accept, while insanity may well create its own world that is forever alien to the reader— not only alien but also repugnant, one that he won't willingly enter. If the reader is permitted to peep into a madhouse, much as the visitors to the eighteenth-century asylums did with safety, then he will usually do so. But he doesn't want to have to go there to live, even briefly. Distance, through a more objective viewpoint, is often this measure of safety that he demands. Also, the internal, stream-of-consciousness viewpoint is more effective as recapitulation than as a continuing narration of events that are happening within the framework of the story. In the flow of thoughts of the internal viewpoint, the stream of consciousness, there is mediation of events; the character has had time to assimilate them, to come to terms with them as they relate to him.

In "The Planners" I wanted to tell the story of a man who is beset by self-doubts, whose marriage is a failure, whose work is troubling his conscience. Although things are happening in the real world of the story, it is about the inner man. Originally I opened with Darin leaning against the compound fence, doing battle with his conscience. Too long, too wordy, too heavy. Also it gave the effect of retrospection, and I wanted the feeling of the story to be that it is happening now. In the published version there is the same functioning scene to open it, this time with his conscience personified. In half a page I accomplished what had taken two pages in the original draft, and set the tone for the rest of the story. Here is a matter-of-fact man who knows that he fantasizes, who says as much, when he tells Stu that he was talking to himself and again later when he takes the roles of analysand and analyst. He isn't alarmed by his fantasies. He is in control, and through the escape offered him by his fantasies he is able to function very well.

From the start it is clear that everything we see, hear, perceive, is coming through Darin. By keeping a dispassionate tone, using an objective third-person viewpoint, I can have him make comparisons between the chimps and man that would have been self-conscious if they had been internalized, and impossible in first person. The first time we hear the monkeys that are ". . . screeching, howling, singing, cursing . . . Darin grunted and headed toward . . ." This is Darin's perception, but he doesn't make a big deal of it. I couldn't have written, "I grunted and headed toward . . ." Too self-conscious, even silly, because Darin would not have said such a thing so directly.

Sometimes the limitations of a given point of view work for the author. Because everything comes through Darin's awareness, only those traits of the people around him that directly bear on this story need be described. In fact, to tell more about any of them would have to be false to the story. Dr. Jacobsen is allergic to monkeys. Stu can't manage his love life. Kelly is a Barbie doll, deliberately rejecting an eligible man who loves her in favor of a married man. Lea is a failed woman. All Darin's assessments. It doesn't matter that all of them must have other dimensions: these are the things that Darin responds to in the story. By focusing on these traits and faults Darin himself is revealed. Even the scenery is a reflection of his mind. He drives home through the darkening forests on a narrow, straight road.

He has a series of fantasies that reveal him in several ways. By being externalized, instead of handled as thoughts, they are made real and more meaningful. With Greta he is the man who understands women, and himself. Then, as his own analyst, he describes what he is doing, and demonstrates his control over the fantasies.

In first person this would not have worked. It would have called for a different tone altogether; it would have been a different story. I wanted these scenes short, concise, into them and out again as quickly as the scenes of reality. I wanted to turn the spotlight on the inner screen in the same way that it has been turned on the outer one. Stream of consciousness would have slowed it down impossibly and would have called for his reactions to his own imaginings, another thing I wanted to skirt.

In the scene with Adam and Eve, the full despair of Darin surfaces for the first time. This is one of the original images that I had in working out the story; it was there from the start. I found there was no way to write it except to be as objective as possible, write from a distance, and let Darin's fantasy reveal that he is not merely a man

unhappy because of a bad marriage, or a guilty conscience over his work, but a man caught up in a much
deeper dilemma. It defines his mind and soul by existing.
It is its own question. To have had him belabor it would
have been out of character. He fantasizes in order to
avoid the very problems his fantasies deal with. This scene
is one that over and over has been mused upon in fiction,
dwelled upon, agonized over. Was it a flaw in the God
that created man that made his fall possible, even inevitable? Why, if so, must man be made to do penance?
I could have had Darin thinking about this at great length,
questioning the experiments, making the connection consciously, admitting his despair. In almost any other viewpoint I would have had to do it that way. By externalizing
the fantasy, I avoided yet another long passage that has
been done often enough. I think it works this way; the
scene is telling, and amusing in itself, and utterly despair-
ing. It, like all the other fantasy scenes, comes directly
from Darin's mind without getting into the morass of
symbolism that would have followed through the use of
a truly internal viewpoint.

He sees the committee members and has his revenge
on them in his fantasy. By now I hope it is clear that he
fantasizes in order to cope with reality. He has sex fantasies that revolve around his wife and his relationship
with her. He has fantasies about the committee members
in which he reduces them to animal status. Only in connection with his own experiments with the Driscoll boy
does he confront his own conscience, personified in the
female figure, Rae. Toward the end, when he thinks of
the boy and of the convicts he injected with the boy's
RNA, Rae confronts him.

> "But you can always console yourself that your
> motives were pure, that it was all for Science, can't
> you, Dr. Darin?" Rae asked mockingly.
> He looked at her. "Go to hell," he said.

I could have stopped that scene before her entrance.
He is brooding about his experiments. He has played God
with these people. He has damaged them irremediably
and he knows it. For him to say, "But we had to find out.
We had to be sure," isn't enough. This, in effect, is what
is said, through Rae, but in a way that allows him to
deny his guilt. Also, he denies Rae, who is his anima,
his soul, his inner self. And this is the final key to Darin.
He will get by. He will continue his work, continue with

his bad marriage, although he will wander from that straight and narrow road he saw earlier, and he will deny his soul, or conscience, wall it off by giving it a separate identity. And it will come back again and again to mock him.

FOR A WHILE THERE, HERBERT MARCUSE, I THOUGHT YOU WERE MAYBE RIGHT ABOUT ALIENATION AND EROS

by Robin Scott Wilson

HARLEY JACOBS became a veteran of Chicago when he hitchhiked to that toddlin' town in late July, 1968, out of a profound sense of personal alienation and because he was bored waiting for his draft board to summon him; because Senator McCarthy had stimulated his activist's itch, his desire to hook into a cause; because he was curious—with a small town resident's naivete—about Hippies and Yippies; and because—whatever the fortunes of McCarthy, the Democratic Convention, the Youth International Party, and the National Mobilization Committee—it looked like there might be a good supply of poontang in the balmy summer evenings in Grant Park.

Now this is not to imply that most of those brave souls at Chicago were, like Harley, about equally interested in politics and poontang. Such was clearly not the case. And unlike most Chicago veterans, because of his dual motivation, Harley found his experience in the Windy City painfully dichotomous: it seemed that whenever he began to establish himself with a young lady—in a bush, under a park bench, back of the statue of General Jonathan Logan —someone shouted: "Here comes the fuzz!" or "Let's go! Let's go!" and Harley's consummation remained only to be desired, however devoutly. Likewise, no sooner did Harley begin to pelt cops with baggies full of excrement, join in a Japanese-style snake dance, or march up Michigan Avenue, than his attention was captured by a flash of thigh or the gleam of black-lined eyes, and he found himself out of the action, off hunting for a bush, a park bench, or the back of a statue.

Frustrated by this alternation of events, torn by opposing motivations, Harley's net alienation increased. Once, in an elevated language gleaned from *The Pocket Guide to*

Freud, he appealed his dilemma to those he milled with
in front of the Hilton. "How," he asked, eyes streaming
piteously from tear gas, "how does a person overcome
his personal estrangements without at the same time com-
promising his commitments to principles of social significance?"

"What you talkin' about, man?" asked a bearded
young man who might have sat for a cheap two-color
litho of Christ.

"I mean, as soon as I begin to establish a satisfactory
interpersonal relationship, events compel me to. . ."

"He means," translated another beard, "he ain't gettin'
any."

"Well, hell," said the first youth, wiping his eyes,
"who is?"

"But," protested Harley, "the requirements of the whole
man, of total reconciliation. . ."

"Look, man. When you protestin', protest. When you
ballin', ball. You mix 'em up and your head's gonna
get all fucked up."

Harley shook his head. No one seemed to understand
the importance of a simultaneous, broad-spectrum cure
for alienation. But he persevered. He was about to press
for a better answer when he suffered what many in Chicago suffered during that turbulent week: a policeman
whacked him in the groin with a very large night stick.

After the whack, Harley rapidly lost interest in both
poontang and the politics of dissent. He returned to Reading, Pennsylvania, feeling greatly depersonalized, politi-
cally impotent, totally alienated, and sore. And, after a
week of recovery from his wounds—spiritual and cor-
poreal—in the best tradition of American pragmatism, he
decided the answer to his and the nation's problems must
lie in education, that panacea of progressivism. Perhaps,
he thought, he could find a cure for his own difficulties by
relating to the vast overworld of learning. Perhaps he
could begin his reform of this world he had never made,
his own odyssey out of alienation, by going to college.
And anyway, it would placate the draft board for a
while.

But it did not take Harley long to discover that colleges, too, are depersonalizing institutions, that they are
exceedingly fine-grinding mills dedicated to statistical
definitions of the good life which are only accidentally
and occasionally congruent with the needs of individual
inmates. Thus, as a faceless number in numbered courses

taught by professors whose numbers, not names, appeared on the IBM card that served as his class schedule, Harley spent his first semester at Bangsville State College, Bangsville, Pa., one of those instant colleges that had sprung up in the sixties in the rich humus of federal money; a college of raw, cheap buildings, classrooms crowded with students named Al or Karen, an indifferent and poorly paid faculty, and a computerized records system employing hardware rivaled only be the First Air Defense Command in expense and complexity. Such were educational priorities in 1968.

"It was depersonalizing," said Harley one night, speaking of his Chicago experience during a rare dormitory bull session. "I mean, like you were just a thing and not a person. And here it's even worse. Here you aren't even a thing any more. Just a number. I guess I'd rather be a thing than a number."

"Indeed," said a world-weary upperclassman, a sociology major named Group Al. "It is the inevitable result of the post-industrial society."

"Yes," said Red Al, a neo-Marxist who enjoyed great repute among campus radicals for having visited Havana, Cuba, although he did not let it be known that the visit had resulted from the hijacking of an Eastern Airlines jet on which he had been bound for a week with his parents at their Miami Beach estate. "It is the inevitable result of colonialist oppression by the fascist pigs in the Pentagon."

"Horseshit," said Dirty Al, the dormitory's resident dealer. "When that cop busted you in the jewels, Jacobs, you weren't a bit depersonalized. No way. I mean, that has got to be considered a act of intimacy."

Harley, who was an honest and open-minded sort, had not considered it that way before, and he gave the proposition some thought, the group silent for a moment, awaiting his reaction. He was much respected as a Chicago veteran. "Perhaps you are right, Dirty Al," he said after a bit, with some gravity. "At least I was not ignored the way we all are here."

"Right, Harley. Right!" said Pretty Al, the resident fag, eager to ingratiate himself with the younger man. "However painfully, you managed to establish a meaningful relationship with the big policeman while in the very act of achieving communion with a situation of social significance. It is these meaningful relationships that count! You must be able to relate personally with—ah—someone!"

Harley nodded. He was flattered by the attention, grateful for the advice from older and wiser heads. "Maybe it is like this professor I got for 2722 says. . ."

"Which one?"

"403 or maybe 405. I forget. Anyway, he says you got to overcome alienation by relating to everything you can. . ."

"Indeed! Indeed!" said Group Al. "The Learyan doctrine of dropping out has been thoroughly discredited by social psychologists. You must seek to penetrate the institutional infrastructure of society, accommodate to the personal-societal interface!"

"Uh?"

"But at the same time you dare not compromise with the forces of imperalist reaction," said Red Al.

"Uh?"

"While remembering the primal value of interpersonal relations—ah—relation*ships*," said Pretty Al.

"Uh?"

"And it don't hurt to turn on now and then," said Dirty Al.

Harley rose to stride among the chromium and vinyl chairs and stained coffee cups and intertwined students in the shabby cinder-block lounge. It was good of the older men in the dormitory to take an interest in him, to help him in his search. He would take their advice, or as much of it as he could. "All right," he said, chin up, arms outflung like a young Lenin at the Finland Station. "You are all right. I will find a girl who is active in some socially significant endeavor directed against the establishment, and perhaps I can relate to her and the endeavor simultaneously and thus cease to be alienated."

All but Pretty Al nodded their approval.

The socially significant endeavor directed against the establishment—a violent demonstration in support of a separate department of studies in bracero folklore—was very much a success. So was the girl, at least at first. But Harley quickly discovered it was Chicago all over again. No sooner did the girl begin to simmer nicely than Harley found their nights consumed with group planning, mixing Fels Naptha soap flakes with gasoline, and debating the details of Che Guevara's instructions for making a grenade launcher out of a .410 shotgun and a broomstick. Then, during the demonstration, it was another night stick in the groin; and after the campus had quieted down, after Harley and the girl had been bailed out by the Student Activities Fund, after he was once again able to move the girl back to the front burner of his amatory range, he suffered from a physiological disability—the result of the night stick—which he could only hope would prove temporary.

Fortunately it did. Harley recovered satisfactorily over Christmas vacation, that season of peace, and by the end of the semester he found he had succeeded finally in establishing a fully satisfactory interpersonal relationship with the girl. Of course, at the same time, his alienation in other areas was nearly total: he found he had also established a failing record in his classes, a permanent estrangement with the family back in Reading, a threat of 1-A classification by his draft board, a hide-and-seek relationship with the man who was trying to repossess his 1964 Mustang, and a running skirmish with the Dean of Students who wanted to know why he no longer occupied the dormitory room assigned to him.

Now it is the beginning of Harley's second semester at Bangsville State, and he ponders the establishment of further relationships, the diminution of his estrangement from all the world external to the girl. He has yet to try Group Al's notion of "accommodating to the personal-societal interface" mostly because he does not understand what Group Al was talking about. But standing in the long registration line snaking down the hall of the administration building, he conceives an interesting variation of that notion in the course of an idle conversation which incidentally displays his rapid mastery of the language of student discourse.

"Jeez," he says to Sally Grundig, the girl with whom he has established the viable interpersonal relationship and with whom he has come to share a plywood room above the Kollege Korner Waffle and Do-Nut Shop, "this registration's a drag."

"Yeah," says Sally, a Bryn Mawr reject despite her Main Line accent. "Definitely messed up."

"I mean, here we are, you and me, with a fine viable interpersonal relationship all established and everything. How come I can't establish a good relationship with all this other shit?" He waves an arm around to include the

line of students, the tables of professors and clerks, the
multicolored pillars of stacked IBM cards.

They shuffle past a table of cards and take one each
of white, green, yellow, and blue, as a sign directs. "I
mean," continues Harley, "you feel just like another IBM
card. Nobody *looks* at you. Just at your cards. I'd rather
be a thing or a number than a *card,* for chrissake."

Sally shrugs. Her mind is largely elsewhere.

"It is a strongly dichotomous situation."

"Di-*what*omous?"

"It's a word I learned in 2345. Means all split in two."

"Oh."

"I mean, no matter what I do, I can't seem to relate to
everything at once. One side of things is all fixed up. No
alienation there, hey babe? But the other side of things
is all screwed up. I can't relate to all this administrative
Mickey Mouse."

Sally sighs and shifts her swollen ankles, which have
begun to bother her a good deal of late. "Yeah," she says
with some resignation. "But maybe you and I could use a
little more alienation ourselves. And maybe a little less
relations."

Harley is too busy pondering the paradox of private
felicity and public alienation to listen. He holds up an
IBM card at arm's length and looks at a fluorescent ceiling fixture through its holes. He draws the card back
until it touches his nose and sights, one eye closed, through
a hole, swinging his head around until Sally's round face
and long dark hair are framed in a fuzzy square. Sally
sticks out her tongue and waggles her fingers at her ears.
Startled, Harley removes the card. "You looked good that
way," he says. "Until you stuck out your tongue. Like
a picture on a wall, only brighter."

They pass a table where a bored professor takes the
yellow and green cards and replaces them with puce and
red. He does not look up at Harley or Sally or at the long
line of students in which they are linked in impersonal
lock step. Harley recognizes him as 226, the man he had
the past semester for 1471.

"Life through an IBM card hole," says Harley, sighting
again, this time at his own reflection in a glass door. "It
is simpler. Everything has square edges."

Sally says, "Harley, I think I'm going to get sick."

Harley removes the card from his face. "But it's after
two. I thought you were only supposed to get sick in the
mornings."

"I think I better go home. I think I'm going to barf." She has this worried look that Harley has come to associate with pregnancy. Harley peers at her through the IBM card, tilting his head to bring her slightly swollen abdomen into view. "Okay," he says. "Gimme your cards and I'll get you registered."

Sally leaves and Harley shuffles on. The line is not perceptibly diminished by her departure, would not be perceptibly increased by her return. It has a viperine existence of its own, many times greater than the sum of its parts.

Everything Harley looks at through his IBM card takes on a new clarity and freshness, a simplicity and purity of line and color. He experiments with different holes. After a bit he decides that his favorite is really two holes punched very close together whose dividing strip of cardboard almost disappears close to his eye. He no longer looks where he is going, but peers at professors, walls, lights, fire extinguishers, and the sinuous line in front of and behind him which can be made—flat and linear—to curve sensuously from corner to corner of the square of his vision.

The line conveys him past the registration stations. He holds his and Sally's cards out in his left hand, and he is dimly aware that from time to time cards are removed and replaced with others.

After a timeless time, he grows aware that someone is addressing him. A voice repeats: "Your blue fee card, please. Your blue fee card." He removes the card from his eye. It is blue. He does not wish to surrender it; it contains his favorite pair of holes. A large grey lady in rimless spectacles is looking up at him from her seat behind a table full of blue cards. It is the first time anybody has looked at him since Sally left. "Your blue fee card, please. In your hand. Yes, that one." Wordlessly, confused, Harley shakes his head. He smiles pleadingly. "Uh—you see—I can't. . ."

"Come on, young man!" There is exasperation in the large grey lady's voice. Reflected light bobs up at him from her spectacles. "You can't complete your registration until your blue fee card is stamped and sent to the Bursar!"

Harley makes a strangled sound deep in his throat, clutches the blue card tightly, and turns out of the line to flee down the corridor. He does not yet quite understand why he must flee. He knows only that there is the inkling of a broad-spectrum cure for his alienation, and whatever it is, it involves the IBM card.

Out in the cold midafternoon gloom of the campus, Harley briefly halts his flight. He debates returning to the grey lady and surrendering his card, behaving rationally. But now the idea of giving up the card is unthinkable, or thinkable to him only in the way that such theoretical propositions as love and death and good and bad are thinkable. He is very confused. The card, suddenly so dear to him, is the obvious symbol of the depersonalization he has sought to overcome, and yet—and yet—the view, the fuzzy, square view, the rectilinear organization of everything seen through the card, is oddly comforting, suggests possibilities for new relations . . .

As solace to his confusion, he peers through the double holes of the card at the ugly campus, at the winter-torn trees, at the shrubbery bright with candy wrappers and browning copies of the *BS Daily Bulletin*, at the water tower high up on McNamarra Hill whose elevation requires him to turn the card to the horizontal so that the long way of the holes will be vertical.

How clean and bright and logical everything looks! How simple and positive and *understandable!*

And peering thus, Harley permits his mind to dash back through the tangled, steaming, implausible jungles of memory, and then upward in time again to that point in the registration line when he has been captured by simplicity. And he seizes on a splendid new notion: that there is no real distinction between the conglomerate of illusions, passions, lusts, hopes, tumescences, headaches, infidelities, and gastric upsets that are Harley Jacobs and the clean, sharp-edged, slope-cornered, geometrically holed, purely colored perfection of the IBM cards that are also Harley Jacobs. Only, thinks Harley, the cards-Harley—despite the disclaimers they bear—can far better withstand being bent, spindled, folded, shuffled, and—yes—*duplicated* than can the flesh-Harley. Perhaps, he thinks, perhaps he has found—eureka!—the personal-societal interface, Perhaps, having found it, he can now accommodate himself to it. Perhaps it is the end of alienation. It is worth some thought.

The campus full of ugly new buildings and the plywood room over the waffle shop are the loci of Harley's life, the pressure points at which the tourniquet of his alienation is applied. Ultimately, all his troubles come home to roost in the plywood room. And there too is pregnant Sally and the laundry to be taken to the Wash-O-Mat and the letters from parents and notices from his draft board and notes from his landlady and reminders from GMAC and duns from the doctor and that other IBM card bearing the dismal record of his first semester grades.

While Sally is busy in the bathroom throwing up supper, Harley ponders the contrast between cards-Harley and flesh-Harley. He likes Sally, he likes the plywood room, he likes going to college, he even likes the idea of the duplicate Harley Sally is working on with such assiduity. What he doesn't like are grades and being broke and getting drafted and leaving the comfortable, ugly little campus and the snug, warm, syrup-smelling plywood room.

Like, ever.

And apart from the draft, he does not want someday to graduate and become an Accountant, Advertising Man, Airlines Representative, Chemist, Comptroller (with or without the voiced "p"), Designer, Engineer, Insurance Agent, Management Trainee, Personnel Man, Salesman, Spy, Teacher, Technician, Writer, or Zoologist, and work forty hours a week doing one thing in one place and buy bonds through the Payroll Savings Plan and stand in line to screw the Comptometer Operator (no silent "p") at Christmas parties and grow old and retire with a gold watch that says "Forty Years Service Award."

And so Harley sits at his packing-crate desk, Dionne Warwick bitching about her and some man out of the radio, the sound of Sally busy at her pregnancy in the bathroom, and decides the nature of the current division of labor and responsibility between IBM card-Harley and flesh-Harley is not really in his best interests, that if the cards will just take on that part of Harley so vulnerable to, so alienated from, parents, banks, credit companies, landladies, draft boards, and college administrators, the other part will be happy to handle all the remaining business, will be quite content and fully related to the ugly little campus and the sweet plywood room above the waffle shop.

At midnight, Harley is outside the administration building picking the lock with a paper clip and the flattened tube of a BiC ball-point pen. It is an art he learned from the older brother of one of his colleagues in Boy Scout Troop 502, which met sporadically in the basement of the First Lutheran Church of Reading, Pa., for sessions of military drill, knot tying, and grab-ass during Harley's junior high school years.

Inside, Harley checks to make sure there are no janitors about and goes to work on the Registrar's files. He spends most of the night studying the system: green card for Curriculum file, pink card for Housing, white card for Master Machine Room Control file, yellow card for Cumulative Grade Record, blue card for Fees, and red card for Student Deferment file, purple card for Financial Aids, puce card for Student Employment Payroll, mauve card for Personal History index, and brown card for Student Identification ("affix picture in upper right-hand corner; do not use staples or other metal fasteners"). Just before dawn, he finishes his study and skulks across campus to home, watchful for campus rent-a-cops.

The next night he returns and begins his work in earnest. He registers himself for a heavy twenty-one-hour load; stamps his fee card PAID and signs it with an illegible scrawl very like the Bursar's; alters his first semester grade record to a flattering mixture of A's and B's and makes a Xerox copy of it to enclose in a letter ostensibly from the Dean of Instruction addressed to "Local Board No. 47, Reading, Pa.," which explains that earlier reports on Jacobs, Harley, were in error; grants himself permission to occupy off-campus housing; establishes himself as the recipient of a $2000 annual scholarship; puts himself on the payroll as a student assistant in "Department 145," wondering as he does so what department that can be; and files a power-of-attorney directing that both scholarship and payroll checks be sent automatically by the computer to his bank for deposit. Again it is nearly dawn when he has finished, and he returns home to sleep through the day.

On the third night, he is busy with his paper clip and ball-point pen all over campus. It is necessary that he insert the cards in the proper files, that appropriate aspects of the new card-Harley be properly distributed among the Bursar, Registrar, Dean of Instruction, Dean of Students, Dean of Liberal Arts, the Housing Office, and the Office of Student Aids. And of course, most important of all, the white Master Machine Room Control card, the very informing spirit of the new Harley, must be carefully inserted in the long skinny file cabinets that surround the clicking, light-blinking, machine-oil-smelling god in the basement of Hubris Hall.

As each card nestles in its appropriate file, Harley feels a progressive lightening of his spirits, a burgeoning sense of communion with the once-hostile world. He has re-written, tailored, shaped the vulnerable, external, IBM card-Harley into something fine and brave and solvent, something immune to the thrusts of night sticks; and he has filed its manifold presences into the manifold file drawers in which it belongs as surely as cell belongs to flesh, neuron to thought, passion to spirit. For the next semester at least, the Harley-cards will operate in intimate electro-mechanical harmony with one another, with the draft board, with the bank, and with the college adminis-' tration. And the flesh-Harley will be free to enjoy the ugly little campus and the sweet plywood room.

And freely enjoy he does, at first. Initially, he is fully satisfied with the results of the nonaggression pact he has so slyly negotiated with the harsher realities of life, the public sources of his alienation. He attends his classes, and because he in now unconcerned about grades, he learns a great deal. He pays his back rent and resumes his monthly remittances to the finance company. The draft board restores his 2-S classification, and he finds himself honorably mentioned on the Dean's list, which brings an illiterate but enthusiastic letter from home enclosing a modest check. For the first time, Harley finds the whole man integrated harmoniously with all aspects of its existence; no jarring alienation from anything; peace, comfort, pleasure everywhere; every hole in the siren flute of desire is stopped.

He tries to explain his satisfaction, his accomplishment, to Sally. He wants her to know of his remarkable achievement. But she is totally intent on her own thing, and only nods sweetly, a little vacantly, and says, "That's real nice, baby." When she thinks of Harley at all, it is of a future Harley, a father-Harley. She is not much interested in IBM card-Harley and finds flesh-Harley comfortably less importunate in bed, which she mistakenly ascribes to her altered figure and which she confidently foresees will end; she has no doubt that an ardent Harley and a flat belly will return with the simultaneity and necessity of apple blossoms and bees.

The disinterestedness of a preoccupied Sally triggers— does not originate—an odd new dissatisfaction in Harley. The necessarily secret nature of his treaty with society has rendered him an unperson as surely as any secret East

European purge; he dare not participate in campus political activities lest he draw on himself investigation; his
classroom accomplishments, such as they are, are trans-
cended by the cards in the files. And of course the clever
treaty itself must remain secret, at least from the college
administration.

In quiet but growing discontent, Harley visits his old
dormitory to flirt with the revelation of his scheme, to
display his calm mastery of his own fate in front of *someone.*

"I kind of took your advice, Group Al," he says in-
gratiatingly to the sociology major. "And it worked out
great."

"Advice? What advice?"

"You know. About accommodating to the personal-
societal interface, or whatever. It works."

"How about that," says Group Al, fingering his new
beard. "Tell me about it."

"Well, I can't say too much, but what I did was. . ."

"I advised you to accommodate to the personal-
societal interface, huh?"

". . . Yes, and what I did was. . ."

"That's very interesting and I'm glad it worked for you.
The thing is, there's a lot of new evidence about the validity of personal integration. . ."

". . .But let me *tell* you! You see what I did was. . ."

"The thing is, sociometrists have determined to *my* satisfaction that the real intellectual in American society
has been forced into internal emigration. Only shallow
thinkers and cultural Philistines can find identity in a society based upon psychic and material domination. Now
you take your problem. . ."

"But I don't *have* any problem now. I've got it
whipped. . ."

". . .You'll find the solution, as I have, in group therapy. There's a bunch of us meet in the basement of the
Methodist Church, and you'll be welcome if you want to
come along tonight."

"Well—ah—thanks. I guess not tonight." Harley is
deeply disappointed in Group Al.

"Okay, Jacobs. But anytime you want to. . ." He
leaves, a beatific smile flashing here and there around the
lounge.

To the neo-Marxist, Harley says, "I took your advice,
Red Al. I think I've found a way to exploit the exploiters."

"Did I advise you to do that?"

"Yes, and I figured out a way. You see, what I did was analyze the fascist-imperalist establishment like you said and develop a system to beat. . ."

"Good, Harley. Great! You're obviously on the right track. Like this stuff here. You know what it is?"

"No. But let me tell you about. . ."

"It is a prep sheet for the Foreign Service Entrance Examination. I'm going to take it tomorrow."

"Fine. But what I want to tell you is. . ."

"It's a tough exam, but professor 321 thinks I stand a good chance because of my knowledge of the Cuban situation."

"Gee, Al, good. I hope you do okay on it. But there's this thing with the computer. . ."

"Thanks, Harley. If I make it, I'll put in a good word for you in Washington. You'll be a senior in a couple of years, and you might want to kind of aim for the Foreign Service. Great bunch of people there." Red Al returns to his prep sheet.

Again disappointed, Harley says, "One last thing, Red Al. Is Pretty Al still around?"

Red Al looks up from his papers. "Why, no, Harley. The lucky stiff passed the exam last month. He's already in Washington."

To the pot man, Harley says, resignation in his voice, "Gimme a nickel bag, will you Dirty Al?"

As the spring semester and Sally ripen toward their respective commencement exercises, Harley sinks into a kind of lethargy. He finds it almost impossible to communicate with his fellow students, who are interested, after all, in grades, administrative repression, jobs, and girls, none of which affect Harley in the least. He feels a new boredom, a satiation with peace. He spends more and more time in bed peering through the holes in his blue IBM card, now worn and fuzzy. But even the card ceases to give him much solace. There is nothing he can put his finger on, at first. He remains convinced that he has discovered the best of all possible worlds, and he wonders if his dis-ease may not stem from something amiss in his diet. It does not yet occur to him that he has eaten too much lotus.

And then June comes. Harley makes a midnight trip to the Registrar's office to enter his spring semester grades. A few days later Sally brings forth Harley, Jr., in pain and triumph.

And then July comes and Sally's belly flattens and she lies at night, expectant (in a new sense of the word), but there is little or no Harley.

It is not now a matter of damage from a night stick.

Sally questions. Harley questions, as baffled as she. After much soul-searching and a great deal of peering through the IBM card, Harley begins to suspect the truth: that he has delegated too much, that his frightening disability is psychological, a part of the miasma of boredom and nullity in which he finds himself

By August he is near despair; Sally is morose and uncommunicative. Can it be, he wonders, that he has purchased peace at too dear a rate? Are the two sides of his nature, the public card-Harley and the private flesh-Harley now themselves alienated one from the other? Must he now, upon retiring, ask himself: "Will the real Harley Jacobs please stand up?"

Harley cannot be sure. He thinks back to Chicago, to his chaotic first semester at Bangsville S. C. "There must," he says to Sally one night after a particularly disappointing experience, "there must be a lesson to be learned in all this."

Sally, deflated in belly and libido, says in her best Main Line, "Okay, Clyde. You find it, or me and the baby haul ass."

And thus is the terrible dichotomy of his times revealed to Harley. The lesson is there. The exhortation and the threat are clear. In matters of alienation, Harley comes to realize, there are no permanent broad-spectrum cures, no magical molds and miraculous molecules that can simultaneously zap the virus of isolation, the bacillus of loneliness, the fungal flowers of love. The best he can hope for, he comes to realize, is to choose the disorder that will get him in the end.

It is no small boon.

Slowly, not without considerable pain, sitting at his packing-crate desk, Harley pushes a Venus No. 2 pencil through his favorite pair of IBM card holes. What was square and simple becomes roughly round, enlarged, bordered with irregular torn blue fibers. Thus spindled and violated, subsequently folded and mutilated, the card drops to the plywood floor, and Harley goes out into the night.

It takes only a little while with the paper clip and the BiC. He does not wish to go too far. He leaves his grades alone: even though they have not been assigned him by his professors, he believes he has earned them, the ABRACADABRA of IBMery, minus the C's, D's, and R's. But the paper employment in Department 145 goes. So does the scholarship. So does the twenty-one-hour course load: with professors to please and a living to get, he will need more time.

Later that night, after a splendid exhibition of the stimulating powers of alienation, Harley lies smoking a cigarette and tries to understand.

"It will mean that man from GMAC will be around bugging us. And the landlady."

"Um," says Sally.

"It will mean that I'll be uptight a lot of the time."

"Um."

"It means that I am incapable of achieving meaningful relationships with society as a whole and with you at the same time."

"Um."

"It means that I will be full of ups and downs. I will be hard on you. I may sometimes beat little Harley. I may beat you. I will be a mess of contradictions. I will be forever more or less hung up, and when I am not hung up I will be disgustingly straight and conformist and square, and I will probably always be alienated to everything but you and little Harley and the plywood room, wherever we wind up having our plywood room."

"Um," says Sally. *"Mais il faut cultiver notre jardin."*

"What?"

"It's French. Number 6904. Professor 175. It means 'never mind, baby, let's us cultivate the old garden again.' "

POINT OF VIEW: THE QUICK-CHANGE ARTIST IN THE TYPEWRITER

by Robin Scott Wilson

THERE IS no way a story can be presented to a perceptive reader in such a way that the hand of the author does not show. Whatever point of view the author employs— omniscient, detached, first or third person, narrator in- or outside story—the simple fact that *someone* has selected the material, shaped it, and caused words to be put on paper reveals the auctorial presence. I labor this obvious point because I want to take a shot at the critical position which would attach special virtue to that fiction in which the author is effaced, in which narration is as "objective" as possible, in which events are almost entirely shown and not told, in which, as E. M. Forster proclaims rightfully, the author does not take "the reader into his confidence about his characters . . . at the expense of illusion and nobility."

In fact, I am not the least offended by Henry Fielding's practice of stepping on stage to talk to me from time to time; it does not bother me that H. G. Wells tells me at least as much as he shows me; and Frederik Pohl's running commentary in "Day Million" is what makes *that* story work. I am not saying that a strong or obvious auctorial presence is the secret of a good story. Far from it. But it is surely as effective a way to handle some material as is its contrary technique, the almost perfectly effaced author in Hemingway's "The Killers," and I think it far preferable to the literary contortions of Sartre's "durational realism," in which all evidence of auctorial presence—even the shaping and selecting hand—is ruthlessly extirpated.

If we accept the inevitability of the auctorial presence, our judgments then are not about whether or not the author is somehow "in" the story but about how much of him is there, how his presence is manifest, and what it contributes to the realization of other aspects of the story.

If the narrator is in the story as its principal character, the auctorial presence will usually be pretty well submerged in him. He is most likely to be the primary spokesman for the author, and even if some subsidiary character is the instrument of the author's opinions, we can learn of them only as they are filtered through the perceptions of the first-person narrator. If central character George is convinced that chastity is important and subsidiary character Sam shares the author's belief that it is foolish, George—appearing as the "I" of the story—may be a poor transmission channel for the author's belief, although it can be done. Mark Twain does it with Huck Finn, who believes he is sinful for his aid to Jim, the runaway slave, but who is carefully depicted by Twain—primarily through Jim—as virtuous in this regard.

On the other hand, if the narrator is in the story but is a subsidiary character, his utility as a locus for the auctorial presence is much greater. Relatively free from other duties in the story, he can speculate, make philosophical observations, provide background and insight, and characterize with some objectivity his fellow actors. In much of Robert Penn Warren's *All the King's Men,* Jack Burden—the passive newspaper reporter—is Warren's vehicle for comment on the more central characters of Anne Stanton, Dr. Adam Stanton, and Willie Stark, the political boss drawn from Louisiana's Huey P. Long.

But it is under conditions of omniscience, the narrator clearly outside the story, that the auctorial presence becomes most apparent. While the author may employ one or several characters inside the story as his spokesmen, every word that is not dialogue, every scrap of information not delivered by one character to another, reveals the author's hand. And that is why showing usually implies little auctorial presence; telling often entails strong or obvious auctorial presence.

It follows then that one great advantage of a strong auctorial presence, particularly in certain kinds of short fiction, is the freedom it grants the author to employ more summary passages and fewer time-consuming dramatic scenes. In "For A While There, Herbert Marcuse . . ." I chronicle about a year in the life of Harley Jacobs in something less then six thousand words. There are several brief scenes—in front of the Chicago Hilton, in the plywood room, in the return to the dormitory—and two slightly more extensive ones—the dormitory bull-session and Harley's ruminations in the registration line; all the rest of the story is told in rapid narrative summary. While each of these scenes is seen largely through Harley's eyes, I feel no embarrassment at commenting on them directly, consulting as necessary the biographies and unexpressed sentiments of those around him. To have dramatized it all, given the slender plot and rather minor theme of the story, would have been to bore my readers and send them searching for another, more rapidly paced story.

Another great advantage of the strong auctorial presence, of course, is precisely the matter of commentary. Because I am by choice and temperament a didactic writer and, I guess, something of a ham, I am eager in some stories to get on the stage with the characters and add my two cents' worth. In "For A While There, Herbert Marcuse . . ." I deliver this commentary in a number of ways, exploiting the story without scruple to say some things I just damn-well want to say. I do this—

In direct statement: "Now this is not to imply that most of those brave souls at Chicago were . . . equally interested in politics and poontang." Or, "Such were the educational priorities in 1968."

In the use of figurative language: ". . . arms outflung like a young Lenin at the Finland Station" or ". . . the virus of isolation, the bacillus of loneliness, the fungal flowers of love."

In statements of motive and intent: Sally "has no doubt that an ardent Harley and a flat belly will return with the simultaneity and necessity of apple blossoms and bees." Or, ". . . said Pretty Al, the resident fag, eager to ingratiate himself with the younger man."

Yet another advantage of obvious auctorial presence lies in the matter of reader identification. I think we can all agree that such identification is important, but identification with *whom?* With Harley? With people who have Harley's problem? With the general plight of young people undergoing some sort of maturation? Or is it possible that the auctorial presence itself can become a kind of "character" with whom the reader can identify? I believe so, and here I must state that there is a vast difference between the author of a story and the presence of that author in the story. I have been referring to "I" so far in my discussion of my presence in "For A While There, Herbert Marcuse . . . ," but there is no proper pronoun for the fellow I've been talking about. He sits on my typewriter, a quick-change artist (now in a ringmaster's top hat and jodhpurs), and makes obscene comments to me; he jumps into my stories with varying degrees of enthusiasm; he deals with my characters and my readers and my personal beliefs without much attention to my real desires; and I learn from him. But he is not "I." He is not a "he" either, but something between "I" and "he."

In any case, auctorial presence (let's call him "AP" and give him masculine gender; his sibling, the Muse, is feminine) *is* an object for reader identification, and to the degree I can control AP, I try to take advantage of this. It can be tricky, because I am aware, even if AP isn't or just doesn't give a damn, that readers vary, and something in AP that appeals to some may put others off entirely. An example:

AP says he doesn't want to imply that the protestors at Chicago in the summer of 1968 were interested in anything but the exercise of their idealism, doesn't want to imply that some might also have been interested in the

possibility of a little fun and games. Reader A, a Mc-
Govern Democrat, says to this: "Right on, man!" Reader
B, a Daley Democrat, says to this: "Horsefeathers! All
them long-hair hippie freaks wanted was to stir up
trouble and lay around in the parks bombed outta their
gourds." Then AP goes a little too far, following his relatively straightforward denial with, "Such was clearly not
the case." He doth protest a bit too much, and the Daley
Democrat nods and smiles and suspects that maybe a bit
of irony just zipped past him and it is okay and AP is
perhaps on the side of right and justice after all. The
McGovern Democrat thinks, "Say, what's this guy pulling
on me?" If neither one is sure, the propaganda content
of the passage is lessened, the comedy is a bit heightened,
and AP and I have gotten away with it, because we're
the only ones who really know.

Indeed, a well-controlled AP is almost essential to
comedy, particularly black comedy and satire. Most people do not readily identify with the desires and triumphs
of characters in de Sade; most don't feel much like going
along with de Sade and his AP either. But substitute for
de Sade and his AP Voltaire and *his* AP in *Candide* or
Nathanael West and his AP in *A Cool Million* and the
adventures of poor little Justine could be made pretty
funny. Murder is indeed most foul, but the murders in
Kind Hearts and Coronets are hilarious. Unrequited love
is a very real human torment, but it is the stuff of which
a thousand comic episodes have been built. The realization that a fully integrated personality, a life of clear
purpose and broad satisfaction, is not possible in our civilization (if it ever was, anywhere) might be shown as
devastatingly tragic; I hope Harley's discovery of this fact
is at least mildly comic.

In summary, a good, well-controlled AP can provide
the author a voice for expressing ideas that lie somewhat
outside the story (and here he jumps out of my typewriter
and onto the reader's page, dressed in cap and gown,
sporting a goatee, clearing his throat to lecture as he
points at things on a little blackboard); he can deliver
deeply personal information about what's going on in
characters' heads (here he still has the goatee and wears
pince-nez, but now there is a diploma on the wall and a
couch behind him still warm from its occupant, and he
reads from a notepad); he can clarify and amplify the
author's words with language inappropriate to the characters, with allusions to events and ideas beyond their

comprehension, and with rhetorical devices appropriate
only to written, not spoken, discourse (here the AP is an
earnest young woman with hornrim glasses, earphones,
and a microphone, peering at the proceedings in the story
from within a UN-style glass booth); and he can provide
the kind of distance between the events of the story and
the reader which allows the reader to accept a world in
which "right" and "wrong" are local options, are reversed, are irrelevant, or are comic (here he holds a re-
ducing glass before the story, and depending on the focal
length, everything in it is flipped upside down or diminished to an insignificant speck of no importance to anyone, but interesting).

All this, of course, is the mediating role of the Auctorial
Presence. The AP stands between author and material
and characters and readers and comments on them and
speaks for them and explains to them and sorts out the
morality and values and importance of what's going on,
telling the little old Methodist lady from Dubuque that
sure, Harley is living in sin with Sally, but they love one
another and the baby and it doesn't really matter anyway;
telling the Democrats of all stripes that sure, Chicago in
1968 was a bad scene, but the party and the Republic
will probably survive it; telling the proprietors and students
at all the little colleges around the country that sure, this
ain't no Harvard, but it is still a very good thing that all
the Harleys and Sallys and Als and Karens can learn to
quote Voltaire and train for the State Department and
figure out the societal-personal interface; telling everybody everywhere who will listen that sure, there aren't
any permanent cures for being a human being, but hang
tough, the human condition is like sex: when it's good,
it's very, very good; and when it's bad, it's not so bad.

STYLE:
The Dress of Thought

Expression is the Dress of Thought,
and still Appears more decent as
more suitable.

To SAY that every good writer has a style uniquely his
own, a way of going about artistic creation that is as
individual as his fingerprints, is profoundly true but implies a comprehensiveness for the term "style" that makes
it too unwieldy and vague for ready use as a critical term.
Style considered as the choice of words, their arrangement
in sentences, and their exploitation as sources of sensuous
imagery does some violence to the word but is convenient.

Words delivered to the reader are ink marks on paper,
symbols of great abstraction, largely meaningless in themselves, a *medium* through which meaning is triggered in
the mind. Words, even if not vocalized, carry sound, can
be musical, can carry such intellectual freight as music
is capable of, but that is all; the writer is aware of the
musical quality of words and phrases and he takes whatever advantage of it he can. His real concentration, however, is on the ability of the words he chooses to tap the
reader's store of remembered sense-images, intellectual
associations, and emotions.

Words can deliver *denotative* and *connotative* meanings. The essayist or technical writer seeks the former—
meanings as given in the dictionary, as little confused by
additional, equivocal meanings as possible. The fiction
writer depends heavily on the latter, choosing words which
can trigger in the reader's mind all sorts of additional
meanings—emotional, intellectual, or sensuous. "Sensuous" and "sensual," for example, carry much the same
denotative meaning; they connote very different things.

When a writer combines words in a sentence, he pays
attention to the shape and structure of the sentence. He
manipulates the natural *rhythm* of a series of words and

exploits its ability to reinforce their meaning. He avoids awkward concatenations of eye-obstructing polysyllables and the fractionally distracting action of unconscious jingles, and he tries to suit the pace of his phrasing to the action he is describing. He is more likely to construct a *loose* or *cumulative* sentence, one whose meaning is complete well before it ends, in passages of little physical movement, when the loose sentence's capability for subtle rhythmic effects can be employed for all its musical worth, and additional meanings can be strung like beads on a string in a succession of clauses. He uses the *periodic* sentence to suspend full meaning, however many interruptions he permits, however complex the sentence may be, to the end. Either sentence may employ the device of *balance*—equal rhetorical elements on either side of a conjunction whose meanings are complementary—or *antithesis*—balanced elements whose meanings contrast. Loose sentences are the meandering streams of language; periodic, are the breaking waves; balanced, convey the antiphonal rhythm of the diurnal tides.

The preceding sentence attempts to make certain fairly abstract notions concrete through a series of sense-images. There are a great many such rhetorical devices, and if you have a fondness for Greek you may wish to take a look at *litotes, hyperbole, apostrophe, synecdoche,* and the like. Two such devices—*metaphor* and *simile*—are worth distinguishing. *Metaphor* is an implied comparison between two unlike things (usually one is abstract, the other concrete and sensuous in its appeal): "Life is just a bowl of cherries. . . ." *Simile* is explicit comparison: "My luv is like a red, red rose. . . ." Language—and particularly slang—is full of one-word metaphors. "Hey, dude, dig that chick with all the bread . . . ," which are more properly described as *kennings*. Good writers coin them with delight.

Most of style is conscious, although not self-conscious. But experienced writers have usually so internalized the rhetorical elements of style they have adopted as theirs that they exercise full conscious control primarily in revision, the process by which competent writing becomes beautiful. And here I offer you four rules handed down to me by my father along with a ten-dollar bill, a bottle of whisky, and a used bible. Wilson's Four Rules of Good Writing (which I all too often violate) are:

1. Never use a big word if a little one will do.
2. Never use two words if one will do.

3. Avoid the passive voice like the plague.
4. And let the verbs carry the load.

THE LISTENERS

by James E. Gunn

"Is there anybody there?" said the Traveler,
Knocking on the moonlit door. . . .

THE VOICES BABBLED.

MacDonald heard them and knew that there was meaning in them, that they were trying to communicate and that he could understand them and respond to them if he could only concentrate on what they were saying, but he couldn't bring himself to make the effort. He tried again.

"Back behind everything, lurking like a silent shadow behind the closed door, is the question we can never answer except positively: Is there anybody there?"

That was Bob Adams, eternally the devil's advocate, looking querulously at the others around the conference table. His round face was sweating, although the mahogany-paneled room was cool.

Saunders puffed hard on his pipe. "But that's true of all science. The image of the scientist eliminating all negative possibilities is ridiculous. Can't be done. So he goes ahead on faith and statistical probability."

MacDonald watched the smoke rise above Saunders' head in clouds and wisps until it wavered in the draft from the air duct, thinned out, disappeared. He could not see it, but the odor reached his nostrils. It was an aromatic blend easily distinguishable from the flatter smell of cigarettes being smoked by Adams and some of the others.

Wasn't this their task? MacDonald wondered. To detect the thin smoke of life that drifts through the universe, to separate one trace from another, molecule by molecule, and then force them to reverse their entropic paths into their ordered and meaningful original form.

All the king's horses, and all the king's men. . . . Life itself is impossible, he thought, but men exist by reversing entropy.

Down the long table cluttered with overflowing ash trays and coffee cups and doodled scratch pads Olsen said, "We always knew it would be a long search. Not years but centuries. The computers must have sufficient data, and that means bits of information approximating the number of molecules in the universe. Let's not chicken out now."

> *"If seven maids with seven mops*
> *Swept it for a half a year,*
> *Do you suppose," the Walrus said,*
> *"That they could get it clear?"*

". . . ridiculous," someone was saying, and then Adams broke in, "It's easy for you to talk about centuries when you've been here only three years. Wait until you've been at it for ten years, like I have. Or Mac here who has been on the Project for twenty years and head of it for fifteen."

"What's the use of arguing about something we can't know anything about?" Sonnenborn said reasonably. "We have to base our position on probabilities. Shklovskii and Sagan estimated that there are more than one thousand million habitable planets in our galaxy alone. Von Hoerner estimated that one in three million have advanced societies in orbit around them; Sagan said one in one hundred thousand. Either way it's good odds that there's somebody there—three hundred or ten thousand in our segment of the universe. Our job is to listen in the right place or in the right way or understand what we hear."

Adams turned to MacDonald. "What do you say, Mac?"

"I say these basic discussions are good for us," MacDonald said mildly, "and we need to keep reminding ourselves what it is we're doing, or we'll get swallowed in a quicksand of data. I also say that it's time now to get down to the business at hand—what observations do we make tonight and the rest of the week before our next staff meeting?"

Saunders began, "I think we should make a methodical sweep of the entire galactic lens, listening on all wavelengths—"

"We've done that a hundred times," said Sonnenborn.

"Not with my new filter—"

"Tau Ceti still is the most likely," said Olsen. "Let's really give it a hearing—"

MacDonald heard Adams grumbling, half to himself,

"If there is anybody, and they are trying to communicate, some amateur is going to pick it up on his ham set, decipher it on his James Bond coderule, and leave us sitting here on one hundred million dollars of equipment with egg all over our faces—"

"And don't forget," MacDonald said, "tomorrow is Saturday night and Maria and I will be expecting you all at our place at eight for the customary beer and bull. Those who have more to say can save it for then."

MacDonald did not feel as jovial as he tried to sound. He did not know whether he could stand another Saturday night session of drink and discussion and dissension about the Project. This was one of his low periods when everything seemed to pile up on top of him, and he could not get out from under, or tell anybody how he felt. No matter how he felt, the Saturday nights were good for the morale of the others.

> *Pues no es possible que esté continuo el arco armado*
> *ni la condición y flaqueza humana se pueda sustenar*
> *sin alguna lícita recreación*

Within the Project, morale was always a problem. Besides, it was good for Maria. She did not get out enough. She needed to see people. And then. . . .

And then maybe Adams was right. Maybe nobody was there. Maybe nobody was sending signals because there was nobody to send signals. Maybe man was all alone in the universe. Alone with God. Or alone with himself, whichever was worse.

Maybe all the money was being wasted, and the effort, and the preparation—all the intelligence and education and ideas being drained away into an endlessly empty cavern.

> *Habe nun, ach! Philosophie,*
> *Juristerei und Medizin,*
> *Und leider auch Theologie*
> *Durchaus studiert, mit heissem Bemühn.*
> *Da steh' ich nun, ich armer Tor!*
> *Und bin so klug als wie zuvor;*
> *Heisse Magister, heisse Doktor gar,*
> *Und ziehe schon an die zehen Jahr*
> *Herauf, herab und quer and krumm*
> *Meine Schüler an der Nase herum—*
> *Und sehe, dass wir nichts wissen können!*

Poor fool. Why me? MacDonald thought. Could not some other lead them better, not by the nose but by his real wisdom? Perhaps all he was good for was the Saturday night parties. Perhaps it was time for a change.

He shook himself. It was the endless waiting that wore him down, the waiting for something that did not happen, and the Congressional hearings were coming up again. What could he say that he had not said before? How could he justify a project that already had gone on for nearly fifty years without results and might go on for centuries more?

"Gentlemen," he said briskly, "to our listening posts."

By the time he had settled himself at his disordered desk, Lily was standing beside him.

"Here's last night's computer analysis," she said, putting down in front of him a thin folder. "Reynolds says there's nothing there, but you always want to see it anyway. Here's the transcription of last year's Congressional hearings." A thick binder went on top of the folder. "The correspondence and the actual appropriation measure are in another file if you want them."

MacDonald shook his head.

"There's a form letter here from NASA establishing the ground rules for this year's budget and a personal letter from Ted Wartinian saying that conditions are really tight and some cuts look inevitable. In fact, he says there's a possibility the Project might be scrubbed."

Lily glanced at him. "Not a chance," MacDonald said confidently.

"There's a few applications for employment. Not as many as we used to get. The letters from school children I answered myself. And there's the usual nut letters from people who've been receiving messages from outer space, and from one who's had a ride in a UFO. That's what he called it—not a saucer or anything. A feature writer wants to interview you and some others for an article on the Project. I think he's with us. And another one who sounds as if he wants to do an exposé."

MacDonald listened patiently. Lily was a wonder. She could handle everything in the office as well as he could. In fact, things might run smoother if he were not around to take up her time.

"They've both sent some questions for you to answer. And Joe wants to talk to you."

"Joe?"

"One of the janitors."

"What does he want?" They couldn't afford to lose a janitor. Good janitors were harder to find than astronomers, harder even than electronicians.

"He says he has to talk to you, but I've heard from some of the lunchroom staff that he's been complaining about getting messages on his—on his—"

"Yes?"

"On his false teeth."

MacDonald sighed. "Pacify him somehow, will you, Lily? If I talk to him we might lose a janitor."

"I'll do my best. And Mrs. MacDonald called. Said it wasn't important and you needn't call back."

"Call her," MacDonald said. "And, Lily—you're coming to the party tomorrow night, aren't you?"

"What would I be doing at a party with all the brains?"

"We want you to come. Maria asked particularly. It isn't all shop talk, you know. And there are never enough women. You might strike it off with one of the young bachelors."

"At my age, Mr. MacDonald? You're just trying to get rid of me."

"Never."

"I'll get Mrs. MacDonald." Lily turned at the door. "I'll think about the party."

MacDonald shuffled through the papers. Down at the bottom was the only one he was interested in—the computer analysis of last night's listening. But he kept it there, on the bottom, as a reward for going through the others. Ted was really worried. *Move over, Ted.* And then the writers. He supposed he would have to work them in somehow. At least it was part of the fallout to locating the Project in Puerto Rico. Nobody just dropped in. And the questions. Two of them caught his attention.

How did you come to be named Project Director? That was the friendly one. *What are your qualifications to be Director?* That was the other. How would he answer them? Could he answer them at all?

Finally he reached the computer analysis, and it was just like those for the rest of the week, and the week before that, and the months and the years before that. No significant correlations. Noise. There were a few peaks of reception—at the twenty-one-centimeter line, for instance—but these were merely concentrated noise. Radiating clouds of hydrogen, as the Little Ear functioned like an ordinary radio telescope.

At least the Project showed some results. It was feeding star survey data tapes into the international pool. Fallout. Of a process that had no other product except negatives.

Maybe the equipment wasn't sensitive enough. Maybe. They could beef it up some more. At least it might be a successful ploy with the Committee, some progress to present, if only in the hardware. You don't stand still. You spend more money or they cut you back—or off.

Note: Saunders—plans to increase sensitivity.

Maybe the equipment wasn't discriminating enough. But they had used up a generation of ingenuity canceling out background noise, and in its occasional checks the Big Ear indicated that they were doing adequately on terrestrial noise, at least.

Note: Adams—new discrimination gimmick.

Maybe the computer wasn't recognizing a signal when it had one fed into it. Perhaps it wasn't sophisticated enough to perceive certain subtle relationships. . . . And yet sophisticated codes had been broken in seconds. And the Project was asking it to distinguish only where a signal existed, whether the reception was random noise or had some element of the unrandom. At this level it wasn't even being asked to note the influence of consciousness.

Note: ask computer—is it missing something? Ridiculous? Ask Olsen.

Maybe they shouldn't be searching the radio spectrum at all. Maybe radio was a peculiarity of man's civilization. Maybe others had never had it or had passed it by and now had more sophisticated means of communication. Lasers, for instance. Telepathy, or what might pass for it with man. Maybe gamma rays, as Morrison suggested years before Ozma.

Well, maybe. But if it were so, somebody else would have to listen for those. He had neither the equipment nor the background nor the working lifetime left to tackle something new.

And maybe Adams was right.

He buzzed Lily. "Have you reached Mrs. MacDonald?"

"The telephone hasn't answered—"

Unreasoned panic. . . .

"—oh, here she is now. Mr. MacDonald, Mrs. MacDonald."

"Hello, darling. I was alarmed when you didn't answer." That had been foolish, he thought, and even more foolish to mention it.

Her voice was sleepy. "I must have been dozing." Even drowsy, it was an exciting voice, gentle, a little husky, that speeded MacDonald's pulse. "What did you want?"

"You called me," MacDonald said.

"Did I? I've forgotten."

"Glad you're resting. You didn't sleep well last night."

"I took some pills."

"How many?"

"Just the two you left out."

"Good girl. I'll see you in a couple of hours. Go back to sleep. Sorry I woke you."

But her voice wasn't sleepy any more. "You won't have to go back tonight, will you? We'll have the evening together?"

"We'll see," he promised.

But he knew he would have to return.

MacDonald paused outside the long, low concrete building which housed the offices and laboratories and computers. It was twilight. The sun had descended below the green hills, but orange and purpling wisps of cirrus trailed down the western sky.

Between MacDonald and the sky was a giant dish held aloft by skeleton metal fingers—held high as if to catch the star dust that drifted down at night from the Milky Way.

> *Go and catch a falling star,*
> *Get with child a mandrake root,*
> *Tell me where all past years are,*
> *Or who cleft the Devil's foot;*
> *Teach me to hear mermaids singing,*
> *Or to keep off envy's stinging,*
> *And find*
> *What wind*
> *Serves to advance an honest mind.*

Then the dish began to turn, noiselessly, incredibly, and to tip. And it was not a dish any more but an ear, a listening ear cupped by the surrounding hills to overhear the whispering universe.

Perhaps this was what kept them at their jobs, MacDonald thought. In spite of all disappointments, in spite of all vain efforts, perhaps it was this massive machinery, as sensitive as their fingertips, which kept them struggling with the unfathomable. When they grew weary at their electronic listening posts, when their eyes grew dim with looking at unrevealing dials and studying uneventful graphs, they could step outside their concrete cells and renew their dull spirits in communion with the giant mechanism they commanded, the silent, sensing instrument in which the smallest packets of energy, the smallest waves of matter, were detected in their headlong, eternal flight across the universe. It was stethoscope with which they took the pulse of the all and noted the birth and death of stars, the probe with which, here on an insignificant planet of an undistinguished star on the edge of its galaxy, they explored the infinite.

Or perhaps it was not just the reality, but the imagery, like poetry, which soothed their doubting souls, the bowl held up to catch Donne's falling star, the ear cocked to catch the suspected shout that faded to an indistinguishable murmur by the time it reached them. And one thousand miles above them was the giant, five-mile-in-diameter network, the largest radio telescope ever built, which men had cast into the heavens to catch the stars.

If they had the Big Ear for more than an occasional reference check, MacDonald thought practically, then they might get some results. But he knew the radio astronomers would never relinquish time to the frivolity of listening for signals that never came. It was only because of the Big Ear that the Project had inherited the Little Ear. There had been talk recently about a larger net, twenty miles in diameter. Perhaps when it was done, if it were done, the Project might inherit time on the Big Ear.

If they could endure until then, MacDonald thought, if they could steer their fragile vessel of faith between the Scylla of self-doubt and the Charybdis of Congressional appropriations.

The images were not all favorable. There were others that went boomp in the night. There was the image, for instance, of man listening, listening, listening to the silent stars, listening for an eternity, listening for signals that would never come, because—the ultimate horror—man was alone in the universe, a cosmic accident of self-awareness which needed and would never receive the comfort of companionship. To be alone, to be all alone, would be like being all alone on earth, with no one to talk to, ever—like being alone inside a bone prison, with no way to get out, no way to communicate with anyone outside, no way to know if anyone was outside. . . .

Perhaps that, in the end, was what kept them going—to stave off the terrors of the night. While they listened there was hope; to give up now would be to admit final defeat. Some said they should never have started; then they never would have the problem of surrender. Some of the new religions said that. The Solitarians, for one. There is nobody there; we are the one, the only created intelligence in the universe. Let us glory in our uniqueness. But the older religions encouraged the Project to continue. Why would God have created the myriads of other stars and other planets if He had not intended them for living creatures; why should man only be created in His image? Let us find out, they said. Let us communicate with them. What revelations have they had? What saviors have redeemed them?

These are the words which I spake unto you, while I was yet with you, that all things must be fulfilled, which were written in the law of Moses, and in the prophets, and in the psalms, concerning me. . . . Thus it is written, and thus it behoved Christ to suffer, and to rise from the dead the third day: and that repentance and remission of sins should be preached in his name among all nations, beginning at Jerusalem. And ye are witnesses of these things.

And, behold, I send the promise of my Father upon you: but tarry ye in the city of Jerusalem, until ye be endued with power from on high.

Dusk had turned to night. The sky had turned to black. The stars had been born again. The listening had begun. MacDonald made his way to his car in the parking lot behind the building, coasted until he was behind the hill, and turned on the motor for the long drive home.

The hacienda was dark. It had that empty feeling about it that MacDonald knew so well, the feeling it had for him when Maria went to visit friends in Mexico City. But it was not empty now. Maria was here.

He opened the door and flicked on the hall light. "Maria?" He walked down the tiled hall, not too fast, not too slow. "*¿Querida?*" He turned on the living room light as he passed. He continued down the hall, past the dining room, the guest room, the study, the kitchen. He reached the dark doorway to the bedroom. "Maria Chavez?"

He turned on the bedroom light, low. She was asleep, her face peaceful, her dark hair scattered across the pillow. She lay on her side, her legs drawn up under the covers.

Men che dramma
Di sangue m'e rimaso, che no tremi;
Conosco i segni dell' antica fiamma.

MacDonald looked down at her, comparing her features
one by one with those he had fixed in his memory. Even
now, with those dark, expressive eyes closed, she was the
most beautiful woman he had ever seen. What glories
they had known! He renewed his spirit in the warmth of
his remembrances, recalling moments with loving details.

C'est de quoy j'ay le plus de peur que la peur.

He sat down upon the edge of the bed and leaned over
to kiss her upon the cheek and then upon her upthrust
shoulder where the gown had slipped down. She did not
waken. He shook her shoulder gently. "Maria!" She turned
upon her back, straightening. She sighed, and her eyes came
open, staring blankly. "It is Robby," MacDonald said,
dropping unconsciously into a faint brogue.

Her eyes came alive and her lips smiled sleepily.
"Robby. You're home."

"*Yo te amo,*" he murmured, and kissed her. As he
pulled himself away, he said, "I'll start dinner. Wake up
and get dressed. I'll see you in half an hour. Or sooner."

"Sooner," she said.

He turned and went to the kitchen. There was romaine
lettuce in the refrigerator, and as he rummaged further,
some thin slices of veal. He prepared Caesar salad and
veal scallopine, doing it all quickly, expertly. He liked to
cook. The salad was ready, and the lemon juice, tarragon,
white wine, and a minute later, the beef bouillon had been
added to the browned veal when Maria appeared.

She stood in the doorway, slim, lithe, lovely, and
sniffed the air. "I smell something delicious."

It was a joke. When Maria cooked, she cooked Mexican,
something peppery that burned all the way into the stomach and lay there like a banked furnace. When Mac-
Donald cooked, it was something exotic—French, perhaps,
or Italian, or Chinese. But whoever cooked, the other had
to appreciate it or take over all the cooking for a week.

MacDonald filled their wine glasses. "*À la très-bonne,*
à la très-belle," he said, "*qui fait ma joie et ma santé.*"

"To the Project," Maria said. "May there be a signal
received tonight."

MacDonald shook his head. One should not mention
what one desires too much. "Tonight there is only us."

Afterward there were only the two of them, as there had been now for twenty years. And she was as alive and as urgent, as filled with love and laughter, as when they first had been together.

At last the urgency was replaced by a vast ease and contentment in which for a time the thought of the Project faded into something remote which one day he would return to and finish. "Maria," he said.

"Robby?"

"*Yo te amo, corazón.*"

"*Yo te amo,* Robby."

Gradually then, as he waited beside her for her breathing to slow, the Project returned. When he thought she was asleep, he got up and began to dress in the dark.

"Robby?" Her voice was awake and frightened.

"*¿Querida?*"

"You are going again?"

"I didn't want to wake you."

"Do you have to go?"

"It's my job."

"Just this once. Stay with me tonight."

He turned on the light. In the dimness he could see that her face was concerned but not hysterical. "*Rast ich, so rost ich.* Besides, I would feel ashamed."

"I understand. Go, then. Come home soon."

He put out two pills on the little shelf in the bathroom and put the others away again.

The headquarters building was busiest at night when the radio noise of the sun was least and listening to the stars was best. Girls bustled down the halls with coffee pots, and men stood near the water fountain, talking earnestly.

MacDonald went into the control room. Adams was at the control panel; Montaleone was the technician. Adams looked up, pointed to his earphones with a gesture of futility, and shrugged. MacDonald nodded at him, nodded at Montaleone, and glanced at the graph. It looked random to him.

Adams leaned past him to point out a couple of peaks. "These might be something." He had removed the earphones.

"Suppose you're right. The computer hasn't sounded any alarms."

"After a few years of looking at these things, you get the feel of them. You begin to think like a computer."

"Or you get oppressed by failure."

"There's that."

The room was shiny and efficient, glass and metal and plastic, all smooth and sterile; and it smelled like electricity. MacDonald knew that electricity had no smell, but that was the way he thought of it. Perhaps it was the ozone that smelled or warm insulation or oil. Whatever it was, it wasn't worth the time to find out, and Mac-Donald didn't really want to know. He would rather think of it as the smell of electricity. Perhaps that was why he was a failure as a scientist. "A scientist is a man who wants to know why," his teacher always had told him.

MacDonald leaned over the control panel and flicked a switch. A thin, hissing noise filled the room. It was something like air escaping from an inner tube—a susurration of surreptitious sibilants from subterranean sessions of seething serpents.

He turned a knob and the sound became what someone—Tennyson?—had called "the murmuring of innumerable bees." Again, and it became Matthew Arnold's

> *. . . melancholy, long withdrawing roar*
> *Retreating, to the breath*
> *Of the night wind, down the vast edges drear*
> *And naked shingles of the world.*

He turned the knob once more, and the sound was a babble of distant voices, some shouting, some screaming, some conversing calmly, some whispering—all of them trying beyond desperation to communicate, and everything just below the level of intelligibility. If he closed his eyes, MacDonald could almost see their faces, pressed against a distant screen, distorted with the awful effort to make themselves heard and understood.

But they all insisted on speaking at once. MacDonald wanted to shout at them. "Silence everybody! All but you —there, with the purple antenna. One at a time and we'll listen to all of you if it takes a hundred years or a hundred lifetimes."

"Sometimes," Adams said, "I think it was a mistake to put in the speaker system. You begin to anthropomorphize. After a while you begin to hear things. Sometimes you even get messages. I don't listen to the voices any more. I used to wake up in the night with someone whispering to me. I was just on the verge of getting the mes-

sage that would solve everything, and I would wake up."
He flicked off the switch.

"Maybe someday somebody will get the message," Mac-
Donald said. "That's what the audio frequency translation is intended to do. To keep the attention focused. It
can mesmerize and it can torment, but these are the conditions out of which spring inspiration."

"Also madness," Adams said. "You've got to be able to
continue."

"Yes." MacDonald picked up the earphones Adams had
put down and held one of them to his ear.

"Tico-tico, tico-tico," it sang. "They're listening in
Puerto Rico. Listening for words that never come. Tico-
tico, tico-tico. They're listening in Puerto Rico. Can it
be the stars are stricken dumb?"

MacDonald put the earphones down and smiled. "Maybe there's inspiration in that, too."

"At least it takes my mind off the futility."

"Maybe off the job, too? Do you really want to find
anyone out there?"

"Why else would I be here? But there are times when
I wonder if we would not be better off not knowing."

"We all think that sometimes," MacDonald said.

In his office he attacked the stack of papers and letters
again. When he had worked his way to the bottom, he
sighed and got up, stretching. He wondered if he would
feel better, less frustrated, less uncertain, if he were working on the Problem instead of just working so somebody
else could work on the Problem. But somebody had to do
it. Somebody had to keep the Project going, personnel
coming in, funds in the bank, bills paid, feathers
smoothed.

Maybe it was more important that he do all the dirty
little work in the office. Of course it was routine. Of
course Lily could do it as well as he. But it was important
that he do it, that there be somebody in charge who believed in the Project—or who never let his doubts be
known.

Like the Little Ear, he was a symbol—and it is by
symbols men live—or refuse to let their despair overwhelm
them.

The janitor was waiting for him in the outer office.

"Can I see you, Mr. MacDonald?" the janitor said.

"Of course, Joe," MacDonald said, locking the door of
his office carefully behind him. "What is it?"

"It's my teeth, sir." The old man got to his feet and with

a deft movement of his tongue and mouth dropped his teeth into his hand.

MacDonald stared at them with a twinge of revulsion. There was nothing wrong with them. They were a carefully constructed pair of false teeth, but they looked too real. MacDonald always had shuddered away from those things which seemed to be what they were not, as if there were some treachery in them.

"They talk to me, Mr. MacDonald," the janitor mumbled, staring at the teeth in his hand with what seemed like suspicion. "In the glass beside my bed at night, they whisper to me. About things far off, like. Messages, like."

MacDonald stared at the janitor. It was a strange word for the old man to use, and hard to say without teeth. Still, the word had been "messages." But why should it be strange? He could have picked it up around the offices or the laboratories. It could be odd, indeed, if he had not picked up something about what was going on. Of course: messages.

"I've heard of that sort of thing happening," MacDonald said. "False teeth accidentally constructed into a kind of crystal set, that pick up radio waves. Particularly near a powerful station. And we have a lot of stray frequencies floating around, what with the antennas and all. Tell you what, Joe. We'll make an appointment with the Project dentist to fix your teeth so that they don't bother you. Any small alteration should do it."

"Thank you, Mr. MacDonald," the old man said. He fitted his teeth back into his mouth. "You're a great man, Mr. MacDonald."

MacDonald drove the ten dark miles to the hacienda with a vague feeling of unease, as if he had done something during the day or left something undone that should have been otherwise.

But the house was dark when he drove up in front, not empty-dark as it had seemed to him a few hours before, but friendly-dark. Maria was asleep, breathing peacefully.

The house was brilliant with lighted windows that cast long fingers into the night, probing the dark hills, and the sound of many voices stirred echoes until the countryside itself seemed alive.

"Come in, Lily," MacDonald said at the door, and was reminded of a winter scene when a Lily had met the gentlemen at the door and helped them off with their overcoats. But that was another Lily and another occasion and another place and somebody else's imagination. "I'm glad you decided to come." He had a can of beer in his hand, and he waved it in the general direction of the major center of noisemaking. "There's beer in the living room and something more potent in the study—190 proof grain alcohol, to be precise. Be careful with that. It will sneak up on you. But—*nunc est bibendum!*"

"Where's Mrs. MacDonald?" Lily asked.

"Back there, somewhere." MacDonald waved again. "The men, and a few brave women, are in the study. The women, and a few brave men, are in the living room. The kitchen is common territory. Take your choice."

"I really shouldn't have come," Lily said. "I offered to spell Mr. Saunders in the control room, but he said I hadn't been checked out. It isn't as if the computer couldn't handle it all alone, and I know enough to call somebody if anything unexpected should happen."

"Shall I tell you something, Lily?" MacDonald said. "The computer could do it alone. And you and the computer could do it better than any of us, including me. But if the men ever feel that they are unnecessary, they would feel more useless then ever. They would give up. And they mustn't do that."

"Oh, Mac!" Lily said.

"They mustn't do that. Because one of them is going to come up with the inspiration that solves it all. Not me. One of them. We'll send somebody to relieve Charley before the evening is over."

> *Wer immer strebens sich bemüht,*
> *Den können wir erlösen.*

Lily sighed. "Okay, boss."

"And enjoy yourself!"

"Okay, boss, okay."

"Find a man, Lily," MacDonald muttered. And then he, too, turned toward the living room, for Lily had been the last who might come.

He listened for a moment at the doorway, sipping slowly from the warming can.

"—work more on gamma rays—"

"Who's got the money to build a generator? Since nobody's built one yet, we don't even know what it might cost."

"—gamma-ray sources should be a million times more rare than radio sources at twenty-one centimeters—"

"That's what Cocconi said nearly fifty years ago. The same arguments. Always the same arguments."

"If they're right, they're right."

"But the hydrogen-emission line is so uniquely logical. As Morrison said to Cocconi—and Cocconi, if you remember, agreed—it represents a logical, prearranged rendezvous point. 'A unique, objective standard of frequency, which must be known to every observer of the universe,' was the way they put it."

"—but the noise level—"

MacDonald smiled and moved on to the kitchen for a cold can of beer.

"—Bracewell's 'automated messengers'?" a voice asked querulously.

"What about them?"

"Why aren't we looking for them?"

"The point of Bracewell's messengers is that they make themselves known to us!"

"Maybe there's something wrong with ours. After a few million years in orbit—"

"—laser beams make more sense."

"And get lost in all that star shine?"

"As Schwartz and Townes pointed out, all you have to do is select a wavelength of light that is absorbed by stellar atmospheres. Put a narrow laser beam in the center of one of the calcium absorption lines—"

In the study they were talking about quantum noise.

"Quantum noise favors low frequencies."

"But the noise itself sets a lower limit on those frequencies."

"Drake calculated the most favorable frequencies, considering the noise level, lie between 3.2 and 8.1 centimeters."

"Drake! Drake! What did he know? We've had nearly fifty years experience on him. Fifty years of technological advance. Fifty years ago we could send radio messages one thousand light-years and laser signals ten light-years. Today those figures are ten thousand and five hundred at least."

"What if nobody's there?" Adams said gloomily.

Ich bin der Geist der stets verneint.

"Short-pulse it, like Oliver suggested. One hundred million billion watts in a ten billionth of a second would smear across the entire radio spectrum. Here, Mac, fill this, will you?"

And MacDonald wandered away through the clustering guests toward the bar.

"And I told Charley," said a woman to two other women in the corner, "if I had a dime for every dirty diaper I've changed, I sure wouldn't be sitting here in Puerto Rico—"

"—neutrinos," said somebody.

"Nuts," said somebody else, as MacDonald poured grain alcohol carefully into the glass and filled it with orange juice, "the only really logical medium is Q waves."

"I know—the waves we haven't discovered yet but are going to discover about ten years from now. Only here it is nearly fifty years after Morrison suggested it, and we still haven't discovered them."

MacDonald wended his way back across the room.

"It's the night work that gets me," said someone's wife. "The kids up all day, and then he wants me there to greet him when he gets home at dawn. Brother!"

"Or what if everybody's listening?" Adams said gloomily. "Maybe everybody's sitting there, listening, just the way we are, because it's so much cheaper than sending."

"Here you are," MacDonald said.

"But don't you suppose somebody would have thought of that by this time and begun to send?"

"Double-think it all the way through and figure what just occurred to you would have occurred to everybody else, so you might as well listen. Think about it—everybody sitting around, listening. If there is anybody. Either way it makes the skin creep."

"All right, then, we ought to send something."

"What would you send?"

"I'd have to think about it. Prime numbers, maybe."

"Think some more. What if a civilization weren't mathematical?"

"Idiot! How would they build an antenna?"

"Maybe they'd rule-of-thumb it, like a ham. Or maybe they have built-in antennae."

"And maybe you have built-in antennae and don't know it."

MacDonald's can of beer was empty. He wandered back toward the kitchen again.

"—insist on equal time with the Big Ear. Even if nobody's sending we could pick up the normal electronic commerce of a civilization tens of light-years away. The problem would be deciphering, not hearing."

"They're picking it up now, when they're studying the relatively close systems. Ask for a tape and work out your program."

"All right, I will. Just give me a chance to work up a request—"

MacDonald found himself beside Maria. He put his arm around her waist and pulled her close. "All right?" he said.

"All right."

Her face was tired, though, MacDonald thought. He dreaded the notion that she might be growing older, that she was entering middle age. He could face it for himself. He could feel the years piling up inside his bones. He still thought of himself, inside, as twenty, but he knew that he was forty-seven, and mostly he was glad that he had found happiness and love and peace and serenity. He even was willing to pay the price in youthful exuberance and belief in his personal immortality. But not Maria!

Nel mezzo del cammin di nostra vita
Mi ritrovai per una selva oscura,
Che la diritta via era smarrita.

"Sure?"

She nodded.

He leaned close to her ear. "I wish it was just the two of us, as usual."

"I, too."

"I'm going to leave in a little while—"

"Must you?"

'I must relieve Saunders. He's on duty. Give him an opportunity to celebrate a little with the others."

"Can't you send somebody else?"

"Who?" MacDonald gestured with good-humored futility at all the clusters of people held together by bonds of ordered sounds shared consecutively. "It's a good party. No one will miss me."

"I will."

"Of course, *querida.*"

"You are their mother, father, priest, all in one," Maria said. "You worry about them too much."

"I must keep them together. What else am I good for?"

"For much more."

MacDonald hugged her with one arm.

"Look at Mac and Maria, will you?" said someone who

was having trouble with his consonants. "What god-damned devotion!"

MacDonald smiled and suffered himself to be pounded on the back while he protected Maria in front of him. "I'll see you later," he said.

As he passed the living room someone was saying, "Like Eddie said, we ought to look at the long-chain molecules in carbonaceous chondrites. No telling how far they've traveled—or been sent—or what messages might be coded in the molecules."

As he closed the front door behind him, the noise dropped to a roar and then a mutter. He stopped for a moment at the door of the car and looked up at the sky.

E quindi uscimmo a riveder le stelle.

The noise from the hacienda reminded him of something—the speakers in the control room. All those voices talking, talking, talking, and from here he could not understand a thing.

Somewhere there was an idea if he could only concentrate on it hard enough. But he had drunk one beer too many—or perhaps one too few.

After the long hours of listening to the voices, Mac-Donald always felt a little crazy, but tonight it was worse than usual. Perhaps it was all the conversation before, or the beers, or something else—some deeper concern that would not surface.

But then the listeners had to be crazy to begin with—to get committed to a project that might go for centuries without results.

Tico-tico, tico-tico. . . .

Even if they could pick up a message, they still would likely be dead and gone before any exchange could take place even with the nearest likely star. What kind of mad dedication could sustain such perseverance?

They're listening in Puerto Rico. . . .

Religion could. At least once it did, during the era of cathedral building in Europe, the cathedrals that took centuries to build.

"What are you doing, fellow?"

"I'm working for ten francs a day."

"And what are you doing?"

"I'm laying stone."

"And you—what are you doing?"

"I am building a cathedral."

They were building cathedrals, most of them. Most of them had that religious mania about their mission that would sustain them through a lifetime of labors in which no progress could be seen.

Listening for words that never come. . . .

The mere layers of stone and those who worked for pay alone eliminated themselves in time and left only those who kept alive in themselves the concept, the dream.

But they had to be a little mad to begin with.

Can it be the stars are stricken dumb?

Tonight he had heard the voices nearly all night long. They kept trying to tell him something, something urgent, something he should do, but he could not quite make out the words. There was only the babble of distant voices, urgent and unintelligible.

Tico-tico, tico-tic. . . .

He had wanted to shout "Shut up!" to the universe. "One at a time!" "You first!" But of course there was no way to do that. Or had he tried? Had he shouted?

They're listening with ears this big!

Had he dozed at the console with the voices mumbling in his ears, or had he only thought he dozed? Or had he only dreamed he waked. Or dreamed he dreamed?

Listening for thoughts just like their own.

There was a madness to it all, but perhaps it was a divine madness, a creative madness. And is not that madness that which sustains man in his terrible self-knowledge, the driving madness which demands reason of a casual universe, the awful aloneness which seeks among the stars for companionship?

Can it be that we are all alone?

The ringing of the telephone half penetrated through the mists of mesmerization. He picked up the handset, half expecting that it would be the universe calling, perhaps with a clipped British accent, "Hello there, Man. Hello. Hello. I say, we seem to have a bad connection, what? Just wanted you to know that we're here. Are you there? Are you listening? Message on the way. May not get there for a couple of centuries. Do be around to answer, will you? That's a good being. Righto. . . . ."

Only it wasn't. It was the familiar American voice of Charley Saunders saying, "Mac, there's been an accident. Olsen is on his way to relieve you, but I think you'd better leave now. It's Maria."

Leave it. Leave it all. What does it matter? But leave

the controls on automatic; the computer can take care of it all. Maria! Get in the car. Start it. Don't fumble! That's it. Go. Go. Car passing. Must be Olsen. No matter.

What kind of accident? Why didn't I ask? What does it matter what kind of accident? Maria. Nothing could have happened. Nothing serious. Not with all those people around. *Nil desperandum.* And yet—why did Charley call if it was not serious? Must be serious. I must be prepared for something bad, something that will shake the world, that will tear my insides.

I must not break up in front of them. Why not? Why must I appear infallible? Why must I always be cheerful, imperturbable, my faith unshaken? Why me? If there is something bad, if something impossibly bad has happened to Maria, what will matter? Ever? Why didn't I ask Charley what it was? Why? The bad can wait; it will get no worse for being unknown.

What does the universe care for my agony? I am nothing. My feelings are nothing to anyone but me. My only possible meaning to the universe is the Project. Only this slim potential links me with eternity. My love and my agony are me, but the significance of my life or death are the Project.

HIC • SITVS • EST • PHAETHON • CVRRVS • AVRIGA • PATERNI
QVEM • SI ᕋ NON • TENVIT • MAGNIS • TAMEN • EXCIDIT AVSIS

By the time he reached the hacienda, MacDonald was breathing evenly. His emotions were under control. Dawn had grayed the eastern sky. It was a customary hour for Project personnel to be returning home.

Saunders met him at the door. "Dr. Lessenden is here. He's with Maria."

The odor of stale smoke and the memory of babble still lingered in the air, but someone had been busy. The party remains had been cleaned up. No doubt they all had pitched in. They were good people.

"Betty found her in the bathroom off your bedroom. She wouldn't have been there except the others were occupied. I blame myself. I shouldn't have let you relieve me. Maybe if you had been here— But I knew you wanted it that way."

"No one's to blame. She was alone a great deal," MacDonald said. "What happened?"

"Didn't I tell you? Her wrists. Slashed with a razor.

Both of them. Betty found her in the bathtub. Like pink lemonade, she said."

Percé jusques au fond du coeur
D'une atteinte imprévue aussi bien que mortelle.

A fist tightened inside MacDonald's gut and then slowly relaxed. Yes, it had been that. He had known it, hadn't he? He had known it would happen ever since the sleeping pills, even though he had kept telling himself, as she had told him, that the overdose had been an accident.

Or had he known? He knew only that Saunders' news had been no surprise.

Then they were at the bedroom door, and Maria was lying under a blanket on the bed, scarcely making it mound over her body, and her arms were on top of the blankets, palms up, bandages like white paint across the olive perfection of her arms, now, MacDonald reminded himself, no longer perfection but marred with ugly red lips that spoke to him of hidden misery and untold sorrow and a life that was a lie. . . .

Dr. Lessenden looked up, sweat trickling down from his hairline. "The bleeding is stopped, but she's lost a good deal of blood. I've got to take her to the hospital for a tranfusion. The ambulance should be here any minute." He paused. MacDonald looked at Maria's face. It was paler than he had ever seen it. It looked almost waxen, as if it were already arranged for all time on a satin pillow. "Her chances are fifty-fifty," Lessenden said in answer to his unspoken question.

And then the attendants brushed their way past him with their litter.

"Betty found this on her dressing table," Saunders said. He handed MacDonald a slip of paper folded once.

MacDonald unfolded it: *Je m'en vay chercher un grand Peut-être.*

Everyone was surprised to see MacDonald at the office. They did not say anything, and he did not volunteer the information that he could not bear to sit at home, among the remembrances, and wait for word to come. But they asked him about Maria, and he said, "Dr. Lessenden is hopeful. She's still unconscious. Apparently will be for some time. The doctor said I might as well wait here as at the hospital. I think I made them nervous. They're hopeful. Maria's still unconscious. . . ."

O lente, lente currite, noctis equi!

The stars move still, time runs, the clock will strike. . . .

Finally MacDonald was alone. He pulled out paper and pencil and worked for a long time on the statement, and then he balled it up and threw it into the wastebasket, scribbled a single sentence on another sheet of paper, and called Lily.

"Send this!"

She glanced at it. "No, Mac."

"Send it!"

"But—"

"It's not an impulse. I've thought it over carefully. Send it."

Slowly she left, holding the piece of paper gingerly in her fingertips. MacDonald pushed the papers around on his desk, waiting for the telephone to ring. But without knocking, unannounced, Saunders came through the door first.

"You can't do this, Mac," Saunders said.

MacDonald sighed. "Lily told you. I would fire that girl if she weren't so loyal."

"Of course she told me. This isn't just you. It affects the whole Project."

"That's what I'm thinking about."

"I think I know what you're going through, Mac—" Saunders stopped. "No, of course I don't know what you're going through. It must be hell. But don't desert us. Think of the Project!"

"That's what I'm thinking about. I'm a failure, Charley. Everything I touch—ashes."

"You're the best of us."

"A poor linguist? An indifferent engineer? I have no qualifications for this job, Charley. You need someone with ideas to head the Project, someone dynamic, someone who can lead, someone with—charisma."

A few minutes later he went over it all again with Olsen. When he came to the qualifications part, all Olsen could say was, "You give a good party, Mac."

It was Adams, the skeptic, who affected him most. "Mac, you're what I believe in instead of God."

Sonnenborn said, "You are the Project. If you go, it all falls apart. It's over."

"It seems like it, always, but it never happens to those things that have life in them. The Project was here before I came. It will be here after I leave. It must be longer lived than any of us, because we are for the years and it is for the centuries."

After Sonnenborn, MacDonald told Lily wearily, "No more, Lily."

None of them had had the courage to mention Maria, but MacDonald considered that failure, too. She had tried to communicate with him a month ago when she took the pills, and he had been unable to understand. How could he riddle the stars when he couldn't even understand those closest to him? Now he had to pay.

Meine Ruh' ist hin,
Meine Herz ist schwer.

What would Maria want? He knew what she wanted, but if she lived, he could not let her pay that price. Too long she had been there when he wanted her, waiting like a doll put away on a shelf for him to return and take her down, so that he could have the strength to continue.

And somehow the agony had built up inside her, the dreadful progress of the years, most dread of all to a beautiful woman growing old, alone, too much alone. He had been selfish. He had kept her to himself. He had not wanted children to mar the perfection of their being together.

Perfection for him; less than that for her.

Perhaps it was not too late for them if she lived. And if she died—he would not have the heart to go on with work to which, he knew now, he could contribute nothing.

Que acredito su ventura,
Morir querdo y vivir loco.

And finally the call came. "She's going to be all right, Mac," Lessenden said. And after a moment, "Mac, I said—"

"I heard."

"She wants to see you."

"I'll be there."

"She said to give you a message. 'Tell Robby I've been a little crazy in the head. I'll be better now. That "great perhaps" looks too certain from here. And tell him not to be crazy in the head, too'."

MacDonald put down the telephone and walked through the doorway and through the outer office, a feeling in his chest as if it were going to burst. "She's going to be all right," he threw over his shoulder at Lily.

"Oh, Mac—"

In the hall, Joe the janitor stopped him. "Mr. Mac-Donald—"

MacDonald stopped. "Been to the dentist yet, Joe?"

"No, sir, not yet, but it's not—"

"Don't go. I'd like to put a tape recorder beside your bed for a while, Joe. Who knows?"

"Thank you, sir. But it's— They say you're leaving, Mr. MacDonald."

"Somebody else will do it."

"You don't understand. Don't go, Mr. MacDonald!"

"Why not, Joe?"

"You're the one who cares."

MacDonald had been about to move on, but that stopped him.

Ful wys is he that can himselven knowe!

He turned and went back to the office. "Have you got that sheet of paper, Lily?"

"Yes, sir."

"Have you sent it?"

"No, sir."

"Bad girl. Give it to me."

He read the sentence on the paper once more: *I have great confidence in the goals and ultimate success of the Project, but for personal reasons I must submit my resignation.*

He studied it for a moment.

Pigmæi gigantum humeris impositi plusquam ipsi gigantes vidant.

And he tore it up.

TRANSLATIONS

1. *Pues no es posible . . .*
   The bow cannot always stand bent, nor can human frailty subsist without some lawful recreation.
   Cervantes, *Don Quixote*

2. *Habe nun, ach! Philosophie, . . .*
   Now I have studied philosophy,
   Medicine and the law,
   And, unfortunately, theology,
   Wearily sweating, yet I stand now,
   Poor fool, no wiser than I was before;
   I am called Master, even Doctor,
   And for these last ten years have drawn

My students, by the nose, up, down,
Crosswise and crooked. Now I see
That we can know nothing finally.
>   Goethe, *Faust,* opening lines

3. *Men che dramma . . .*
Less than a drop
Of blood remains in me that does not tremble;
I recognize the signals of the ancient flame.
>   Dante, *The Divine Comedy,*
>   Purgatorio

4. *C'est de quoy j'ay le plus de peur que la peur.*
The thing of which I have most fear is fear.
>   Montaigne, *Essays*

5. *À la très-bonne, à la très-belle, qui fait ma joie et
ma santé.*
To the best, to the most beautiful, who is my joy
and my well-being.
>   Baudelaire, *Les Epaves*

6. *Rast ich, so rost ich.*
When I rest, I rust.
>   German proverb

7. *Nunc est bibendum!*
Now's the time for drinking!
>   Horace, *Odes,* Book I

8. *Wer immer strebens sich bemüht, . . .*
Who strives always to the utmost,
Him can we save.
>   Goethe, *Faust,* Part I

9. *Ich bin der Geist der stets verneint.*
I am the spirit that always denies.
>   Geothe, *Faust,* Part I

10. *Nel mezzo del cammin di nostra vita . . .*
In the middle of the journey of our life
I came to myself in a dark wood,
Where the straight way was lost.
>   Dante, *The Divine Comedy,*
>   Inferno, opening lines

11. *E quindi uscimmo a riveder le stelle.*
And thence we issued out, again to see the stars.
>   Dante, *The Divine Comedy,*
>   Inferno

12. *Nil desperandum.*
There's no cause for despair.
>   Horace, *Odes,* Book I

13. *HIC • SITVS • EST • PHAETHON . CVRRVS .
AVRIGA • PATERNI . . .*

Here Phaeton lies: in Phoebus' car he fared,
And though he greatly failed, more greatly dared.

Ovid, *Metamorphoses*

14. *Percé jusques au fond du coeur* . . .
Pierced to the depth of my heart
By a blow unforeseen and mortal.

Corneille, *Le Cid*

15. *Je m'en vay chercher un grand Peut-être.*
I am going to seek a great Perhaps.

Rabelais on his deathbed

16. *O lente, lente currite, noctis equi!*
Oh, slowly, slowly run, horses of the night!

Marlowe, *Dr. Faustus*

(Faustus is quoting Ovid. He waits for Mephistopheles
to appear to claim his soul at midnight. The next
line: "The devil will come and Faustus must be
damn'd.")

17. *Meine Ruh' ist hin,* . . .
My peace is gone,
My heart is heavy.

Goethe, *Faust*, Part 1

18. *Que acredito su ventura,* . . .
For if he like a madman lived,
At least he like a wise one died.

Cervantes, *Don Quixote*
(Don Quixote's epitaph)

19. *Ful wys is he that can himselven knowe!*
Very wise is he that can know himself!

Chaucer, *The Canterbury
Tales*, "The Monk's Tale"

20. *Pigmæi gigantum humeris impositi plusquam ipsi
gigantes vidant.*
A dwarf standing on the shoulder of a giant may see
further than the giant himself.

Didacus Stella, in
Lucan, *De Bello Civili*

ON STYLE

by James E. Gunn

*"Before you can become a real writer
you must develop your own style."*

EVERY NOVICE writer has heard these words at some

time in his life, or has seen them written on some hopeful exercise, probably by his high school English teacher. Some high school English teachers suffer from two handicaps: they have accumulated a great deal of misinformation about writing, and they must oversimplify that.

One might say the same thing about everyone who has never written fiction for publication.

But before we can discuss style, we must clear away the underbrush which obscures our view. The apprentice writer who sets out to develop "his own style" is starting the process from the wrong end.

Style is the appropriate expression of story. It emerges from story; it is not imposed on it. Good style is transparent; it is a window through which the story can be seen to move and live and work out its destiny.

C. Hugh Holman in *A Handbook of Literature* has defined style as "the arrangement of words in a manner which at once best expresses the individuality of the author and the idea and intent in his mind." I would agree with the second half of Holman's definition but not the first. A writer attempting to express the idea and intent in his mind cannot help but arrange his words in an individual manner; that process is largely unconscious once the writer has freed himself from the influence of his reading. In this sense, his high school English teacher was right: the writer who wishes to be more than an echo must recognize and shun the merely imitative and even the derivative. But this is different from "expressing the individuality of the author."

Style, Holman continues, is expressed in such general qualities as "diction, sentence structure and variety, imagery, rhythm, repetition, coherence, emphasis, and arrangement of ideas."

Style is primarily a product of revision. Revision sometimes is performed in the head before the writing begins, but most writing, however carefully thought out beforehand, would profit from revision. Gunn's first law of writing is: good stories are not written, they are rewritten. Put that beside Wilson's Four Rules. At the same time I must caution the apprentice writer that in an art every rule has its exceptions. Although I agree completely with Wilson's Four Rules of Good Writing, I remember occasions when I have violated every one of them—with good reason and with good effect.

If you could see what I am writing in first draft, you

would see a page and a quarter of typed words speckled with xxxxxes like fly droppings. "Fly droppings"—there is an exercise in style: the choice of a simile which describes the appearance of the page appropriately but might as easily, and even more accurately, have been "like a child's jacks cast upon the page," but aside from the fact that "fly droppings" is shorter and connotes a blemish, it also serves to stop the reader, to remind him, hopefully, that writing is a subject as real and as earthy as, say, garbage collecting.

Each xxxxxed out portion of my first draft (in my final draft I make it neater with one of the relatively new chalk tapes) represents a change of mind after the word or phrase was typed. In the second sentence, for instance, I had typed "complain," intending to write "I do not wish to complain about high school English teachers," but xxxxxed it out and inserted "denigrate" (which violates Wilson's first rule but follows his second) because it not only was shorter but a bit better in expressing my meaning. I could have used "run down"—and considered it— but "run down" is a bit too colloquial at this position and might lead to a brief confusion as to whether "run down" is a verb or adjective phrase. If you're looking for that sentence, forget it: I eliminated it as unnecessary in the revision.

(A good principle followed by many writers is to get through that first draft as rapidly as possible and worry about the niceties in revision.)

I have made copies for my students of the first drafts of my stories (a favorite is "The Old Folks," published in *Nova Two*) to show how I changed my mind during the composition and why and what the changes did. Another reason is to demonstrate that the stories they read in books do not spring forth complete, like Athena out of the head of Zeus, but in labor and suffering like any real child; even professional writers succumb to the fallacy that everyone else's work is easy.

Gunn's second law is that you can't teach creativity. In fact, it's almost impossible to teach fiction writing. What you can teach in a fiction-writing class is critical judgment: the ability to know when something is good or bad, right or wrong for the particular story or the particular position in the story, and how to fix it. The writer must not be easily satisfied. The beginning writer tends to clutch at his first idea as if he will never have another, to set down the first word that springs to mind as if the English language were not rich in synonyms; the experienced writer knows that ideas and words are cheap, that he must discard ten or more to get a good one, and that the only good ones are those that work and work uniquely.

If what I have written about style is true (don't let me get by with that! disagree!), why do teachers and even some writers insist that you should "develop your own style"? Why, indeed, are most of the great writers known as "stylists"?

There, you have pushed me against the wall! If style emerges from story, then no author should have a recognizable style. Unless—unless those authors who write in the same consistent style, who seem to have followed the advice of your high school English teacher, always write the same story.

There are two kinds of writers in the world: Storytellers, who seem to say, "Let me entertain you"; and Artists, who seem to say, "I'm going to tell you a Great Truth." Storytellers find life so rich and varied, so full of stories, that they tell a different one each time they sit down to write, and each one is told in a different way because each is a different aspect of life. Artists find in life a single pattern which recurs in different ways; their problem is expressing this vision of reality in the unique way it demands. For this task they develop a choice of words, a sentence structure, images, rhythms, repetitions, coherences, emphases, and arrangements of ideas which become a style; and since they see life as unitary, they write the same story many times.

(Distinctions are seldom this sharp; there are Storytellers with style, who also tell us a Great Truth or two, and Artists who entertain us, who tell a great story.)

And why are the Artists, the stylists, considered greater than the Storytellers? Why are the Flauberts, the Henry Jameses, the James Joyces, and in our times the William Faulkners and the Ernest Hemingways considered superior to the de Maupaussants, the Charles Dickenses, the Rudyard Kiplings, the H. G. Wellses, the O. Henrys?

(Henry James and Joseph Conrad, conscious literary artists both, admired the stories and novels of H. G. Wells and nagged him to write more carefully, more artistically, more stylistically, but Wells, who was tempted, finally turned his back on them: " 'I am a journalist,' I declared, 'I refuse to play the artist! If sometimes I am an artist it is a freak of the gods. I am a journalist all the time and what I write *goes now*—and will presently die.' " He was a better writer than a prophet—his science fiction, at least, continues to live.)

The answer to the question about the greatness of the stylists, as so many answers are, is tentative and multiple: 1) the Artists are more concerned with the way things are said, that is, with technique; the Storytellers, with story; and the Artists, therefore, tend to be more skilled in the use of words and their arrangements; 2) the Artists, because they are concerned with new forms of expression, are more likely to be experimental and, when they succeed, to become important in literary histories; 3) the critics, who write the literary histories and make the literary judgments, are more interested in experiment, in technique, in style, than in story—which anyone can enjoy and understand without help; and 4) who says they're greater anyway? If literary survival is an appropriate measure of quality, the work of the Storytellers seems to survive longer than that of the stylists. H. Rider Haggard's *She* has never been out of print since it was first published in 1886 while Henry James's *The Bostonians,* published the same year, isn't read even by college students. The hasty, stylistically impoverished novels of Edgar Rice Burroughs continue to sell hundreds of thousands of copies annually sixty years after they first were printed.

The work of many stylists changed over the years: Henry James's early novels were simple and clear compared to the involutions of his later fiction; James Joyce's *Dubliners* and *Portrait of the Artist as a Young Man* are not *Ulysses* or *Finnegans Wake,* but excellent fiction for all that; William Faulkner's early stories were the work of a Storyteller, and only his later novels are written in the kind of stream-of-consciousness that some call Faulknerese.

Critics may say that these writers were groping their way toward their style, but their earlier works and shorter works are not lesser fiction, only less experimental, and their styles changed to fit different stories or the same stories differently perceived as they grew older and life seemed more complex.

Style is the meat of the parodists. Stylists find themselves held up, magnified, so that every eccentricity seems like a blemish. Parody makes style funny by making it obvious, by exaggeration—and also by applying it to an inappropriate subject, as Wolcott Gibbs pilloried Hemingway's style by turning his epic description of bullfighting,

Death in the Afternooon, to the perils of highway driving in "Death in the Rumble Seat."

If a stylist like Ray Bradbury should try to write a Robert Heinlein novel in Bradbury's lush, metaphorical style, the result would be ridiculous or humorous. Style emerges from story; when it does not, when a stylist tackles a story which does not suit his style, the result often seems like self-parody, which some critics say that Hemingway achieved in *Across the River and Into the Trees.*

The worst sin of the stylist, however, is to allow his style to become a wall in front of his story rather than a window, to allow the syle in which he tells a story to become so obtrusive that the reader is constantly reminded of the stylist's (and the author's) presence. We live, to be sure, in an age of personalities, and sometimes the author's presence or his voice or his antics are more interesting than what he has to say; to learn how to be a salable character or to perfect the art of selling yourself, however, is not the same thing as learning how to write fiction.

(Another reservation: in one sense every experimental work calls attention to its style because it is new; the successful ones, the really successful ones, find their styles becoming transparent and then invisible as readers learn how to read them.)

Which brings us to the work at hand. Now that I am exposed as a writer who prefers story to style—and I will confess that some of what I have said above is personal preference—let me get to the story which precedes this essay, a story with which two literary agents found some of the same faults I have denounced in stylists. One said "The Listeners" was "overartistic for the available audience and actually for any audience; it is overartistic for the story content and the kind of story it is"; the other, that it was "a curiously remote story." Both objected to the foreign language quotations as "alienating" or "irritating." I had to sell the story myself.

In defense of "The Listeners," I should add that I had no trouble selling it; I sent it to *Galaxy* and Fred Pohl brought it immediately, asking only that I provide translations for the quotations, which I was happy to do. The story was nominated for a Nebula award of the Science Fiction Writers of America; although it didn't win, it was included in *Nebula Award Stories Four.* It was picked up immediately for another anthology. It formed the first chapter of my novel *The Listeners,* published by Scribner's in 1972. It is included in a collection of my short fiction,

Breaking Point, published by Walker. I would be surprised if the saga of "The Listeners" ends there.

Well, a story needs no defense—or rather, if it needs one a defense won't help—but it may explain the circumstances that surround the work and those illustrate another fact about the writing business that apprentice writers should understand. In fact, we might call it Gunn's Third Law: agents, editors and publishers are not infallible; because they work in a creative field, they actually are more fallible than most men. Case histories prove again and again that what one agent or editor or publisher finds unpublishable will be seized upon by another with cries of joy.

"The Listeners" is a prime example of the truth that style emerges from story. All the decisions that an author makes in the course of writing a story—and writing a story is nothing but a flash of inspiration followed by an incredible number of decisions (a good story is one in which the right decisions have been made)—affect the style in which the story is written: the situation, its resolution, the characters, the setting, the mood, the theme, the viewpoint—most of all the viewpoint. So it was with "The Listeners."

The story idea came out of a book by Walter Sullivan, *We Are Not Alone,* a description of the long effort by man to communicate with life on other worlds, a dream which recent scientific developments has converted from a speculation into a possibility. The situation that occurred to me was the incredible difficulty involved in a project which must endure a century or more without results— indeed, with negative results: there would be problems of continuing financial support, of maintaining morale, of sustaining enthusiasm. . . . Undergirding this would be the Project's problem: how to communicate with intelligent life on other worlds. Counterpoint to this would be the Project's problem of communicating about itself with people outside the Project. The Project could have been viewed from outside, but I decided to place the story within the Project (other stories which make up the novel and other devices provide an external viewpoint). The characters, then, would be the personnel on the Project. The mood would be quiet and the plot, uneventful, reflecting the predominant motif of the Project: lack of meaningful events.

But an uneventful story means no story. The theme was legitimate; how could I convert it into effective narrative? Perhaps if I made the Director of the Project the viewpoint character for the story: keeping the Project going would be *his* problem, and that problem would dominate his life to the—to the what? To the detriment of his other relationships.

Gradually his character and his background took shape in my mind: he would be a competent man or he never would have become head of the Project, but he must be a reflective man or he could not understand the real nature of the problem he faced. He would be a good man, a kind man, a loving man, but he also would be a man obsessed by a goal. Surely that would tear him apart. He would doubt his ability to handle the situation, as what sensitive man would not? He would be married, and therein would lie another conflict, another counterpoint to the other two problems: for the members of the Project also must communicate on a personal level. What if the Director, who is trying so desperately to communicate with intelligent creatures on other worlds, cannot communicate with his wife?

I decided that this story, as well as the others in the series, would be told from the viewpoint of a person who not only would have the basic problem of extraterrestrial communication, but a problem of interhuman communication as well. So the story assumed added dimensions: it began to feel heavy, alive with emotional currents; it began to achieve the feeling of reality that a good story in being develops for a writer; it became *possible* and then *inevitable*.

Further considerations of character followed, and other possibilities began to develop from them: what would be the Director's qualifications (he is asked that question in the story)? He should have some engineering background, electrical or electronic probably, for the Project inevitably is associated with radio communications. I could have made him an astronomer, but, perhaps unconsciously, I wished to leave the stars a bit mysterious, the subject for metaphor rather than analysis. The whole process would be dominated by symbols for communication or the absence of communication or the inability to communicate; and this would become another level of narrative: denser and denser, more like life. And he would be a communicator—not a speech major but a man who communicates with aliens, a linguist.

This would provide an opportunity for another level of narrative: it is easy enough to *state* that a character has certain qualities, but it is difficult to *show* it; and the difference between stating and showing is the difference between ineffective and effective narration. Every statement of the author must be *proved*. How else can one show a man as a linguist unless he speaks and thinks in other languages? From this came the foreign language quotations. Originally I didn't much care if the reader understood the meaning of the quotations, at least on first reading, or the meaning of everything that went on in the story; although the quotations had meanings which added a further level of understanding to what was going on, a reader could get their gist and flavor from the events and dialogue surrounding them. But I didn't resent translating them. I was a bit sorry to see them used as footnotes in the magazine version; I thought the footnotes were distracting, and in the Nebula anthology I changed them to an appendix. Those readers who wished to savor more of the story afterward could go back and put the translations into place; it became a bit like life when in imagination we relive a scene or a series of events with the added perspective provided by distance or experience.

What of the style? By describing the conditions which govern style, I may have said as much about the style of "The Listeners" as I can say. But I will go on: the diction, as a whole, is pedestrian, colloquial, commonplace; here and there some technical language occurs and occasionally some reflections which call for a bit of poetic diction and imagery. What the men are doing is their commonplace (one of the technical discoveries of science fiction writers some thirty years ago was that the future will not be marvelous but commonplace to those who live in it); technical terms are the language in which technical men communicate (the fragments of conversation at the party all are parts of recorded scientific speculations); and the sensitive mind phrases its reflections in images, poetry, and metaphor.

The story begins in the middle of things, which is usually a good place to begin, and in spite of the fact that it describes the end result of nearly fifty years of effort the events of the story are packed into approximately forty-eight hours; this, too, helps a story. Critics say that there are two kinds of narration: scenic (dramatized) and panoramic (summary). Almost all the individual scenes (I write in scenes; I am able to visualize the story better this way, almost as if I were writing a little play) are completely dramatized; there is virtually no summary. And

I try to make the setting seem real by following Flaubert's precept that every scene must be established by appeals to at least three (of the five) senses.

One aspect of the story: why include the janitor and his false teeth? Call it comic relief, like Shakespeare's porter. Call it one more concession to realism: everything in life isn't serious. Call it another level of story, another counterpoint. I can tell you where the janitor came from: a long time ago I jotted down an idea for a story I might write some day, about a janitor for a Project Ozma who began picking up signals on his false teeth that the engineers, with all their fancy equipment, could not receive; and no one would believe him. The only resolution I could think of, however, was: how ironic!—which is an ineffective resolution, a cop-out, to which student writers often resort when they can't think of an ending which really resolves the problem. So I put the modest subplot into "The Listeners," as I put in everything else I knew or thought about the topic; and, as such things have a way of doing, the janitor turned out to be the factor which stops MacDonald from carrying out his intention to resign, and his willingness to try anything, including listening to the janitor's teeth, is a symbol of his renewed openness to the Project and to life.

Does the story work? Some may feel, like my agent, that "it is overartistic for the story content and the kind of story it is." Others may feel that it justifies itself.

Looking back upon a life divided between two worlds—one academic and literary, one creative and commercial—it seems to me sometimes that I have attempted to bring the two together, to build bridges between commercial fiction and literary fiction, to use the technical skills of the latter to improve the former but in an evolutionary way, without sacrificing the values, the narrative strengths, of popular fiction.

If I have done this in "The Listeners" for some, perhaps for many, I can ask no more.

GRANDY DEVIL

by Frederik Pohl

MAHLON BEGAT Timothy, and Timothy begat Nathan, and Nathan begat Roger, and the days of their years were long on the Earth. But then Roger begat Orville, and Orville was a heller. He begat Augustus, Wayne, Walter, Benjamin and Carl, who was my father, and I guess that was going too far, because that was when Gideon Upshur stepped in to take a hand.

I was kissing Lucille in the parlor when the doorbell rang and she didn't take kindly to the interruption. He was a big man with a burned-brown face. He stamped the snow off his feet and stared at me out of crackling blue eyes and demanded, "Orvie?"

I said, "My name is George."

"Wipe the lipstick off your face, George," he said, and walked right in.

Lucille sat up in a hurry and began tucking the ends of her hair in place. He looked at her once and calmly took off his coat and hung it over the back of a chair by the fire and sat down.

"My name is Upshur," he said "Gideon Upshur. Where's Orville Dexter?"

I had been thinking about throwing him out up until then, but that made me stop thinking about it. It was the first time anybody had come around looking for Orville Dexter in almost a year and we had just begun breathing easily again.

I said, "That's my grandfather, Mr. Upshur. What's he done now?"

He looked at me. "You're his *grandson?* And you ask me what he's *done?*" He shook his head. "Where is he?"

I told him the truth: "We haven't seen Grandy Orville in five years."

"And you don't know where he is?"

"No, I don't, Mr. Upshur. He never tells anybody where he's going. Sometimes he doesn't even tell us after he comes back."

The old man pursed his lips. He leaned forward, across Lucille, and poured himself a drink from the Scotch on the side table.

"I swear," he said, in a high, shrill, old voice, "these Dexters are a caution. Go home."

He was talking to Lucille. She looked at him sulkily and opened her mouth, but I cut in.

"This is my fiancée," I said.

"Hah," he said. "No doubt. Well, there's nothing to do but have it out with Orvie. Is the bed made up in the guest room?"

I protested, "Mr. Upshur, it isn't that we aren't glad

to see any friend of Grandy's, but Lord knows when he'll be home. It might be tomorrow, it might be six months from now or years."

"I'll wait," he said over his shoulder, climbing the stairs.

Having him there wasn't so bad after the first couple of weeks, I phoned Uncle Wayne about it, and he sounded quite excited.

"Tall, heavy-set old man?" he asked. "Very dark complexion?"

"That's the one," I said. "He seemed to know his way around the house pretty well, too."

"Well, why shouldn't he?" Uncle Wayne didn't say anything for a second. "Tell you what, George. You get your brothers together and——"

"I can't, Uncle Wayne," I said. "Harold's in the Army. I don't know *where* William's got to."

He didn't say anything for another second. "Well, don't worry. I'll give you a call as soon as I get back."

"Are you going somewhere, Uncle Wayne?" I wanted to know.

"I certainly am, George," he said, and hung up.

So there I was, alone in the house with Mr. Upshur. That's the trouble with being the youngest.

Lucille wouldn't come to the house any more, either. I went out to her place a couple of times, but it was too cold to drive the Jaguar and William had taken the big sedan with him when he left, and Lucille refused to go anywhere with me in the jeep. So all we could do was sit in *her* parlor, and her mother sat right there with us, knitting and making little remarks about Grandy Orvie and that girl in Eatontown.

So, all in all, I was pretty glad when the kitchen door opened and Grandy Orvie walked in.

"Grandy!" I cried. "I'm glad to see you! There's a man——"

"Hush, George," he said. "Where is he?"

"Upstairs. He usually takes a nap after I bring him his dinner on a tray."

"*You* take his dinner up? What's the matter with the servants?"

I coughed. "Well, Grandy, after that trouble in Eatontown, they——"

"Never mind," he said hastily. "Go ahead with what you're doing."

I finished scraping the dishes into the garbage-disposer and stacked them in the washer, while he sat there in his overcoat watching me.

"George," he said at last, "I'm an old man. A very old man."

"Yes, Grandy," I answered.

"My grandfather's older than I am. And *his* grandfather is older than that."

"Well, sure," I said reasonably. "I never met them, did I, Grandy?"

"No, George. At least, I don't believe they've been home much these last few years. Grandy Timothy was here in '86, but I don't believe you were born yet. Come to think of it, even your dad wasn't born by then."

"Dad's sixty," I told him. "I'm twenty-one."

"Certainly you are, George. And your dad thinks a lot of you. He mentioned you just a couple of months ago. He said that you were getting to an age where you ought to be told about us Dexters."

"Told what, Grandy Orville?" I asked.

"Confound it, George, that's what I'm coming to! Can't you see that I'm trying to tell you something? It's hard to put into words, that's all."

"Can I help?" said Gideon Upshur from the door.

Grandy Orville stood up straight and frosty. "I'll thank you, Gideon Upshur, to stay the be-dickens out of a family discussion!"

"It's my family, too, young man," said Gideon Upshur. "And that's why I'm here. I warned Cousin Mahlon, but he wouldn't listen. I warned Timothy, but he ran off to America—and look what *he* started!"

"A man's got a right to pass on his name," Grandy Orville said pridefully.

"Once, yes! I never said a man couldn't have a son—though you know I've never had one, Orvie. Where would the world be if all of us had children three and four at a time, the way you Dexters have been doing? Four now—sixteen when the kids grow up—sixty-four when *their* kids grow up. Why, in four or five hundred years, there'd be trillions of us, Orvie. The whole world would be covered six layers deep with immortals, squirming and fidgeting and I—"

"Hush, man!" howled Grandy Orville. "Not in the front of the boy!"

Gideon Upshur stood up and yelled right back at him. "It's time he found out! I'm warning you, Orville Dexter, either you mend your ways or I'll mend them for you. I didn't come here to talk; I'm prepared to take sterner measures if I have to!"

"Why, you reeking pustoon," Grandy Orville started, but then he caught sight of me. "Out of here, George! Go up to your room till I call you. And as for you, you old idiot, I'm as prepared as you are, if it comes to that——"

I went. It looked like trouble and I hated to leave Grandy Orville alone, but orders were orders; Dad had taught me that. The noises from the kitchen were terrible for a while, but by and by they died down.

It was quiet for a long, long time. After a couple of hours, I began to get worried and I went back downstairs quietly and pushed the kitchen door open a crack.

Grandy Orville was sitting at the kitchen table, staring into space. I didn't see Mr. Upshur at all.

Grandy Orville looked up and said in a tired voice, "Come in, George. I was just catching my breath."

"Where did Mr. Upshur go?" I asked.

"It was self-defense," he said quickly. "He'd outlived his usefulness, anyway."

I stared at him. "Did something happen to Mr. Upshur?" I asked.

He sighed. "George, sometimes I think the old blood is running thin. Now don't bother me with any more questions right now, till I rest up a bit."

Orders were orders, as I say. I noticed that the garbage-disposal unit was whirring and I walked over to shut it off.

"Funny," I said. "I forgot I left it running."

Grandy Orville said nervously, "Don't give it a thought. Say, George, they haven't installed sewer lines while I was away, have they?"

"No, they haven't, Grandy," I told him. "Same old dry well and septic tank."

"That's too bad," he grumbled. "Well, I don't suppose it matters."

I wasn't listening too closely; I had noticed that the floor was slick and shiny.

"Grandy," I said, "you didn't have to mop the floor for me. I can manage, even if all the servants did quit when——"

"Oh, shut up about the servants," he snapped testily. "George, I've been thinking. There's a lot that needs to be explained to you, but this isn't the best time for it and maybe your dad ought to do the explaining. He knows you better than I do. Frankly, George, I just don't know how to put things so you'll understand. Didn't you ever notice that there was anything different about us Dexters?"

"Well, we're pretty rich."

"I don't mean that. For instance, that time you were run over by the truck when you were a kid. Didn't that make you suspect anything—how soon you mended, I mean?"

"Why, I don't think so, Grandy," I said, thinking back. "Dad told me that all the Dexters always healed fast." I bent down and looked under the table Grandy Orville was sitting at. "Why, that looks like old clothes down there. Isn't that the same kind of suit Mr. Upshur was wearing?"

Grandy Orville shrugged tiredly. "He left it for you," he explained. "Now don't ask me any more questions, because I've got to go away for a while and I'm late now. If your Uncle Wayne comes back, tell him thanks for letting me know Mr. Upshur was here. I'll give your regards to your dad if we happen to meet."

Well, that was last winter. I wish Grandy would come back so I could stop worrying about the problem he left me.

Lucille never did get over her peeve, so I married Alice along about the middle of February. I'd have liked having some of the family there at the wedding, but none of them was in town just then—or since, for that matter—and it wasn't really necessary because I was of legal age.

Alice is a very attractive girl and a good housekeeper, which is a good thing—we haven't been able to get any of the servants back. But that's good, too, in a way, because it keeps her inside the house a lot.

It's getting on toward nice weather, though, and I'm having a tough time keeping her away from the third terrace, where the dry well and septic tank are. And if she goes down there, she's bound to hear the noises.

I don't know. Maybe the best thing I could do would be to roll the stone off the top of the septic tank and let what's struggling around in there come out. He's had plenty of time to get himself back together, I think.

But I'm afraid he's pretty mad.

DAY MILLION
by Frederik Pohl

ON THIS DAY I want to tell you about, which will be about ten thousand years from now, there were a boy, a girl and a love story.

Now, although I haven't said much so far, none of it is true. The boy was not what you and I would normally think of as a boy because he was a hundred and eighty-seven years old. Nor was the girl a girl, for other reasons. And the love story did not entail that sublimation of the urge to rape, and concurrent postponement of the instinct to submit, which we at present understand in such matters. You won't care much for this story if you don't grasp these facts at once. If, however, you will make the effort you'll likely enough find it jam-packed, chockful and tiptop-crammed with laughter, tears and poignant sentiment which may, or may not, be worthwhile. The reason the girl was not a girl was that she was a boy.

How angrily you recoil from the page! You say, who the hell wants to read about a pair of queers? Calm yourself. Here are no hot-breathing secrets of perversion for the coterie trade. In fact, if you were to see this girl you would not guess that she was in any sense a boy. Breasts, two; reproductive organs, female. Hips, callipygian; face hairless, supraorbital lobes nonexistent. You could term her female on sight, although it is true that you might wonder just what species she was a female of, being confused by the tail, the silky pelt and the gill slits behind each ear.

Now you recoil again. Cripes, man, take my word for it. This is a sweet kid, and if you, as a normal male, spent as much as an hour in a room with her you would bend heaven and Earth to get her in the sack. Dora—we will call her that; her "name" was omicron-Dibase seven-group-totter-oot S Doradus 5314, the last part of which is a color specification corresponding to a shade of green— Dora, I say, was feminine, charming and cute. I admit she doesn't sound that way. She was, as you might put it, a dancer. Her art involved qualities of intellection and expertise of a very high order, requiring both tremendous natural capacities and endless practice; it was performed in null-gravity and I can best describe it by saying that it was something like the performance of a contortionist and something like classical ballet, maybe resembling

Danilova's dying swan. It was also pretty damned sexy. In a symbolic way, to be sure; but face it, most of the things we call "sexy" are symbolic, you know, except perhaps an exhibitionist's open clothing. On Day Million when Dora danced, the people who saw her panted, and you would too.

About this business of her being a boy. It didn't matter to her audiences that genetically she was male. It wouldn't matter to you, if you were among them, because you wouldn't know it—not unless you took a biopsy cutting of her flesh and put it under an electron-microscope to find the XY chromosome—and it didn't matter to them because they didn't care. Through techniques which are not only complex but haven't yet been discovered, these people were able to determine a great deal about the aptitudes and easements of babies quite a long time before they were born—at about the second horizon of cell-division, to be exact, when the segmenting egg is becoming a free blastocyst—and then they naturally helped those aptitudes along. Wouldn't we? If we find a child with an aptitude for music we give him a scholarship to Julliard. If they found a child whose aptitudes were for being a woman, they made him one. As sex had long been dissociated from reproduction this was relatively easy to do and caused no trouble and no, or at least very little, comment.

How much is "very little"? Oh, about as much as would be caused by our own tampering with Divine Will by filling a tooth. Less than would be caused by wearing a hearing aid. Does it still sound awful? Then look closely at the next busty babe you meet and reflect that she may be a Dora, for adults who are genetically male but somatically female are far from unknown even in our own time. An accident of environment in the womb overwhelms the blueprints of heredity. The difference is that with us it happens only by accident and we don't know about it except rarely, after close study; whereas the people of Day Million did it often, on purpose, because they wanted to.

Well, that's enough to tell you about Dora. It would only confuse you to add that she was seven feet tall and smelled of peanut butter. Let us begin our story.

On Day Million, Dora swam out of her house, entered a transportation tube, was sucked briskly to the surface in its flow of water and ejected in its plume of spray to an elastic platform in front of her—ah—call it her rehearsal hall. "Oh, hell!" she cried in pretty confusion, reaching out to catch her balance and finding herself tumbled against a total stranger, whom we will call Don.

They met cute. Don was on his way to have his legs renewed. Love was the furthest thing from his mind. But when, absent-mindedly taking a shortcut across the landing platform for submarines and finding himself drenched, he discovered his arms full of the loveliest girl he had ever seen, he knew at once they were meant for each other. "Will you marry me?" he asked. She said softly, "Wednesday," and the promise was like a caress.

Don was tall, muscular, bronze and exciting. His name was no more Don than Dora's was Dora, but the personal part of it was Adonis in tribute to his vibrant maleness, and so we will call him Don for short. His personality color-code, in angstrom units, was 5290, or only a few degrees bluer than Dora's 5314—a measure of what they had intuitively discovered at first sight; that they possessed many affinities of taste and interest.

I despair of telling you exactly what it was that Don did for a living—I don't mean for the sake of making money, I mean for the sake of giving purpose and meaning to his life, to keep him from going off his nut with boredom— except to say that it involved a lot of traveling. He traveled in interstellar spaceships. In order to make a spaceship go really fast, about thirty-one male and seven genetically female human beings had to do certain things, and Don was one of the thirty-one. Actually, he contemplated options. This involved a lot of exposure to radiation flux—not so much from his own station in the propulsive system as in the spillover from the next stage, where a genetic female preferred selections, and the subnuclear particles making the selections she preferred demolished themselves in a shower of quanta. Well, you don't give a rat's ass for that, but it meant that Don had to be clad at all times in a skin of light, resilient, extremely strong copper-colored metal. I have already mentioned this, but you probably thought I meant sunburned.

More than that, he was a cybernetic man. Most of his ruder parts had been long since replaced with mechanisms of vastly more permanence and use. A cadmium centrifuge, not a heart, pumped his blood. His lungs moved only when he wanted to speak out loud, for a cascade of osmotic filters rebreathed oxygen out of his own wastes. In a way, he probably would have looked peculiar to a man from the twentieth century, with his glowing eyes and seven-fingered hands. But to himself, and of course to Dora, he looked mighty manly and grand. In the course of his voyages Don had circled Proxima Centauri, Procyon and the puzzling worlds of Mira Ceti; he had carried agricultural templates to the planets of Canopus and brought back warm, witty pets from the pale companions of Aldebaran. Blue-hot or red-cool, he had seen a thousand stars and their ten thousand planets. He had, in fact, been traveling the starlanes, with only brief leaves on Earth, for pushing two centuries. But you don't care about that, either. It is people who make stories, not the circumstances they find themselves in, and you want to hear about these two people. Well, they made it. The great thing they had for each other grew and flowered and burst into fruition on Wednesday, just as Dora had promised. They met at the encoding room, with a couple of well-wishing friends apiece to cheer them on, and while their identities were being taped and stored they smiled and whispered to each other and bore the jokes of their friends with blushing repartee. Then they exchanged their mathematical analogues and went away, Dora to her dwelling beneath the surface of the sea and Don to his ship.

It was an idyll, really. They lived happily ever after— or anyway, until they decided not to bother any more and died.

Of course, they never set eyes on each other again.

Oh, I can see you now, you eaters of charcoal-broiled steak, scratching an incipient bunion with one hand and holding this story with the other, while the stereo plays d'Indy or Monk. You don't believe a word of it, do you? Not for one minute. People wouldn't live like that, you say with a grunt as you get up to put fresh ice in a drink.

And yet there's Dora, hurrying back through the flushing commuter pipes toward her underworld home (she prefers it there; has had herself somatically altered to breathe the stuff). If I tell you with what sweet fulfillment she fits the recorded analogue of Don into the symbol manipulator, hooks herself in and turns herself on . . . if I try to tell you any of that you will simply stare. Or glare; and grumble, what the hell kind of love-making is this? And yet I assure you, friend, I really do assure you that Dora's ecstasies are as creamy and passionate as any of James Bond's lady spies', and one hell of a lot more so than anything you are going to find in "real life." Go ahead, glare and grumble. Dora doesn't care. If she thinks of you at all, her thirty-times-great-great-grandfather, she thinks you're a pretty primordial sort of brute. You are. Why, Dora is further removed from you than you are from the australopithecines of five thousand centuries ago. You could not swim a second in the strong currents of her life. You don't think progress goes in a straight line, do you? Do you recognize that it is an ascending, accelerating, maybe even exponential curve? It takes hell's own time to get started, but when it goes it goes like a bomb. And you, you Scotch-drinking steak-eater in your relaxacizing chair, you've just barely lighted the primacord of the fuse. What is it now, the six or seven hundred thousandth-day after Christ? Dora lives in Day Million. Ten thousand years from now. Her body fats are polyunsaturated, like Crisco. Her wastes are hemodialyzed out of her bloodstream while she sleeps—that means she doesn't have to go to the bathroom. On whim, to pass a slow half-hour, she can command more energy than the entire nation of Portugal can spend today, and use it to launch a weekend satellite or remold a crater on the Moon. She loves Don very much. She keeps his every gesture, mannerism, nuance, touch of hand, thrill of intercourse, passion of kiss stored in symbolic-mathematical form. And when she wants him, all she has to do is turn the machine on and she has him.

And Don, of course, has Dora. Adrift on a sponson city a few hundred yards over her head, or orbiting Arcturus fifty light-years away, Don has only to command his own symbol-manipulator to rescue Dora from the ferrite files and bring her to life for him, and there she is; and rapturously, tirelessly they love all night. Not in the flesh, of course; but then his flesh has been extensively altered and it wouldn't really be much fun. He doesn't need the flesh for pleasure. Genital organs feel nothing. Neither do hands, nor breasts, nor lips; they are only receptors, accepting and transmitting impulses. It is the brain that feels; it is the interpretation of those impulses that makes agony or orgasm, and Don's symbol-manipulator gives him the analogue of cuddling, analogue of kissing, the analogue of wild, ardent hours with the eternal, exquisite and incorruptible analogue of Dora. Or Diane. Or sweet Rose, or laughing Alicia; for to be sure, they have each of them exchanged analogues before, and will again.

Rats, you say, it looks crazy to me. And you—with your aftershave lotion and your little red car, pushing

papers across a desk all day and chasing tail all night—
tell me, just how the hell do you think you would look to
Tiglath-Pileser, say, or Attila the Hun?

ON VELOCITY EXERCISES

by Frederick Pohl

IF TWO communications experts come face to face,
though they come from the ends of the earth, they can
jibber-jabber together happily on the subject of parabolic
dishes and megabits per second and bandwidths. They may
not agree, but each will understand what the other is saying. If, on the other hand, two writers come together,
however well they know each other and however much
they may have in common, they can hardly discuss even
the basics of their common trade without misunderstanding. Writing is unique among professions of which I
have much personal knowledge in that it lacks a really
useful vocabulary. We all more or less agree to use
words like "plot" and "style" and "theme" and "character" . . . but we don't always mean the same things by
them, and anyway a story does not usually come apart
into these discrete and definable pieces without serious
damage to the story. Not if it is a good story in the first
place, it doesn't.

I have always found this situation to be a trial for me.
In thirty-odd years as an editor I have had to talk about
their stories (in a tangible way, urging them to do one
thing rather than another, asking them to make changes,
complimenting them on what they do well) with perhaps
a thousand writers all over the world. As a teacher I
have had my writing class stare at me in incomprehen-
sion, and glance furtively at each other, when I thought
I was making a point so pellucid that my son's pet pigeons
could have pecked it out in half a dozen trials. One
way or another I have dealt with these communications gaps successfully enough, but I had feedback and
the question-and-answer period to help me. In writing
about writing, which is what I am doing now, I find all this
particularly troublesome. You see, what I really want to

say to you about the writing of the preceding stories does not readily lend itself to the standard literary language. It is not the language I think in when I think about how to write a given story.

So if you will bear with me, I will try to tell you how I think of these stories, in my own rather idiosyncratic way. And then, if I can, I will try to translate it into Standard Literary.

"Grandy Devil" belongs to a class of my stories which I sometimes call "three-word stories" and sometimes "velocity exercises." If you happen to have read a lot of my work, you may remember stories like "Punch" and "Pythias," which are in the same category. They are "three-word stories" (not that every one of them is exactly *three* words; it may be a little more or less) because in every case they offer a snapper at the end that is intended to give you an insight you have not previously had, so rapidly and overwhelmingly that the whole cast of the story changes instantly for you.

In the technical jargon of the writing trade, this kind of story is sometimes called a "twist ending" or a "one-punch" story. I don't like to use either of these terms because they do not represent what I want to do. I do not want the end to "twist" what has gone before. I want it to *illuminate* what has gone before. In "Punch," the story concerns aliens who have given Earthmen all sorts of technological gifts, including the secret of building space warships. The hero forms a friendship with one of the aliens and takes him duckhunting, in the course of which venture he happens to mention that Earthmen prize good sportsmanship and therefore they never shoot sitting prey. The alien who has given us space travel looks at him with surprise and delight and says, "Neither do we." In "Pythias" the narrator (it is a first-person story) describes how a friend of his mastered the secret of tele-kinesis (*you* know what telekinesis is: the ability to move objects by the power of the mind alone) and so developed such enormous powers that he threatens to take over the dictatorship of the world. The narrator murders his friend on the grounds that the friend simply cannot be trusted with a secret so dangerous to the peace and security of the world. Then he says his three words: "But I can."

Nor do I like to think of them as "one-punch." What goes before the three words at the end is not meant to be mere spacing. It is meant to have—and to the extent that I am able to put down on paper what I envision in my head it does have—a life and substance of its own. What I say in the opening sections of these stories I try to say economically, in an absolute minimum of words. ("The secret of writing well is leaving out the dull parts.") But that minimum is meant to include enough to make you feel that something real is happening. You are meant to feel that these are real people, doing real things, and not simple lay figures erected, like the traveling salesman and the farmer's daughter or the two Irishmen named Pat and Mike, solely for the purpose of supporting a punchline.

There is a technical problem involved here. It is easy enough to set up a punchline in very few words. The problem is making the words mean something. You cannot allow your reader to feel that he is being led toward a punchline. The stories in which he does feel that are the ones which gave the "one-punch" its name. Slick magazines like *Collier's* and *Liberty* used to thrive on them. But you don't see many stories like that any more (in fact, you don't see *Collier's* and *Liberty* any more) because after a while even the dullest reader began to understand what was being done to him. It became quite clear that if a very short story didn't have much excuse for being there in its first few hundred words, it was certain that the excuse would turn up in a "surprise" in the last line.

Once readers are educated to this point there is terrible trouble. The reader begins to try to outguess the writer. ("Now, let's see, what will the surprise be? Oh, I know. The police officer is a *woman*.") When he does that you have lost the ballgame. Sometimes he will in fact guess what you are going to surprise him with, and that's a disaster for you. Once in a while he will guess a better surprise than you have in store for him, and then you are in *real trouble*. But even if he doesn't outguess you, you are dead anyway. The mere fact that he expects *a* surprise diminishes the excitement of *any* surprise.

So to me the important thing in writing a "three-word story" is in keeping as much as possible going on, giving the opening sections of the story enough validity and interest so that the score is jammed with notes and chords and glissandos; you keep the reader too busy to try to outguess you. (This process is sometimes described as "throwing dust in the eyes of the reader," but I don't much like that description either; I don't want just to distract his attention, I want to keep him involved with me and my story.) And because I try to do these things as rapidly and economically as possible, I call them "velocity exercises."

"Grandy Devil," for personal reasons, is one of my favorite stories of this kind; the story itself will tell you what our inadequate common vocabulary has not allowed me to explain.

"Day Million" is quite a different kind of story, although still a velocity exercise of sorts.

I really do not very much like talking about my own stories, especially in an evaluative way, but I do think "Day Million" is quite a good story. With no more than half a dozen possible exceptions, all of them far longer, "Day Million" is probably the most *successful* story I ever wrote in, let's see, thirty-five years this month of writing professionally.

Not at all coincidentally, I am sure, it is also one of the most conceptually difficult stories I have ever tackled. The actual writing itself was a breeze; I sat down about two o'clock one morning and put the first page in the typewriter; before six the first draft was written; I ate some breakfast, rolled clean white paper into the machine and had it complete and in the mail by nine. But the bits and pieces that make it up had been rolling around in my head for years.

What I wanted to do was to write a love story that might be meaningful for people who lived more than a thousand years from now (in the sense that *Love Story* is meaningful to millions of readers this year, and *Romeo and Juliet* was meaningful to Elizabethans); and I wanted to write it in terms that would be comprehensible to people who live right this minute.

It is a little bit as though I were going to try to translate *Sonnets from the Portuguese* into terms that would be comprehensible to the brood bitches and sires at the neighborhood stud kennels. I do not believe that our frames of reference in the area of love will match at all well with those of our remote descendants.

I did not expect, actually, to describe "love" (whatever you or I or anyone means by that cloudy and much-used word) in the sense that it will *really* exist a thousand years from now. I don't know what the world will be like a thousand years from now any more than you do. In a sense that made the job easier, because I could select possible patterns of love that I could describe, instead of being limited to patterns for which no words exist as yet. But the basic job was to show how *different* love might be, and that was job enough for me.

And the other thing was that I had set myself the goal of making it a "velocity exercise." That is, I wanted to do it in as close to two thousand words as I could.

Why did I set myself an arbitrary limit like that?

For the same reason that the Japanese write haiku and Petrarch wrote sonnets. The challenge of a fixed form imposes a kind of discipline on me to which I respond with better work than I would produce otherwise.

I first found this to be true in writing poetry. (I still think it is true for me with poetry, and—all you free-verse writers who don't want to trouble to master your craft out there—I think it would be true for most of you too.) I relearned it as to fiction during the years when I was working under the tempery and arbitrary lash of Horace Gold, a quirky and demanding editor who made everybody write better stories for him than they were writing for anyone else.

I do not just mean to say that Horace was a good editor. He was, but that's beside the point. What Horace wanted me to do to my stories was seldom essential to any reasonable view of what the story should be, and sometimes it was plain crazy. But in shaping what I wanted to say to his known prejudices and demands, son of a gun, the stories came out a lot better than they ever did with any other editor I had ever worked with.

Since I don't have Horace around any more, I impose my own arbitrary standards. If I had known how to do that in the first place I might not ever have needed Horace; but I didn't, and I did; and anyway, that's why I set myself a limit on "Day Million."

So in "Day Million" I tried not to put in one single word that did not bear directly on what I was trying to do: to make the reader feel the grotesqueness, the incongruity, and ultimately the validity of a kind of love which no one today has ever experienced, in a setting as unlike our own as ours is unlike that of Boadicea or Erik the Red. I have always liked "throwaway lines." (My favorite, you did not ask but I will tell you anyway, is from the novel of competing advertising agencies of the future, *The Space Merchants,* in which one character dismisses all of organized religion by saying, "It's a Taunton account.") "Day Million" is full of throwaways. The disadvantage of a throwaway is pecuniary. You waste on a few words a notion which a R * b * rt S * lv * rb * rg (to disguise beyond recognition the name of an esteemed writing friend who has one writing habit I deeply deplore) could milk into half a novel. The advantage of it, however, is that you give the reader something to do for himself. The line is not thrown away. It is only that the reader himself develops it. And I think that what I personally like most about "Day Million" is that it is in a sense a throwaway story: I could have used the same material and made a novel out of it, but by keeping it all to the least possible number of words I let the reader write his own novel.

Now let me tackle the translation into Standard Literary.

To me the above discussion falls mostly under the heading of "style." My definition of style is not my own, but I am sorry to say I don't remember whose it is: "Style is the problem solved." Plot, character, setting, theme—all of these things, it seems to me, must reflect themselves in the style; "style," in the sense of being an idiosyncratic word order, use of metaphor, coinage or whatever, seems to me a distraction from what it is in the story that impels a writer to write it and a reader to read it.

In fact, what I really think is that all these elements of story writing are interdependent and pretty nearly inseparable. Parodists have fun every now and then by writing, say, an account of a football game in the "style" of Hemingway, Joyce, Shakespeare, Proust, and even Samuel R. Delany. I do not deny that the thing can be done; I only point out that when style is inappropriate to the rest of the story the results are comic.

Each element of your story imposes problems on you: how to show the inner person of a character, how to move your plot from scene to scene, how to display the setting, how to elucidate your theme. In the act of solving these problems style is created. If it is appropriate, it is good; if it is inappropriate it is bad; and that is the Whole of the Law.

Biographical Notes

Samuel R. "Chip" Delany was born in New York in 1942. He has been honored with numerous Hugo and Nebula Awards for his novels and short stories, which include *Babel-17, Nova, Dhalgren, Triton,* and *Stars in My Pocket Like Grains of Sand.* He is also one of science fiction's most important critics; his essays and reviews have been collected in such volumes as *The Jewel-Hinged Jaw, Starboard Wine,* and *Silent Interviews.* His 1988 memoir *The Motion of Light in Water* was honored with a Hugo Award. He has taught writing at many Clarion Workshops and he recently served as the chairman of the Department of Comparative Literature at the University of Massachussetts in Amherst. His most recent books include *Atlantis: Three Tales* and *Longer Interviews.*

Harlan Ellison was born in Cleveland in 1934. At last count he had published more than seventeen hundred stories, essays, columns, and film and television scripts. Among his many books are *Deathbird Stories, Mefisto in Onyx, The Glass Teat, Alone Against Tomorrow, Shatterday, Angry Candy,* and *The Harlan Ellison Hornbook.* He has also edited novels and stories, including the landmark *Dangerous Visions* anthologies. He has been honored with the World Fantasy Lifetime Achievement Award, the British Fantasy Award, the Mystery Writers of America Edgar Award (twice), the P.E.N. Award for journalism, and more Hugo and Nebula Awards than any other writer. His recent books include *Mind Fields* (with Jacek Yerka) and the forthcoming volume *Slippage.*

James Gunn was born in 1923 in Kansas City, Missouri. His many novels include *This Fortress World, The Joy Makers, The Immortals,* and *The Listeners.* He was honored with the Pilgrim Award for his contributions to science fiction criticism, which include such books as *Alternate Worlds: The Illustrated History of Science Fiction* and *The New Encyclopedia of Science Fiction,* as well as the four volumes of *The Road to Science Fiction* that he edited. At the University of Kansas he founded the Center for the Study of Science Fiction, and as a teacher he has helped shape the careers of many important writers, including novelists John Kessel, Pat Cadigan, and Bradley Denton. He is currently at work on a variety of projects, including a new novel, *Catastrophe!*

Daniel Keyes was born in Brooklyn in 1927. He was educated at Wayne State University and at Ohio University, where he went on to teach. His first novel, *Flowers for Algernon,* has become a classic and was honored with the Nebula Award in 1966; it also served as the inspiration for the 1968 movie *Charly.* His other novels include *The Touch, Unveiling Claudia,* and *The Minds of Billy Milligan.* He currently lives in Florida.

Damon Knight was born in Bend, Oregon, in 1922. He is the author of many classic short stories and novels, including *The Man in the Tree, A for Anything,* "To Serve Man," *CV,* and *Why Do Birds.* As an editor, he is responsible for many important anthologies, including the long-running *Orbit* series. As a critic, his Hugo-winning collection *In Search of Wonder* has been among the most influential books in the field of science fiction. He and his wife, Kate Wilhelm, helped found both the Science Fiction Writers of America and the Clarion Writers' Workshops. He has been honored with the Pilgrim Award, the Science Fiction Writers of America Grand Master Award, and the C.E.S. Wood Award for a distinguished career in letters. He lives in Eugene, Oregon, and is currently at work on a new novel.

Ursula K. Le Guin was born in California in 1929. She is the author of such classic novels as *The Lathe of Heaven, The Dispossessed, A Wizard of Earthsea,* and *The Left Hand of Darkness.* Her groundbreaking reviews and essays—for which she has been honored with the Pilgrim Award—have been collected in the such volumes as *Dancing at the End of the World* and *The Language of the Night.* She has been honored with ten Hugo and Nebula Awards and she recently received the World Fantasy Lifetime Achievement Award. A veteran teacher at writers' workshops, she lives with her family in Portland, Oregon.

Frederik Pohl was born in Brooklyn in 1919. He has been one of science fiction's most influential writers and editors. Among his many masterworks are *Gateway* and its sequels, *JEM, The Years of the City,* and his classic collaborations with C. M. Kornbluth, including most notably *The Space Merchants.* He has edited many magazines, books, and anthologies, and while he was its editor, *If* magazine received three successive Hugo Awards for Best Magazine. He has been honored with many other awards, including the Grand Master Award of the Science Fiction Writers of America. His most recent novel is *The Voices of Time,* and he is at work on a new book. He lives in Palatine, Illinois.

Joanna Russ was born in New York in 1937 and rose to prominence in the early 1970s with her novels *Picnic on Paradise, And Chaos Died,* and *The Female Man.* She has won Hugo and Nebula Awards for her short fiction, which has been collected in such volumes as *Extra(ordinary) People, The Zanzibar Cat,* and *The Hidden Side of the Moon.* In 1988 she received the Pilgrim Award for her criticism, which includes the classic *How to Suppress Women's Writing* and the recent volume *To Write Like a Woman.* After teaching for many years at the University of Washington, she recently moved to Arizona, where she is at work on a major new volume of criticism.

Robert Silverberg was born in New York in 1935 and published his first novel in 1955. He has gone on to write hundreds of novels and short stories, including such masterworks as *Dying Inside, Tower of Glass, Lord Valentine's Castle,* and *A Time of Changes,* as well as many works of nonfiction. He has won many Hugo and Nebula Awards for his work. As an editor, he has assembled scores of anthologies, including the *New Dimensions* volumes and volume one of *The Science Fiction Hall of Fame.* Among his most recent books are *Kingdoms of the Wall* and *Hot Sky at Midnight.*

Kate Wilhelm was born in Cleveland in 1928 and published her first novel in 1962. Since then, she has gone on to publish more than thirty novels and collections of short stories, including mysteries, courtroom thrillers, and such masterworks of speculative fiction as *Where Late the Sweet Birds Sang, Juniper Time, Margaret and I,* and *Death Qualified.* With her husband, Damon Knight, she was a mainstay of the Clarion Writers' Workshops for more than twenty years, during which time she helped develop the talents of scores of science fiction writers. She lives in Eugene, Oregon, where she is now at work on a new novel, *Malice Prepense.*

Jack Williamson was born in 1908 in the Arizona Territory and sold his first science fiction story to *Amazing Stories* in 1928. He has gone on to write many more books, including such classics as *The Legion of Space, Darker Than You Think,* and *The Humanoids.* He taught for many years at Eastern New Mexico University and he received a Pilgrim Award for his criticism, which includes such books as *Teaching SF* and *H. G. Wells: Critic of Progress.* He received a Hugo Award for his memoir *Wonder's Child: My Life in Science Fiction.* His most recent novels are *Beachhead* and *Demon Moon.*

Robin Wilson was born in Columbus, Ohio, in 1928. He served four years in the Navy and eight years in the CIA before entering the world of academia. As a professor at Clarion State College in Pennsylvania, he founded the Clarion Writers' Workshops— modeling it on the Milford Workshops that Kate Wilhelm and Damon Knight founded—and served as an instructor for many years. He edited three *Clarion* anthologies and coauthored one novel, *To the Sound of Music.* From 1980 to 1993 he served as President of California State University, Chico, before retiring to pursue his writing career again. In 1994 he published a mystery novel, *Death by Degrees,* and he edited a new anthology of science fiction, *Paragons.* He is currently at work on another mystery novel.